DAWN BEFORE DARKNESS

DAWN BEFORE DARKNESS

Liz Lazarus

Published in the United States by Mitchell Cove Publishing, LLC.

For resources regarding stalking, visit **https://www.stalkingawareness.org**. While SPARC (Stalking Prevention, Awareness, & Resource Center) does not directly work with individual victims, it provides extensive resources, training, and technical assistance to professionals who support victims, such as law enforcement, victim service providers, and health professionals.

For resources regarding guardianship and conservatorship abuse, visit **https://www.cearjustice.org.** CEAR (Center for Estate Administration Reform) is a not-for-profit advocate with a mission to educate and seek justice for Americans when they are threatened by the growing problem of abusive probate, trust and guardianship fraud.

ISBN: 978-0-9909374-7-0

Edited by Evelyn Fazio, Brooke Berthelsen and Janie Mills
Cover Design & Jacket by Josh Wirth
Interior by Jill Dible of Jill Dible Design
e-book by BookNook.biz
Author Photograph by Tony Deferia of tdeferiamedia, Inc.
Author Logo by Amber Clark of Wildcraft Designs

Websites: www.dawnbeforedarkness.com | www.lizlazarus.com

To Travis …

You turned my world from black & white to Technicolor.

The pen is mightier than the sword.
— Edward Bulwer-Lytton

This novel was inspired by real events.

Prologue

Dawn had never practiced a breakup speech before—never gave it a second thought—but now she was rehearsing how to end her summer romance without stirring up drama or provoking retaliation.

I think it's best if we cool things off for a while. She replayed this phrase in her mind while gripping her phone so tightly that her fingertips turned pink. Finally, she called him and blurted her declaration without even saying hello.

"Why?" he asked. "Everything's been great between us."

"It's not you," she lied. "Things have just been hard lately with work and my mom."

"I can help." His voice lowered, taking on a seductive tone. "You know, hard isn't all bad. I've got something hard that brings you a lot of pleasure."

A chill ran down Dawn's spine, as if he'd slithered through the phone and traced an ice cube down her back. She'd jumped into this relationship far too quickly, and it was time—no, past time—to get out. Dawn struggled to feign a breezy attitude, if there was such a thing.

"I've just got a lot going on right now. I think it's best if we take a break."

"How can I change your mind?" he persisted.

Her attempt at a casual parting of ways was failing, leaving Dawn no choice but to become more assertive. "You can't."

The line went dead.

Chapter 1

"He's going to hit us!" shouted Stuart.

Dawn, who'd been scrolling through Instagram, looked up. From the passenger seat of her boyfriend's car, she saw the back of a maroon Chevy Blazer reversing at high speed toward them. Stuart grabbed the gearshift and hesitated, clearly debating which was worse—to back into oncoming traffic or to let the SUV crash into the front of his car. They were in a tight spot, having just pulled into a gas station next to a Thai diner. Because there'd been no open spots in front of the restaurant, Stuart had opted for the station's small lot next door.

Before the SUV could reach them, it side-swiped a parked gray Honda. The high-pitched sound of metal on metal made Dawn cringe, and the scraping continued until the Blazer broke free and stopped directly in front of them.

Dawn snapped a picture of the license plate, which provided both evidence of the collision and the time: 7:32 p.m. She waited, expecting the driver to emerge and inspect the damage he'd caused. Instead, the Blazer sped forward, its tires squealing as it traversed the lot, cut in front of oncoming traffic, and disappeared out of sight.

"I can't believe that jerk," exclaimed Dawn. "He hit that car and took off."

"C'mon," said Stuart. "Let's go someplace else."

Dawn's chest tightened. Her body was revealing what her mind had chosen to ignore. *Stuart isn't the right guy for you.* The *right guy* would do the *right thing*—not leave the scene of an accident he'd just witnessed.

"We have to report this," she said. "Call 911 or something."

"He saw it." Stuart pointed to a guy in a hoodie who was using an antiquated pay phone by the side of the gas station.

The hoodie guy turned his back toward the accident and continued his conversation. Before Stuart could protest, Dawn hopped out of the car and walked toward the damaged Honda. The left rear was completely mangled.

An elderly Asian man who'd been pumping gas approached. He spoke in Mandarin as he clapped his hands, mimicking the crash.

She nodded, confirming their mutual observation, although she couldn't understand a word he was saying.

"Dawn, what are you doing? C'mon," Stuart beckoned. He'd pulled next to one of the pumps and motioned for her to return.

She planted her fists on her hips and stood firm. The two had been dating for only a few months, and although they'd been spending nearly every weekend together, he had no right to dictate orders. Betting the owner of the Honda was inside the restaurant, Dawn ignored Stuart and headed toward the front door.

As she neared the entrance, she sensed a presence behind her, as if the heavy August air was gently blowing on her neck, causing the baby hairs to tingle. The sensation made her whip around. A tall White guy was just inches away. He seemed to have come out of nowhere and was uncomfortably close. Dawn took a step back.

"Sorry. I didn't mean to scare you. Did you see the accident?" He spoke quickly, as if taking swift action was a matter of life or death.

Dawn looked up to make eye contact. Being five feet nine, she noticed tall men as they made her feel normal. She nodded and held up her phone, which displayed a photo of the license plate: JAZ 260.

"Got the license plate of the car," she confirmed.

As the man studied the photo, she studied him—wavy brunette hair, intense brown eyes, smooth thin lips, and thick lashes, the kind that women covet.

"Dawn, let's go," Stuart shouted from a distance. He stroked his curly blond hair and glared with piercing green eyes, not hiding his impatience.

"Look, if you need to go, I can find the owner," said the man. "I assume one witness is enough."

Dawn hesitated. She wasn't raised to leave the scene of a crime. She was raised to follow the rules, obey the speed limit and return the grocery cart *inside* the store—the corral *outside* wasn't good enough.

"Could you text me that photo, though?" the man requested. "I didn't think to get proof. That was smart."

Dawn's face flushed. People, especially men, rarely noticed her intelligence. As a slender blonde with ocean-blue eyes, the compliments about her model-like appearance were routine, even expected. But this man saw her mind without focusing on her beauty.

"Where were you?" she asked.

He pointed across the street to an upscale five-story condo building. "I live over there. Walk here all the time for takeout. I'm Nick."

Just then, she felt a tug on her arm. The Asian man was talking to her again. He pointed to Dawn, then to Nick, and to the Honda. She tried to gesture that they would take care of things and that he didn't need to worry. This earnest old man was making more of an effort than Stuart, and he couldn't even speak English.

"Maybe I should come with you," she suggested. "To see if we can find the owner?"

"No need to have both of our evenings interrupted. I'll call you and let you know what happens." He paused. "If you'd like."

"Yes, please do." Dawn texted him the photo, and with no reason to linger, she retreated toward Stuart's Lexus, all the while yearning to stay longer. She searched for something to say but came up empty. All she could muster was a simple "thank you."

"Hey, I'm just doing what I hope someone would do for me, you know?" He shrugged and smiled.

Chapter 2

On Monday morning, Dawn awoke to the sound of her 6:00 a.m. alarm. She crawled out of bed and splashed water on her face. There was no need for makeup—the animals didn't care. She pulled her hair into a ponytail and put on her uniform: short-sleeved navy scrubs. Her purple Crocs, the only part of her outfit that allowed for individuality, were stationed next to the front door of her duplex. Not only were they comfortable for standing all day, but they were practical for the fur, pee and poop that would inevitably be splattered on them.

On the way to the Village Veterinary Clinic, she made her regular stop at the Dunkin' Donuts for a large iced coffee, which she chugged in her Jeep. Once the Monday morning chaos began, odds were that she wouldn't make it back to the break room. The veterinary clinic appointments were overbooked, much like the airlines, in anticipation of no-shows. But if every pet owner kept his or her time slot and a few emergencies arrived, the day would be nonstop mayhem. On top of that, and unlike the airlines, the clinic kept the number of staff to a minimum, which put undue stress on the entire system.

She parked at the far edge of the lot, entered the back door using a key card and clocked in just before 7:00 a.m. All the techs had lockers, by seniority. She had the best location in a far corner, away from the door to the reception room. Dawn stored her wallet and keys, took another swig of coffee and joined the team in the break room to review the day's schedule.

Her first appointment was a female Dachshund name Daisy who was having her teeth cleaned. Small dogs like Dachshunds and Chihuahuas were challenging patients. They had the same number of teeth as any other dog, but they were crammed into a tiny mouth. These breeds were prone to exposed roots and often required an unfair share of extractions.

Dawn entered the exam room where a man was engrossed in his cell phone. His pronounced biceps stretched the seams of his suit. A little brown dog stood on the metal exam table, observing her owner's every move. Dawn mused that these two didn't *go together*. The old saying that people and their animals favored each other was true, and this hulk of a guy and the tiny dog didn't seem like a match. Not to mention, he wasn't making any effort to comfort her, being far more interested in his phone. Dawn glanced at his ring finger, which had a gold band.

Probably her dog, she thought.

"Good morning," she said, with a cheerful smile. "I'm Dawn, and I'll be taking care of Daisy today."

The guy barely looked up.

"I wanted to confirm that she's having her teeth cleaned and that she hasn't had any food or water this morning?"

"Yeah, I'm pretty sure she hasn't eaten."

Dawn's eyebrows rose. "Well, it's pretty important that we know for certain because she'll be under anesthesia."

"If you guys told us not to feed her, then I'm sure my wife followed your directions. I'm just here for the drop-off."

Dawn smiled, which was more of a smirk if he'd bothered to notice. This was definitely not his dog. "Do you know if Daisy has been under anesthesia before?"

"No idea."

"Maybe we should call your wife?"

"You won't catch her," he retorted. "She's on a plane. This got sprung on me this morning."

Dawn had the urge to reply, *Oh, you just realized this morning that you have a dog?* But she didn't dare. The Village Veterinary Clinic was the only privately owned clinic in Laurel, South Carolina. Veterinarians Neil and Smita Patel, the married owners, had opened the practice so residents wouldn't have to drive forty-five minutes to the larger city of Greenville. They'd resisted offers from the big chains to sell, fearing the relentless pursuit of revenue would impact the level of care. As much as Dawn wanted to smack the guy for calling this precious little girl a *this*, she couldn't afford to alienate a customer.

"Do you have any requests while *she* is under anesthesia?" asked Dawn. "We can trim her nails or clean her ears. It's easier when they're asleep."

"Nope, just the teeth."

Dawn bristled at the word, *nope*. She found it to be dismissive and would have preferred a mere *no*, or even better, *no, thank you*. Growing up on her parents' farm, she'd spent her childhood dreaming of a life helping animals. Graham, the horse, and Betty, the cow, were her favorite siblings, much preferred over her half brothers. She knew some days would be challenging, but what she hadn't expected from this vocation was the amount of frustration that came from dealing with people.

She gently stroked Daisy, whose little head was still tracking every movement of her owner. "What a pretty girl you are. Can I have a quick look in your mouth?"

With the practiced hand of an experienced vet tech, Dawn gently pinched the back of the dog's jaw, forcing the mouth to open. A fair amount of plaque coated the front teeth. Releasing her grip on Daisy's mouth, the Dachshund promptly started licking her gums.

"It looks like she has some tartar buildup that we'll need to remove. I won't know her full condition until after we clean her teeth. If we find cavities, we have a few options, depending on your budget. We can take care of them up to a specific cost or call you to get approval for any additional procedures that may be necessary."

The guy looked up from his phone for the first time and scoffed. "My wife is already making me pay two hundred dollars just to clean its teeth. I don't want any upcharges."

"I understand, but it's my job to let you know her condition once we're able to get a better look."

"Sure, whatever."

Normally, Dawn would allow time for the owner to give a goodbye pet or kiss, but with this guy, she didn't bother. Instead, she scooped Daisy into her arms, wished the man a good day and exited the exam room. Daisy looked up and licked Dawn's nose. "Oh, you sweet girl. I sure hope your mamma loves you."

The treatment room had a metal table in the center and a stainless-steel sink in the corner. The floor was cream tile like the rest of the clinic, and the walls were painted light blue. Glass containers of Q-Tips, tongue depressors and gauze were neatly lined up on the counter next to a large jar of treats. Dawn drew up the meds and administered a sedative by inserting a needle just under the skin between Daisy's shoulder blades. Because the needle was small and Dawn knew exactly where to pinch the skin, the little dog didn't even flinch. She placed an IV catheter in Daisy's leg, taped the hub and took Daisy to the kennel.

Dawn knew she had just enough time to sneak another sip of coffee before the surgery room would become available. In the break room, Kelly Howell, Dawn's coworker and best friend, was stocking clean scrubs. Kelly was a petite brunette with owl-like brown eyes and short curly hair. She'd joined the vet clinic ten years ago, not long after Dawn, although the two women had chosen different paths. Dawn had worked summers while earning her bachelor's in biology from Clemson. She was president of the pre-veterinary society and had passed a two-year certification program. Kelly, on the other hand, had started as a receptionist and worked her way up. From an experience standpoint, they were peers, but Dawn's education earned her ten dollars an hour more than Kelly. The truth of the matter was that neither woman was in it for the money. They loved the animals.

"How was your weekend?" asked Kelly.

Dawn shrugged.

"Uh oh. Are you tired of Stuart already?"

"I don't know. He's good to me, but I'm not sure he's a good man."

"What do you mean?"

"It's like what my mom says. 'Watch how a man treats the janitor.' Then you can tell what he's really like. I'm pretty sure if Stuart ran over the janitor, he'd just keep on driving."

Kelly laughed. "Just the kind of guy you want to be the father of your children."

Before Dawn could respond, Regan Mead, one of the other vet techs, poked her head in the break room. "Room one is open," she said.

Dawn swiped her hands under the sanitizer dispenser and exited the break room to retrieve Daisy. The dog was like putty, relaxed and content, which was just what Dawn needed to make injecting the Propofol into the IV catheter an easy task. Within seconds, Daisy's head flopped to the side, allowing Dawn to insert a breathing tube. Next, she placed a mouth gag and started to administer a mixture of oxygen and Isoflurane, an anesthetic that would keep Daisy under sedation once the Propofol wore off.

As Dawn started cleaning Daisy's teeth, a large chunk of plaque broke off, revealing smelly rot underneath. She sighed—this tooth needed to come out. She fetched Dr. Patel, who examined Daisy's X-rays and inspected the rotten tooth.

"Mr. Hill only wanted a cleaning," reported Dawn. "He was adamant about not paying for anything else."

"Well, it's our job to educate him. Let's get him on the phone, please."

Dawn dutifully looked up the contact information for Brody Hill and handed the phone to the doctor.

"Mr. Hill, this is Dr. Patel. We have Daisy here and I wanted to give you an update. She's fine, still sedated. We've found a substantial amount of calculus on her teeth. Once it was removed, we could see tooth 106 was severely diseased, with significant pocketing, grade 4 mobility and evident bone loss. The gum has recessed leaving room for bacteria. If we leave it as is, she's prone to getting an abscess, which is extremely painful. My advice would be to extract the tooth. I'll pass you over to Dawn, who can discuss your options."

With that, Dr. Patel handed the phone to Dawn and left the room, oblivious to the position he'd put her in.

"I told your girl I just want the cleaning." Brody's voice was firm.

"Uhm, this is Dawn. We spoke earlier when you dropped off Daisy. If you choose to proceed with the extraction, that will be one hundred and fifty dollars."

"A hundred and fifty dollars," he exclaimed. "That's insane."

"I understand, but taking out the tooth now, before it creates additional complications, will be less expensive in the long run. And based on the severity of decay, Daisy's probably already in pain."

"She doesn't act like she's in any pain."

"Animals hide pain well, plus the bacteria could affect her heart."

"Look, I told you before, just do the cleaning. I don't pay that much for my own teeth. Why would I pay one hundred and fifty dollars for a dog?"

Dawn rolled her eyes. If she had a dollar for every time a pet owner made that unoriginal comment, she'd be retired on the beach.

"You're just trying to upsell me, but I know that game."

It wasn't like the money was going into Dawn's pocket, and Daisy needed the treatment. She clinched her teeth. "So you're declining the treatment?"

"Damn right I am."

"Okay, we'll give you a call when she's ready to be picked up—"

The line went dead before she could finish speaking. Dawn's chest tightened, just like the night of the car crash. She bet if Stuart owned Daisy, he'd leave the poor dog in pain, too. A striking clarity overcame her—she was ending the relationship. Then, she made a second bold decision. She was going to help this sweet dog. It wasn't Daisy's fault that she'd ended up with a jackass for an owner.

Dawn put an elevator, a tool used to sever the periodontal ligament, under the rotten tooth. Even under anesthesia, Daisy's jaw chattered due to the nerve pain. With a pair of sterile pliers and a strong tug, Dawn extracted the tooth. She pressed gauze against the gum to slow the bleeding. Fortunately, this tooth didn't require stitches, evidence that would've exposed her crime and possibly gotten her fired.

When they called Brody Hill to have Daisy picked up, she would explain that the tooth had simply fallen out due to the magnitude of decay. She'd congratulate him on his good luck of getting a free extraction. What they didn't know wouldn't hurt them, and her actions had helped Daisy. Most of all, she'd reached the limit of what she could tolerate, and bending the rules was the only way to keep her sanity.

Chapter 3

The rest of the day was the usual Monday chaos. The surgery room was backed up with sterile procedures: spaying, neutering and wound treatments. Non-sterile procedures like vaccinations and nail trims were done in the treatment room and overflowed to the intake rooms.

At 5:00 p.m., Dawn's phone buzzed. She expected it to be a call from her mom, Marie, adding one last item to the shopping list. Monday was grocery day, which Dawn did for herself and her housebound mother. But when she looked at the screen, she had a voicemail from an unknown number.

"Hi, this is Nick—from the Thai place. I was the other witness to the car accident."

Dawn smiled. How endearing that this Good Samaritan, who she met just two days ago, felt the need to reintroduce himself. Truth be told, she'd thought about him the entire evening after their brief encounter. When she hadn't heard from him by Sunday, she figured he wasn't going to call. She silently berated herself for not accompanying him inside the restaurant to see if the spark was mutual. Instead, she stayed faithful to her dwindling relationship and let Stuart drag her off, so the opportunity was lost. But now, maybe it wasn't.

"I wanted to let you know I found the owner of the Honda," the voicemail continued. "He was at the restaurant. I can tell you more about it if you want to call me back. Thanks."

A flicker of excitement grew in Dawn's belly. On her way home, she rushed through the aisles of the Ingles supermarket, checking off items from her mother's handwritten shopping list. The cursive was becoming larger and more noticeably jagged, an indication of Marie's declining eyesight. Eggs had been listed twice. Dawn wasn't sure if her mom's forgetfulness had become worse since her father's death a year earlier, or if he had concealed the extent of her condition. Still, it wasn't until Dawn helped sell the family farm and moved her mother to the duplex next door that she really noticed the decline.

She entered the kitchen of her mom's unit and began to unload the groceries. Marie, who'd been watching a Turner Classic movie, stood up from the couch. She was a tall woman with shoulder-length sandy hair and Coke-bottle glasses that made her blue eyes appear enlarged. In her late sixties, she was young to be a widow, but she'd married a man fifteen years her senior, and they'd had Dawn, their only child.

Dawn gave her mom a quick peck on the cheek before walking across their connected porch to her own unit. She kicked off her Crocs and headed for the bathroom, where she peeled off her scrubs and stepped into the steamy shower. She smiled as she recalled the day's events and how she'd helped Daisy. Then a troubling thought occurred to her. If Dr. Patel looked closely at the notes, he'd know that Daisy's tooth wasn't likely to fall out on its own. He'd know what she'd done. But he was a kind man and not the type to stir up trouble. Beyond that, his life had recently become quite busy. As a new father, raising baby Devin with Smita, one of the smartest, sweetest women Dawn had ever met, he wouldn't have the time to review her work. In any case, there was nothing she could do now—the damage, or rather the repair, was done.

In comfy sweatpants and a T-shirt, Dawn settled into the thick pillows of her couch to return Nick's call. He answered on the first ring, making her heartbeat quicken.

"Hi Nick, this is Dawn from the other night."

"Oh, hello. I wanted to let you know I found the owner of the Honda at the restaurant. I told him what happened and gave him the photo you took. He really appreciated having that kind of proof. He called the police and has my information in case he needs a statement. I told him there were other witnesses, but he probably just needs the one."

"I'm glad you found him. Have you heard anything more?"

"No. I meant to ask you, did your husband see the SUV drive away?"

"Oh, he isn't my husband. We were just on a date. Nothing serious."

The line went quiet. Dawn wondered if something in her voice revealed her lie. She and Stuart had never talked about being exclusive, but she was downplaying their relationship.

"In that case, would you like to meet at the Thai place for dinner this Friday? I know their best dishes, the ones they don't put on the menu. They kind of know me there."

Dawn bit her lower lip. Was he actually asking her on a date? He seemed so casual.

"Sure," she replied.

"How about we meet there at seven?"

"That sounds great. See you then." As she hung up, Dawn was already thinking about how she'd break up with Stuart.

Chapter 4

On Friday night, Dawn entered the restaurant wearing a sleeveless black dress and sandals. The dining area had small wooden tables. Larger booths upholstered in bright red vinyl lined the walls. Every surface was covered in decorative art: pictures of gold elephants, rows of framed bhat, the Thai paper currency, and exotic birds made of paper mâché. Each table had a fresh yellow rose in an ornate vase. The restaurant looked like the living room of an Asian grandmother who'd crammed all of her keepsakes into a tiny space.

Nick was already seated at a booth. When Dawn approached, he stood, towering over her. He wore designer jeans and a red polo shirt with a Porsche emblem.

A petite Asian woman arrived with a platter of steaming appetizers: Tom Ka soup, Thai dumplings and shrimp cakes. The aroma of curry, coconut and seafood filled her nostrils.

"I ordered a few things to get started," he said. "What would you like to drink?"

"A white wine," Dawn replied, looking at the waitress.

The woman shook her head. "No alcohol."

"They don't have a liquor license." Nick reached into a cooler by his side and pulled out a bottle of Sauvignon Blanc, two wine glasses and a corkscrew. "But they let me bring my own." He proceeded to uncork the bottle and poured two glasses, handing one to her. As he raised his hand, he asked, "To what shall we toast?"

Dawn blushed. It had been a long time since a guy had made her so nervous that she was tongue-tied.

"How about to being in the right place at the right time?" he offered.

Dawn nodded, clinked her glass with his and took a sip. "So, how did you find the owner of the Honda?"

"The staff knew him. Guess he's a regular, too."

"Have you heard back from him?"

"No, but he has the license plate of the perpetrator, thanks to you. I imagine his insurance will pursue it."

As Dawn took another sip of wine, a man dressed in a white chef's apron and hat placed a dish on the table. "Mr. Nick, Good to see you. I brought you my special roti canai, on the house."

"Thanks, Aroon." Nick gestured for Dawn to dig in, which she did. The chef waited momentarily for Dawn's approval before heading back to the kitchen.

"I guess they *do* know you here," she remarked.

"I come here a lot after work."

"What do you do?"

"I oversee the loan department at the Wells Fargo branch downtown."

"That's impressive."

He shrugged. "I have a good team. Now that I've trained them, I pretty much just sit back and let them run the show. What about you?"

"I'm a vet tech at the Village Veterinary Clinic."

"That sounds fun. Playing with puppies and kittens all day."

Normally, Dawn would've been irritated by such a gross misconception of her job, but somehow Nick's remark didn't set her off. "Actually, playing with puppies and kittens is a tiny part of what I do. Most of the animals I see are sick or dying, so I spend more time euthanizing them than playing with them. It can be more heartbreak than fun."

"I'm sorry. I didn't realize—"

"It's okay. Most people don't understand how hard it can be. I mean, I got into this kind of work because I love animals, but there's a reason we have mandatory compassion fatigue courses every six months."

"Compassion fatigue? That's when you don't care anymore?"

"Kind of. It's easy to become indifferent because we see the same trauma day after day. Last week, I treated three dogs with heatstroke. One owner refused to accept that leaving his dog in the car was the problem—because, he argued, the windows were cracked. Can you imagine sitting in ninety degrees for an hour wearing a fur coat? Or this week, I had the sweetest little Dachshund. Her owner refused to pay to extract a tooth that was clearly infected and painful."

Nick was about to take a bite of dumpling but placed his fork back on the plate.

"I'm sorry," she apologized. "I get wound up sometimes when I talk about my work."

"It's understandable. How do you deal with it?"

"Well, I try to trust my instincts. For Daisy, I pulled out the tooth anyway and just said it fell out."

"What about the dog with the heatstroke?"

"He barely survived. That day required a cold beer in a hot shower."

"Hmm. A beautiful girl in the shower with a beer. Care for company?" He flashed a grin.

Dawn felt the chemistry between them sizzle. Even in the early days with Stuart, she'd never experienced this level of connection. Just then, her phone buzzed. It was silenced, but they both could hear it vibrating against the vinyl seat.

She glanced at the screen to see a text from Stuart: *Let me know when you're back.*

Dawn knew what he wanted—a late-night booty call once she'd returned from girls' night out, a fib she'd told to have the night free. She knew lying was wrong, but what if Nick was simply updating her on the car accident?

"Do you need to get that?" he asked.

"It's nothing."

"Shall we order?" Nick raised his hand, signaling the waitress.

With an entire table full of appetizers, Dawn couldn't imagine eating anything more, but Nick took the liberty of ordering the main course and poured each of them another glass of wine.

"Did you grow up here?" he asked.

Dawn nodded.

"Your family is still here?"

"Just my mom. My dad passed away last year—cancer." Dawn reached for the gold, heart-shaped locket that never left her neck. She opened the side lock, which revealed miniature portraits of her parents. "My folks," she said, and waited for the obligatory condolence. Over the past year, there'd been hundreds of "I'm sorrys" and dozens of "Let me know how I can help." All of them had good intentions, but each one had left her feeling hollow.

"What was the worst part of losing your dad?" he asked.

No one had ever asked her how she'd felt. "You'd probably think it was no longer having him around, but he was suffering. He'd become so thin and was being fed from a tube. That was no way to live. I was relieved to know he was finally at peace. The worst part was my brothers from his first marriage. Dad left everything to Mom and me, and they were horrible about it. Even tried to contest the will. They always picked on me as a kid, but I never expected them to get so ugly over money."

"How'd they pick on you?"

"You name it. Made me eat worms, dragged me down the stairs in a sleeping bag, told me a monster lived in my closet. As a kid, I avoided them as much as I could. After school, I'd go to the barn to escape them."

"That's terrible."

"It's why I don't miss them. We weren't close before, and now we don't talk at all. But enough of me, what about your family?"

"They're still in Holland. I'm the only one who crossed the pond."

"You're Dutch?"

"Yes. My family name is VanBroklin. We kind of own the banking business in Amsterdam, but I wanted to make my own way."

"How'd you end up in South Carolina?"

"If I'd used our connections, I could've skipped the hard part, landed in New York, and had a thriving business, but I didn't want that, so here I am with *all y'all*." Nick's attempt at a Southern drawl was pathetic, making Dawn burst into laughter.

When the main course arrived, a mixture of beef, noodles and vegetables, Dawn could hardly eat. The appetizers had been filling, plus her stomach was in knots—in a good way. For the first time in a long time, she'd met someone who really listened. At the end of the meal, the waitress placed a leather folder on the table between them.

"You know the Dutch custom about picking up the check?" he asked.

Dawn knew the term, Dutch treat, meaning they'd split the bill. Was that what he meant?

"We pick up the bill," he said.

Dawn breathed a sigh of relief. He'd ordered so many pricey dishes without asking her. Naturally, she assumed he'd pay.

"We pick up the bill," he repeated, "Look at it and put it back down." As he spoke, he retrieved the folder, glanced inside, and placed it back on the table without adding any form of payment.

Before Dawn could react, Nick began laughing. He pulled a wad of cash from his pocket and slapped two crisp hundred-dollar bills on the table.

"You get it?" he asked. "We pick up the bill?"

"I get it." Dawn rolled her eyes. His amusement with the wordplay was far more entertaining than the joke itself. "At least let me get the tip."

"Already taken care of. You ready to go?"

As the pair exited the restaurant, the hostess waved. "Thank you, Mr. Nick. See you soon."

Outside, the cool air of the restaurant gave way to the muggy summer heat. Dawn scanned the spot where the damaged Honda had been parked. Had it not been for the actions of a bad guy, she would not have met this good guy.

At her Jeep, she leaned against the driver's side and faced Nick. "I had a really good time. Thank you," she said.

He reached for her hand and softly kissed it, all the while staring into her eyes as if mentally undressing her. Dawn's whole body quivered. She wanted more. She knew there would be more. But first, she had to officially call things off with Stuart.

Nick opened the door and helped her inside. "Be safe," he said, then patted the roof, as if giving the okay for her to leave.

At home, Marie's kitchen light was still on. Dawn burst into her mom's duplex ready to share every detail of her evening.

"You just missed Stuart," said Marie.

"What?" Dawn's brows furrowed.

"He knew you were out with your girlfriends, but he stopped by to give me a present." Marie pointed to a brand-new Alexa perched on the kitchen counter. "He showed me how to ask her questions and play music. I can even tell her to make a phone call. Isn't that clever?"

"How dare he. This wasn't a gift, Mom, but an excuse for him to stop by unannounced."

In the past, Dawn might've considered his actions kind, but now they felt overbearing and presumptuous. A troubling thought crossed her mind, knowing Stuart worked in IT. "Those things can eavesdrop. Did you know that?"

"Eavesdrop? How?" asked Marie.

"I don't know exactly, but I don't trust it. Haven't you heard the stories? You talk about needing a new pair of shoes, then ads for shoes start popping up on your phone?"

The excitement Dawn had felt from her date with Nick had evaporated, turning into anger at Stuart for pulling such a stunt. She marched over to the device and pressed the power button. The illuminated blue ring extinguished.

"I don't want you using it," declared Dawn. "I'm telling Stuart to take it back. In fact, I'm telling him we're done."

Back at her place, Dawn's attention returned to Nick. She searched for him on Instagram but found nothing. She tried TikTok and Facebook—still nothing. Dawn googled: *VanBroklin Amsterdam Banking*. Several articles about his family, primarily his prominent father, were featured. A few photographs of his parents dressed for a black-tie event were available, and a short mention of their six children, but no additional pictures.

The next morning, Dawn had just finished her Saturday run when Stuart called. "I'm going to pick up dinner later. What do you want?"

His offer to bring over dinner used to please Dawn, and he often ordered a third plate for Marie. Given how he pampered her mom, Dawn shouldn't have been so annoyed by the Alexa. And given they'd spent the last few months together, it was reasonable for him to expect to come over.

"I think I'm just going to stay in tonight," she said.

"That's fine. We can watch a movie. What do you want to eat?"

"I mean, I'd rather have the night to myself."

"I didn't see you last night," he protested, then added. "Look, if you're still mad about that stupid car accident, I told you I was sorry. I thought we were past that."

"I am so past that."

"What does that mean? What do you want from me?"

"Right now, I want some space."

The line was quiet for a moment. "What about Fort Lauderdale?" he asked. They had planned the trip weeks ago. Stuart was flying down to help his parents move, and Dawn had planned to join him over the weekend for a short beach vacation.

"I think you should go without me."

"Go without you?" he repeated. "I already bought your plane ticket, and my mom really wants to meet you."

Dawn shook her head. She couldn't meet his parents. That would send the absolute wrong message. She wasn't looking to get more serious with him.

"I can't go. I'm sorry, but I just can't."

"What am I supposed to tell my parents?"

"Tell them we're taking a break."

"You're seriously not going?" Stuart exhaled into the phone. "I can't believe you, Dawn. You know if I cancel your ticket now and you change your mind, the fare is going to double."

Had he not heard her? This conversation wasn't about her changing her mind about a trip. She'd changed her mind about *him*. Before she could say anything further, he yelled a string of obscenities into the phone and hung up.

Chapter 5

Dawn's first appointment Monday morning was an eight-year-old female golden retriever named Lucky, owned by Allie Church. Because the town of Laurel had only one high school, the women knew each other, although Allie was a few years younger. When Dawn entered the room, the dog was sprawled on the floor with her head resting on her paws. Allie was sitting cross-legged next to Lucky, stroking her thick fur.

"Something's wrong," said Allie. "She's been sleeping more than usual and she's barely eating."

Dawn listened to the dog's heart. Everything sounded normal. She checked the color of Lucky's gums, which could indicate a loss of blood or shock. When she pressed gently against Lucky's abdomen, the dog let out a sharp yelp.

"Has she been constipated?" Dawn suspected something could be stuck in Lucky's intestines.

"Doesn't seem to be."

"I'd suggest we do an X-ray of her belly and draw blood to get a better idea of what's going on."

"How much will that cost?" asked Allie.

"Around four hundred dollars."

The girl winced. "That's a lot."

"I could start with just the X-rays. That's about two hundred. If they're inconclusive, we'll need to discuss the blood work as a second step."

Allie agreed, so Dawn took Lucky to the treatment area and hoisted her onto the table. She called her colleague, Alex Camp, to assist. Alex was a big guy, towering over the girls, which was especially handy with Great Danes and St. Bernards, but his help wasn't necessary. Lucky lowered her head and closed her eyes, as if saying, "I'll do my part and sit still if you'll just find out what's wrong with me."

The X-rays of the mid-section provided a definitive answer—Lucky's uterus was filled with fluid. Dawn reflected on the many animals she'd treated named Lucky. In her experience, that name was a guaranteed curse.

"Well, the good news is we found the problem," Dawn told Allie as she returned to the exam room. "Lucky has pyometra—an infection of the uterus. This condition requires surgery, but at her age, the probability of a full recovery is quite good."

"How much is the surgery?" asked Allie.

"Could be anywhere between two and three thousand dollars."

"Are you kidding?" Allie's voice was strained. "I can't afford that. What happens if she doesn't have it?"

"If we don't operate, she'll get septic and die."

The girl's eyes started to water. "You mean if I can't pay for the surgery, she'll die?"

Dawn nodded.

"And y'all would just let her die?"

"Well, that's not our decision," corrected Dawn. "Maybe you could start a GoFundMe? I've seen that work before to raise money. Or take out a credit card?"

"I already have three maxed out." Allie pressed her hands against her forehead and started to pace. She muttered to herself, "What am I going to do? I can't watch her suffer. I can't." Suddenly, she jerked to a stop. With what seemed like absolute resolve, Allie declared, "You need to keep her from suffering. If you won't do the surgery, then put her down."

"You want us to euthanize her?" clarified Dawn.

"If you really loved animals, you'd do the surgery for free. But if you won't, then yes. I won't let her suffer."

Dawn ignored the jab—one she'd heard many times before. If the clinic covered every surgery, it would be bankrupt. She spoke slowly and deliberately, trying to determine if Allie was really willing to put Lucky down or if she was bluffing to get a free procedure.

"Have you ever put an animal to sleep before?" asked Dawn.

"No."

"Well, let me explain the process. We inject a sedative to relax her and then administer a second injection that is simply an overdose of an anesthetic. After the second injection, Lucky will go to sleep and her heart will stop beating. Her body may have a few reflexes—she might gasp or flinch—but she's not suffering. Then it will be over."

Allie recoiled in horror, but Dawn pressed on. "Her eyes will stay open. The eyes don't shut when you die—that only happens in movies. You may even think she's staring at you, but she isn't. Her bowels will void, so she'll likely defecate or urinate."

Dawn wasn't sharing these grisly details to be unkind—her motive was the opposite. She needed to be certain Allie was serious. The girl had come to the decision so quickly. She added, "Once it's done, there's no going back. Maybe you'd like to take her home for a few days and think about it?"

Allie bowed her head and whispered, "No. I can't afford three thousand dollars, and someone has to ensure she doesn't suffer."

Dawn lowered her head—another senseless death. She fetched Lucky from the kennel to allow the pair some final moments together. "Take as long as you'd like," she offered, secretly hoping Allie might change her mind.

After about fifteen minutes, Dawn poked her head into the room. Allie sat cross-legged on the floor, sniffling and stroking Lucky's back. Seeing Dawn, she withdrew her hand. "Go ahead. You can take her."

"I can administer the drugs in here, so you can be with her. I know it's the hardest part of being a pet owner, but your presence will comfort her."

Allie shook her head. "I can't watch."

Don't be so selfish, thought Dawn. *Suck it up for your pet. You're not the one dying today.* This wasn't the first time Dawn had to perform an unnecessary euthanasia, yet this one particularly stung. Maybe it was because she'd lost her dad a year earlier, which brought a heightened awareness of the finality of death.

"Are you sure?" asked Dawn. "You won't regret not being there for her? I'm sure she'd be there for you."

"Don't you understand?" Allie exploded. "I don't want this. I can't watch."

Dawn walked over to Lucky, who today, she thought, was the unluckiest dog alive. She took her by the collar and pulled her toward the door, but Lucky wasn't having it. The dog's paws scraped against the linoleum floor in a desperate attempt to rejoin Allie, which forced Dawn to carry her out of the room.

Once in the treatment area, Dawn alerted the other vet techs, Kelly, Regan, and Alex, to the impending procedure. All work paused. All joking ceased. The room became silent. Everyone took a moment to love on poor Lucky. Regan retrieved a chocolate bar from her locker and fed small pieces to Lucky, which she eagerly lapped up. No one needed to worry about the stomachache that would ensue. At that moment, spoiling Lucky for the last few moments of her life was all that mattered.

Dawn spoke softly as she stroked the dog. "It's okay, girl. You'll get to play in puppy heaven and chase all the squirrels you want and have endless treats."

With a deep breath and a silent prayer, Dawn placed the IV catheter in Lucky's leg. Alex wrapped his giant arms around Regan and Kelly as they watched in silence. Dawn injected Propofol, a short-lasting sedative that relaxed the body, and Lucky's head fell to the side.

"Wait!" shouted Suzanne, the red-headed receptionist, as she barged into the room. "Allie Church came back. She wants more time. Please tell me you haven't—"

Dawn froze. She was literally seconds away from injecting the Euthasol.

Chapter 6

That evening, Dawn was supposed to have a second date with Nick. She considered cancelling. The rollercoaster of emotions over Lucky's stay of execution had left her completely drained, but her excitement to see Nick again won out. At 6:30 p.m., she heard the revving of a motorcycle outside. Nick dismounted a bright green Kawasaki Ninja and swaggered up the front path, helmet in hand.

"I guess your Porsche is in the shop," she joked as she opened the door, remembering his shirt from their first date.

"It is," he replied. "Hope you don't mind the bike."

Outside, Nick handed Dawn a spare helmet and gently buckled it under her chin. She found this simple task, him fastening the clasp, to be so sensual. He mounted and steadied the bike, and Dawn climbed aboard. She wrapped her arms around his waist, and they sped off, the wind in her face.

At a local pizza joint, Nick picked a table in the back, ordered a pitcher of beer and the house special. "How was your day?" he asked.

"I don't even know where to start," said Dawn. "Let's just say for once, the dog I treated has a fitting name." She recounted how they'd barely escaped a tragedy. If Allie Church had shown up seconds later, Lucky would've already been gone.

"Sounds like the dog is still going to die," he surmised.

"True." Dawn realized the relief she was feeling for Lucky was only temporary. "Without surgery, she'll deteriorate over the next few weeks. Instead of a quick death by Euthasol, she'll suffer. The really unfortunate part is that all of this could've been avoided if Lucky had been spayed."

"I'm starting to see why your job isn't playing with puppies and kittens all day." Nick reached forward and took her hand. "You said the operation is three thousand dollars? What if I were to pay for it?"

Dawn nearly spit out her beer. "Pay for it? Why would you do that?"

"I don't know. You've kind of got me feeling for this dog, Lucky, and I bet the owner isn't going to do anything."

"Three thousand dollars is a lot of money for a dog you don't even know."

"My family wastes that much on a weekend getaway. Why not put the money to good use? What do you need? A credit card?"

"You're serious?" Dawn studied Nick's face, looking for some indication that he was joking.

"*Dead* serious." He laughed. "I'm kidding, but yes, I'm serious." He casually took a swig of beer as if shelling out thousands of dollars was nothing.

"It's a lot of money, and I don't think the owner will pay you back," cautioned Dawn. "And if we're going to date, and I'm going to tell you about every sob story at the clinic, you can't offer to pay for each one."

With a charming smile, Nick replied, "So we're going to date?"

The next morning, before Dawn called Allie to bring in Lucky for the surgery, she texted Nick. "Had a great time last night. Are you sure about Lucky?"

"100 percent. Need my credit card?" he replied.

"Not yet. Suzanne from the front desk will reach out to you."

Dawn thought about asking again if he was absolutely certain, but she didn't want to offend him. Apparently, Nick didn't consider three thousand dollars to be a lot of money. Something about letting him pay didn't feel entirely ethical, but she wasn't breaking the law. She dismissed her uneasiness, knowing that Lucky was going to be saved.

When Dawn shared the good news with Allie, the girl burst into tears. After the sedative, Lucky had slept the rest of the prior day and refused to eat that morning, which ended up being a blessing. They could perform emergency surgery that morning. In the daily meeting, Dawn announced that they'd need to add an unscheduled ovariohysterectomy for Lucky. The room erupted into applause—except for Kelly.

"I never expected Allie to find a way," said Kelly, who also knew Allie Church from high school. "I was certain she'd take Lucky home, do nothing and let that sweet girl suffer."

Dawn wanted to share the full story with her best friend, but she remained quiet. What Nick was doing was altruistic but also so unusual. Beyond that, money was a sensitive topic with Kelly. Dawn made more, was able to spend more and had her mom for support. Kelly wasn't as fortunate. She and her siblings had been left to fend for themselves from an early age. She often described her childhood as a daily episode of *The Hunger Games*—eat or be eaten, kill or be killed. It was a peculiar thought, but Dawn was certain that if Kelly knew about Nick's involvement, she'd find a reason not to like him.

Dawn thought about the previous evening when she and Nick had stood on the porch after dinner. He'd taken her hands and wrapped them behind her back. Gripping her wrists firmly, he'd inched forward, forcing her to step back until she was pinned against the front door. Then, he'd leaned in and gently kissed her for the first time.

"There's someone out front to see you," said Suzanne, interrupting Dawn's daydream.

"Allie Church? How'd she get here so fast?"

"No, it's a guy."

Dawn and Kelly exchanged a quizzical look.

When Dawn entered the front reception, she saw Stuart holding a bouquet of red roses. He looked different and not in a good way. His curly blonde hair, which once had seemed wild and sexy, reminded her of an over-sprouted Chia Pet. His muscular arms, which she'd once thought manly, appeared to be bulging and unnatural. And his clear green eyes now looked reptilian.

"What are you doing here?" she asked. In the months they'd been dating, he'd never shown up at her work.

"Look, I know you're pissed about that car wreck, but can we get past that? Please?"

Dawn motioned Stuart to the side of the waiting area. There were no customers yet as the clinic had just opened, but she didn't need Suzanne eavesdropping. "You can't be here," she said. "I have a busy day. We have an emergency surgery."

Stuart gestured toward an empty waiting room and sneered. "I can see it's standing room only."

"This is not the right time or place." Stuart's sarcasm irked Dawn. Whether he understood her job or not, she did have to prep for Lucky's operation.

"Do you know how many girls would cream if their boyfriend brought them flowers to work?"

"Don't be crass." Dawn crossed her arms. The two stood in silence, glaring at each other.

Suddenly, a middle-aged woman dressed in a designer jogging suit barged through the front door with her leashed German Shepherd. Dawn immediately recognized Mrs. Rhodes and her dog, Hunter. He was a frequent flier, constantly getting into skirmishes.

Seeing Dawn, Mrs. Rhodes rushed toward her. "Help. Please. I need your help. Hunter's been hurt."

Dawn looked at Stuart. "We'll finish this later."

He flung the roses to the floor and stormed out of the clinic like a petulant child, trampling the flowers on his way out.

Chapter 7

That evening over dinner, Dawn told her mom how Nick had saved Lucky. Sharing some good news after the year they'd endured was a welcome change. Losing her dad was Dawn's first blow, followed by the battle with her two half brothers contesting the will. The women had prevailed in the lawsuit thanks to their lawyer, Benjamin Clayton, and the indisputable clarity of the estate documents. But the unanticipated animosity, layered over their grief and mourning, had taken its toll.

"I'd like to meet this generous young man," said Marie. "Why don't you invite him for dinner?"

"Mom, we just started going out," protested Dawn. Although Dawn usually reserved introducing her parents until months into a relationship, the complicating factor was that her mom lived next door. Deciding it was better to orchestrate an introduction rather than having Nick run into Marie on the front porch, she extended Nick an offer of a home-cooked meal.

On the evening Nick was to meet Marie, Dawn waited outside in the rocking chair. As the rocker pitched back and forth, creaking against the wooden boards, her anxiety intensified. What would Nick think of her humble duplex and the fact that her mother lived next door?

Her thoughts were interrupted by the rumble of a motorcycle. She watched, biting her lower lip as Nick dismounted and sauntered up the walk. At the top of the steps, he retrieved a bottle of red wine and a bouquet of flowers from his backpack.

"Flowers for me?" she asked, playfully outstretching her hands.

He drew the bouquet away like a kid protecting a prized toy. "For your mom. Is she here yet?"

"Right, about that. She lives there." Dawn pointed to her mother's door on the other side of the porch and held her breath. Nick didn't respond, but she could see his mind churning. She backtracked, explaining quickly. "She moved next door after my dad died. I just wanted her close by to make sure she's okay. She can be a little forgetful at times, but she totally respects my privacy."

He smiled, his deep brown eyes seeming to twinkle with amusement. "I think that's perfect."

Dawn exhaled a sigh of relief and led him inside her mother's unit. The savory aroma of a stewing roast filled the air. Marie wiped her hands on her apron before graciously accepting the flowers and wine. Her smile broadened—the same radiant smile that her daughter had inherited. The two women even stood in a similar pose, leaning slightly on one hip.

"Why don't you two have a seat in the dining room?" said Marie. "I'll be right in."

Dawn and her mom typically ate in the kitchen, but Marie had chosen the dining room for this special meal. From the head of her antique table, looking through the back sliding glass door, Nick would have a view of her lush flower and vegetable garden.

"Mind if I use your water closet?" he asked.

"Of course, dear. Down the hall to the right."

Once Nick was out of earshot, Marie whispered, "Stuart never washed up before dinner."

Dawn rolled her eyes but was secretly delighted that Nick was earning her mom's approval. Out of the corner of her eye, Dawn spotted the Alexa perched on the kitchen counter with its blue band illuminated. "I thought I asked you to turn that thing off."

"It's useful," said Marie. "If I forget something, I can ask her."

An image of Stuart secretly listening to their conversation popped into Dawn's mind. It was an outrageous thought, but still, it was conceivable. She imagined him pounding his fist into the wall when he heard her introduce Nick. She pictured him racing over, uninvited, and provoking a confrontation. Nick was taller, but Stuart was more muscular. In a fistfight, he'd likely win.

Dawn marched over to the device and yanked the cord from the wall. The light went out, giving her an immediate sense of relief. "If you like it so much, I'll get you a new one, but you're not using *that* one."

"Is something wrong?"

Nick's voice made both women jump. Dawn blushed as if she'd been caught red-handed talking about Stuart. Marie, avoiding the question, invited everyone into the dining room. The table was set with her Sunday best: china plates, salad and dinner forks, dessert spoons and crystal water glasses. Marie served Nick first, spooning large chunks of roast beef topped with carrots, potatoes and onions onto his plate. Dawn took these home-cooked meals for granted, but Nick appeared to relish every bite.

"So, Nick," said Marie. "Dawn says you're from the Netherlands. What brought you to the States?"

"College, but then I decided to stay. My family is in banking. I wanted to be in the business but make it on my own."

"Is any of your family here?" asked Marie.

"Just me. My parents and five brothers and sisters are still over there. I go back a few times a year to visit, but America is home for me now."

Marie smiled and, as if rewarding his answer, refilled Nick's wine glass, which finished the bottle.

"Let me run next door to get another," offered Dawn. At her place, she scanned her wine rack. Nothing she had was as fancy as the bottle he'd brought. She grabbed a ten-dollar Cabernet and headed back. As soon as she entered Marie's kitchen,, Dawn could hear Nick's panicked voice.

"Are you okay? How can I help? Let me take your arm," he said.

In the dining room, Dawn found Marie sprawled face down on the floor, arms flailing, while Nick kneeled next to her.

"Mom! What happened?"

"I must have lost my balance."

"She just fell," said Nick. "I tried to catch her, but she was too far away."

Dawn took one of Marie's arms, and Nick took the other. They lifted her to a chair where she fanned her face and tried to catch her breath.

"How'd you lose your balance?" asked Dawn.

"I don't know."

Dawn noticed her mom's empty wine glass on the table. "Oh no."

"What?" Nick and Marie asked in unison.

"You shouldn't have been drinking alcohol with your blood pressure medication. Did you get dizzy? Is that why you fell?"

"I don't think I was dizzy," replied Marie.

"This is my fault," said Nick. He kneeled next to Marie's chair. "I should've asked before bringing wine."

"It's not your fault," said Dawn. "It's mine. I didn't think about her mixing alcohol with her Lisinopril. She doesn't usually drink." Dawn turned to her mom. "Are you okay? Do you think you should go to the emergency room to get checked out?"

"No, dear. I'm fine. Just a bit winded." Marie started to get up. "We still have dessert."

Dawn put her hand on her mom's shoulder. "I'll get it."

When she returned from the kitchen carrying a plate of fried dough balls covered in powdered sugar, Dawn began to wonder if her mom was losing it. "You made donuts for dessert?" she asked.

"Those aren't donuts, dear. I bet Nick knows what they are."

Nick scanned the plate but didn't speak.

Marie's brow furrowed, as if she'd made a terrible mistake. "I was trying to make oliebollen, to give you a taste of home."

"Oh, I'm sorry. I didn't—"

"No need to apologize. I obviously didn't make them right."

"I really appreciate the effort." Nick smiled sheepishly. He reached for one of the pastries and took an oversized bite. "They're delicious. Better than Mom's."

As if he hadn't already won Marie over, that proclamation sealed the deal. After dessert, Marie excused herself to take an Advil and lie down, declining their offers of assistance.

Dawn took Nick's hand, leading him outside. On the porch, he stopped her, pulled her close and kissed her. "I've been wanting to do that all night," he said.

"I'd invite you over, but I need to make sure Mom isn't just putting on a brave face. Maybe we can see each other this weekend?"

"I'm going camping this weekend."

Dawn's heart sank.

"You can come with me, if you want," he offered.

Her face brightened as she leaned in for another kiss, but Nick pulled away and squinted as he stared over her head.

"What is it?" she asked.

"Do you recognize that car?"

Dawn whipped around to see a silver sedan parked down the street. She couldn't say for certain, because it was dark, but it looked like Stuart's Lexus.

"Isn't that the guy you were with the other night?" he asked.

Dawn hadn't spoken to Stuart since he'd stormed out of the clinic—no phone calls, no texts, nothing. Frankly, she didn't care, but if he was spying on her, that was creepy. Her suspicions about the Alexa had been half joking, but now she wondered if he had planted some sort of listening device. He was clever enough to do it. She studied the car more carefully. It was parked just beyond the streetlamp, making it impossible to tell if anyone was inside.

"I'm not sure," she replied. "It could be him."

"Want me to check it out?"

"No, that's okay. If it's him, I'll make sure he knows not to come around again."

After the couple said goodnight, Dawn checked on Marie, who had a bruised knee but was otherwise okay. Before loading the dishwasher, she stepped outside and peered down the dark street. The silver car was gone.

Chapter 8

On Saturday morning, Nick pulled up in a white Ford pickup truck. The cargo bed was fully loaded with camping gear: a tent, coolers, backpacks and other supplies.

"How many vehicles do you have?" asked Dawn. There was the Porsche, the motorcycle and now a truck.

"Well, I need this one for camping," he said, as he escorted her to the passenger seat.

The two drove northwest to the Blue Ridge Mountains and Oconee State Park. Nick sang along to music from a classic rock station as he tapped the steering wheel. Every once in a while, he'd try for a high note and go wildly off-key, making them both laugh.

They followed signs toward backcountry camping, away from the more populated tent grounds. A few miles in, Nick veered off the main road and onto a dirt path leading into the woods.

"Have you been here before?" asked Dawn.

"In the general area." Once they parked, he handed her a lanyard with a silver whistle. "In case you get lost, just blow me and I'll know where to find you."

Dawn suppressed a giggle. Every once in a while, Nick would say something that reminded her that English wasn't his first language. She was tempted to explain the real meaning of what he'd just said, but the sexual suggestion had her tongue-tied.

"How about I just call you?" she suggested. But when Dawn looked at her phone, she understood his point—no service. As much as she wanted this trip to be adventurous, even romantic, she immediately had second thoughts. What if her mom needed to reach her?

Nick started scouting for a location to pitch the tent. In his olive hiking shorts, untucked tan T-shirt and brown ankle boots, he could've been a model for Patagonia. He spotted an area with a gradual slant and raked the spot clear. He anchored the ground tarp with a mallet, unrolled the tent and secured the edges before threading the two cross poles over the top.

"I thought I'd leave the top open," he said. "It's not supposed to rain and will give us some breeze. How about you put down the sleeping bags while I get the fire started?"

While Dawn unrolled the sleeping bags, Nick dug a dirt ring about fifty feet from the tent. He stacked small dry branches in the center and lit the fire. As the flame took hold, he added larger sticks, prodding them with a piece of metal rebar. Dawn joined him, sitting on a log that he'd positioned by the fire. She hadn't noticed before, but he'd also brought two plastic coolers for drinks and food.

"Beer is for starting the fire," he said, as he handed her a bottle. "And wine goes with dinner." Nick opened the cooler to reveal two steaks and corn on the cob wrapped in foil.

"Is this how you rough it?" she teased.

"If you weren't here, I'd be eating a pouch meal and boiling my water, so thanks for keeping me civilized." He leaned over and kissed her on the cheek.

"Speaking of which, I don't suppose there's an outhouse around here?"

"Afraid not." He reached for his backpack and pulled out a hand shovel, a roll of toilet paper and wet wipes. "You'll need to go away from the camp, dig a hole and cover it up. Don't want any bears tracking your scent."

"Bears, really? There are bears out here?"

"They won't bother us. And if they do, I'm prepared." Nick lifted the hem of his T-shirt to expose an HK VP9 pistol holstered at his waist. Dawn had seen the slight bulge when admiring his body, but never imagined he was carrying a firearm.

"You have a gun?" Her voice went up an octave.

"Just a precaution. I don't plan on using it."

"I have a whistle, but you need a gun? Maybe I'll skip going to the bathroom."

"I can stand guard," he offered.

Dawn shook her head. Like it or not, she was going to have to traipse into the woods with nothing more than a whistle for protection. As she squatted, exposed from the waist down, she scanned the forest, looking for any signs of movement. Everything was eerily still. Suddenly, a flock of birds scattered like black confetti thrown into the air. Dawn gasped. She placed the whistle between her lips, hastily wiped herself and hurried back to the campsite.

When she returned, the fire was already crackling. Nick offered her a glass of red wine, and they enjoyed their steak dinner as the sun set over the trees, casting brilliant shades of orange and crimson. Dawn marveled at the man sitting next to her. Never before had she been so attracted to someone.

For dessert, he cored an apple, filled it with marshmallows and chocolate and roasted it over the hot coals. Of all of the elaborate pastries Marie had ever made, this simple delicacy was just as tasty. The thought of her mom, alone and unable to contact her daughter, soured Dawn's appetite. She tried to dismiss her concern—it was only one night.

"Something wrong?" he asked.

Dawn was taken aback. How was Nick so perceptive? She shook her head and tried to brush off her uneasiness.

"I'll have to show this dessert to Mom," she said. She held up the apple, leaned toward Nick and took a selfie. The photo came out fuzzy because of the dim light, but it was their first official picture together. In the weeks to follow, she'd regret not having taken a better one.

After dinner, as the fire smoldered, Nick lit a lantern and pulled Dawn close. They sat in silence, listening to the sounds of the crickets chirping in the summer heat.

"That's how the males attract a mate," he said. "They rub their wings together so the females will hear them—the louder, the better."

"Sounds like a guy," she said. "Showboating to sleep with the girl."

Nick cupped his hands over his mouth and imitated the sound of the crickets. "Is it working?" he asked with a smile.

"Oh yeah, it's working."

Without speaking, he took Dawn by the hand and led her to the tent. He pulled his T-shirt over his head, revealing his toned abs. Not taking his eyes off her, he unzipped his shorts, carefully placing the holstered gun on the ground. He stepped out of his hiking boots and, without inhibition, removed his briefs. There he stood in front of her, naked, muscular and hard. Nick scooped Dawn into his arms and gently placed her on the sleeping bag. He unzipped her shorts and pulled her panties to her ankles. Leaning forward, he lowered his head between her legs.

Dawn's whole body tensed. Normally, she would've stopped him. She would've pulled his face to hers and guided him inside of her, intercepting the oral sex, which felt too intimate. But with Nick, she was strangely willing to be more vulnerable. In that moment, she shut her eyes and relaxed, letting her body feel the flit of his tongue.

That was her first orgasm of the night, followed by another one once he was inside of her. What they shared was a tenderness unlike anything she'd felt before. She'd only known Nick for a few short weeks. Was it possible that she was already in love?

Sleep came easily—satiated with a hearty dinner, flowing wine and steamy sex—but a few hours later, Dawn jerked awake. Had she heard a noise or just dreamed it? Light from the stars beamed through the mesh tent, making a grid-like pattern on Nick's empty sleeping bag.

"Nick?" she whispered, as she sat up.

No answer.

Just as she was about to crawl outside to look for him, she heard twigs snapping, as if someone —or something —was lurking around the back of the tent. Dawn held her breath and listened. Were those footsteps? Two-legged or four? Curious or malicious? Her whistle was somewhere in the tent, carelessly discarded in the heat of passion. She groped around the sleeping bag, desperately trying to find it.

The crunching outside continued, moving closer. Dawn froze, paralyzed with fear. Whatever was out there started jabbing into the tent's sheer nylon.

"Nick!" she shouted.

Still no answer.

Dawn caught sight of the metal rebar Nick had used to poke the fire. She gripped it like a spear, feeling her rapid heartbeat pulse in her hand. Summoning every ounce of her resolve, she charged out of the tent, naked and screaming at the top of her lungs. She was prepared to confront whatever was out there—but all was quiet.

Dawn was alone. No bear. No intruder. Nothing.

Suddenly, the crunching started again, behind her. She whipped around to see a shadow moving in the distance.

"Who's there?" she demanded.

From the darkness, a naked figure emerged, wearing nothing but a gun belt and holster.

"It's me. What's wrong?" he asked.

Dawn recognized Nick's voice before she could see his face.

"Where've you been? I was calling you. Why didn't you tell me you were leaving?"

"I didn't want to wake you up. You were snoring so peacefully."

"I don't snore," she snapped. "There was something outside the tent."

Nick didn't react.

"Didn't you see it?" she asked, still panicked. "It was right there." She pointed to the back of the tent.

Nick switched on the flashlight in his hand. "I don't see anything. Whatever it was, it's gone now."

The next morning, Dawn awoke to light beaming through the top of the tent. Being able to see her surroundings—the trees, ground and footpath leading to the truck—made the scare from the night before seem silly. It had probably been a small animal, but her mind sure had played tricks on her in the dark.

Nick was by the pit, preparing to light another fire.

"Good morning," he said. "I brought eggs and sausage. Thought we could take a hike after breakfast."

She glanced at the screen of her phone and frowned. Still no service.

"You're worried about your mom?" he asked.

"I know I'm being silly, but I didn't realize she wouldn't be able to reach me. I told her I was going camping with you, and I'm sure she'll remember, but—"

"Why don't we return?" he suggested. "I'll make you both breakfast."

"You sure?"

"Positive. Just have to pack up camp." Nick doused water on the firepit, carried the coolers to the truck and repacked the ground tarp, tent and stakes. In no time, everything was secured in the cargo bed of the truck. They hopped inside the cab, and he pressed the ignition button.

Nothing happened.

He pressed the button again and shot a worried look Dawn's way.

"What's wrong?" she asked.

"I don't know. The truck won't start."

"Could the battery have drained?"

He shook his head and pressed the ignition button again. Still nothing.

"Could it be the starter?" she asked.

"I don't know." Nick's voice was getting louder. He wasn't yelling at Dawn, not like Stuart had done, but her questions seemed to unnerve him.

She pulled out her phone. It wasn't going to miraculously have reception, but she couldn't help but check. What had been precious seclusion the night before was quickly turning into unwelcome isolation.

"How far are we from the entrance?" she asked.

"It's Sunday. No one's there."

"Well, how far until we get cell phone reception?"

"At least thirty kilometers." He repeatedly jabbed the ignition button as if that would make a difference.

"Can you pop the hood?" Dawn's voice was calm and steady. Dealing with life and death situations at the clinic had taught her not to panic. Emergencies didn't fluster her—they propelled her to take control.

Nick didn't respond at first, so Dawn repeated her request. With the hood unlatched, she lifted the metal cowling and peered inside. Having half brothers who were gearheads and a father who repaired his own tractors had its benefits. Dawn knew her way around an engine.

The problem was obvious, even glaring. The negative battery cable was detached from the terminal and dangling loose in the air. Now, for the first time, Dawn panicked. This malfunction wasn't something that could happen by accident. It required the nut to be unscrewed—by force.

She recalled the footsteps outside the tent the night before. She pictured Stuart's car parked down the street from her home. She imagined Alexa listening as she shared her plans to go camping with Nick. Dawn had seen Stuart's temper before, like when he threw the flowers to the floor at the clinic. He could become angry when he didn't get his way, but this would be a new low.

She refastened the cable. "Try it now."

The engine turned over and started without a hitch.

Dawn didn't share her suspicion, and Nick didn't seem to know enough about engines to realize his had been sabotaged. On the way home, as soon as she could get a signal, she called her mom's mobile phone. It went to voicemail.

"No answer?" asked Nick.

She shook her head.

He pressed the gas pedal, thrusting the truck into the next gear.

Dawn told herself that Marie not answering didn't mean anything. Her mom could still be asleep, though she was usually an early riser. When they finally reached the duplex, everything appeared normal. The street was quiet. A car passed. Neighbors dressed in their Sunday best were headed to church. Before Nick's truck stopped, Dawn hopped out and ran up the walkway, her pulse racing with every step. She burst through Marie's unlocked front door. In their small town, no one locked their doors, but suddenly, that didn't feel as reassuring as it used to.

"Mom!" she called.

No reply.

Marie's Jitterbug phone with the oversized touchpad was on the kitchen counter. Where was her mother and why didn't she have her phone? Dawn rushed down the hall to the bedroom. Marie's bed was made but empty.

Dawn silently admonished herself. What if her mom had forgotten about the camping trip? What if Marie had tried to call Dawn and couldn't reach her? She'd probably go looking for her daughter. Dawn pictured Marie wandering the streets, lost and without a phone.

She met Nick in the kitchen. Her face told him everything.

Chapter 9

A flash of movement outside caught Dawn's attention. She hurried to the back sliding glass door, shoved it open and ran into the yard. At the edge of the fence, wearing a brimmed hat and gardening gloves, was Marie, oblivious to the worry she'd caused. The tension that had filled Dawn's body escaped like a deflating balloon.

Nick joined the women outside, putting his arm around Dawn and rubbing her shoulders. "Marie," he said. "I'm making breakfast. How do you take your eggs?"

Dawn offered to help, but Nick told her making breakfast was "a little egg," a Dutch expression for an easy task. Once they'd finished eating, Marie stood and started gathering the dishes. She stopped abruptly, set the plates on the table and clutched the back of the chair.

"Are you okay?" asked Dawn.

"I must've stood up too quickly. Got a bit dizzy."

Dawn moved to her mom's side, taking her arm. "Why don't you sit down?"

Marie placed her hand on her chest and whispered, "I feel a little breathless."

Nick stood, but before he or Dawn could help, Marie collapsed. Her limbs went limp, and her eyes rolled into the back of her head.

Dawn clung to Marie's arm, bracing but not stopping the fall. She managed to cradle the back of her mother's head, preventing it from bashing onto the hardwood floor.

"Call 911," she directed Nick. Dawn placed two fingers on her mom's carotid artery and checked for a pulse—it was there but faint. All she could do was kneel helplessly next to her mother until the ambulance arrived.

Nick escorted the medical team, an EMT and paramedic, inside. Just as they entered the duplex, Marie's eyelids started to flutter and open. The two young men introduced themselves and started asking questions. The EMT took Marie's glucose and oxygen levels and started her on a nasal cannula.

"Are you taking any medications?" the paramedic asked.

Marie feebly pointed toward the kitchen cabinet.

Dawn, who oversaw her mother's medications, interjected. "Lisinopril, Levothyroxine, fish oil, calcium and hematinic." The first two were for high blood pressure and an underactive thyroid. The other three were nutritional supplements.

"Marie, your heart looks fine, but your blood pressure is low," said the paramedic. "I think we should take you to the hospital to get checked out, just to be on the safe side. Are you okay with that?"

Marie looked at Dawn, "Do I have to?"

"Probably should, just to be sure."

The medical team moved Marie onto a gurney.

"Can I ride with her?" asked Dawn. "I'm her healthcare power of attorney. I need to be there to help her make decisions."

Dawn looked at Nick. "It's okay," he said. "Go. Call me when you know more."

Inside the ambulance, the paramedic started a saline IV. Dawn sat on a bench holding her mom's pale hand, thankful they'd returned early from the camping trip. She couldn't understand how her mom had *low* blood pressure. Marie's medications were to combat *high* blood pressure.

En route, she called Nick. "Have you left yet?"

"No. I'm cleaning up breakfast."

"Can you do me a favor? Check my mom's medications."

"Sure. Where are they?"

"In the kitchen. If you're facing the sink, open the far left cabinet. There's a turntable with her pill bottles. I want to check how many tablets of Lisinopril are left. I just refilled the prescription."

Dawn heard the cabinet squeak open.

"I don't see it," he said.

"What do you mean?"

"I see Advil, calcium, Excedrin, fish oil, hematinic and Levo-something. That's it."

"No Lisinopril?" she asked.

"Correct."

"What the hell?" Dawn's mind raced. She rummaged through Marie's purse but found nothing. How could the medication vanish into thin air? The only people who knew where it was stored were Marie, Dawn and now Nick.

No. There was one more person who knew—Stuart.

At the hospital, Marie's color began to return. Samples of her bloodwork were sent to the lab, and she continued to receive fluids intravenously. By late afternoon, she'd recovered enough to be discharged.

When they arrived home, a vase of fresh flowers brightened the kitchen table. Marie read the get-well card from Nick while Dawn checked the kitchen cabinet. As Nick had reported, the Lisinopril was missing. She checked the bathroom and bedroom but still came up empty. Dawn questioned her mother repeatedly. Could she have misplaced the bottle? But Marie was adamant that she hadn't moved her pills.

That night, Dawn fell asleep on Marie's couch. She missed her morning alarm and arrived late to work without her iced coffee. The other vet techs were huddled in the break room, cautiously admiring their unofficial mascot, Kelly's cat, Kia. Appropriately named as she'd been thrown from a Kia automobile, the cat had been brought to the clinic by the people who'd seen the cruel act. They'd been driving behind the Kia when the passenger extended his arm out of the window and let the cat dangle in the air. Then he deliberately tossed the cat over the roof. Miraculously, the cat landed on her feet and was unharmed. Kelly had offered to foster the gray and white tabby, although everyone knew how that story would play out.

Kia had earned her reputation as a fractious, ornery cat. She was perfectly content at home with Kelly, but the moment she was put in a carrier and brought to the vet, she turned into a monster. The other techs would rather handle a pit bull than deal with this cantankerous feline, so it was always left to Dawn to give Kia her annual exam.

Kelly brought the carrier into the exam room and placed it on the table. Kia's eyes were dilated into black orbits, and she emitted a low guttural growl.

"Sweet girl, it's okay," cooed Kelly.

"Can you hold her so I can inject the DKT?" asked Dawn.

DKT, also known as "kitty magic," would sedate Kia so Dawn could get through the exam without ending up scratched and bleeding. She unhooked the top of the carrier, placed a thick blanket on top of the cat and lifted her onto the table. The growl turned into a hiss as the cat thrashed wildly. Although the techs weren't allowed to treat their own pets, Kelly could assist. She pinned Kia's head so Dawn could administer the shot. With the hard part done, Dawn left Kelly to tend to her baby girl.

Twenty minutes later, evil Miss Hyde had transformed into the well-mannered Dr. Jekyll. Kia still protested mildly when touched, but she didn't try to mutilate the first thing she could sink her claws into.

"She's going to be so pissed at me," said Kelly. "After her last exam, she ignored me for two days."

The door to the exam room opened. "Sorry to bother you," said Suzanne, looking grim. "It's about Lucky."

Dawn's heart dropped. "After all we did to save that dog—what happened?"

"Oh, it's not that. Lucky's fine. It's the payment for her surgery. I got the credit card from the man who was covering the cost, but the card was declined. He's going to be able to pay, isn't he?"

Dawn smiled. The head of loans at the bank who owned a truck, motorcycle and sports car would certainly be able to pay. Plus, she'd seen the wad of cash he carried around. Undoubtedly, it was some sort of glitch.

"Don't worry," assured Dawn. "I'll call him."

Nick answered on the first ring. "Good morning, beautiful. How's your mom?"

"She's well. Loved the flowers. Thank you." Dawn hesitated, feeling uneasy about bringing up the money. "I'm really sorry to bother you, but I'm calling about the payment for Lucky's surgery. Our receptionist said there was a problem with the credit card you used?"

"Oh, right. I just got a notification. The card expired. American Express never sent me a new one so I didn't notice. I've been so busy at work."

"It's no problem. Everyone here is just so grateful that you were willing to cover the surgery."

He added, "What's your American saying: The shoemaker's kids have to wait for their shoes? I organize everyone else's finances but neglect my own."

Dawn laughed. "It's the cobbler's kids have no shoes." She hesitated. "So, do you think you could give me the new expiration date?"

"I could if they'd send me the new card. I still don't have it."

Dawn didn't appreciate the position Suzanne had put her in, making her feel like a debt collector when Nick had been so generous.

"I could call them," he offered.

"It's okay. Our receptionist, who is also the bookkeeper, just brought it up. She won't close out the month for another week. We have time."

"Nonsense. I'll have a cashier's check made out to the clinic. Would that work?"

Dawn breathed a sigh of relief. "Yes, that's perfect. Thank you. Oh, and I'll probably stay close to Mom for a few days, but you're welcome to stop by."

"I was hoping you'd be free Friday night. There's a black-tie charity auction at the governor's mansion in Columbia. The bank is a sponsor, so I have to go. What do you say? You'd make a dull evening a lot more exciting."

Chapter 10

On Friday evening, Dawn did a twirl in Marie's kitchen, modeling the black dress she'd worn to a fraternity formal in college. The slit up the leg and the low back were a sexy contrast to the conservative lace overlay. Wearing two-inch heels, she was approaching six feet tall. For once, she didn't have to think about her height. Nick would still tower above her.

"Oh, honey, you look so lovely," said Marie. "Wait a minute. I've got something for you." Marie left the room and returned with a velvet jewelry box containing one-carat diamond earrings.

"Oh no, Mom. I can't. Dad gave you those."

"And what better occasion for you to borrow them?" said Marie. "There may be fancy ladies there, but no one will outshine you."

Outside, a black stretch limo turned into the driveway. Nick emerged wearing a tuxedo, pressed white shirt and black bow tie. He looked like a model for GQ, with the exception of the drab brown duplexes as the backdrop.

When Dawn opened the front door, he did a double take. "Wow, you look amazing." He leaned in and kissed her cheek. Brushing her hair behind her ear, he admired the earrings.

"I know. Aren't they gorgeous? On loan from Mom."

Nick turned to Marie and handed her a business card. "Here's my number if you need anything. It's only an hour drive, and we won't be back too late."

"Don't worry about me. You two go enjoy yourselves."

Nick held Dawn's hand as she climbed into the limo. She slid over to the window seat, marveling at the spacious leather interior. A bottle of champagne was chilling next to crystal flutes on a silver tray. Nick gave some instructions to the driver and closed the privacy window. He popped open the champagne, poured two glasses and offered a toast.

"Proost," he said.

Dawn clinked her glass and repeated timidly, "Proost." Then she asked, "How's your English so good? You don't even have an accent."

"We start English lessons in grade one, but really it's years of watching your American movies." He switched to an Austrian accent and cited the famous line from *Terminator*, "I'll be back."

Dawn burst into laughter. The couple talked and laughed so much that she barely noticed the hour-long drive to Columbia or that they'd finished the bottle of champagne. When they arrived, she wobbled out of the limo.

"Careful there," said Nick. He swept an arm around her waist to steady her.

The decorations outside the governor's mansion set the tone: a red-carpet entrance, glittering trellises of lights and violinists serenading the well-heeled party goers. The venue for the auction was next door at a two-story colonial home converted into an event space. Nick and Dawn glided up the brick steps to the foyer where a volunteer took their tickets and handed them auction packets. Each packet contained a booklet of the items for sale and an individual bidding number.

Once checked in, the couple mingled in the crowd as they explored the venue. Every room was immaculately decorated with stately furniture, antique rugs and priceless artwork. The main dining hall offered a dinner buffet. Waiters circulated with trays of hors d'oeuvres, and several rooms had an open bar. Tables covered with white linen tablecloths displayed the items for auction, including watches, jewelry, signed sports memorabilia and exclusive trips. Nick admired a Breitling watch and scribbled his number below the last bidder. Dawn's eyes widened when she saw the amount—five thousand dollars.

"Come on, let's get a drink," he suggested. Nick ordered two more glasses of champagne and handed her a flute.

"I probably should eat. I'm a little lightheaded," she admitted.

Just then, Nick pointed to an adjacent room. "There's the governor. Let's say hello."

Nick took Dawn by the hand and led her to a group of people who were surrounding a distinguished-looking gentleman. Dawn didn't pay much attention to politics. She knew the governor's name but couldn't have picked him out of a lineup. They joined the circle, and Nick jumped into the conversation.

"Governor," said Nick. "I'd like you to meet Dawn Smith."

The man offered his hand. "Nice to see you." He leaned toward

Nick and remarked, "Such a beauty deserves a beautiful piece of jewelry, don't you think? Hope you're bidding. It's for a good cause."

"We're just getting started," assured Nick.

More people crowded in to speak with the governor, and Nick had more bidding to do. He led Dawn into the next room and jotted his number next to a few more items with the excitement of a kid at Christmas.

"Do you want anything?" he asked.

Dawn thought, *Yes, food.* Normally, she would've been more outspoken, but she felt so out of place. With her modest wages, she couldn't afford to bid on anything. On top of that, she felt fatigue setting in, probably from too much champagne. As she followed Nick from room to room, she managed to snatch a bacon-wrapped scallop from a passing waiter.

Finally, Nick noticed. "We should get some dinner."

On the way back to the main dining room, Nick checked on the Breitling. Two people had outbid him. He entered a new offer, now at five thousand seven hundred and fifty dollars. He also grabbed two more glasses of champagne before they joined the buffet line.

A volunteer circled the room, ringing a tiny bell and proclaiming like the town crier, "Ten more minutes before bidding closes."

A few people abandoned the buffet line to hover protectively near their treasures, standing guard by the bid sheet. In the last ten minutes, bidding escalated into a flurry, with each person jockeying to be the final number on the card.

"Do you want to stand next to the watch?" asked Dawn.

Nick took her hand and kissed it. "No. You've been patient enough with my bidding obsession. Let's get you fed."

The auction ended when Nick and Dawn finally sat down to eat. She touched her hand to her forehead, feeling faint. Although she'd consumed half a bottle of champagne in the limo, she'd been discreetly setting aside the flutes at the party. But why, then, was she still so dizzy? It didn't make sense.

Nick strolled by the table with the Breitling and glanced at the bidding card.

"Did you win?" she asked when he rejoined her.

He shook his head. "It's fine. I can always buy one. Was just trying to help the charity." He noticed her droopy eyes. "Hey, are you okay?"

"I'm just tired."

"It's a long drive back. I'll get us a room at the Hilton. You can rest tonight, and we'll go back early tomorrow." He pulled out his phone to make the reservation.

Dawn touched his forearm. "That's really thoughtful, but I'd rather go back tonight. Did the limo wait for us?"

Nick seemed disappointed. "I'll give him a call. Just need to check if any of my other bids came through."

He went to the volunteer table while Dawn found a bathroom. In the mirror, her reflection looked distorted. The mirror was fine. She, however, was not. She splashed some cold water on her face while she waited for an open stall.

Back in the foyer, Nick helped her down the stairs to their limo. The night air was thick and humid, intensifying her fatigue like a heavy blanket covering her body. Inside the car, Dawn could've curled up on the seat and slept the whole way home, but she forced herself to stay awake. She soon found her lips pressed against Nick's. He unzipped her dress and eased her back onto the leather seat. She felt his weight on top of her. She pressed his chest, pushing him away. From the glow of the interior lights, Dawn could see the confused expression on his face. She slid from the seat onto the floor and knelt in front of him. Reaching forward, she unzipped his pants and took him into her mouth.

Chapter 11

On Monday afternoon, Suzanne's demeanor showed signs of visible stress, far beyond the usual frenzy of the clinic. "I have to close the month," she said to Dawn. "I thought you said your donor was issuing a cashier's check for Lucky's surgery? Is he going to bring the check here, or are we supposed to go pick it up?"

Dawn had never finalized that detail with Nick, and although she didn't want to pester him about the payment, she liked having an excuse to stop by his office. She'd been lovesick ever since her Cinderella date at the governor's mansion.

The Wells Fargo bank was a three-story red brick building near the town square, next door to the Baptist church and down the street from the Methodist one. Dawn parked in the back surface lot and walked to the front entrance. Cool air engulfed her as she stepped inside, triggering a grim flashback. The last time she'd been there, just a year ago, was shortly after her father's death. She and her mom had to notarize Marie's new healthcare and financial power of attorney documents, putting Dawn in charge of her mother's affairs.

An armed guard gave a slight nod as she passed by. Dawn looked around, not knowing where the loan department would be. To her left was an open area with thick carpet and plush couches. A few offices lined the walls to her right, but none of the name plates were for Nick. Tellers manned stations at the back of the room behind a center island with office supplies.

Just then, Dawn saw Nick.

He wasn't at a desk or in an office but sitting at one of the teller booths. A nameplate with gold lettering read, *Nicholas VanBroklin.*

What? she thought.

A few people were queued behind a velvet rope. Dawn took her place in line, all the while watching Nick accept deposits and cash checks. The visual was a stark contrast to what she'd envisioned when she'd pictured him at the bank. When it was finally Dawn's turn, she approached the counter, her eyes squinting.

"What are you doing here?" asked Nick, not masking his surprise.

"What are *you* doing *here*?" She tapped her finger on the counter.

"I'm pulling double duty. We're short-staffed."

"The head of the loan department is covering for a teller?" she asked, tilting her head.

"It's called servant leadership. I've always believed the culture of an organization comes from the top. I try to set an example that none of us are too good to do any job at this bank."

Dawn felt like a fool, wrongly judging Nick for covering for a teller. She'd never experienced that kind of philosophy at the clinic. As kindhearted as Dr. Patel was, he'd never practice *servant leadership* and clean the kennel.

"What brings you here?" Nick's voice was cheerful, apparently missing her unfounded accusation.

She avoided eye contact. "I wasn't sure if you were bringing the cashier's check by the clinic or if we were supposed to pick it up."

"Oh. I put it in the mail. I thought you said your bookkeeper could wait. I'm sorry. I didn't realize you were coming by."

For the second time that afternoon, Dawn felt like a fool. "You're right. I did say she could wait."

Nick reached forward, gently tilting her head up so their eyes could meet. "If you want, I'll issue a new check. I'll have to cancel the one in the mail, but I can do that."

Dawn glanced at her phone: 4:40 p.m. By the time she made it back to the clinic, Suzanne would already be gone. "No, it's fine. I'll tell them it's on the way."

"Any other day and I'd take you to dinner," he said. "But we're slammed with month-end and we're short-staffed. Looks like it'll be a late night."

"I understand. I need to check on Mom anyway. I'll call you later?"

He nodded and winked at her.

As Dawn exited the bank, the security guard held the door open. Outside, the humidity felt like she'd stepped into a swamp. She tugged at her scrubs, which stuck to her body.

If Nick were a teller, would that matter? she wondered.

It wasn't his job that had set her off. It was the fact that she thought he'd lied. Dawn immediately felt bad for how quickly she'd jumped to the wrong conclusion. Even if he hadn't noticed, she wanted to make amends. An idea came to her—she'd surprise him with dinner at the bank since he had to work late.

In her Jeep, she blasted the air-conditioning and scanned her phone for nearby restaurants. When she glanced up, several cars had exited the parking lot, which opened her view to a row of vehicles at the far corner. One SUV in particular caught her attention—a maroon Chevy Blazer. Dawn put her Jeep into gear and pulled behind it.

Her mouth fell open when she read the license plate: JAZ 260.

This was the car—the hit-and-run driver.

She pressed the gas pedal, jerked the steering wheel and sped behind a group of parked cars, concealing her position. There, Dawn readied the camera on her cell phone and waited. She eyed each person who exited the bank, watching intently to see who would approach the SUV.

She thought about calling the police, but they already had the license plate. By now, they'd probably tracked down the perpetrator. For all she knew, he'd paid for the damage and been levied a fine for leaving the scene. She waited a while longer, torn between wanting to pick up dinner for Nick and needing to check on her mom, but she was unable to budge, not until she learned the identity of this criminal.

A few more people exited the building, getting into their cars.

The next person immediately caught her attention with his lanky swagger. He strolled down the sidewalk at the edge of the bank, approached the maroon SUV and opened the door.

Chapter 12

Dawn's mind went into overdrive. Was there any reasonable explanation? She recalled how Nick had shown up at the accident, seemingly out of nowhere, and offered to find the owner of the damaged Honda. Had that been a diversion tactic? Did he redirect her to ensure the owner would never receive her photograph of *his* license plate?

But how? He would've had to ditch his SUV beyond the gas station and pretended to be on foot. It seemed so implausible, but the more she thought about it, the more it seemed probable. But why would he ask her out and take her back to the scene of the crime? It reminded Dawn of a TV show where the murderer covertly attended his victim's funeral, gleefully witnessing the anguish he'd caused.

She shuddered.

Wait a minute, she thought. *I bet he actually is a teller.*

Dawn searched for the bank's website and clicked on the executive team. The Director of Commercial Lending was listed as Carl Cristoff. Nick's name was nowhere to be found. This wasn't conclusive evidence—a call to the bank would be concrete proof—but she was starting to put the pieces together.

A pit formed in her stomach as she thought about Lucky's surgery. Who doesn't notice an expired credit card? And how convenient it was that the cashier's check was already mailed, making it unavailable. The realization that she might be on the hook for a three-thousand-dollar operation made her feel nauseous.

Dawn's phone rang, making her jump. A picture of Stuart flashed across the screen.

"Hello," she said.

"Hello? That's it? Just hello. Why haven't you called me?" he demanded.

They hadn't spoken for almost two weeks, which seemed like a lifetime ago.

Before she could reply, he continued. "What's going on with you? Why don't you just tell me what I did wrong instead of giving me the silent treatment?"

Dawn was confused. Stuart had hung up on her. He'd stormed out of the clinic. She thought *he'd* ghosted *her*. Moreover, he seemed to think they were still in a relationship.

"You could've called *me*," she countered.

"I was trying to give you some space; plus I had to go to Florida to help my parents, remember? I was hoping you'd change your mind about the trip. Man, it was brutal. We had to fit four bedrooms into two, and my mom didn't want to give anything away."

Dawn immediately pictured the mysterious silver car that had been parked down the street from her duplex. It couldn't have been Stuart. He was out of town that week. And her camping trip with Nick had been the following weekend. Stuart couldn't have followed her and Nick into the woods and disabled the truck battery. He was still in Florida.

"You there?" he asked, pulling her back into the conversation.

"I'm here," she whispered. Dawn felt like her brain would implode with these new revelations.

"Look. I can come over. I'll bring dinner and we can talk. I've missed you."

Stuart was grasping at their old, familiar pattern, but Dawn had already moved on. The question now consuming her was—who exactly had she moved on with?

"It's not a good time. I'm sorry."

"What's up with you?"

"I have to take care of my mom. She was hospitalized."

"What happened? Is she okay?" he asked.

"She'll be fine, but I really need to go."

Dawn glanced at the time: 4:55 p.m. She had five minutes before the bank closed. She darted back inside and asked the security guard for the head teller.

"I'm Cecilia Park," said the woman, with a heavy Southern drawl. "How can I help you?"

"Hi. I was in your bank earlier and one of your tellers was so helpful. I wanted to send a thank-you note, but I forgot his name. It was Nicholas Van-something. I think he's from Amsterdam. Does he work for you?"

"Oh, you must mean Nick VanBroklin. Yes, he works for me. But honey, he's not from Amsterdam. He's from South Carolina. His mama and I went to high school together. She'll be so tickled to hear he received a compliment."

Dawn's mouth gaped. She stumbled backward without saying another word and hurried out of the bank. On the drive home, a myriad of questions raced through her mind. Why hadn't she done more research on Nick before agreeing to date him? Why had she taken everything he'd told her at face value instead of checking for herself? And what was his endgame? At some point, she was bound to find out the truth—like if she surprised him at the bank again, and he was still behind the teller desk. She wondered what other lies he'd told her. She'd never seen the Porsche that was supposedly in the shop. Now she wondered if the only Porsche emblem he owned was on his polo shirt.

She allowed herself a small amount of vindication—he'd not fooled her for too long. But in the short time they'd dated, she'd fallen for him. He'd seduced her in the woods. That night had been consensual, but now she felt completely violated. The thought of him inside of her made her want to puke, and what she'd done in the limo to please him made her visibly gag.

The cashier's check, she thought. She was certain he'd lied about that, too. Suzanne would be on a warpath when she found out they weren't getting paid. Unfortunately, Dawn had no choice but to deal with that inevitability straight on.

Chapter 13

The next morning, Dawn took a deep breath as she entered Dr. Patel's office. "Do you have a minute?" she asked.

He bobbled his head from side to side and gestured toward a chair.

"I think I may have messed up," she confessed.

He smiled and spoke with a pleasant, syllabic rhythm common to those who grew up in Bengaluru. "Dawn, you're one of our best employees. Smita says *the best,* although I'm not allowed to play favorites. Hypothetically, if you *messed up* and pulled a dog's tooth that needed to come out, I don't think anyone would be the wiser."

Dawn gulped. He knew what she'd done with Daisy, but that wasn't the confession she needed to make. Hers was much worse. Dawn stammered, struggling to find the words. She couldn't bring herself to admit to a second, more serious mistake. Instead, she excused herself and texted Smita, who was still home on maternity leave. *Sorry to bother you. Can I stop by? Need to talk.*

Smita replied right away. *Please do. I could use some adult conversation.*

Later that afternoon, Dawn arrived at the Patel's craftsman-style home, with its wide columns and pitched gable roof. They lived in a middle-class neighborhood twenty minutes from the clinic. Dawn had been there before for holiday parties and housesitting when the couple had taken a rare vacation. She'd been there most recently to meet baby Devin just after his birth. He was now approaching ten weeks old, and Smita would soon be returning to the clinic.

When she opened the door, Smita's chestnut-colored eyes were as warm and welcoming as ever, although they showed slight bags. Her typical immaculate living room was filled with plastic bottles, pacifiers, a bouncy chair and blankets. The baby monitor displayed Devin sleeping in the nursery.

"Would you like some tea?" offered Smita. Her voice carried an inexplicable tranquility. She had a rare gift—able to calm people and animals with a single word or touch.

"No thanks. I actually need to talk to you about work if that's okay."

Smita's eyes narrowed, undoubtedly concerned that whatever was going on couldn't be handled by her husband. Dawn should've confessed to Dr. Patel, but she'd lost her nerve. Smita was the easier choice and certainly more likely to understand.

"Did Dr. Patel tell you about the pyo surgery he performed on Lucky, Allie Church's dog?" asked Dawn, as the two women sat down.

"He did. That was quite a miracle."

"Did he tell you that the fee was covered by the guy I'm dating?"

"He didn't, but that was very generous of Stuart."

Dawn exhaled. "It wasn't Stuart. I started dating someone else—Nick. He offered to pay for the surgery, but then his credit card was declined. He said he was mailing a check, but I'm pretty sure he's stalling. And now I just found out he's been lying to me about who he is. Suzanne needs to close out the month, and she's waiting for the payment. But now, I don't think it's coming."

Smita put her finger to her mouth and tapped her lips.

"I was going to tell Dr. Patel, but I—" Dawn's voice trailed off. "I can't pay it back right away, but you can deduct a portion from my paycheck each week."

"How'd you discover this guy was lying?" asked Smita.

Dawn bowed her head, embarrassed at how gullible she'd been. "A few things. Nick told me he was the head of loans at the bank, but when I went there to surprise him, I found out he's a teller. The rest unraveled from there. He told me he was from Amsterdam, but he's really from here. He pretended to be a witness to a car accident, but I think he caused it. And he keeps stalling on paying for Lucky's surgery, so I'm guessing he's not going to."

Smita nodded, taking in the information.

"Trust me," said Dawn. "I'm going to confront him about all of these lies. He doesn't know I've found out."

"Do you think he could be dangerous?"

Dawn shrugged. Nick had never shown a temper.

"Does he own any weapons?"

"A gun."

Smita's expression, which was perpetual pleasantness, turned to stone. She inched closer to Dawn, although no one else was within earshot. "What I'm going to tell you stays between us, okay? Neil knows, but no one else."

Dawn nodded.

"Several years ago, before I met Neil, I was dating a guy. He passed himself off to be someone he wasn't, like your Nick. When I tried to break up with him, he became violent. His threats were so extreme that I had to move. I hid at my aunt's house for half a year. This turned out to be a blessing because I met Neil. But still, this guy put us through hell. He harassed my entire family, trying to track me down."

"Wow. I had no idea."

"I'm telling you this because I don't want you to go through a similar situation. My advice—don't confront him. Don't let him know what you've discovered. Make up an excuse to distance yourself, but make it all about you and your circumstances, not about him."

Dawn let the warning sink in. She didn't think Nick would be like the guy who'd pursued Smita, but then again, she didn't know the *real* Nick.

"Why should I have to placate him? I want him to know I'm no fool."

"I understand, but a guy who will lie and steal like this, who owns a gun? You want him out of your life. Do a breezy breakup. I know it's not fair, but your safety is what's most important. Promise me?"

If Dawn had learned one thing in all the years of working with Smita, it was that her instincts were flawless, almost supernatural. If she was this worried about Nick, that he could be dangerous, Dawn couldn't ignore her advice.

"Okay. I promise."

"One more thing," added Smita. "I'll talk to Neil and Suzanne. If writing off a pyo is the worst outcome, we can all consider ourselves lucky."

Chapter 14

Dawn had never practiced a breakup speech before—never gave it a second thought—but now she was rehearsing how to end her summer romance without stirring up drama or provoking retaliation.

I think it's best if we cool things off for a while. She replayed this phrase in her mind while gripping her phone so tightly that her fingertips turned pink. Finally, she called him and blurted her declaration without even saying hello.

"Why?" he asked. "Everything's been great between us."

"It's not you," she lied. "Things have just been hard lately with work and my mom."

"I can help." His voice lowered, taking on a seductive tone. "You know, hard isn't all bad. I've got something hard that brings you a lot of pleasure."

A chill ran down Dawn's spine, as if he'd slithered through the phone and traced an ice cube down her back. She'd jumped into this relationship far too quickly, and it was time—no, past time—to get out. Dawn struggled to feign a breezy attitude, if there was such a thing.

"I've just got a lot going on right now. I think it's best if we take a break."

"How can I change your mind?" he persisted.

Her attempt at a casual parting of ways was failing, leaving Dawn no choice but to become more assertive. "You can't."

The line went dead.

She looked at the dark screen. Had they been cut off? Had he hung up? Maybe it was for the best. More talking wasn't going to change anything. At least he hadn't gotten belligerent. She shrugged, putting him totally out of her mind.

Dawn grabbed a beer and hopped in the shower. With grocery shopping still to do, she dressed in shorts and a T-shirt and pulled her wet hair into a ponytail. When she opened the front door, she froze.

Nick was standing on her front porch as if he'd been waiting for her.

"What are you doing here?" she asked.

"I needed to see you."

Dawn studied his arm—bicep flexed, elbow bent, hand hidden behind his back. She envisioned his fingers coiled around the grip of a pistol. He was only a few feet away, so close she could smell his breath.

"I thought I was clear on the phone. I can't be in a relationship right now." Her voice quivered as she fixated on his arm.

"If you're worried about your mom, I can help. I'll stop by at lunch to check on her."

A lump formed in Dawn's throat at the thought of this psycho anywhere close to her mom.

"Come on. We're great together, and that was one hell of a limo ride." He grinned and took a step forward, wedging his foot in the door frame. Nick's smile was no longer boyish or charming. It was cunning, aggressive and determined.

Dawn had a singular thought. She couldn't let him power his way inside. Once that threshold was broken, he could force her to do a whole lot more. She held up Marie's handwritten grocery list and slipped past him.

"I'm headed to the store." It took every ounce of her resolve to pretend they were still having a normal conversation.

"I'll come with you," he persisted. "We can save this for when we get back."

Nick pulled his arm from behind his back. Time slowed as Dawn watched his hand emerge, holding something. She was overwhelmed with a feeling of total helplessness. If he meant to harm her, there was absolutely nothing she could do to stop him.

Out of the corner of her eye, she spotted her neighbor, Cindy Steinert. The petite blonde had just stepped onto her front porch to feed Snowball, her equally petite cat. Dawn's instinct was to cry for help. Maybe a witness would be enough to deter him. Her gaze jumped from Snowball's fluffy white fur and pink collar to Nick's hand. She blinked, trying to make sense of what she saw. His fingers weren't gripping a gun but a bottle of Cabernet.

Dawn nearly collapsed with relief.

"We can take my bike," he said, as he nodded toward the Kawasaki.

"Sorry, I already promised to go with my neighbor." Dawn pointed to Cindy and shouted, "Hi, Cindy, I'm ready when you are."

Her neighbor, puzzled by Dawn's remark, put down the bowl of Friskies and walked over. "What'd you say?"

"This is my friend, Nick," said Dawn. She stared intently at Cindy and spoke firmly. "I told him that you and I were just about to head out. He was just leaving." Dawn held her breath, fearful that Cindy wouldn't catch on.

Nick turned toward the girl. "This street is full of beautiful women."

Cindy immediately stood taller. She glanced from Nick to Dawn, clearly confused.

Nick handed the bottle to Dawn. "Can't let this go to waste. You ladies enjoy it. I'll see *you* later." He turned, sauntered back to his motorcycle and sped off.

"Who was that?" asked Cindy, nearly drooling. "And why aren't you having a drink with him? I sure would."

Chapter 15

Later that night, Dawn was watching TV when her phone started pinging with text messages from Nick.

9:15 p.m. Hope you liked the wine...should have been us drinking it
9:18 p.m. We're good together...don't get spooked
9:19 p.m. I can make your life better
9:21 p.m. Don't give up on us!!!
9:25 p.m. Remember the camping trip??? I can take you on more trips...I can show you the world

Her phone rang. It was Nick. Dawn silenced the ringer. The text messages continued.

9:26 p.m. I just called...pick up the phone so we can talk
9:29 p.m. We need to talk
9:30 p.m. You can't quit on us...I won't let you!!!
9:33 p.m. If ur testing if I will fight for us...I will
9:34 p.m. You can quit on other guys...NOT ME

Dawn finally replied.

9:35 p.m. I need some space. Please. Good night.

Nick didn't call or text anymore that night. The next day, every time Dawn received a spam call or social media ping, her shoulders tensed. By the end of the day, when all had been quiet on the Nick front, she finally allowed herself to relax.

That evening, as she was enjoying a homemade chicken potpie at her mom's kitchen table, Marie dropped a bomb.

"Nick stopped by today. He told me you'd called things off with him. He looked so sad."

Dawn nearly choked. "He came *here*? What'd you say to him?"

"I told him I'd talk to you, and I gave him a potpie to take home."

Dawn leaned forward and pointed her finger at Marie like a teacher admonishing a pupil. "If he shows up again, I don't want you answering the door. I don't want you talking to him. Do you hear me?"

"For heaven's sake, why are you so upset?"

"He's a liar. He's not the head of loans at the bank. He's a teller. And he's not from Amsterdam. He's from South Carolina. He has the same last name as a famous banking family, but he's not Dutch. That's why he didn't recognize the dessert you made for him."

"Oh honey, I remember when I first met your father. He embellished his job at the factory. He was just trying to impress me, but that's what men do. If I'd held a little white lie against him then, I wouldn't have you now."

Dawn pressed her hands against her forehead and shook her head. How could she make her mom understand? "Look. You have to trust me on this. Nick is *nothing* like Dad. He's not a good man, and I don't want him anywhere near us."

Marie put down her fork. "But he seems so much better suited for you than Stuart."

"How about neither of them, Mom? There are more than two men in the world. I don't want either of them."

She pulled out her phone and pounded out a text message to Nick.

7:14 p.m.   Stay away from my mom. Goodbye.

He immediately replied.

7:14 p.m.   Potpie was delicious!!!

Dawn became so angry, she started shaking. She hurled her phone against the wall, shattering the front glass. When she finally calmed down enough to retrieve it from the floor, the screen was dead. For the rest of the evening, she became keenly aware of how often she checked her phone. Every time she glanced at the cracked, black screen, she wanted to hurl it again.

The next morning at the clinic, Dawn's spirits were lifted by a special visitor. Allie Church had stopped by with Lucky and cupcakes to thank the staff. The golden retriever pranced around the waiting room like she'd never been sick a day in her life. Allie spoiled her with a cupcake, which she gobbled in one bite. Dawn glanced at

Dr. Patel, who gave her a quick nod. No one else in the clinic knew the full story, and Dawn appreciated his discretion. Even though the surgery was performed because of Nick's lie, Dawn couldn't begrudge today's celebration.

After work, Dawn stopped by the Apple store. Her phone was beyond repair, so she was forced to buy a new one. A young clerk, who looked like he couldn't be a day out of high school, reloaded her life onto the device. Once the setup was completed, he rebooted the phone and handed it to her.

The screen displayed five missed calls and sixty-one text messages, all from Nick, starting from the time she'd smashed the phone.

7:17 p.m.	Ur mom said we shouldn't break up...I agree
7:18 p.m.	Ur mom wants us to stay together
7:22 p.m.	I'm the best man you will ever meet...you need to realize this
7:24 p.m.	I'm the one who can take you away from this small town and ur small life
7:28 p.m.	Missed Call from Nick
7:29 p.m.	Pick up the damn phone when I call you!!!
7:35 p.m.	DO NOT DISRESPECT ME!!!
7:36 p.m.	REALLY??? THIS IS HOW YOU THINK IT ENDS???
7:41 p.m.	TAKE YOUR GOODBYE AND SHOVE IT UP YOUR ASS UR QUITTING I'M NOT I'M GOING NOWHERE!!! DO YOU UNDERSTAND ME??? NOWHERE!!!

Dawn scrolled through the pages of messages. The lower case progressed to full capital letters with lots of exclamation points. She randomly selected the third voicemail and played it.

"Look, Dawn. You better listen to me. No one, and I mean no one, dumps me. I decide if and when we are done, and I have decided we are not done. You don't get to give up your pussy one time and decide it's over. If I want more, I get more. I get it when I want it and for as long I want it. Do you understand me—"

Dawn stopped the playback. She'd only listened to the first twenty-five seconds of a three-minute message, but she'd heard enough.

"Is something wrong?" the clerk asked.

Dawn looked up. "What? Oh no, the phone's fine."

Back at her Jeep, she googled: *If you block a number, will the person know?*

Her search provided the answer: *When you block a phone number, the sender can still leave a voicemail, but you won't get a notification. Messages can be sent, but they won't be delivered and the sender won't get a notification that the call or message was blocked.*

She considered how Nick had become more maniacal the longer she'd remained silent. Even if her phone had been working, she probably would've ignored him. Then she recalled Smita's cautionary tale about a guy so crazed that she had to move. Nick had already shown up uninvited to their place, and Marie was at home all day—alone and defenseless.

Dawn needed to de-escalate the situation. She crafted a text.

5:42 p.m. My phone broke, I was not ignoring you
Please respect my wishes
You'll find the right girl, it's just not me

He replied immediately.

5:43 p.m. I'm sorry
I drank too much…was having a hard time saying goodbye
Want the best for you…tot ziens

Dawn typed "tot ziens" in her Google translator. It meant "goodbye" in Dutch.

Yes, she thought. *Good riddance, you lying freak.*

Chapter 16

Friday couldn't come soon enough for Dawn, eager to put this tumultuous week behind her. She could hardly believe how she'd gone from feeling like a princess to realizing she'd been played for a fool. Fortunately, Nick hadn't texted or called since their last exchange, but Dawn couldn't shake a looming sense of dread. She was in the break room, packing up for the day, when Kelly joined her.

"Want to grab a drink?" her friend asked.

"That sounds like a great idea."

Dawn's phone rang—it was Stuart. She hadn't spoken to him all week and felt guilty about how easily he had been forgotten. Stuart wasn't *the one*, but at least he was trustworthy.

"What's up?" Dawn tried to recall how they'd left things. She thought they were broken up, but maybe he felt he still had a chance?

"Looks like you've been keeping yourself busy." His tone was harsh, even hateful.

"What do you mean?"

"Is there something you want to tell me?"

"Tell you? About what?"

"I got a call today. From a guy named Nick."

Dawn gulped. *How did Nick get Stuart's number?* she wondered. *And what did he say?* As if on cue, Stuart provided that answer.

"He said the two of you are sleeping together, and he thought I should know. I told him that wasn't possible because we're dating, so he sent me a photo."

"A photo?" she repeated.

"Yeah, a photo. I'll text it to you."

Dawn put her phone on speaker so she could see the incoming text. When she clicked on the message, she gasped. The picture was of her lying face down, naked, on Nick's sleeping bag. Her round butt cheeks were fully illuminated as if he'd pointed a flashlight directly at them.

"What is it?" asked Kelly.

Dawn covered her mouth with her hand. Both Kelly and Stuart awaited an explanation, but she had none.

"Stuart, I'm sorry," she groveled. "That was a big mistake."

"A mistake, Dawn, really? I'm not an idiot. Was Marie even hospitalized or was that just an excuse to spend time with *him*?"

"No, she did go to the hospital. And I'm done with him. Shit. I can't believe he did that."

"Did what?" asked Kelly.

Dawn turned her screen toward Kelly.

"Shit," her friend repeated.

Stuart continued. "I would've never cheated on you, Dawn. I thought you had class. Boy, was I wrong. You know, I'm glad you didn't meet my folks. I would never introduce a slut like you to them."

The line went dead.

"WTF," exclaimed Kelly. "Nick took that? What if he posts it? What if he has more of them?"

Dawn slumped onto the bench next to her locker. "I definitely need a drink."

At the bar, Dawn ordered a pitcher of margaritas and shared the whole ordeal with Kelly, starting with the car accident and ending with his latest stunt, the nude photo.

"He's trying to get Stuart out of the way, so you'll go back to him," surmised Kelly.

Dawn shook her head. "I'd already chosen him over Stuart. He knew that. But this photo tells me that he's not done messing with me."

"What are you going to do?"

"I don't know. I'm still trying to figure out how he got Stuart's number. He must've accessed my phone, but how? It's password protected."

"Maybe he held it up to your face while you were sleeping?"

"It won't unlock if my eyes are shut."

Kelly shrugged as Dawn poured another drink.

"He would've sent the worst photo to Stuart," said Kelly. "He probably just has the one. And so what? We see your butt. Big deal. It's the same as wearing a thong on the beach."

Dawn gave a halfhearted smile. Wearing a thong on the beach would've been her choice. This photo was not.

When their drinks were empty, the two parted ways. Dawn pulled into her driveway and immediately noticed something was amiss. The porch was dark. She scaled the front steps and heard a crunch under her shoes—the front light bulb had been crushed into shards. It could've been neighborhood kids playing a prank or Stuart taking his revenge, but Dawn knew better.

Chapter 17

On Saturday morning, as Dawn awoke, she cringed at the thought of how she'd spent the last two weekends. How, after just three dates, had Nick convinced her to accompany him alone into the woods? He'd been so nonchalant. If she wanted to spend time with him, she could join him, but his plans were set. His approach was cunning—a subtle difference from a direct invitation. And what about the fancy auction at the governor's mansion? For a second time, he'd put her in a situation where getting home wasn't as simple as a quick Uber ride. She recalled how she'd become so lethargic, to the point Nick had offered to pay for a hotel. Would he have taken more naked photos of her if she'd agreed? An alarming thought popped into her mind. Had her fatigue been induced by more than the champagne?

She climbed out of bed and slipped on a tank top, shorts and a pair of Nikes. With her schedule, Dawn didn't exercise during the week, but her Saturday runs kept her in shape. She exited through the back sliding glass door. Her patio looked like a barren desert compared to Marie's oasis of flowers, plants and vegetables.

Dawn checked the time, adjusted her earbuds and set out on a light jog. Christina Aguilera played on Pandora, setting the pace. Her feet pounded against the chipped pavement. Dawn's duplex was a far cry from the expansive farmhouse of her childhood, but she was close to work and to her mom. That was good enough. Thirty minutes later, she was on the home stretch down her street.

Inside, Dawn charged her phone and poured a glass of ice water. She took a few gulps and leaned against the sink to stretch her calves. Sweat dripped from her brow, stinging her eyes. As she was reaching for a paper towel, she heard pounding on the front door.

"Dawn, open up. I know you're in there." Nick's voice was insistent.

Her heartbeat spiked. How did he *know* she was home? Had he been spying on her duplex?

The pounding stopped.

Dawn wanted to look through the peephole but was afraid she'd see an eyeball staring right back at her. A streak of color flashed past the kitchen window. She darted into the hallway to escape being seen. Dawn wiped her eyes with her tank top and listened intently.

All was quiet.

She kneeled without making a sound, hoping he'd eventually give up and leave. The sound of sliding metal reverberated across the room. Only then did Dawn realize she hadn't locked the back door.

"Where are you, Dawn? I know you're here," he taunted.

Heavy footsteps clacked against the hardwood floor. He'd let himself inside. Dawn's blood pulsed loudly in her ears. Her breathing was so pronounced, she was certain he would hear her. Crouched in the hallway, she frantically considered her options. Leap for her phone on the counter and call 911 or retreat down the hall.

Escape, escape, escape replayed in her mind.

Dawn scurried down the hall and into her bedroom. She scanned for potential hiding spots. *Under the bed? No, too obvious. Inside the closet? No, the next place he'll look.* She wished she could contort herself into an impossibly small space, somewhere he'd never think to check. *Stop wishing. Start acting,* she thought.

She unlocked the window, lifted the frame and wrapped her leg over the sill. Without hesitation, she half-jumped, half-tumbled outside, banging her ankle. Dawn suppressed a scream. On the ground, she reached up, slid the window shut and limped to the front corner of the duplex. From that vantage point, she could see Nick's motorcycle, but he wouldn't be able to spot her.

Suddenly, she felt something touch her leg. She flipped around, losing her balance, and fell backward. Dawn crawled on all fours to distance herself from Nick. She'd kick. She'd scream. She'd sprint to the neighbors for help.

But there, prancing delicately, one paw crisscrossing over the other, was Snowball. Dawn exhaled in relief until the cat started mewing—an insistent, prolonged cry.

"Shhh," she pleaded, scooping up Snowball to quiet her.

"Nick, I'm surprised to see you." Dawn heard her mother's voice on the front porch.

No! she silently screamed.

"I'm looking for Dawn. Have you seen her?" he asked.

"She's not home? She must've gone for a run."

"I'll wait for her. Could I trouble you for a glass of water?"

"Don't let him inside," hissed Dawn, under her breath.

"Why don't you have a seat on the rocking chair. I'll bring you some." A few moments of silence passed. Then Dawn heard her mother's voice again. "Here you go. Since you're here, Nick, could I ask a favor? Our light bulb broke, and I don't have any replacements. Would you be a dear and go to the store? Here's five dollars. If you hurry, you'll probably beat her back."

Dawn wasn't sure if her mom was simply sending Nick on an errand or if she was finding a clever way to get rid of him. Either way, he walked to his motorcycle, revved the engine and tore off down the street.

Once he was out of sight, Dawn released Snowball and rushed to the front porch.

Marie took a step back. "My word, you startled me. Where'd you come from? Nick was just looking for you."

"I know." Dawn took her mom by the hand, led her inside and locked the door. She checked the back sliding glass door to confirm it was secure, too. "He was banging on my door. When I didn't answer, he let himself in."

Dawn waited for Marie's reaction, expecting her to be just as appalled and terrified, but her mom's face remained blank.

"Who does that, Mom? He's obsessed. He's sending me all kinds of text messages and calling nonstop. I need to use your phone—I have to call the police."

About ten minutes later, a uniformed officer in his mid-thirties pulled up in a patrol car. Dawn met him on the porch.

"We received a call reporting a break-in?" he said. "Are you Dawn Smith?"

"Yes, a guy I used to date, Nick VanBroklin, broke into my house."

"How do you know it was him?" the officer asked.

"I'd just returned from a run, and he started banging on my front door. When I didn't answer, he came in through the back."

"He broke your back door?"

"Well, no, it was unlocked, but he just let himself in."

"Did you tell him not to come in?"

"I hid so he wouldn't see me."

"Okay." The officer spoke slowly. "So, once he was inside, what'd he do?"

"He walked around my place calling my name."

The officer waited as if expecting to hear more.

"I had to jump out of my bedroom window. I had to hide outside so he couldn't find me."

"So, you never had any interaction with him while he was here?"

"Well, no, I got away."

The officer shifted from one foot to another. He was holding a notepad and pen but hadn't jotted a single word. "Did he threaten you or do anything to indicate he might cause you harm?"

"He broke into my house," said Dawn, exasperated.

"Well, ma'am, actually, he entered an unsecured door and appeared to be looking for you, based on what you're telling me."

"I broke up with him. He shouldn't be here. And he's been sending me threatening text messages. I'll show you." Dawn let the officer scroll through the thread on her phone.

After scanning the texts, he looked up. "Ma'am, based on these messages, I wouldn't want to date this guy either. But I don't see anything that's a direct threat."

"You don't consider these messages threatening?" Her voice grew sharper.

"Not legally. There's no indication he means to cause you bodily harm. Did he take anything or damage any of your property while he was here?"

"He was coming for *me*, not my stuff. When he couldn't find me, he confronted my mom. He told her that he was looking for me."

"Then what happened?"

"She gave him money to replace our lightbulb, one that I think *he* broke."

The officer started to speak but stopped himself. After a few seconds, he asked. "At any point have you specifically told him that he cannot be on your property?"

"I broke up with him. Why should I have to specifically tell him not to come over? Isn't that obvious?"

"Just because you ended the relationship doesn't legally prohibit him from visiting your property. If there was a protection order in place or a previous criminal trespass warning, or if he'd committed a crime inside your home, then I'd have something to work with here."

"So, you can't do anything?"

"Ma'am, what you're reporting is that he came to your house looking for you, entered through an unsecured door, you hid from him and your mom sent him on an errand. This was called in as a break-in, which means a burglary, but none of the information you've given me meets that threshold. I can make a report to document the incident. What is your ex-boyfriend's name and date of birth?"

"Nick VanBroklin. I don't know his birthday."

The officer's eyebrows rose, his only reaction in an otherwise stoic demeanor. Dawn felt the judgment.

"If he returns and you don't want him on your property, call the police. We'll come out and issue a criminal trespass warrant." The officer pointed to the bolt. "And be sure to lock your doors. Have a nice day, ma'am."

Chapter 18

The exchange with the officer made Dawn feel helpless. Yes, she'd left her door open, but that didn't give Nick permission to invade her home. Left unchallenged, she feared he would become emboldened, and she was right. The barrage of obscene text messages began later that day.

2: 15 p.m. YOU DIDN'T TRY…DON'T THINK I DIDN'T NOTICE!!!
2: 17 p.m. YOU GAVE UP ON A REAL MAN!!!
2: 18 p.m. I WAS UR BEST LAY AND YOU KNOW IT!!!
2: 18 p.m. I CAN MAKE YOU CUM ALL NIGHT
WHO ELSE CAN DO THAT FOR YOU??? NOT STUART!!!
2: 21 p.m. DID IT FEEL GOOD WHEN I SLID DEEP INSIDE YOU???
2: 22 p.m. I KNOW YOU GET WET THINKING OF ME STICKING IN MY BIG ONE
YOU KNOW YOU WANT MORE!!!

You don't get to send me this crap, she thought. Not only was she going to block his number, but she wanted him to know. She replied.

2: 23 p.m. This number has been permanently blocked.
No calls, voice messages or texts can be delivered from this number.
Any further harassment will result in police action.

The man who had such charming manners, who'd kissed her hand on their first date and brought wine and flowers for dinner, was a farce. And obviously, he could only continue the charade for so long. Now she was seeing the *real* Nick.

Dawn decided she wouldn't share the text messages with her mom—Marie lived in a world where men were gentlemen. Still, she couldn't allow Marie to offer Nick another potpie or ask him to run another errand. Dawn decided to share how he'd stiffed her and the clinic for Lucky's surgery.

"What kind of man leaves a woman in the lurch like that?" scoffed Marie when she heard the story.

"That's right, Mom. The Patels covered the surgery, or it would've come out of my paycheck. Nick lied about paying and he's lied about so many other things. He's not a good man."

Chapter 19

On Monday morning, Dawn was about to greet her first appointment when Dr. Patel stopped her in the hallway and asked her to come to his office. To Dawn's surprise, Smita was there with baby Devin but without her typical sunny smile. Dr. Patel had never said a word about the debacle with Lucky's payment or how Dawn had gone to Smita instead of him. Now, she wondered if there was a problem.

Smita handed Dawn a piece of paper. She read the bright red capital lettering, which took up the entire page: DAWN SMITH IS A WHORE.

She was speechless.

"I assume this was done by the fellow who didn't pay for Lucky's surgery?" asked Dr. Patel.

Dawn knew this was Nick's doing. Stuart probably shared those sentiments, but he wasn't a psycho. Plus, the capital letters were Nick's trademark.

"Where'd you find this?" she asked.

"Taped to the front door."

Dawn shook her head in disbelief. "This has to be Nick."

"I'm going to cover your appointment while you and Smita talk over some things," said Dr. Patel. He stood, exited the office and quietly shut the door behind him.

Smita outstretched her arms, beckoning Dawn closer. "I'm guessing the breakup didn't go so well?"

Something about Smita's caring nature allowed Dawn to be more vulnerable than normal, especially at work. She started to explain but burst into tears.

Smita wrapped her arm around Dawn's shoulder and offered a tissue.

Through choppy breaths, Dawn relayed the recent drama with Nick.

"I did what you said. I told him I needed to focus on my work and my mom, but he won't leave me alone. He came inside my place over the weekend. I was so scared, I jumped out the window. I even called the police, but they said there was nothing they could do."

Smita gently rubbed Dawn's back. "What else has he done?"

Dawn bowed her head. "He has a compromising photo of me. He sent it to Stuart, and he may have more."

Smita nodded. "Anything else?"

Dawn handed Smita her phone with the vile text messages.

"Good," said Smita.

"Good?" Dawn lifted her head.

"For you to file a restraining order, he has to commit at least two acts of stalking, harassment or other threatening behavior. We can't prove he left the note here, but you have the messages on your phone and the police report of him entering your home."

"You think I should file a restraining order?"

"I do."

"How does that work?"

"You'll fill out an online form with his name, address and details of each incident. Once he's served, a hearing date will be set by the magistrate court. Within fifteen days—"

"Fifteen days? Why so long? Can't I get some kind of emergency order?"

"That's called an *order of protection,* where you'd request an emergency hearing before the judge. But I'm afraid your situation won't qualify. In South Carolina, your abuser must be a spouse, ex-spouse, live-in partner of the opposite sex or someone with whom you share a child in order to request an order of protection."

"That's archaic."

"I agree, but the best you can do for now is to file a restraining order. Once the date for a hearing is set, you'll testify as to what he's done. He'll be able to testify, too, but it'll be hard for him to deny his behavior. Then the judge will decide if there's cause to sign the order."

"I know his condo building, but I don't know his exact address."

"You'll need it. He has to be served in person by the sheriff. Can you find out without putting yourself in danger?"

Dawn nodded. She didn't think the bank would provide his home address, but maybe the condo leasing office would if she said she was his girlfriend.

"Is that what you did?" Dawn asked. "Filed a restraining order?"

"Yes. With my case, he was prohibited from contacting me for six months."

"So if you had a restraining order, why'd you still have to move?"

Smita sighed. "Someone clever can find other ways to harass you, but it's still worth filing so the court has a record of your complaint."

Before going back to work, Dawn called the leasing office of Nick's condo building, prepared to lie to get his unit number. Either they'd give her the information with no hassle, or they'd refuse to share details about their residents. Either way, it was worth a try. What she didn't expect was a third response—they had no record of a Nick VanBroklin living there.

Toward the end of the day, Dawn found Kelly, who was restocking treats in the exam room. "Could we trade cars for a night?" she asked.

"We can trade cars forever," joked Kelly. Dawn's Jeep was much nicer than Kelly's Nissan. "Seriously, what's up?"

"I need to find out Nick's address, for a restraining order."

"A restraining order?" Kelly's eyes widened.

"Things have gotten worse." Dawn showed Kelly the text messages and described the scare Nick had given her over the weekend. "I need his address for the restraining order, but if I follow him in my Jeep, he might recognize me."

"Can't you find his address online?" asked Kelly.

"I've tried. There's nothing. I have to leave soon. The bank closes at five."

"Okay, but I'm coming with you."

Kelly shoved the half-filled treat jar against the wall and grabbed her keys. Twenty minutes later, the women pulled into the Wells Fargo parking lot to begin their stakeout. Dawn gathered her long blonde hair into a bun and slipped on sunglasses.

"He can still recognize you," said Kelly.

"He won't be looking for me in your car. Can we turn on some air?"

"It's broken." Kelly shrugged.

Dawn sighed and manually rolled down the window.

At 5:10 p.m., Nick turned the corner of the building and walked along the sidewalk. As he pulled away, Kelly shifted her car into gear and followed the Blazer out of the lot, keeping some distance.

"He lives in the condos across from Little Bangkok," said Dawn. "They didn't recognize his name, so maybe he's subleasing. We can park outside the building and follow him inside to get the unit number."

The maroon SUV turned onto Nick's street. It passed the Thai restaurant and, at the entrance to the condo building, continued down the road.

"What?" said Dawn. "Why isn't he turning?"

"What should I do?" asked Kelly.

"Keep following."

About half a mile down the road, Nick's SUV turned into a four-story complex with chipped paint and dead shrubbery. The building, originally a motel, had been converted into apartments. Each unit had an exterior entrance with a single window next to the door. Nick parked and ascended the rusted stairs to the fourth floor, taking them two at a time.

"Of course," said Dawn. "The night of the accident, he said that he walked to the restaurant, but he was actually driving. He didn't live within walking distance. That SOB couldn't even tell me the truth about where he lives. Quick. We have to follow him."

The women exited Kelly's Nissan and scampered up the stairs that Nick had just used. Dawn's long legs and weekly runs made the climb effortless, but Kelly doubled over, panting once they'd reached the top floor. In the time it had taken them to mount the stairs, Nick had disappeared—likely into one of the many doors along the fourth-floor hallway.

"Did you see where he went?" whispered Dawn.

Kelly shook her head.

"Damn. We should've just watched him from the car and gotten the number later." She crept to the first unit and put her ear to the door.

"Let me do that," huffed Kelly. "What if he comes out and sees you?"

Just then, one of the apartment doors midway down opened. Dawn and Kelly leapt into the open stairway, out of sight. When Dawn peered around the corner, she saw a Hispanic woman with a young boy walking toward them. She quickly stepped forward so their paths would cross.

"Excuse me," she said. "I'm supposed to meet a guy named Nick VanBroklin here, but I've forgotten which one is his unit. Could you help me?" Dawn pulled out her phone and scrolled to the fuzzy selfie she'd taken during the camping trip.

"I'm sorry," said the woman, barely looking at the photo. "We just moved here. I haven't really met anyone." The woman continued down the stairs with the boy.

Kelly touched Dawn's arm. "Don't you think having the apartment building will be enough? The court can send the letter to the front office, and they can deliver it to his place?"

"The sheriff has to serve him *in person*," replied Dawn.

"What about serving him at the bank?"

"Maybe, but the online application requires his home address. Come on. Let's get out of here. We're not going to find him tonight."

The women descended the stairs and headed to the parking lot. About ten feet before they reached Kelly's car, she stopped abruptly.

"What's wrong?" asked Dawn.

"Look." Kelly pointed. The front driver's side tire was fully deflated, causing the wheel rim to touch the ground.

"Shit," exclaimed Dawn. "Do you have a spare?"

Although Kelly had a spare tire in the trunk, there was no jack—something Dawn's father would've never allowed. Before Dawn was given permission to drive, she had to first prove that she could change a tire. She could've fixed Kelly's flat if she'd had the right equipment. Instead, they were forced to call roadside assistance, which had a forty-five-minute estimated wait time.

"Let's get some dinner," offered Dawn. "My treat for this mess. Just need to call Mom and tell her to eat without me."

The women walked to a nearby fast-food restaurant and dined on greasy burgers and soggy fries. When the tow truck finally arrived, the mechanic was able to change the flat using Kelly's spare tire and his heavy-duty jack.

"Ma'am, I don't mean to alarm you," he said. "But I don't think this happened by accident."

"What do you mean?" asked Kelly.

The mechanic took a toothpick from his mouth and used it to point to the valve of the flat tire. "This stem here has been cut off. That doesn't happen by itself."

Kelly and Dawn exchanged a worried look. In unison, they turned to face Nick's apartment building. Exterior stairs bookended each side. Nick could've scaled one side, traversed the length of the building and descended using the stairs on the other side. He could've sliced the tire valve while they were talking to the Hispanic woman.

A chill came over Dawn as she recalled the camping trip and the loose battery cable on the truck.

"You bastard," she muttered, realizing this was the second time he'd sabotaged a vehicle.

"How could he have seen us?" questioned Kelly.

Nick knew where Dawn worked. The profane note taped to the front door proved he'd been there. If he'd visited during business hours, he would've seen her Jeep parked around back, right next to Kelly's blue Nissan.

Chapter 20

Once home, Dawn kicked off her Crocs, grabbed a beer and headed to the bathroom. She undressed, tossing her scrubs, bra and panties onto the floor, and was about to step into the shower, but stopped. Something felt off. The air was different. It was moist.

Dawn dismissed the weird feeling and reached for the shower door. In that instant she realized what was wrong. She jerked her arm back as if the metal handle were on fire. Fresh water droplets formed beads against the glass pane. Dawn had showered the night before. The glass should've been dry. Someone had been in her house. Maybe he was still there.

Dawn snatched a towel and wrapped it around her naked body. She grabbed a pair of scissors from her makeup drawer, gripping the handle like a knife. Standing as stiff as a statue, she listened for any unfamiliar sounds—a footstep or creaking floorboard. Hearing nothing unusual, she tiptoed into her bedroom. There, she flung open the closet door, prepared to stab the intruder hiding inside.

Nothing. All was still.

Shaking, she hastily slipped on a pair of jeans and a shirt—there was no time for undergarments.

She crept down the hall and into the den. Her grip on the scissors was so tight that her knuckles were turning white. She tugged at the back sliding glass door, confirming it was still locked. Everything looked normal in the kitchen, until Dawn noticed a single plastic container of yogurt resting in the trash can. The thin aluminum lid had been peeled back and the contents eaten. Dawn had skipped breakfast, and she'd taken the garbage out the night before. She gasped, bolted outside and across the porch to Marie's unit, but the front door was locked.

"Mom, open up. It's me."

She pounded on the door while trying to convince herself that the locked door was a good thing. That's what she'd told her mom to do.

Marie, who was dressed in a nightgown, greeted her daughter. "What is it, dear?"

"Have you been in my place? Did you shower there? Eat a yogurt?"

"Of course not. Why do you ask?"

"Has Nick been here?"

"I don't think so."

"He broke into my place. I don't know how, but I'm changing the locks. Yours, too. For tonight, get dressed and pack a bag. We're going to a hotel."

"A hotel?" Marie questioned. "Do you really think that's necessary?"

Dawn was tempted to show her mom the explicit text messages, to tell her about the naked picture he'd sent to Stuart and the profane note he'd taped to the clinic door. She considered revealing his latest stunt, vandalizing Kelly's car, but she didn't want to scare Marie.

"Yes, it's necessary," she replied firmly.

Back at her place, she grabbed an overnight bag and stuffed it with clothes. The last time she'd used that bag was for the camping trip, a thought that made her feel sick. She hurried to the dresser to retrieve her locket, but the jewelry stand was bare. Dawn dropped to her knees and crawled around the floor, frantically searching for her most valued possession. The necklace was nowhere to be found.

In her heart, she knew.

The sense of loss overwhelmed her, rekindling the intense grief that came in the early days after her father's death.

Dawn sank to the floor and wailed.

The next morning, Dawn took time off from the clinic to have the locks changed. She wasn't sure how Nick had accessed her place but guessed he'd copied the key. He could've copied Marie's key, too, and she wasn't taking any chances. While the locksmith worked, Dawn sat at the kitchen table and downloaded the application for a restraining order.

The form required her to list her information as the plaintiff and Nick's as the defendant. She entered his address, without the unit number, and checked all three boxes for the type of offense: *first degree harassment*—unwanted surveillance and damaging property, *second degree harassment*—texting and calling, and *stalking*—unwelcomed pursuit.

She described each incident, including the date, time and place, and checked the boxes requesting specific restrictions—that he be barred from threatening her or her family; barred from entering or attempting to enter her residence or place of employment; and barred from communicating or attempting to communicate with her in any way.

When the locksmith finished both residences, Dawn charged three hundred dollars to her credit card, adding it to the ninety dollars for Kelly's replacement tire and the hundred and thirty dollars for the hotel. Her nostrils flared at the thought of how much money Nick was costing her.

The restraining order required a notary's signature, so Dawn stopped by the UPS store. There was no way she was going to the bank. With the form officially sealed, she headed to the Laurel courthouse to file the paperwork with the magistrate clerk. Dawn wondered if Nick had harassed other women. She knew so little about him and couldn't uncover any trace of him online.

Then an idea hit her. Nick's boss, Cecilia Park, said she'd gone to high school with his mother. This woman could be the key to finding out more about him. Dawn sat on a bench in a quiet corner of the courthouse lobby and opened Facebook. She quickly found Cecilia, and below her place of work at the bank, Cecilia had listed her high school in Simpson, the next town over. She'd also listed her graduation year, which gave Dawn another idea. She mulled over her plan, made the call to the bank's main line and was transferred to the head teller.

"This is Cecilia Park. How can I help you?" The woman dragged out each vowel of her name as she spoke.

"Hi, Ms. Park. This is Kelly Smith calling from Simpson High School. I'm on the committee to plan the next reunion for your class, and I've been tasked with tracking down everyone's contact information."

"Oh how fun. I didn't know they had any plans for a reunion."

"Well, it's kind of an impromptu thing. We're trying to recapture some of that old school spirit."

"School spirit?" Cecilia scoffed. "It's hard to have any of that when your football team loses every game."

"I understand," said Dawn. "What's the best number and email to send you some follow-up information?"

Without hesitation, Cecilia rattled off her contact information.

"And is there anyone else you stay in touch with that I can add to the list?"

"Let's see. My husband, Bill, of course. But he won't come unless I make him, so just send everything to me."

"I sure will," said Dawn. "Anyone else?"

Cecilia provided a few more names, but none were VanBroklin. Dawn noted them anyway. Maybe one of them would know Nick's mother.

"Oh and how could I forget, Amanda Graham. Her son works for me."

"Do you have Amanda's information by chance?"

"It's been years since we spoke, but I think she's still in Simpson. She moved back home after the divorce. Wait, I can get Nick. He'll know how to reach her."

"That's okay," stammered Dawn. "No need to bother him. I'll reach out to Amanda directly."

Dawn couldn't believe her good luck. With one phone call, she'd found Nick's mother. She wondered what the woman would be like. Was she a sweet lady, oblivious to her son's derangement, or a monster who'd spawned a child just like herself?

Chapter 21

Having spent the morning waiting on the locksmith and filing the restraining order, Dawn headed to work in the afternoon. She knew the stress she was putting on the others. Time off was planned well in advance to manage the schedule, and the clinic was already down one vet with Smita on maternity leave.

Suzanne met her in the break room. "I'm glad you're finally here," said the receptionist, not hiding her exasperation. "Can you take a walk-in? A cat named Princess."

Cats named "Princess" were typically a Persian or Ragdoll. She probably wore a sparkly collar and had a matching bedazzled carrier. No doubt she had at least one comfy cat bed but was allowed to sleep with the humans.

When Dawn pushed open the door to the exam room, she confirmed her theory. On the table sat a fluffy white Ragdoll that looked a lot like Snowball, minus the pink collar. Dawn beamed at her ability to guess correctly but then skidded to a stop.

Leaning against the wall, sporting a wicked grin, was Nick.

"You need to leave now," she said. Her voice was firm but shaky.

"My cat needs to be treated." He spoke with an earnest yet mocking tone. His stare, the one she'd once found to be so alluring, made her shudder.

The cat started to walk toward her, one paw crisscrossing over the other. Dawn's mouth dropped open. This cat didn't *look like* Snowball—she *was* Snowball.

"How dare you steal my neighbor's cat," she exclaimed.

"What are you talking about?" Nick played innocent, but his grin told her otherwise.

"I'm calling security if you don't leave immediately." The clinic didn't actually have security, but Dawn hoped the threat would make him go.

Ignoring her warning, Nick approached the table and grabbed Snowball by the scruff of the neck. The cat mewed.

"Put her down," shouted Dawn. She charged forward and wrapped her arms around Snowball's belly, forcing a tug-of-war. Nick jerked the cat toward him, drawing Dawn within inches of his face. The last time they'd been that close, they were sharing a kiss. Now, everything about him repulsed her. She tugged again. Snowball bleated like a goat. Just at the moment Dawn pulled, Nick let go. She stumbled backward, with Snowball clutched in her arms, and slammed into the wall with a loud thud.

Nick swept the corner of his jacket back with his right hand and placed his fist on his hip. The movement revealed his pistol, holstered on his right side. All he had to do was draw, aim and shoot. In a matter of seconds, Dawn knew that he could easily take her life. Her thoughts felt like they were moving in slow motion.

Scream? Run? Beg?

Just then, there was a soft knock on the door, followed by Dr. Patel entering the room. "Excuse me, I thought I heard—"

He halted mid-sentence after seeing Dawn pressed against the wall with a look of terror in her eyes. She darted behind him, still clutching Snowball. Nick, surprised by the interruption, let his jacket fall over the firearm.

"What's going on here?" the vet asked.

"That's Nick. We need to call the police."

As Dr. Patel reached for his phone, Nick shoved past both of them and out of the room.

"911, what is your emergency?" asked the operator.

"My employee's ex-boyfriend was here," said Dr. Patel. "He's been harassing her."

"Is the suspect still there?"

"No, he ran out."

"Is your employee injured or in need of medical care?"

"Hold on." Dr. Patel put his phone on speaker. "Are you injured? Do you need medical attention?"

"I'm okay." Dawn felt Snowball's claws pressing against her chest and realized she was squeezing the cat too tightly.

"The suspect is your ex-boyfriend?" asked the operator.

"We dated briefly. He's crazy. I just filed for a restraining order."

"What's his name?"

"Nick VanBroklin."

"Is that his full legal name?"

"No, I'm sorry. It's Nicholas."

"Middle name?"

"I don't know."

"And his date of birth?"

Dawn rolled her eyes, annoyed that she couldn't provide that information, either. She described his height, weight, vehicle and address—basically everything she did know about him.

"An officer is on the way. Please don't leave the scene," said the operator.

A few minutes later, a middle-aged African American officer arrived.

"Sir," said the officer to Dr. Patel, "As you were a witness, I'll need to interview you separately, after I'm done speaking with Ms. Smith." The officer turned toward Dawn, "Do you have a trusted friend or coworker who can support you while we talk?"

"I can send Kelly," said Dr. Patel. "You can use my office."

A few moments later, Kelly rushed to Dawn's side.

As the three stood in Dr. Patel's office, Dawn recounted the incident. "Nicholas VanBroklin, a guy I dated a few times, showed up here pretending to be one of my appointments. He had my neighbor's cat that he'd stolen. I told him to leave, but he refused. Thankfully, Dr. Patel walked in and scared him off."

"How do you know he had your neighbor's cat?"

"I recognized her. I chipped her myself when she was a kitten. I can scan her to prove it."

"Okay. I'm going to need the contact information of the cat's owner in case they want to press charges for the theft of the animal."

Dawn hadn't realized that the abduction of Snowball would be a crime, but it made sense. Given her last interaction with the police, she was relieved that this officer seemed to be taking the situation more seriously.

"Our dispatch noted that you filed for a restraining order," he said. "When did you file it?"

"This morning. He broke into my house last night and stole my favorite necklace."

"What?" exclaimed Kelly. "You need to get some security cameras."

Dawn nodded in agreement, another expense courtesy of Nick.

The officer jotted on his notepad. "If you filed the order this morning, I doubt the sheriff has had time to serve it. Now, walk me through what happened here this afternoon."

"I told Nick to leave, but he wouldn't. He grabbed Snowball by the neck. He was hurting her, so I pried her free. I thought he was going to kill me."

"Why'd you think he was going to kill you?"

"He moved his jacket, and I saw his hand right next to his gun."

"He had a gun?" exclaimed Kelly. "Why didn't you mention that before?"

"I don't know. I just wanted to get Snowball and get out."

"Sometimes we forget details in the heat of the moment," explained the officer. "Luckily, it appears Dr. Patel came in and put a stop to it." He reached into his pocket, pulled out a card and scribbled on it. "Here's my information with the case number. An investigator will follow up with you. In the meantime, if Nicholas does anything else, you should file a police report, okay?"

"I don't know his birthday, but I know he works at the Wells Fargo bank downtown. VanBroklin isn't a common name. He shouldn't be hard to find."

"I'll pass that on to the investigator," replied the officer.

Chapter 22

Once the officer left, Dr. Patel suggested that Dawn return Snowball to her rightful owner. Another day of work was lost—thanks to Nick. On her way home, she replayed the confrontation in her mind. *What would Nick have done if Dr. Patel hadn't interrupted them? Was the gun meant to intimidate her, or would he have actually used it?*

Dawn stopped at her place long enough to deliver Snowball and look up Amanda Graham's address. Thirty minutes later, she was parking in front of a modest one-story house by the railroad tracks in Simpson. A large, decaying satellite dish sat prominently in the overgrown grass. The carport was empty. Dawn walked up the footpath to the front door. Inside, sappy music from a daytime soap opera was playing. She rang the bell and waited.

An elderly woman opened the door. Her coarse gray hair needed a good brushing. The skin around her eyes and neck sagged. She was tall like Nick, but her age led Dawn to believe that she couldn't be his mother.

"I'm looking for Amanda Graham," said Dawn.

"Who are you?" The woman's tone was curious. She looked past Dawn as if expecting the crew from the Publishers Clearing House to appear with her million-dollar check.

"I'm Dawn Smith. I used to date Nick VanBroklin. I'm looking for his mom."

There was no recognition of his name, nor denial. The woman overtly eyed Dawn's belly. "Are you pregnant?"

"Are you Amanda Graham?"

The woman squinted. "What do you want with me and my son?"

"May I come in?" asked Dawn. "I'm not pregnant."

Nick's mom seemed to lower her guard, apparently relieved she was not about to become a grandmother. She retreated into her living room, not bothering to hold the door open for Dawn. Inside, her place was dimly lit and decorated in dull shades of brown: tan vinyl walls, an oatmeal-colored couch and a sagging taupe recliner. She pointed to the worn-out sofa and Dawn took a seat.

"I don't mean to bother you," started Dawn. "Nick and I had a bad breakup."

Dawn thought she glimpsed a momentary comprehension in the woman's eyes, as if she didn't need any further description of her son's behavior. However, she didn't respond to the comment or ask a question. Instead, the two women sat in awkward silence.

Dawn looked around the room. There were no pictures or artwork. Even the drapes were a flat, unappealing shade of beige. She happened to glance out the back window and her heart jumped into her throat. Nick's white pickup truck was parked behind the house. She jumped to her feet.

"Is he here?" Dawn asked in a panic.

"No, why?"

"His truck." Dawn pointed outside.

"That's *my* truck. He borrows it sometimes for camping."

"I thought he had a Chevy Blazer?"

"That's his sister's car. She's in the Army, stationed overseas. Nick is keeping it for me. Don't need the neighbors thinking I'm taking on airs."

Dawn's fear subsided, although for the first time, she realized what a risk she was taking by simply being there. As she retook her seat, she marveled at the ever-growing list of lies. Nick didn't own *either* vehicle.

"Is VanBroklin his father's name?"

"Yes. We're divorced."

"Where's his father now?"

"No idea." The woman gestured to her dreary surroundings. "He certainly isn't helping me. Never did."

"You've been divorced for a while?" asked Dawn.

"Nick and Sophie were teenagers."

"And your other children?"

Nick's mother stared blankly.

Dawn repeated her question. "Your other children? Nick said he was one of six?"

"You must've misunderstood," she said, though a fleeting look of recognition surfaced and then vanished, just as it had done before.

Both women knew Dawn hadn't misunderstood. Nick had told her that he was the eldest of six children, all of whom were still in the Netherlands, which was also a lie. When she'd imagined his wealthy banker family, she'd pictured lavish mansions, luxury cars and designer clothes. She certainly hadn't pictured a beleaguered, resentful divorcée who was living by the railroad tracks. And Dawn didn't need Nick to have money or status. Ironically, what had attracted her to him in the first place, besides his good looks, was his character.

"Nick has my necklace, a locket given to me by my father. But, like I said, we had a bad breakup. I don't think he plans to give it back. Maybe you could help me?"

Amanda Graham simply shrugged, leaving Dawn with a newfound regret. She doubted Nick's mother could persuade him to return the locket, even if she was willing to try. Worse, Dawn had signaled how much it meant to her. She tried a different approach. "Have you met any of Nick's other girlfriends?"

The woman stood. "I'm sure my son plans to return your necklace. Probably just hasn't had the time. I think it would be best if we didn't communicate any further."

This woman's words felt like a harsh slap across the face, one that Dawn didn't deserve. Clearly, Nick's mother was taking sides, even if her loyalty was grossly misplaced.

The next day, Dawn received a call from a local number she didn't recognize.

"This is Detective Clyde," the female voice said. "I'm calling to follow up on a police report you filed yesterday. It's regarding an incident at the Village Veterinary Clinic. Do you have a minute to talk?"

"Yes, I can talk," said Dawn.

"I've read the report and just wanted to see if there was anything additional you wanted to share, now that you've had a chance to reflect."

Not knowing what was in the report, Dawn relayed the events from Nick showing up with Snowball to him brandishing the gun. She shared how, thankfully, Dr. Patel had interrupted the confrontation, which made Nick leave.

"And when you say that Mr. VanBroklin brandished the gun, can you describe to me exactly what happened?" asked the detective.

"He pulled back his jacket and showed me his gun."

"Did he take it out?"

"No."

"Did he touch the firearm at all?"

"Well, no, but he made sure I saw it."

"Did he make any direct threats toward you?" asked the detective. "Did he say anything about what he was going to do?"

"He didn't have to *say* what he was going to do. He was carrying a *gun*." Dawn couldn't believe that this detective couldn't understand her point.

"Ms. Smith, it's not illegal to carry a gun. I understand from the responding officer that you and Mr. VanBroklin dated for a period of time. During that time, did you know him to carry a firearm?"

"Well, yes, but that was when we went camping. He had no reason to bring a gun into a veterinary clinic. Don't you see? He was trying to scare me. He wanted me to know that he could get to me—anywhere."

"So, when Mr. VanBroklin was at the clinic, did you feel like he was going to hurt you?"

Dawn exhaled in frustration. "I didn't know what he was going to do."

"And the two of you are no longer dating?"

"Of course not."

There was a brief pause, as if the detective was collecting her thoughts. "Ms. Smith, the responding officer titled the report as a violation of the terroristic threats law and theft of your neighbor's cat. But in order for me to charge Mr. VanBroklin with a terroristic threat, you'd have to be in fear of receiving an injury or death, and the threat would have to be corroborated by a witness or a recording. We don't have that. You're telling me that he came to your place of work to harass you. Even so, harassment isn't always a crime in the eyes of the law. Now, the theft of the cat is a more clear-cut issue and a potential crime that I can investigate. I'm going to follow up with Mr. VanBroklin and see how he explains himself. I'll be back in touch once I've spoken with him."

Dawn was speechless. How could stealing Snowball be Nick's only crime?

Chapter 23

Over the next few days, Nick had gone quiet. There were no signs he'd been to Dawn's home and there were no further attempts to reach her at the clinic. She wasn't sure if the police investigator had spooked him or if her newly installed security camera was keeping him at bay.

On Friday, she was wrapping up at work and thinking about her solitary weekend ahead. Before, with Stuart, it was understood they'd spend time together. They'd developed a comfortable routine that she was starting to miss. Deep down, she knew she was craving companionship more than the man himself. Still, she regretted how their relationship had ended, a gradual disintegration instead of a mature, decisive split. Most of all, she regretted Nick's manipulation, showing Stuart her naked photo. The thought of that image appearing in other places, like on social media or a porn site, loomed in the back of her mind.

Her phone rang. Marie sounded flustered. "I've just been served with some kind of legal paperwork. A courier delivered it. I had to sign for it and for yours, too. I don't understand. Are we being sued?"

Dawn immediately suspected her half brothers, David Jr. and Doug, were stirring up trouble again. They'd already lost the battle over their father's will. What new grievance could they possibly have? She glanced at the clock. It was just past 5:00 p.m. and probably too late to call their lawyer.

"Sit tight, Mom. I'm on my way home. I'll look at everything when I get there."

Dawn was so preoccupied with the thought of another lawsuit that she didn't notice the small object on her windshield, at first. An amber-colored plastic vile with a white turn cap was resting on the wiper blade of her Jeep. She picked up the empty pill bottle and examined it. The label read: TAKE ONE TABLET BY MOUTH EVERY MORNING. Below the dosage instruction was the name of the drug: LISINOPRIL 20 MG TABLET. On the top right of the label, in tiny print, was the patient's name: SMITH, MRS. MARIE.

For a split second, Dawn struggled to make the connection. Obviously, this was her mom's medication, but what was it doing on her

Jeep? The image of bracing Marie's fall flashed in Dawn's mind. She recalled holding her mom's hand in the ambulance and calling Nick from the hospital to ask if he could check the kitchen cabinet. He'd said the medication was missing. At the time, she'd believed him.

Dawn quickly phoned her mom. "I'm on my way home. On the paperwork, look at the top. Who's it from?"

"Nicholas VanBroklin," said Marie. "I don't understand—"

"What does it say? Can you read it to me?"

"It says: *Certificate of Service, State of South Carolina, County of Laurel, Nicholas VanBroklin, Petitioner, versus Marie P. Smith and Dawn R. Smith, Respondents. The undersigned hereby certifies that she has caused the summons and petition for appointment of guardian in the above-captioned case, to be served via courier on the parties listed below."*

"Go on." Dawn's heart was racing. Nick hadn't retreated, he'd retrenched.

"It has the date, our names and address, and is signed by Denise Hatcher, assistant to Charles B. Hood of the Hood Law Firm, LLC. There's a second page that looks the same."

"Hang tight, Mom. I'll be right there." Dawn floored the gas pedal. She needed to read these legal documents for herself. Once home, she plowed through the paperwork as Marie nervously watched.

"You are hereby summoned and required to answer the Petition herein, a copy of which is herewith served upon you, and to serve a copy of your Answer to this Petition upon the subscriber, at the address shown below, within thirty (30) days after service hereof, exclusive of the day of such service, and if you fail to answer the Petition, judgment by default will be rendered against you for the relief demanded in the Petition."

The summons was signed by Charles B. Hood, the attorney for the petitioner. Dawn didn't fully comprehend the legalese, but she understood that she and her mom were being sued by Nick and had thirty days to respond or he'd prevail by default.

The next set of documents was the petition for guardianship of Marie. Nick had listed his relationship as a "family friend and caregiver" of the alleged incapacitated person. He stated that Marie needed a guardian as a means of providing continuing care and supervision due to her incapacitated state. He further requested that the court set a time and place for a hearing and listed Dawn as a person required by statute to be given notice, which is why she'd received a duplicate set of documents. Dawn read the section that described his argument.

"The petitioner has witnessed that Ms. Dawn Smith has failed to provide proper oversight and care for her mother, which has put the health and safety of Mrs. Marie Smith at risk. As an example, Mrs. Smith recently fell at her home and was not provided with medical attention. Soon after, she had a second episode where she collapsed and lost consciousness. The petitioner called for medical aid and ensured that Mrs. Smith was treated at the Laurel County Hospital. Had it not been for the actions of the petitioner, Mrs. Smith would not have received the proper medical care. With no other relatives living nearby or willing to assume the role, Mr. Nicholas VanBroklin, who resides in Laurel County and is a trusted family friend of the incapacitated person, should be named the legal guardian. Mr. VanBroklin requests that the court determine the need for the appointment of a guardian is proper and appoint Mr. Nicholas VanBroklin as the guardian for the above person and that letters of guardianship be issued."

Dawn's hands trembled as she read the petition. She connected the dots with the pill bottle, which Nick had clearly left on her Jeep. The morning they'd returned from the camping trip, Nick had made breakfast. He'd been alone in the kitchen. He could've easily laced her mom's food. That would've explained Marie's sudden drop in blood pressure and collapse. But all of this happened *before* she broke up with him. It didn't make any sense.

"What is it?" asked Marie. "What's he trying to do?"

"Nick is trying to become your guardian. He's lost his mind, and what kind of quack lawyer would agree to draft these documents?"

Dawn took Marie's hands into her own. She knew her mother could get confused at times, but not enough to declare her incompetent. Her mom was still capable of voicing her opinions and desires, and the worst thing in the world would be for Marie to lose her independence. Dawn had moved Marie close to keep an eye on her and to avoid putting her in an assisted living facility after she became a widow.

"Don't worry, Mom. I'll talk to Ben. We'll get this sorted out. Nothing is going to change."

She flipped to the second set of documents, petitioning for the appointment of a conservator. Her mom's property, including the duplex, assets and income were listed with shocking accuracy. Also noted were Marie's checking and savings account at the Wells Fargo bank, her account with Vanguard and her spousal Social Security benefits.

How does he know all of this? wondered Dawn.

She read the justification.

"The petitioner is educated and experienced in financial investments and banking. He is currently employed by the Wells Fargo Bank of Laurel, South Carolina, is certified as a notary public and receives stellar performance reviews. Ms. Dawn Smith, who serves as Mrs. Smith's current Power of Attorney, has an assistant-level job at a veterinary clinic and lacks the financial acumen to properly manage the assets of Mrs. Smith. As an example, the home owned by Mr. David Smith Sr., deceased husband of Mrs. Marie Smith, was sold below market value by Ms. Dawn Smith, a mistake the petitioner could have prevented. Mr. VanBroklin requests that the court determine the need for the appointment of a conservator is proper and appoint Mr. Nicholas VanBroklin as the conservator for the above person and that letters of conservatorship be issued."

"Assistant-level job, my ass," shouted Dawn, her face turning red. "I save lives. You cash checks. I'm calling Ben."

Benjamin Clayton, the lawyer who'd put her half brothers in their place, answered his mobile phone on the third ring.

"Ben, it's Dawn Smith. I'm sorry to bother you this late but we have an emergency."

"I'm just about to have my supper. Did something happen to Marie?" he asked.

"Kind of. We received a petition for a guardian and conservator for her."

"From your brothers?" he guessed.

"No. From my deranged ex-boyfriend. He's trying to mess with me by coming after her."

Ben chuckled, which unnerved Dawn. Nothing about this was amusing.

"Can he *do* this?" she asked.

"Of course, he can do it and waste a lot of time and money. The question isn't if he can *do* it, but if he can *win*. He's not family and you're already the POA. I don't think you have anything to worry about."

"But we have to reply, don't we, or go to court?"

"Why don't you come down to my office Monday morning? We'll sort this all out."

"Any way we could meet in the evening?"

"I'm afraid not."

Dawn reluctantly agreed and hung up. She wanted this meritless, spiteful affront resolved, and a Monday appointment would mean more missed work. Even though Kelly, Alex and Regan had been understanding so far, Dawn was sure she was testing their patience.

A knock at the door made the two women jump.

"Do you think we're getting more paperwork?" asked Marie, her eyes wide.

A stocky woman dressed in khakis and a polo shirt waited outside. She stood with her feet wide apart, reminding Dawn of a bulldog.

"I'm looking for Dawn Smith," she said.

Dawn momentarily wanted to deny her identity, as if that could halt the lawsuit. "I'm Dawn Smith," she admitted, halfheartedly.

"I hope I'm not disturbing you. I'm Detective Clyde. We spoke on the phone about the incident at the vet clinic." The woman flashed her badge as she spoke.

Dawn breathed a sigh of relief.

"I wanted to let you know that I met with Mr. VanBroklin. He had a different version of events, as you'd probably expect. When I asked about the theft of the cat, he stated that he'd found it without a collar and was simply bringing it to the clinic to have it scanned."

"That's bullshit," said Dawn. "Snowball has a pink collar. He probably took it off. And why was he even close to my house? Did you ask him that?"

"I did. He said he was running an errand for your mom—picking up a pack of light bulbs?"

"He broke our front porch light last week. That's a bullshit excuse to be at my house a week later."

"I pulled the police report from that day. It documents that your mother gave him five dollars and asked him to buy light bulbs for her." The detective shrugged. "His story checks out."

"Son of a—"

The detective lifted her hands as if to say, *Hold on a minute.*

"I realized pretty quickly that he was ready with answers for everything I asked. Of course, he didn't admit to threatening you or having any intention of harming you."

"Did you ask him about the gun?"

"I did. He regularly carries a handgun in a holster, meeting all legal requirements, as he pointed out to me. He denied ever showing you the gun at the clinic, but said you knew that he carried."

Dawn shook her head. She knew the truth, no matter how this was playing out. "Of course he'd say that. So there's nothing you can do?"

"I checked on the status of the restraining order you filed. It hasn't been served yet, but I imagine it will be soon. My advice is to make your case to the judge, which would prohibit Mr. VanBroklin from showing up at your place of work again."

As the police officer left, Dawn balled her fists in frustration. How had Nick been able to sue her and Marie for guardianship and conservatorship faster than she'd been able to serve him with a restraining order?

Chapter 24

On Monday morning, Dawn and her mother drove to Ben Clayton's office, a white brick ranch home built in the 1950s and converted into commercial space. He shared the quarters with two other lawyers, each of whom had their own practice. They also shared a kitchen, conference room and a seasoned administrator, Donna Percival.

The wood floors creaked as the women stepped into the front reception area. Donna, whose silver hair was styled in a short bob, sat behind an oversized antique desk. She greeted them warmly, offering coffee as she escorted them to the front conference room. An oval cherry table filled the space. Pictures of golf courses adorned the walls, including the famous sixteenth hole at Augusta National.

Ben arrived shortly thereafter, wearing a pressed light blue polo shirt and khakis. He carried a leather-bound notepad and a Mont Blanc pen, which he placed on the table, precisely aligning the edge of the binder with the seam of the wood. Dawn wasn't sure how old Ben was, probably in his early fifties. He was balding with a ring of light brown hair around his ears. Every time she saw him, she couldn't help but imagine what he'd look like with a full head of hair.

"Good morning, ladies," he said. "Did Donna offer you coffee?"

Dawn nodded and handed Ben the paperwork. He studied the documents for several minutes while the women sat in silence, watching him flip through the pages.

"So, who is this Nicholas VanBroklin fellow?" he asked.

"He's a guy I dated briefly until I figured out he was a liar. When I broke it off, he totally changed—texting me nonstop, showing up at my home and work, and now he's pulled this stunt."

Dawn went on to share the details of Nick's offenses, which Ben noted on his legal pad. She had to walk a fine line describing Nick's derangement while not scaring Marie. In hindsight, she wished she'd come alone.

"I took out a restraining order last week but haven't heard anything. I don't understand how everything I need is taking forever, yet he slapped us with a lawsuit in no time at all."

"Do you know if he's been served?" asked Ben.

"Not as of last Friday."

"Okay. I'll look into that."

"I can't believe he's claiming to be a caregiver to my mom. The court will see through that, right? They'll realize this is just an attempt at revenge against me?"

"I don't see how the judge could see anything else."

"Do you know his lawyer, Charles Hood?" asked Dawn.

"He's a young guy without much experience. He was with a local firm but left. I remember some scuttlebutt about him being kicked out, some kind of integrity breach. You know how rumors fly in this town. They can be nasty, but there's usually some truth behind them."

"Can you call him and explain the situation? Maybe he'll drop the case?"

"I can try, but I suspect he'll take any case that pays. We may just have to play this out in court, but I wouldn't worry. There's no way someone who isn't family—and who has a restraining order against him—is going to prevail. Their first hurdle is going to be proving that Marie needs a guardian."

"How do they do that?" asked Dawn.

"No one over eighteen can have a guardian appointed against their will unless they've been deemed incompetent. The court will issue an order for two examiners to evaluate Marie's condition. One will likely be her doctor, and the other is an independent third party, called a visitor, who will meet with Marie at her home."

Marie, who'd been quietly listening throughout the meeting, spoke for the first time. "I don't want anyone coming to my home and judging me. I won't have it."

Dawn took her mom's hand but kept her focus on Ben. "What kinds of questions will the visitor ask?"

"They'll try to assess if Marie is able to make responsible decisions for herself. They may ask basic questions to determine if she's oriented to time and place like the date and who's the president, and they may ask some questions about her healthcare choices—"

"I handle her healthcare, like arranging doctor's visits and getting her medications. Can't they just talk to me?"

Marie chimed in, "Why can't we make Dawn my guardian?"

Ben squinted and mulled over the suggestion. "We could ask for that, but you'd be admitting you need your daughter's help in making decisions."

"She helps me already."

"What about your finances?" he asked. "If I recall, Dawn has signature authority on your accounts."

"That's correct," said Marie.

"Okay, then. I'll file a response requesting Dawn be named your guardian and conservator. As your only child and existing POA, it's the most logical choice."

"What's the difference?" asked Dawn.

"As your mom's financial and healthcare power of attorney, you're authorized to make decisions for her if she were unable. For example, if she were unconscious, you could speak on her behalf. The guardian and conservator go a step further. You can make decisions for her at any time, similar to how she made choices for you when you were a minor."

"So, if you file this response, do we still have to go to court?" asked Dawn.

"That will be up to the judge, but probably so. It could be a few months based on his docket."

"A few months?" questioned Dawn. "We can't possibly have this hanging over us for months."

"I could file an emergency order. That should speed up the hearing, but we'd need a basis for the filing."

"What about her hospitalization?" suggested Dawn. She hadn't told Ben about finding the pill bottle on her Jeep. She planned to, but not in front of her mom.

"Isn't there anything else you can do?" asked Marie.

"I could try a motion to dismiss," said Ben. "But Nick has levied some serious claims against Dawn. I imagine the judge will want to hear the case. Besides, we'll do better to make our arguments in person, in the courtroom."

"Thank you, Ben," said Marie. "I knew you'd be able to help us."

"Just one more thing," he added, speaking to Marie. "The court will appoint a guardian ad litem for you. This is a third-party attorney who will represent you until the case is concluded."

"Why can't it be you?" asked Marie.

"It would be seen as a conflict of interest for me to represent both of you, even though you're in agreement. The GAL is there solely to protect you, Marie."

"How much do you think this is going to cost?" asked Dawn. She hadn't counted on having to pay for two lawyers.

"I don't think we'll need more than a day in court, if that."

"What about prep time?"

"That should be minimal. By law, there's a priority order for appointments that's followed unless there's a valid reason to select someone else. You're already Marie's POA and you're her only blood relative. Once we hear back from the court, I'll have Donna set up a brief call so we can go over the next steps."

Ben looked at his watch and stood. He shook their hands and concluded the meeting. "Don't worry," he said. "I can promise you that this VanBroklin fellow will never become Marie's guardian or conservator."

Chapter 25

On the way to work, Dawn stopped at a local sandwich shop and ordered six lunches to go. She wanted to thank her colleagues and Dr. Patel for covering for her again. The vet techs gathered around the break room table, enjoying a rare break in the day.

"You didn't have to buy us lunch, but thanks," said Regan. She took a giant bite of the sandwich. Where Dawn would just skip lunch if there wasn't time, Regan tended to wolf down her food.

Alex leaned over to Regan. "You gonna eat that cookie?"

Regan elbowed him in the side. "You pig. Go ahead."

Alex gleefully snatched the chocolate chip cookie from Regan's lunchbox and crammed it into his mouth before she could change her mind.

"You don't want it?" asked Dawn. Regan would gladly give up her chocolate to animals, but never to humans.

"I'm trying to lose a few pounds."

"Regan has a new boyfriend," teased Kelly.

"He's not my boyfriend. We've only been out once."

Alex stood and threw away his sandwich wrapper, apparently having no interest in their girl talk or Regan's new suitor.

"Where'd you meet him?" asked Dawn.

"At happy hour last Friday."

Dawn hid her disappointment. Last Friday, she'd missed out on the after-work fun. Instead, she was plowing through legal papers. "Well, you don't need to give up your cookie. You look great the way you are."

"No, you *need* to give up your cookie—and your candy bar," chided Alex.

"Easy for you to say, Dawn," countered Regan. "Every guy in that bar would've asked you out."

There was an awkward silence. Regan's words were true, although Dawn never intended to be in competition with other women. For her, happy hour was simply a way to relax with friends.

"Trust me, I'm done with guys for a while," assured Dawn.

"You've switched teams?" teased Alex.

Dawn ignored him. "So what's this guy like?"

"He's super cool and so good-looking," gushed Regan.

Dawn turned to Kelly. "Did you meet him?"

"No. I'd already left."

"And he's such a good listener," continued Regan. "He wanted to know all about me and my job and friends. Most guys are so into themselves, you know?"

"You mean like Alex?" jabbed Kelly.

The girls laughed.

"Okay, I know when it's my cue to leave." Alex walked to the sink to wash his hands.

"He's even taller than you, Alex," added Regan, boasting about the new man in her life.

Dawn and Kelly exchanged worried glances.

"What's he look like?" asked Dawn.

"Wavy brown hair and the most piercing brown eyes." Regan gazed at the ceiling as she described him.

Dawn and Kelly traded another concerned look. Dawn pulled out her phone and scrolled to the camping selfie. She enlarged the photo so only Nick was in the frame. Turning her screen toward Regan, she asked, "Is this him?"

Regan's forehead creased. Confusion filled her face. "How do *you* have a picture of *my* Joey?"

Dawn shook her head in disbelief.

Kelly, who'd only seen Nick from a distance at his apartment, knew what was going on. "That bastard," she shouted.

"What is it?" pleaded Regan.

"That guy's name is not Joey," explained Kelly. "He's Nick, a certified maniac. He's the one Dawn broke up with."

"You dated him?" Regan's eyes widened. She muttered to herself, "I knew it. Guys like that don't choose me."

Kelly stepped into the roles of both protector and detective. "What kinds of questions did he ask you?"

"I don't know. Everything. He wanted to know about me, work, y'all."

"Did he ask about Dawn?" probed Kelly.

"Not specifically. He asked about the people I work with. It wasn't like I had any top-secret information."

Kelly turned to Dawn. "What if Regan stops seeing him? Is he going to do the same thing to her?"

You have no idea, thought Dawn. She hadn't told them about the lawsuit yet.

"Do what? What's he going to do to me?" Regan's shock had turned to fear. Alex returned to the table and put his arm around her.

"Remember the guy who showed up with the stolen cat, when Dr. Patel called 911? That's him," said Kelly. "Regan, think. Did he get any vital information from you, like the back door code? Did he ever have access to your phone?"

"I don't think so. We're supposed to go out later this week. What should I do?"

"Let me see his photo," demanded Alex. "I'll take care of him if he shows up here again."

Dr. Patel had given Suzanne standing orders to call 911 at the first sight of Nick, but no one had thought to share Nick's picture with the rest of the staff.

For Dawn, it had never occurred to her that Nick would target her friends. She called Ben's office. He was in a meeting, but Dawn implored Donna to interrupt. A few minutes later, he returned the call, and Dawn explained what had transpired with Regan.

"It's a free country," said Ben. "Nick can date your friend."

"But what about the restraining order? He can't come to the clinic, right?"

"About that. Donna called the magistrate's office. Nick was never served. They said your paperwork didn't have a complete address."

Dawn slumped forward. Why was everything one step forward and two steps back? "I didn't have his apartment number."

"The sheriff must have the full address. Let me see if Donna can find it."

"Were they ever going to tell me he wasn't served?"

"Unfortunately, the sheriff isn't obligated to inform you that the form was incomplete."

"So Nick can just show up here or at my home whenever he wants?"

"The restraining order won't go into effect until after you've had the hearing. In the meantime, I filed our response to the guardianship and conservatorship with the probate court. Donna will email you a copy and set up a call for us to prepare."

"Shouldn't we meet in person?" asked Dawn.

"This is a fairly routine matter. Let me know whether or not you want Marie there. Her court-appointed attorney can speak on her behalf and make a recommendation to the judge, so she doesn't have to be present. If you're worried the proceeding could be upsetting, it might be best for her if she stays home. Also, think about any witnesses you want to testify for you. It's not mandatory, but we'd want people who can speak to your character."

"How about my boss? I run the clinic when the Patels are away."

"Fine. I need to return to my meeting. Donna will be in touch." The line went silent.

Dawn stared at her phone. She trusted Ben, and his support had been invaluable in the lawsuit with her half brothers. So why did she feel so uneasy?

Later that week, Regan was supposed to meet Nick. She had planned to lie and say she was sick, but the anxiety of facing him had actually made her break out in hives. Luckily, Nick never contacted Regan again. Dawn guessed he'd pumped her for as much information as he could and didn't care that leading her on romantically was hurtful.

Out of precaution, Dr. Patel changed the keypad entrance code. Dawn locked her doors, looked over her shoulder and had Alex accompany her in the parking lot. Ordinary things like an autumn leaf that had fallen on her windshield sent her into a panic. From a distance, it looked like Nick had left another pill bottle on her Jeep.

As far as the legal progress, the guardian ad litem, Jerry Raven, was appointed by the judge. Jerry paid a brief visit to Marie's home, which she barely tolerated. When the court-appointed visitor, Daniel Odom, showed up asking prying questions, Marie stopped the interview and complained to Ben. The whole process seemed outrageous to Dawn. Wasn't the point of conceding that Marie needed a guardian and conservator to avoid having outsiders involved?

The following week, Ben called to inform Dawn that a date had been set for the emergency guardianship hearing. "We'll need to be at the courthouse next Thursday morning at 9:00 a.m. Do you want your mom there?"

"Will she have to testify?"

"No. Jerry Raven will speak on her behalf. I'm confident he'll recommend you to be named guardian and conservator."

"Well, then maybe she should stay home. Mr. Odom asked her who the president was, and she'd forgotten. She doesn't care about politics and doesn't watch the news or read the paper. Now she's afraid she'll be put on the stand and made to look like a fool. I don't want her going through that kind of stress."

"I would agree. Can you make sure your boss can be at the courthouse next week to be a character witness? They've allowed two days, Thursday and Friday, but I don't think we'll need that much time, so have him there Thursday."

"Okay, what else?"

"Donna hasn't been able to find Nick's home address to submit the restraining order application. He's not registered at the apartment complex you gave us."

"What about having him served at work?"

"I'll see what I can do, but I wanted you to know that we can't mention the restraining order during next week's probate hearing. It's not relevant until the magistrate judge has heard testimony and rendered his opinion."

"This is so frustrating. Can't we show the probate judge Nick's text messages and play his voicemails? We have to prove what a vile, manipulative person he is."

"Let's just focus on the fact that you're the obvious choice to oversee your mother's affairs. The only choice. Let's not start slinging mud concerning your relationship with Nick."

Dawn's stomach tightened. She wasn't *slinging mud*. She wasn't the aggressor—Nick was. Ben's comment made it seem like she shared some of the blame for this legal mess.

"Well, shouldn't we at least hold off on the guardianship hearing until after the restraining order is in place?" asked Dawn.

"I wouldn't advise that. The court won't look favorably on us if we delay now, given we requested an emergency hearing. Let's stay the course. I'll have Donna set up a call so we can prepare, and I'll have her continue to search for Nick's home address so you can refile the restraining order."

Chapter 26

Dawn chose a navy suit and an ivory silk top for court. During her prep call with Ben, he'd cautioned her not to wear anything too flashy. Out of habit, she walked to her dresser to retrieve her locket. A wave of anger and helplessness flooded her mind when she remembered it was gone.

"Not today," she said out loud. "You don't get to win today, Nick VanBroklin. You can take every last one of my possessions, but you can't take my mom."

When Dawn arrived at the courthouse, Ben was sitting in one of the waiting rooms reviewing his notes. He was dressed in a gray suit, a white Oxford shirt and a gray and pink tie. The color of the tie matched the hue of his cheeks and bald head.

"Good morning," she said. In reality, there was nothing about that morning that felt good.

"Good morning. Are you ready?"

She shrugged. "As ready as I'll ever be."

"I saw Charles Hood. He was in the administrative office making copies. Nothing like waiting until the last minute to prepare for court."

Learning that Nick's lawyer was so ill-prepared gave Dawn some satisfaction and a boost of confidence.

"I asked Charles if they could wait in the other room," he added.

Dawn nodded in appreciation. Their small waiting room had only five chairs, which would've been uncomfortably close.

A few minutes after 9:00 a.m., a bailiff poked his head in the room and asked Ben to join him in the courtroom, leaving Dawn by herself. As the minutes passed, she wondered what they were talking about and why she hadn't been included. This scenario was not part of Ben's explanation of how things would proceed.

Twenty minutes later, the bailiff asked Dawn to join Ben, who was seated at a table on the right, in front of the judge's bench. A man in his early thirties, presumably Charles Hood, was at the table on the left. Papers were strewn in front of him in a chaotic fashion, unlike Ben's neat folders. The stenographer, a middle-aged woman, sat dutifully at the front of the room.

Dawn heard a door open behind them. Without looking, she could feel Nick's stare boring a hole through the back of her head. She made a conscious effort to avoid eye contact but could see him peripherally as he approached the other table. The two men whispered and occasionally laughed, which made Dawn fume. Nothing about this court case was funny.

The back door opened again. This time Dr. Patel entered. He mouthed to Dawn, "Sorry I'm late."

She mouthed back, "It's okay. We haven't started yet."

Jerry Raven, Marie's court-appointed guardian ad litem, followed Dr. Patel. The next two people to enter the courtroom were a complete surprise—the Hispanic woman from Nick's apartment complex and her son.

Dawn leaned over to Ben and whispered, "That woman lives in the same building as Nick. I met her once. She said she didn't know him. Why do you think she's here?"

"Could be a witness for him?" said Ben.

"But she doesn't know him."

The woman and her son took seats in the spectator area at the back. Jerry approached Ben, shook his hand and gave a warm nod to Dawn. After a few minutes, the side door opened, and the bailiff entered.

"All rise," he said. "The Honorable Judge Cain presiding."

Everyone in the room stood as a stout elderly man dressed in a black robe ambled to his chair. "You may be seated," he said.

Each party sat at their designated table. Jerry moved to a small desk to their right and the witnesses settled in on the benches behind them. The judge ceremoniously unfolded his reading glasses, perched them on his nose and scanned some paperwork. The room was completely still.

Finally, the judge spoke. "This morning we'll hear the case of Nicholas VanBroklin, petitioner, versus Dawn Smith and Marie Smith, respondents. Mr. Charles Hood, you're here on behalf of the petitioner, is that correct?"

"Yes, sir," said Charles.

"And Mr. Benjamin Clayton, you represent the respondent, Ms. Dawn Smith?"

"Yes, Your Honor," chimed Ben.

"Mr. Jerry Raven is serving as the guardian ad litem for the other respondent, Mrs. Marie Smith?"

"Yes, Your Honor," confirmed Jerry.

"I see two petitions were filed and responses were also filed. A visitor's report was submitted by Daniel Odom and we have a physician's report from Dr. Ron Landis. Are there any other filings that need to be made before we begin?"

Both Ben and Charles indicated that no other filings were needed. Technically, a second doctor's opinion should've been filed—an omission by Charles and oversight by Ben—but neither side seemed concerned. No one was contesting the need for a guardian or conservator for Marie. The dispute was about who was the best choice to serve in that capacity.

"The folks in the back, are they witnesses?" asked the judge. "Do they need to be sequestered?"

Ben spoke first. "Yes, Dr. Neil Patel is a witness for the respondent, but there's no need for him to be sequestered."

"I would agree," said Charles. "There's no need to sequester our witnesses."

"Okay, if there's nothing further, Mr. Hood, call your first witness."

"I would like to call Mr. Nicholas VanBroklin."

Nick wore a tailored black suit with designer cufflinks. His patent black shoes were so shiny they reflected the light from the ceiling. As he approached the witness stand, the bailiff held up a Bible.

Judge Cain rattled off the swearing-in as if he'd repeated it a million times. "Put your left hand on the Bible, face me and raise your right hand. Do you solemnly swear the testimony you are about to give to be the truth, the whole truth, and nothing but the truth, so help you God?"

Dawn wanted to yell, "Objection. He's incapable of telling the truth." Instead, she sat motionless, staring at her lap.

Nick confirmed his oath and took a seat in the witness stand next to the judge.

"Please state your name for the record," said Charles.

"Nicholas VanBroklin."

"And where do you live?"

"Here in Laurel."

"What's your occupation?"

"I work in banking. I'm employed by the Wells Fargo bank."

"For how long?"

"Over five years."

"I understand that you are also a notary public?"

"That is correct."

Dawn rolled her eyes. Anyone who had thirty-five dollars and was literate enough to fill out an application could be a notary public. He spoke as if that title was some kind of prestigious appointment.

"And what is your relationship to Mrs. Marie Smith?"

"We're not related by blood, but she's like a mother to me."

Dawn raised her head for the first time and glared at Nick. He was already looking right at her, as if expecting a reaction. His smile broadened as they locked eyes. To an outside observer, Dawn appeared to be the hostile one sporting a scowl, while Nick presented a calm, agreeable demeanor.

"Can you provide some background as to why you felt the need to file this petition—to be Marie Smith's guardian and conservator?"

"I sure can. As I spent more time around Dawn and her mother, I realized Marie needed more care than Dawn was providing. And sadly, I noticed that Marie's health and safety were at risk. I thought, as Dawn's boyfriend, I could voice my concerns, but she refused to listen, even became angry when I brought it up. I did my best to supplement Marie's care while we were dating, but then Dawn ended our relationship. She forbade me from coming around her or Marie. I can accept that things ended between us romantically, but I cannot accept leaving Marie helpless and potentially in danger."

Dawn clenched her fists. Never in her life had she wanted to physically cause someone harm, but she could've taken a baseball bat to Nick's face without remorse.

"Do you have examples of your concern for Marie?" asked Charles.

"Sadly, I do. There've been quite a few incidents. One time, when we were having dinner at Marie's place, she lost her balance and fell. I helped Marie up. Instead of taking her mom to the emergency room to ensure there were no broken bones, Dawn just let her take an aspirin and go to bed. I tried to convince Dawn that Marie needed to see a doctor, but she refused."

Dawn leaned over to Ben and spoke in a forceful whisper, "That's a lie."

Ben shook his head, tore a piece of paper from his legal pad and slid it in front of Dawn. She took his pen and wrote, "LIE."

"I also pointed out to Dawn that she shouldn't be giving her mom alcohol. Wine doesn't mix with Marie's medications, but instead of listening to me, she opened a second bottle at dinner." Nick shook his head, feigning piety that would rival a priest.

The judge can't be buying this bullshit, thought Dawn. *Surely, he sees enough fraudsters in his courtroom to see through this charade.*

"Have you witnessed other incidents?" asked Charles.

"Yes. Not long after the fall, we were having breakfast at Marie's, and she passed out. I called 911 and Marie was taken to the hospital. But here's the part that scares me. Dawn and I had been camping the night before at Oconee State Park. Dawn's cell phone didn't have reception, which worried me. What if Marie needed to reach us? I suggested we cut our trip short, so we went back early the next morning. Can you imagine if I hadn't changed our plans? Marie could've been passed out for hours without anyone noticing. She might have died without my help."

Dawn took the pen and underlined "LIE" three times. She slid the paper to Ben. He glanced at it but didn't react.

"Your Honor," said Charles. "I'd like to submit into evidence the recent hospital record for Mrs. Marie Smith."

Charles handed the paperwork to the bailiff, gave a copy to Ben and returned to question Nick. "Any other concerns you'd like to share with the court?"

Nick bowed his head and sighed heavily. "I didn't want to believe that Dawn was deliberately ignoring her mother's care, but something happened that put doubt in my mind."

"And what was that?"

"After we broke up, Dawn ordered me to stay away from Marie. I have the text message if you want to see it. Being concerned, I had to do something, so I reached out to Dawn's brothers. I hoped they'd step in and help care for Marie, or at least convince Dawn that she was being reckless. But when I spoke to David Jr., Dawn's oldest brother, I became even more concerned."

"What'd he say?"

"Objection, Your Honor," said Ben. "Hearsay."

"Sustained," said the judge.

"Your Honor," Charles countered, "I would like to submit into evidence an affidavit from David Smith Jr. He couldn't be here in person but wanted to provide a statement."

Charles returned to his table and retrieved the affidavit. He handed one copy to the bailiff, who passed it to the judge, and the other copy to Ben. Dawn read the statement given by her half brother.

"*I am personally afraid for Marie because she is solely reliant on Dawn for her healthcare and financial support. Through her actions, my sister has demonstrated she is clearly more interested in Marie's money than her well-being. Furthermore, I believe Dawn would forgo medical care for Marie in order to save money, which will one day become her inheritance.*"

Dawn's entire body vibrated with anger. If David Jr. had been in that courtroom, she would've strangled him with her bare hands. His affidavit was coming from a place of spite, but Judge Cain wouldn't know the siblings' history.

Dawn scribbled on the notepaper. *Do something!*

Ben placed his palm on her shoulder, less to show empathy and more to prevent an outburst. He tucked the affidavit in his folder as if removing it from her sight would somehow make the damage it had caused go away.

Charles continued his questioning. "Mr. VanBroklin, in your petition, you noted that the respondent, Dawn Smith, sold her mother's house below market value. Can you tell the court more about that concern?"

"Yes, being in banking, I stay abreast of the residential markets. I was surprised to learn that as Marie's financial power of attorney, Dawn sold their family farm well below comparable sales of similar properties."

"Your Honor, I'd like to submit into evidence properties sold in the same neighborhood as Marie Smith's former home." Charles handed another set of copies to the bailiff and to Ben.

"After her father passed," said Nick. "Dawn was so eager to get the money from selling the house that she didn't take the time to properly value it."

"Objection," said Ben. "Speculation."

Dawn leaned over to Ben and whispered, "We had to buy the unit next to me before it sold to someone else. It was worth it to move Mom closer."

Ben nodded but kept his eyes fixed on Charles and Nick, as if he was watching the last seconds of a tied football game.

"Sustained," said Judge Cain. He looked at Nick. "You'll keep your points to specific facts."

"Yes sir, Your Honor."

Dawn wanted to gag. His show of respect was just that—a show. She knew Nick's real character, although he was surely playing the part of a saint.

"Any other financial concerns?" asked Charles.

"Yes, I was shocked at Dawn's behavior at a charity auction we attended. Dawn started bidding on a very expensive Cartier bracelet. When I asked her how she was going to pay for it, she told me she could pawn her mother's diamond earrings. Marie had loaned Dawn those earrings for the night. They weren't hers to sell. She was outbid on the bracelet, thank goodness, but it showed me an unscrupulous, greedy side of her I hadn't seen before."

Once again, Charles retrieved documents from his table, handing a set to the bailiff and to Ben.

"Your Honor, I'd like to submit into evidence a bidding card from the governor's charity auction held last month. You'll see highlighted two bids for a Cartier bracelet by bidder number one hundred and eighty-two. I'd also like to submit a list of the pre-assigned bidding numbers provided by the charity. Number one hundred and eighty-two is registered to Ms. Dawn Smith."

"That bastard," muttered Dawn. She whispered to Ben, "I never made a single bid at that auction. Nick must've used my number when he was bidding."

The judge stared down at Dawn, then at Ben. He didn't have to say a word, but his message was clear: *quiet in my courtroom*. He turned his attention back to Charles as if giving him permission to continue.

"Is there anything else you'd like to share with the court?" asked Charles.

Nick clasped his hands together and looked directly at the judge to make his final point. "Only that I didn't want to do this, to take legal action, but I saw no other choice. Dawn refuses to speak to me or hear my concerns. I couldn't live with myself if something bad happened to Marie. I had to intervene. I'm fiercely protective of my own mother. Dawn knows that. And if anyone were to upset her or cause her harm, that person would have to deal with me."

Dawn glared at Nick for the second time. Again, he anticipated her reaction and was already staring at her with a chilling grin. No one else understood the meaning behind his last statement, but Dawn knew. Not only was he inflicting this legal battle on her because she'd rejected him, but because she'd dared to visit his mother.

Next, it was Ben's turn to cross-examine Nick.

"Good morning, Mr. VanBroklin," said Ben as he stood and approached the witness stand. "How long did you and Ms. Dawn Smith date?"

"Over most of the summer."

"And what do you mean by most of the summer? A few weeks, a month?"

"It was a while."

"And you think because you've known Dawn and Marie for *a while* that you're qualified to serve as Marie's guardian and conservator?"

Ben's tone was mocking, as if the mere idea was absurd. Nick wasn't rattled, however. He spoke calmly and with considerable deference.

"Frankly, I hoped Dawn's brothers would've stepped up, but they expressed no desire to get involved. And you know, maybe it's better that way—to have someone objective taking care of Marie. Why do you think doctors don't treat their own family members? They're too close to the patient. I don't think Dawn sees how neglectful and irresponsible she's been. At least I'd like to believe it's unintentional."

Dawn's blood was boiling. No one on the planet would describe her as neglectful or irresponsible. Nick was taking her best attributes and saying the opposite.

"Mr. VanBroklin," continued Ben. "What experience do you have being a guardian or conservator?"

"I take care of Matthias when his mom is at work." Nick pointed to the Hispanic boy. "His mother trusts me with her young son, and we've never had a problem. And I take care of my family's finances, including those of my aging mother and my sister who is serving our country in the military overseas." Nick put his hand over his heart as if pledging the flag.

What a complete charade, thought Dawn. She studied the judge's stoic face, unable to discern if he was buying Nick's act.

"Did Marie Smith ever ask you to be her power of attorney, guardian or conservator?" asked Ben.

"After Dawn and I broke up, I still visited Marie. Just because I'd stopped dating her daughter didn't mean I didn't still care about her. And I made a promise to Marie—to always take care of her, no matter what. I'm acting on that promise now."

"I'll ask again. Did Marie Smith ever ask you to be her power of attorney, guardian or conservator?"

"She doesn't understand those terms, but she knows who cares about her."

Ben looked at his notes and appeared to regroup. In Dawn's opinion, he was letting Nick be far too evasive.

"Mr. VanBroklin, would you expect to be paid for serving as guardian or conservator?" Ben crossed his arms and smiled, as if confident that he was about to expose Nick's true motivation.

"Those roles are customarily paid, but I would take on the responsibility at no charge. I'd do that for Marie."

"So I'm clear, you're offering to be the guardian and conservator for a woman you've known only a few months, and you don't want to be paid for your time?"

Why is Ben harping on the money? wondered Dawn. *This is about revenge and control.*

Nick leaned forward. "I love Marie like a mother. And after witnessing the incidents that occurred over the summer, I've changed my view on Dawn's ability to take care of her mom. Marie has lost her husband, her stepsons aren't willing to help, and Dawn is incapable. What else would you have me do?"

"Have you read the visitor's report?" asked Ben.

"No, I have not."

"Then let me provide a copy." Ben searched through his file folder and retrieved a printout of the visitor's report from Daniel Odom, which had been sent to him and Charles Hood. "Do you see the paragraph highlighted in yellow? Could you please read it out loud?"

Nick cleared his throat and read. *"Based on the information I have been able to obtain about Mrs. Marie Smith, including my visit with her and my conversation with her daughter, I believe Mrs. Smith is in need of a guardian and conservator. I do not believe she can care for herself without assistance, and she is not able to manage her financial affairs. Therefore, I would recommend the court appoint Ms. Dawn Smith as her mother's guardian and conservator."*

"A court-appointed social worker, someone with years of experience in assessing family dynamics, has recommended that Dawn Smith should be appointed guardian and conservator. Do you think you're more qualified than Mr. Odom to offer an opinion?"

"With all due respect, he visited one time. How can he make a judgment based on a single visit? He obviously didn't spend enough time with Marie to see what's really going on."

Dawn's rage was now divided between Nick and Ben. Her lawyer was doing a pathetic job of pointing out the real facts. She and Nick had been on five dates. Nick had eaten two meals at Marie's house. He'd seen Marie alone one time, after he'd broken their porch light. If Ben had taken the proper time to prepare, he would've been able to counter Nick's points. As it was, Nick was making it sound like he was practically a member of the family.

"I have no further questions, Your Honor," said Ben.

What? fumed Dawn. *You're giving up?*

Chapter 27

The judge ordered a short recess. Everyone rose as he exited through a side door. Dawn followed Ben to the waiting room in silence. In her heels, she was several inches taller than him, giving her a pronounced view of his bald head. Once the door shut and no one was within earshot, she erupted.

"How could you let him get away with that testimony? He's making it sound like I'm a danger to my own mother. *He's* the one who sent my mom to the hospital. He drugged her. And now that I think about it, I wouldn't be surprised if he pushed her, too. I was next door when she fell."

"Drugged her? What are you talking about?" asked Ben.

"The morning she passed out, Mom's blood pressure pills went missing. I thought she'd misplaced them until the empty bottle appeared on my Jeep at work. *He* did that."

"Why didn't you tell me this before?"

"We barely prepared," countered Dawn. "Besides, I have no proof, even though I'd bet my life it was him."

Dawn paced. She had to do something to expel the anger and frustration that was trapped inside of her. "And what about my shit brother? David Jr.'s statement makes me look terrible."

"Don't worry," assured Ben. "You haven't had your chance on the stand. We'll straighten this all out when you testify."

"He's lying in there. It wasn't his idea to come home early from the camping trip. It was mine. And he doesn't have some special bond with my mother. She barely knows him. Maybe we should bring her here. Have her testify that he's practically a stranger."

Ben shook his head. "We're past that point. With the doctor's statement and that of Daniel Odom, your mom has been deemed incompetent."

"So?"

"Any testimony she'd give now won't hold the same weight. Besides, we don't have time to bring her here and we don't know what she'd say. It could backfire." Ben looked at his watch. "We'd better head back in."

Dawn exhaled through gritted teeth and followed Ben into the courtroom. As she passed Dr. Patel, his worried expression confirmed her concern about how poorly the case was going. Before she could take a seat, the bailiff ordered, "All rise," and the judge reentered the courtroom.

"Mr. Hood, are you ready to call your first witness?"

"Yes, Your Honor. We call Ms. Maribel Santos."

The woman, barely five feet tall, was dressed in dark jeans rolled at the bottom and a short-sleeve top. She took her oath and sat down. Not only did she look like a child on the witness stand, but she fidgeted like one.

"Please state your name for the record," said Charles as he approached.

"Maribel Santos."

"And how long have you known the petitioner, Nick VanBroklin?"

"For many years, since Matthias was little." After her answer, she glanced at Nick as if to ask, *Am I doing this right?*

"Matthias is your son, the boy we see over there?" Charles pointed to the boy who appeared to be about eight years old.

She beamed with pride. "Yes, that's my son."

"And what's your relationship with Mr. VanBroklin?"

"We aren't dating or anything like that. He watches Matthias for me on weekends when I have to go to work at the Quick Stop."

Dawn leaned over to Ben and whispered, "How did Nick go camping with me or to the charity auction if he was supposedly babysitting her child?"

Ben didn't respond.

"Have you ever had any problems, accidents or hospitalizations when Mr. VanBroklin was watching Matthias?" asked Charles.

"Never," she said, and glanced at Nick again.

Dawn whispered, "Put the kid on the stand. He won't be able to lie like his mother."

Rather than appreciating the idea, Ben seemed annoyed at Dawn's chatter.

"And how would you describe Mr. VanBroklin?"

"Very responsible. More responsible than Matthias's father."

"So even though he's not family, you trust him to take care of your child?"

"Yes."

"I have no further questions." Charles reclaimed his seat and leaned back in the chair. He stretched his legs, crossing them at the ankles, in a smug pose.

The judge looked at Ben. "Your witness."

"We have no questions, Your Honor."

Dawn glared at her lawyer. A clever cross-examination could reveal Maribel's perjury. For example, how much does she pay Nick to babysit? Who took care of Matthias on the weekend Nick went camping? And why, in the stairway of her apartment, did she say that she didn't know him?

The judge looked at Charles. "Mr. Hood, anything further?"

"No, Your Honor, that's our case."

"Mr. Clayton, do you want to call your first witness?"

Ben stood. "Thank you, Your Honor. Because he needs to return to his veterinary practice, I'd like to call Dr. Neil Patel to the stand."

"Come on up, sir," said the judge.

Unlike the lawyers, who wore suits, Dr. Patel was dressed in blue scrubs and a white lab coat. He was sworn in, took his place on the witness stand and stated his name for the record.

"What is your occupation?" asked Ben.

"I'm a veterinarian. My wife, Smita, and I own the Village Veterinary Clinic in town."

"How long have you owned the clinic?"

"Six years. We purchased the business from the previous owners."

"And how do you know Ms. Dawn Smith?"

"She's one of our employees at the clinic, our lead vet tech."

"How would you describe her as an employee?"

"Very capable. She does a very good job with the animals and is respected by her peers. When my wife and I go out of town, we leave Dawn in charge of the practice."

"Ever had any issues while you were away, when she was running the business?"

"No. Never."

"And to be a vet tech, Dawn has to administer medications, is that correct?"

"Yes, and much more. The life of the animal is often in her hands."

"How would you describe her ability to treat the animals, handle the medications, deal with medical emergencies and such?"

"As I stated before, she is very capable."

Ben promenaded in a small circle past the judge and by Nick's table before heading back to the witness stand. It was as if he was saying, *Let's take time for this testimony to sink in. This is where the real evidence of Dawn's character begins.*

"Do you know Dawn's mother, Mrs. Marie Smith?" he asked.

"Yes. She has visited the clinic before and comes to our holiday party."

"From what you've seen, how would you describe the relationship between mother and daughter?"

"Very close and loving." Dr. Patel looked at Dawn for the first time and smiled.

"And seeing how Dawn takes care of her mother, would you have any concern having her take care of your own mother?"

"She's no longer with us, God rest her soul, but if she were still alive, I'd be honored to have Dawn look after my mother."

"Dr. Patel, I know you're a very busy man. I appreciate you being here to give us some insights about my client."

"It's no trouble."

"Just a few last questions. Do you know the petitioner, Mr. VanBroklin?"

"I met him once, when he was harassing Dawn at the clinic."

"How was he harassing her?"

"She told me—"

"Objection," interrupted Charles. "Hearsay."

"Sustained," said the judge.

Ben changed his approach. "Have you met any of Dawn's boyfriends?"

"Yes. The last boy I met was Stuart. He came to our house with Dawn when my son was born."

"But you've only met Mr. VanBroklin the one time?"

"That's correct."

"I imagine because their relationship didn't last very long."

"Objection," said Charles. "Your Honor, it's not counsel's role to opine on the state of the relationship."

"I'll agree," said Judge Cain. "Mr. Clayton, anything further for this witness?"

"No, Your Honor. Thank you, Dr. Patel. I have no further questions. Now you'll need to answer any questions Mr. Hood may have for you."

Dawn figured Charles would pass, just as Ben had done for Maribel Santos, but he stood and approached the witness stand. "Dr. Patel, to your knowledge, has Dawn Smith ever performed a procedure on an animal without the owner's consent?"

"Excuse me?" said the veterinarian, clearly taken aback.

"I'll repeat the question. Has your employee, Ms. Dawn Smith, ever performed any kind of procedure, major or minor, that required the consent of the pet's owner, but she failed to obtain that consent."

"I suppose, if we have an emergency, we may not have the time. Then we go on past directives or what's best for the animal in the moment."

"What about a more recent case, one that was *not* an emergency? I believe the animal was a Dachshund named Daisy."

Dawn's throat tightened. Dr. Patel knew she'd extracted the tooth without Brody Hill's consent. Her act of mercy, carelessly shared with Nick on their first date, was now backfiring.

"We see a lot of animals. I would have to review that specific case."

Charles turned toward Judge Cain. "If we need to take a short recess so the doctor can call his office to refresh his memory, we are prepared to do so."

Before the judge could rule on the suggestion, Dr. Patel caved. "As I think about it, I believe I remember that one."

"Go on," said Charles.

"That particular animal needed a tooth extraction."

"And did Ms. Smith have permission from the owner to perform the extraction, a procedure that was not a medical emergency?"

Dr. Patel looked helplessly at Dawn. He was under oath and had no choice but to reply. "No, I don't believe she had permission."

"To clarify, you are confirming that Dawn Smith deliberately ignored the wishes of the animal's owner and performed a non-emergent medical procedure when she had no authority to do so?"

"I don't think—"

"Yes or no, sir?"

Dr. Patel hesitated and bowed his head. "Yes."

"And isn't that reckless behavior grounds for her to lose her license?"

The vet's mouth opened but he was unable to speak.

"That's all I have for this witness," said Charles. He didn't need an answer. He'd made his point. Charles sauntered back to his seat with his chest puffed out like a rooster.

"Thank you, sir," said Judge Cain. "You can step down. You are free to go if you like."

Dr. Patel hurried out of the courtroom, averting eye contact with Dawn. What everyone had thought would be a simple and supportive testimony had turned into a trainwreck.

Chapter 28

"Mr. Clayton," said the judge. "Please call your next witness."

"Yes, Your Honor, I'd like to call Ms. Dawn Smith."

"Ms. Smith, come on up."

Dawn's heart started pounding like she'd finished her Saturday run at a full sprint. She was so out of breath that she feared she wouldn't be able to speak. Slowly, she stood and made her way to the stand, trying to buy time to regain her composure. The bailiff swore her in, and she faced Ben.

"Ms. Smith, good morning."

"Good morning." Her voice quivered.

"Pull close to that microphone for me," interjected Judge Cain.

"You are the daughter of Mrs. Marie Smith, is that correct?"

"Yes, I'm her only child." Dawn leaned into the microphone and spoke louder. Her voice settled slightly.

"Can you tell me about your education?"

"I have a bachelor's degree in biology from Clemson and a two-year veterinary certificate."

"And where have you worked since college?"

"At the Village Veterinary Clinic here in Laurel."

"Working for Dr. Patel, who we just heard from, correct?"

"Yes."

"How many people work at the clinic?"

"There are seven of us full-time and some part-time staff."

"Dr. Patel, a veterinarian and business owner, chooses to leave you in charge when he and his wife are not available. Is that correct?"

"Yes, that's correct."

Dawn waited for Ben to ask about Daisy. She could explain that extracting the tooth was an act of mercy.

"Can you tell us about your family, your parents and your brothers?"

Dawn blinked a few times. Ben was switching topics without letting her justify what she'd done for Daisy. "My mom is Marie. My dad, David Sr., died of cancer last year. I have two half brothers, my dad's sons from his first marriage."

"And where do they live?"

"New York and Connecticut."

"Would you say you are close to them?"

"No. They're several years older and we've had some bad blood after my dad's passing."

"What happened?"

"In his will, my dad left everything to Mom and me. I don't think he meant to slight them, but figured they were already established and didn't need the money. They contested the will but lost the case. That affidavit from my half brother was written out of spite."

"Objection, speculation," said Charles.

"Allow me to redirect," said Ben before the judge could rule. "How many times have your brothers witnessed you caring for your mom in the last five years?"

"Once, at the funeral."

"And at that time, did either express any concerns about your mom's care? Anything at all?"

"Nothing."

Ben paused, apparently to let that point resonate with the judge. "After your dad passed, you sold the family home?"

"Yes. Mom and I decided it would be better if she lived closer to me. I was already at my duplex, so we bought the one next door when it came up for sale."

"Did you realize you weren't getting full market value for your mom's house?"

"We did. The unit next to mine had just been listed, and it was the perfect solution. I wasn't making an irresponsible financial decision. We made a choice. Mom wasn't going to miss a few thousand dollars, but she'd miss the chance to be next door if we didn't act quickly." Dawn shot daggers with her eyes at Charles.

"And when it comes to your mom's medical care, can you share what you do for her?"

"I take her to her doctors' appointments and get her medications."

"About how often is that?"

"Well, her doctors' appointments are a few times a year, and I pick up her medications from the pharmacy every month."

"Do you administer her medications?" he asked.

"No, she keeps them in her kitchen cabinet. She knows which ones to take and when."

"Any concerns that she might get confused and take too many or the wrong ones?"

"No, and Dr. Landis never suggested I should administer her meds. If I saw her starting to get confused, I would change that."

"A few weeks ago, your mother was hospitalized. Can you tell us what happened?"

Dawn hesitated. If she shared her suspicion about Nick drugging her mom without any proof, she'd look crazy. That's why he'd left the pill bottle on her Jeep. He wanted her to make an outlandish accusation so she'd look unhinged. She wasn't going to fall for that trap.

"After breakfast, Mom fainted. I caught her so she didn't hit the floor. Nick called 911 because I asked him to. An ambulance arrived, and I went with Mom to the hospital, not Nick. They ran some tests, observed her for a while, and then released her that afternoon."

"Do you know what happened to her?"

"They think her blood pressure might've been low."

"Prior to this hospitalization, when was the last time she was hospitalized?"

"I can't even remember."

"Meaning you don't know, or it's been a while?" Ben clarified.

"It's been years. She had a procedure when I was in high school. My dad took her."

Ben walked to the table and flipped through his notes. Dawn glanced at the wall clock at the back of the room. It was already 12:30 p.m.

"Dawn, what else do you do to assist your mother in her daily living?"

"I do the grocery shopping. Her vision isn't great, so she doesn't drive, but she still cooks at home. We both do the cleaning and laundry."

"What about her bills?"

"I pay her bills. I'm co-signee on her bank account."

"Have you ever been late with a payment?"

Dawn shook her head.

"Please give a verbal response," directed the judge.

Dawn leaned toward the microphone. "No, I've never been late with a payment."

"Have you ever taken or borrowed money from your mom's account without her knowledge?"

"Never, and I never told Nick I'd pawn my mother's earrings. I'd never dream of doing something like that and he knows it. That was a lie." Dawn looked at Nick for the first time since she'd taken the stand. If she had to describe his demeanor it was sheer amusement. Heat started to rise from the pit of her stomach—it radiated into her limbs like fire.

"Do you charge your mother for any of this work you do for her?" asked Ben.

Even if I was down to my last penny, I wouldn't stoop that low, thought Dawn. Not wanting to feed Nick's sadistic pleasure, she replied flatly, "Of course not."

"And as far as guardian and conservator for your mother, what are your wishes?"

"I'm already her power of attorney. I'm already performing a lot of the duties of a guardian and conservator. And it's not just *my* wish, it's *her* wish, too."

"Objection. Hearsay," said Charles.

"Ms. Smith, you'll keep your testimony to your viewpoint, no one else's," cautioned the judge.

The admonishment didn't deter Dawn but spurred her to address Judge Cain directly. "I'm her daughter. I take care of her—always have and always will. A guy I dated for less than a month, who, by the way, was very ugly about the breakup, should not have any say-so in our family."

"Thank you," said Ben. "Your Honor, I have no further questions."

"Mr. Clayton, how many more witnesses do you have?"

"Just Jerry Raven, the guardian ad litem representing Marie Smith."

"Okay. It's twenty till one. Let's take a lunch recess until two," said Judge Cain. "Mr. Hood, you may cross-examine after lunch. Ms. Smith, you may step down."

Chapter 29

Dawn and Ben went to a Mexican restaurant near the courthouse. The waitress brought a basket of chips and a bowl of salsa. Dawn mindlessly shoved chips into her mouth as she railed at her lawyer.

"This isn't going as I expected—not at all. They're making me look reckless. I've been called a lot of things in my life, but I've never been accused of being irresponsible. And look at Dr. Patel's testimony. They turned him against me. You should've asked me about Daisy. I could've explained that I took pity on her. I relieved her pain when her cruel owner was going to let her suffer."

Ben leaned forward and spoke in a hushed voice. "Lower your voice, please. We're not far from the courthouse. Look, I know Judge Cain. He doesn't care if you pulled a dog's tooth. He'll see that you've been your mom's advocate all these years and should remain so."

"Why didn't you ask me more about Nick's testimony? I could've corrected his lies. He made it seem like we dated for months. We went on *five* dates."

"Like I said before, this hearing isn't about your relationship with Nick, and we don't want to turn it into a story about your split. This case revolves solely around who is best qualified to care for your mother. We need to stick to that topic."

"So what do you think Charles Hood is going to ask me?"

"Like we discussed, he'll probably ask how you care for your mom. Answer his questions. Don't elaborate. If you don't understand the question, ask for clarification and try to stay calm."

"Stay calm? You try staying calm when someone is attacking your character and telling lies."

"I understand, but look at the big picture. Part of what Judge Cain is assessing is your maturity level. Don't let Charles Hood unnerve you."

After lunch, Dawn and Ben returned to the courthouse, passed through the metal detectors and reentered the courtroom. Charles and Nick weren't back yet. At 2:00 p.m., they still hadn't returned. By 2:10 p.m., the bailiff asked Ben if he knew where they were. Dawn found his question to be absurd. Why should her lawyer keep tabs on their adversaries? At 2:15 p.m., the two men walked casually into the courtroom, making light of their tardiness. The bailiff stepped out, presumably to notify the judge, who entered the room a few moments later. Everyone rose.

"You may be seated," said Judge Cain. "Ms. Smith, if you'll retake the witness stand. We're back on the record."

What? thought Dawn. *No reprimand for them being late? Do you not see who the responsible one is here?*

She retook her place on the stand and Charles approached with a fake, friendly smile. "Good afternoon, Ms. Smith."

"Good afternoon." Her reply was cordial but cold.

"I appreciate you answering my questions. We all just want to do what's best for Marie. Is it true that Marie fell at her home a few weeks ago?"

"Yes." Dawn glared at Nick, hoping her expression would convey her thoughts.

"And why do you think she fell?"

Unable to express her belief that Nick had pushed her mom, Dawn implied he was at fault. "I had gone next door, briefly. Mom was alone with Nick. When I returned, she was sprawled out on the floor. Nothing like that had ever happened before, not when I'm with her."

"Was your mom drinking alcohol?"

Dawn blinked but didn't answer.

"I'll repeat. Was your mom drinking alcohol?"

"Nick had brought over a bottle of wine."

"So your mom was drinking wine?"

"Just a little."

"Is she supposed to be mixing alcohol with her medications?"

"Well, no, but she only had a little. We don't normally keep alcohol at her place. Nick brought the bottle."

"Ms. Smith, you're asserting that you're the best person to look after your mom. Wouldn't it be your responsibility to ensure she doesn't mix alcohol with her medications?"

"Normally, she doesn't."

"But just one time could be a problem, as we've seen."

"Objection," said Ben. "Argumentative."

"Sustained," said Judge Cain. "Mr. Hood—"

"Understood, Your Honor. Ms. Smith, after your mom fell, did you take her to the emergency room or schedule a doctor's appointment?"

"We didn't need to. She wasn't hurt, just a little winded."

"How do you know that?"

"She said so. She said she wasn't in any pain."

"Do you have X-ray equipment at your veterinary practice?"

"We do."

"And if you suspect an animal's bone is broken, do you take an X-ray?"

"I don't understand your point." Dawn's tone was shifting from cordial to hostile, with frustration beginning to seep into her responses.

Charles turned toward the judge.

"Ms. Smith, please answer the question," instructed Judge Cain.

"We use X-rays for any manner of things—pyometra, pica, fractures." Dawn hoped her use of medical jargon would intimidate Charles and make him back off.

"So why would you not want an X-ray taken of your mother after her fall?"

"What part of her body would you suggest we examine? Her legs, arms? Should we do a full-body CT scan? I'm not a fan of exposing someone to unnecessary radiation when it's clearly not indicated." The sarcasm in Dawn's voice was palpable.

"Was it the cost of the X-rays that prohibited you from having her treated?"

"Like I told you, she wasn't injured." Dawn's voice grew louder—she was losing her cool.

"Does your vet tech background give you a license to treat people?"

Dawn smirked. "Of course not."

"So why were you treating your mother, making a medical judgment that you had no right to make?"

Dawn looked at Ben. He stared blankly back at her.

"I wasn't *treating* my mother. I was merely observing cause and effect. She fell but wasn't injured. If she'd complained of any pain, I would've taken her to the ER, but she didn't."

Charles walked back to his table and reviewed his notes. Dawn waited, feeling like he was restocking his ammunition in order to take another shot.

"You testified earlier that your mother was hospitalized. You said it could've been due to low blood pressure, is that correct?"

"It could've been. We don't know for sure."

"When you were at the hospital, you asked my client, Mr. VanBroklin, to check your mother's medications. I believe you specifically asked him to look for her blood pressure medication, correct?"

"Yes."

"Did he find the medication?"

"No."

"So your mother's blood pressure medication just disappeared?"

Dawn shrugged.

Charles looked at Judge Cain, expecting him to prompt a verbal response. Instead, the judge seemed disinterested, as if he was drifting into an afternoon nap.

"Your Honor," said Charles. "You'll please instruct the witness to respond."

Judge Cain perked up. "Please respond."

Dawn crossed her arms. "Nick said he couldn't find the bottle."

"Is it possible your mother misplaced her medications?"

"I don't think so."

"You testified earlier that your mother administers her own medications. And if she ever became confused, you would take over that duty?"

"Of course."

"How do you know that hasn't already happened and you missed it? That she became confused and misplaced her medications, or God forbid, took too many of them."

"That's not what happened."

"You just said yourself that you couldn't locate the bottle."

Dawn could feel perspiration beading on her forehead and wished she had a tissue to wipe her face. "All I can tell you is that in the short month I dated Nick, my mother fell and was hospitalized. She'd never fallen before and hasn't fallen since."

"Ms. Smith, are you trying to shirk your responsibility of caring for your mother by somehow blaming my client?" Charles spoke with indignation as he pointed toward Nick.

"Objection," said Ben. "Argumentative."

"Sustained," said the judge. "Mr. Hood, please move this along."

"Just a few more questions, Your Honor. Ms. Smith, you testified that you work at the Village Veterinary Clinic. What are your typical hours?"

"I'm there by seven in the morning and leave around six."

"And who is with your mom while you're at work?"

"She's on her own."

"Your mom, who is in need of a guardian per your own admission, is left alone over eleven hours a day?"

"She watches TV, gardens, cooks. She can call me anytime if she needs something."

"What about the time you were camping with Mr. VanBroklin? Could she reach you then?"

"I didn't realize my phone wouldn't have reception. It was my idea, not Nick's, to cut the trip short in case she needed to reach me."

"How long were you unreachable? A few hours, for the day, overnight?"

Dawn knew how bad this looked. She now realized why Nick had chosen Oconee State Park—the poor cell reception. He'd set her up from the beginning.

"We were gone overnight, just the one time. And like I said, once I realized he'd taken us to a place where Mom couldn't reach me, I asked to go home."

"You asked to go home right away, the minute you realized you were unreachable, or did you wait until the next morning?" Charles grinned as he looked at her.

Why so smug? she thought. *You're not so clever. Nick's the one who set me up. You're just delivering the lines.*

"We went home first thing in the morning," she admitted.

"Ms. Smith, you mentioned your mom has poor eyesight. Can you tell us more about that?"

"There's not much to tell. She has poor vision. She needs glasses."

"She needs her glasses to watch TV, garden and cook?"

"Yes."

"If she lost her glasses, would she be able to do those things?"

"Probably not."

"What if she were to lose her glasses? Would she be able to call you?"

Dawn was taken aback. Her father had always been Marie's crutch when it came to her poor vision. This past year, that duty had been passed to Dawn, and so far, there hadn't been any issues. "I don't know," she finally replied.

"Your mom is home alone for more than eleven hours a day, and although you said she could call you for help, without her glasses she wouldn't be able to make a phone call. Isn't that correct?"

"That's never happened."

"But it could," he countered. "Did it ever occur to you that your mother might need to be somewhere that offers more care, more than you're able to provide?"

"She would hate that."

"As a responsible guardian, wouldn't it be your job to do what she needs, which may not always be what she wants?"

"As a responsible daughter, I do what she needs and wants."

"I have no further questions, Your Honor."

"Any redirect?" asked Judge Cain, looking at Ben.

"Yes, Your Honor." Ben stood behind the table rather than approaching the witness stand. "How many times has your mother needed to reach you but been unable?"

"Never."

"Do you think your mother needs a higher level of care than what you're currently providing?"

"At the moment, no. I help her with a few tasks that she used to do before her eyesight worsened, but she's still very capable of living on her own."

"And if it ever got to the point where you or her doctor felt she needed a higher level of care than what you can provide, what would you do?"

Dawn was stunned. She and Ben had never discussed this question. "I don't know, but it's not to that point yet."

"Thank you. Nothing further."

Chapter 30

As Dawn stepped down from the witness stand, Judge Cain turned toward Jerry Raven, who'd been quietly witnessing the proceedings. "Mr. Raven, will you be providing a report or an opinion?"

Finally, thought Dawn. *We'll hear from the person speaking for Mom.*

Ben had indicated that the guardian ad litem's opinion would hold the most sway with the judge, so Jerry's testimony was the most critical part of the day.

"I can do whatever you prefer," said Jerry as he rose. "I'm prepared to provide an opinion now and a recommendation."

"Go ahead."

"Your Honor, I was able to visit the respondents, Dawn and Marie Smith, at Marie's home. I spent a couple hours there and was able to speak with both women. It was clear to me that they share a loving relationship. I appreciate that this young fellow, Nicholas VanBroklin, felt the need to express his concerns, although filing a lawsuit seems a bit extreme."

Yes! thought Dawn. She could've leapt to her feet and shouted.

"Requesting mediation or calling the state ombudsman might've been a more amicable approach. Nonetheless, we're here now and I think his intentions were in the right place."

What? thought Dawn. *Nick's intentions are so not in the right place.*

"Regarding the guardianship—"

Jerry paused.

Everyone waited.

The sound of the wall clock ticking felt like a collective heartbeat.

"I understand that Mr. VanBroklin thinks he could serve as guardian and feels there are no other options. However, babysitting a boy on weekends and being a full-time guardian are two completely different endeavors. And there are indeed other options."

Exactly, thought Dawn. *I'm the other option—the only option.*

Jerry cleared his throat. "Today's hearing brought to light a situation that I hadn't witnessed during the visit. I have no doubt that Dawn loves her mother, but I don't know that she can be objective when it comes to the level of care Marie Smith actually needs. I'm sure it's hard for Dawn to accept her mother's frailty. It's hard for any of us to watch our parents age, which is why I presume Dawn hasn't increased the level of care. But, at the end of the day, Marie is severely handicapped visually and could cause harm to herself if left unsupervised. And she is left unsupervised for most of the day. Your Honor, I didn't hear a plan for the future. I heard an intention to keep the status quo, even if that's not in Marie's best interest. Therefore, my recommendation, what I think is best for Marie, is that a professional guardian be put in place. But more than that, I think it's appropriate to direct the guardian to investigate Marie's current living conditions and determine if they are sufficient."

Dawn's mouth dropped open. Never in her life had she been so blindsided. Jerry Raven was criticizing her judgment. Her job required her to make tough decisions every day, which saved lives. If anything, that was her strongest skill. This man had spent only a few hours in their home, yet he was committing the most heinous betrayal with his testimony. She wished she could shove his words back into his mouth and make him start over.

"Do you have anyone in mind?" asked Judge Cain.

"I'd be happy to report back to the court with a list of suitable names."

Suitable names? thought Dawn. *I'm the only suitable name.*

"Thank you. And do you have an opinion on conservatorship?"

"I do, Your Honor. For the sake of expediency, the professional guardian could also serve as conservator. It avoids the red tape of one person making necessary healthcare recommendations for Mrs. Smith and having a delay while another person has to approve. As we heard today, Dawn Smith spends long hours at her place of employment. And she chose a fine career taking care of animals, but she may lack the sophistication required to deal with complex financial matters. For example, Dawn could've made the purchase of the duplex for Mrs. Smith contingent on the sale of the family farm without incurring a loss, but she didn't. Her father managed the family finances, but with his passing, she's been thrown into the role without proper training. She hasn't enlisted the help of a wealth management adviser, someone who could give her guidance and ensure the family's assets are protected. A conservator could do that for these women. Therefore, my recommendation is that the court appoint a professional guardian and conservator for Marie Smith."

Dawn's breathing seized up. She gasped for air. The blow Jerry Raven had just thrown was worse than if he'd physically punched her in the stomach.

"Anything further from anyone before closing remarks?" asked the judge.

Ben and Charles chimed in unison, "No, Your Honor."

"Mr. Hood, go ahead."

Charles stood. "Your Honor, the unfortunate thing about this case is that my client was not able to get through to Ms. Smith about his concerns. After their split, my client tried repeatedly to speak with her, but she refused to talk to him and forbade him from contacting her mother. Had he been able to, he would've assisted Ms. Smith in finding a suitable care facility for her mother rather than bringing this case to court. His only goal was to ensure no further harm would come to dear Marie. And no matter the outcome of this case, if Marie Smith receives the care she deserves, he will be able to sleep at night. Thank you."

"Mr. Clayton, I'll hear from you," said Judge Cain.

"Your Honor," said Ben as he rose. "As financial power of attorney, Dawn already handles Marie's affairs including paying her bills and overseeing her assets and investments. There has been no evidence of any abuse or misuse of funds. On the contrary, she's done an admirable job. And let's not forget the testimony of Dr. Neil Patel, a respected veterinarian in our community. He and his wife leave their business under Dawn's supervision. That speaks to her level of responsibility and the trust the doctors have in her."

Ben paused and looked around the room. "As to the matter of guardianship, Dawn is the current healthcare power of attorney. She takes her mother to doctors' appointments, picks up medications and the like. Yes, there was one fall, but that could happen anywhere. There was one hospitalization, but my client was right there, ensuring that medical attention was provided, and Marie was released from the hospital the same day. I submit that every time Marie needed care, my client was there to provide it. Regarding the Affidavit of David Smith Jr., it was clearly biased based on the past discord between the siblings. He doesn't have firsthand knowledge of the care Dawn provides for her mother. And how much first-hand knowledge can Mr. VanBroklin really claim? The two dated for what, a summer? My client has been there for her mother all along, and she should be the only choice for guardian and conservator. Thank you."

"Mr. Raven, anything you want to say?" asked Judge Cain.

"Just one point, Your Honor," said Jerry. "We all know that under Section 62-5-308 of the South Carolina Code, a family member would normally have priority to serve as guardian and conservator. However, the court must decide what is in the best interest of the ward. When a daughter fails to make proper decisions, even if she loves her mother, we—as officers of the court—must step in. We've been fortunate that these recent episodes didn't have more serious results, but do we really want to risk a more tragic outcome down the road?"

"Alright. It's been a long day. I'm not going to make a decision right now as I need to go through my notes. While I take this under advisement, I would ask that Mr. Raven recommend three professionals for my consideration. Now, this is no indication of how the court is going to rule. I will try to read through everything tomorrow since we freed up a day and will do my best to render a decision in a timely fashion. That being said, this court is adjourned."

With that, Judge Cain struck his gavel, collected his papers and hobbled out of the room. Ben exchanged a few pleasantries with Jerry and then shook hands with Charles. Nick was in the back of the courtroom sharing a high-five with Matthias as if their team had won the Super Bowl.

Dawn sat shell-shocked, trying to process what had just happened.

When Ben returned to their table, she pointed at Charles and spoke through clenched teeth. "Did you hear his closing? He didn't even fight because Nick doesn't actually want the responsibility. Don't you see? He just wants me to lose. They're going to take away my mom—because of him."

"We don't know that," counseled Ben. "Let's go to the waiting area so we can talk."

Dawn seethed as she followed Ben, avoiding eye contact with everyone, especially Nick. As soon as the door shut, she exploded.

"Why would Jerry Raven say those things? He made it sound like Mom was in danger—with me. That man spent an afternoon in our home. He never gave any indication he would betray us. Aren't you even upset with him?"

Ben shrugged. "I guess Jerry did what he felt was right."

"Right?" screamed Dawn. "Right would've been recommending *me* to be guardian and conservator."

"Let's just wait until we receive the judge's ruling. He said he hasn't decided yet."

"He asked Jerry to provide three potential names. Of course he's made up his mind." Dawn launched a final jab. "And why didn't you bring up Nick's psycho behavior? He came off like Prince Charming. This case turned into my supposed lack of care for Mom, which is a total farce, instead of the real reason we're here—Nick is a vindictive psychopath."

"Introducing a contentious breakup between you and Nick, which was not the subject of this hearing, would've made you both look bad. Like you said, the judge asked for names of professional guardians. I don't think he's considering Nick as an option."

Chapter 31

That evening, Dawn entered her mom's place, unsure how she'd explain the turn of events.

"Is that you, dear? How'd it go today?" Marie rose from the couch and met Dawn in the kitchen.

Dawn sighed. "We're done."

Marie waited, expecting to hear more details.

"The judge won't decide right away. He said he wanted to review his notes."

"What's there to review? Didn't Ben say this was all just a formality?"

"I guess that's how this judge operates." Dawn forced a smile, trying to hide her exhaustion and despair, although she knew Marie would see through it. "Mom," she said. "If you lost your glasses and needed to call me, what would you do?"

Marie's eyes, which were magnified by the thick lenses of her glasses, looked puzzled. "What do you mean, dear?"

"If you somehow lost your glasses or they got broken, and you needed to reach me, how would you see to use the phone?"

"Alexa, call Dawn," said Marie without skipping a beat.

The female robotic voice replied. "Calling Dawn." Seconds later, Dawn's mobile phone rang.

"Remember? Stuart gave me that gadget. He programmed his number and yours. Of course, I wouldn't call him now—"

"Oh, Mom," Dawn fell into Marie's arms and started to cry. "You don't need a guardian."

Over the next few days, life went back to normal. There was no legal talk and no harassment from Nick. Dawn took his silence as a sign of gloating.

The following Thursday afternoon, Dawn received an email from Ben. *Judge Cain provided his ruling. Please have a read and give me a call if you'd like to discuss.*

She opened the PDF, ignoring the summary of the litigants' arguments, and scrolled directly to the ruling.

Based on careful consideration and review of the pleadings, testimony, affidavits, the visitor's report and the recommendation of the guardian ad litem, I find the following:

1. *Mrs. Marie P. Smith, hereinafter referred to as Mrs. Smith, is a resident of Laurel County, and South Carolina is her home state. This Court has proper jurisdiction of all parties and of subject matter of this action.*
2. *Due to medical conditions and in accordance with the opinion of her doctor, Mrs. Smith is an incapacitated adult in need of assistance and protection.*
3. *Mrs. Smith enjoys a loving relationship with her daughter, Ms. Dawn Smith, and has a warm relationship with the petitioner, Mr. Nicholas VanBroklin. Unfortunately, the petitioner has been unable to communicate his concerns about Mrs. Smith's care with Ms. Dawn Smith.*
4. *The petitioner's concerns regarding recent episodes, such as falls and hospitalization, and the concern over Mrs. Smith's deteriorating eyesight and long hours spent alone are valid.*
5. *The petitioner's concerns regarding the financial oversight provided by Ms. Dawn Smith, including the recent sale of the family home at a loss, the attempted sale of assets such as jewelry and the lack of understanding of complex financial matters are valid.*
6. *Therefore, it is in the best interest of Mrs. Smith that a professional with experience in geriatric care serve as guardian and conservator.*

Therefore, it is hereby ordered, adjudged and decreed:

1. *Mrs. Smith is an incapacitated person in need of protection and assistance by appointment of a guardian and conservator.*
2. *Mrs. Nancy Priest, hereinafter referred to as Mrs. Priest, is a fit and suitable person to serve as guardian for Mrs. Smith. Therefore, I appoint Mrs. Priest as guardian for Mrs. Smith, hereinafter referred to as the Ward.*
3. *Mrs. Priest and Ms. Dawn Smith shall meet at least once every three months to discuss the care plan of the Ward.*
4. *Ms. Dawn Smith shall have full access to all medical records of her mother, Mrs. Smith.*
5. *There shall be no restrictions on contact or visitation by either peti-*

tioner, Mr. Nicholas VanBroklin, or respondent, Ms. Dawn Smith, with Mrs. Smith unless limited or restricted by the treating physician or other health care provider.

6. *The existing Healthcare Power of Attorney and Durable Power of Attorney executed by Mrs. Smith shall become invalid after entry of this Order.*
7. *Due to her incapacitated state, Mrs. Smith is not permitted to ship, transport, possess or receive a firearm or ammunition.*
8. *Each year on the anniversary of appointment, the guardian shall file with the Court, the Annual Report of Guardian, and the guardian shall comply with all statutory requirements of the South Carolina Probate Code.*

The document was signed by Judge Cain and dated two days prior. Reality started to sink in. Dawn's position as power of attorney had just been revoked. A stranger, Nancy Priest, was now her mother's legal guardian and conservator. Dawn wasn't exactly sure how this ruling would affect their lives, but she felt like she was losing control.

Her anger simmered—at Judge Cain and Jerry Raven for being so obtuse to Nick's treachery, and at Ben Clayton for downplaying the enormity of the lawsuit. Most of all, she despised Nick for exploiting the flawed legal system to attack her family. She dialed Ben's number.

"Mr. Clayton is in a meeting," said Donna.

"I need to speak with him. It's urgent. Can you interrupt?"

"I'm afraid not. I'll have him call you as soon as he's available."

Dawn hung up in frustration and searched for Jerry Raven's number. When she called his office, his paralegal answered.

"This is Dawn Smith," she said. "Jerry Raven was appointed as my mom's guardian ad litem. I'd like to speak to him about his testimony."

"Hang on a moment," the paralegal directed. The line went quiet. A few moments later, she returned to the call. "I'm sorry, he's not permitted to speak with you about the case."

"Why not?"

"It would be a conflict of interest. He represents your mother."

"That doesn't make any sense. He spoke to me when he came to our home before the trial. And my mom and I are on the same side of this lawsuit. What changed?"

"I'm sorry, but that's all he told me."

"This is absurd," shouted Dawn as she hung up. Unable to suppress her need to vent, she pounded out a reply to Ben's email.

Ben,

You assured us that this lawsuit was basically a formality. I'm extremely disappointed with the judge's ruling. There is no way a stranger can care for my mom better than me. What recourse do we have? Please call me immediately.

Dawn

That evening, when Dawn arrived home, a black Toyota was parked in the driveway. She entered her mom's kitchen to find Marie sitting at the table sharing a slice of homemade apple pie with a woman.

"Hello," said Dawn, curious as to who this stranger might be.

"Oh, this is my daughter who I was telling you about," said Marie.

The woman stood, barely reaching Dawn's shoulders. She had bobbed brown hair and wore a baggy sweater and slacks. She crossed her arms, not attempting to shake hands. "I'm Nancy Priest. I assume you saw the court order?"

"Just today." Dawn turned to her mom. "What have you ladies been talking about?"

"Nancy said the judge asked her to help look after me, so she stopped by to pay a visit. If I'd known she was coming, I would've cleaned up a bit."

Dawn eyed the state of the kitchen. The counters were dusted with white flour and littered with mixing bowls, spilled milk and eggshells.

"Your mom said she cut her hand while baking." The judgment in Nancy's voice was palpable.

"Oh, it's just a nick from the apple peeler." Marie lifted her hand. A blood-stained paper towel was wrapped around her index finger.

"Nothing to worry about, although I had a heck of a time getting the bleeding to stop."

"Mom, why don't you go get a Band-Aid?" suggested Dawn.

"Okay, dear. But it's not bleeding anymore." Marie headed to the bathroom, which gave Dawn the opportunity to speak with Nancy privately.

"I would've appreciated a call first. She doesn't know about the court order. I just got it today."

"It was sent to me two days ago." Nancy's remark carried a hint of condescension, as if being informed first made her the better person.

To Dawn, the delay in sharing Judge Cain's order was another example of how Ben had failed her. "Still, you could've checked with me before just showing up," she said.

Nancy tilted her head and narrowed her eyes. "Let me explain how this works. Marie is *my* ward. It's *my* job to ensure she's safe and healthy. When possible and as a courtesy, I'll try to inform you of my decisions, but I am not obligated to do so."

Nancy sounded like a yappy Yorkshire Terrier, unaware of its small size and barking orders like a big dog.

Dawn realized this meeting could go one of two ways. She could become equally confrontational, or she could bite her tongue for now, until she could talk to Ben. One thing was crystal clear—she needed to challenge the court's decision.

"Well, I would appreciate being notified. Let me give you my mobile." Dawn waited for Nancy to take out her phone, but the woman didn't budge from her defensive stance. So, Dawn found a piece of scrap paper and provided her contact information the old-fashioned way.

"Please thank your mom for the pie." Nancy surveyed the kitchen. "I think I've seen enough."

Seen enough? thought Dawn. The kitchen was cluttered—big deal. The better the chef, the bigger the mess, and everything could be cleaned up in a matter of minutes.

"I'll be in touch." Nancy walked to the front door and looked over her shoulder. "Oh, I'll need copies of your mom's bank accounts, her investment statements and title to her property. I'll be adding myself as co-signee on her accounts."

"What is all of this going to cost?" asked Dawn.

"My fee is one hundred and fifty dollars an hour. Today was two hours."

Three hundred dollars to eat a piece of apple pie? thought Dawn. The absurdity was almost too much to comprehend. The court had given this woman a blank check. Nancy Priest could visit whenever she wanted, for as long as she wanted, and charge Marie for her time. And because she was now Marie's conservator, she could even pay herself.

Chapter 32

After the Friday morning team meeting, Dr. Patel asked Dawn to join him in his office. He'd already apologized for having to admit, under oath, that she'd performed an unauthorized procedure on Daisy. She'd downplayed the damage caused by his testimony to ease his guilt, although she suspected it had weighed into Judge Cain's decision.

"I need to show you something," he said. He swiveled his computer screen so Dawn could see the Google reviews of the clinic. On average, they scored 4.7 stars with mostly 4's and 5's. A single, recent one-star review stood out.

If you care about your pet, do NOT take it to the Village Veterinary Clinic!!! My dog died due to the negligence of Dawn Smith!!!

Dawn was speechless. No dog had died recently at the clinic and certainly none due to her negligence. This was downright libel. She checked the date. The review had been posted earlier in the week.

"This has to be Nick. Can we have it removed?"

"Suzanne says it violates Google's policy regarding misinformation. She reported it, but we don't know if they'll take it down."

The review was so much worse than the note he'd taped to the door—it was public and potentially permanent.

"I'm sorry," said Dawn.

"One bad review is no worry. Is he still harassing you?"

"Not since the trial." Dawn's gaze met the floor. "But he's done his damage."

"Sorry to interrupt, Dr. Patel," said Suzanne, as she knocked on the door. "Regan is ready in surgery, and Dawn, you have a new client in room one. Name is Austin with his Jack Russell, Moose."

"I guess Austin hasn't read my review," she replied.

When Dawn entered the exam room, Moose started barking, expelling his abundant energy. The owner, an attractive man in his early thirties, tried to calm the dog by rubbing his ears.

"Good morning. I'm—" Dawn hesitated. She imagined this man hearing her name and leaving the clinic. Even now, Nick was messing with her head. She continued, "I'm here to see what's going on with Moose."

"We were out in the woods, and he came back with ticks." The whole time Austin spoke, he kept rubbing Moose. Dawn respected owners like this, who instinctively comforted their pets. It said a lot about the person.

"I see. Did our receptionist take a look at him?"

"No. She brought us in here and asked us to wait."

Dawn approached the little dog, who barked again and wagged his tail. She searched his body, parting his short hair so she could see his skin. "Can you show me where you found the ticks?"

Austin picked up Moose and turned him on his back. The dog started to wiggle as if this was a new game—to see if he could turn back over. Austin pointed to a few places on Moose's belly. "I tried ripping them off, but they're stuck pretty deep. So I tried using a lighter, but I must've gotten too close to his skin because he started howling. Do you think you can remove them?"

"Sir, these aren't ticks," said Dawn.

"What are they?"

"These are Moose's nipples."

"No, they can't be. He's a *male* dog."

"Males have nipples, too." Dawn pointed to Austin's chest, blushing slightly. "You're a male. You have nipples."

He looked dumbfounded. "But they're all over his belly."

"Dogs can have up to ten nipples. Humans have just two."

Austin's face turned red. "Well, I'll be damned."

Dawn bit her lower lip to suppress a giggle. "Hey, at least you care enough about Moose to bring him in."

"Care about my dog? I tried to burn off his nipples."

They both burst into laughter. Moose started barking to join the fun. Dawn hadn't had a good belly laugh like that in weeks, maybe months. Everything in her life had been so bereft of anything lighthearted. Moose's "tick problem" brought some levity into her life for a brief moment.

"You won't tell anyone, will you?" asked Austin.

"I don't know." She flashed a coy smile. "Sounds like pretty good blackmail to me."

He glanced at her left hand. It was a quick dart of the eye, but Dawn caught it. "What if I take you out to dinner to buy your silence?"

Dawn's face sobered. As cute and nice as this guy appeared to be, Nick had also started off charming—until he wasn't. She no longer trusted her judgment.

"I don't think so," she said, with no further explanation.

The smile on Austin's face faded, although he brushed off his disappointment. "Well, if you change your mind, ask for Austin over at Bailey Acres."

Dawn knew of Bailey Acres. It was the largest dairy farm in the state. "That's a pretty big place. You sure I'll find you?"

"Just ask for Moose's dad." Austin refastened Moose's leash, lifted him from the table and set him on the floor. The little dog ran up to Dawn. "He likes you, and he's a good judge of character."

Dawn knew that animals were the best judge of character, and this one clearly loved his owner. She reconsidered Austin's offer of a dinner date. "What if I asked to see your driver's license before I agreed to go out with you?" she asked, remembering the pains of not knowing Nick's birthday.

Austin reached into his pocket, pulled out his wallet and slapped his license on the exam table. Not only was this guy a good dad to Moose, but he had no reservations about showing his identification. She took note of his birth date and his last name—Bailey. He was Austin Bailey, the owner of Bailey Acres' son.

"Well?" he asked.

"I'll think about it," she replied, surprising even herself.

Once Austin and Moose left the clinic, Dawn marched straight to Suzanne.

"Ticks? Really? Why didn't you check?" she asked. This wasn't the first time an owner had mistaken nipples for ticks. It happened often enough that Suzanne had been instructed to check the animal before creating a nuisance visit for one of the vet techs.

"That guy was super-hot and no wedding band," replied Suzanne. "I thought you might want to take the appointment."

Chapter 33

On Saturday morning, Dawn set out on her weekly run. Her pace was quicker than usual, letting the frustration from the trial pound onto the pavement. She replayed the day in court and how Nick and his lawyer had so artfully portrayed her as a risk to her mom. With the exception of her dad's illness and death, this past week had been the worst time of her life.

Sweat dripped from her face as she turned the corner for the homestretch. She picked up the pace to sprint the last quarter mile. Suddenly, a passing force knocked her off balance. She stumbled sideways and fell hard onto gravel. The unexpected blow left her short of breath and with skinned knees and palms. Still on the ground, Dawn looked up. A bright green motorcycle was about halfway down the street, speeding away. The rider, dressed in black with a black helmet, deliberately stopped and looked back. His face was covered by the helmet's dark shield, but she could picture Nick grinning.

"What the hell do you want from me?" screamed Dawn.

Her outburst was met with silence. The neighborhood was eerily quiet. The only sound she heard was the revving of the bike's engine as he drove away. Dawn eyed the nearby homes. Had anyone seen them? Had a surveillance camera captured the assault? Unfortunately, she was on the back side of the duplexes, out of sight of any potential cameras. No doubt Nick had carefully planned the location of his attack and, just like when he'd stolen her necklace, she had no proof.

Dawn picked bits of gravel from her bloody knees and hobbled home, vowing to buy a second camera for the back side of the duplex. During dinner that evening with Marie, she brushed off the injury as a clumsy fall. She also downplayed the role of Nancy Priest in their lives. If the worst they had to endure were some intrusive visits and outrageous bills, they'd find a way to cope. Dawn still wanted to challenge the ruling and was awaiting a return call from Ben to determine if that was even possible.

On Monday afternoon, Dawn saw a missed call and voicemail on her phone.

"This is Nancy Priest. I'm giving you a courtesy call to let you know I've decided to place Marie in assisted living. A facility in Laurel has an opening so I'll be moving her today. In these situations, change can be difficult at first, so I suggest you wait to visit until she's had time to settle in."

Dawn couldn't believe her ears. This woman was treating her mother as if she were property, not a human being. She rushed into the exam room where Kelly was bandaging their frequent flyer, Hunter Rhodes, who'd gotten into another fight.

"Can you cover for me? It's urgent. My mom."

"What is it?" asked Kelly.

"Can't talk now. I'll call you."

"Okay. Go."

Dawn raced home. Halfway there, she received a call from Marie.

"The woman from last week, Nancy, said I was going to live at a new place. She said that she already told you. Is that true? Do I have to leave?"

"No, Mom. I'm going to put a stop to this. I'll be right there."

When Dawn arrived, the black Toyota was parked in the driveway. She burst through Marie's front door to find Nancy sitting at the kitchen table. Marie was nowhere in sight.

"What do you think you're doing?" demanded Dawn. "You can't just uproot her."

Nancy rolled her eyes and muttered under her breath, "I knew I should've waited to call."

"So, you were just going to kidnap my mother?"

"Look, I've read the court transcript, and I've visited this home. Jerry Raven, your mother's guardian ad litem, instructed that I assess Marie's living situation, and I have. It's not safe for her to remain here alone. And every day that goes by where I don't take action is a risk for me."

"A risk for you? She's perfectly fine here. And she's happy."

"My decision is made. Are we going to have a problem?" Nancy lifted her phone as if prepared to call for reinforcements.

"Why didn't you discuss this with me first instead of springing this news on us? It's not right."

Nancy shook her head. "Long, drawn-out discussions will only make Marie worry. It's better to rip off the Band-Aid. After she's there, she'll adjust."

So, this isn't the first time you've dropped a bomb on a family, thought Dawn. She stormed out the front door and called Ben.

Before he could finish saying hello, Dawn unleashed her fury. "You never called me back last week about challenging the guardianship, and things have gotten worse. This woman is at our home, trying to move Mom to a facility. Can she do that?"

"Hold on now, what's going on?" he asked.

Dawn explained the situation as she paced across the front porch.

"Well, Dawn, Nancy is a professional. Before you get defensive, maybe you should consider what she's suggesting. It'll give you more freedom in your own life."

"When did I ever say Mom was a burden? I'll tell you when—never. Because she isn't. I won't have an outsider making decisions for our family. How do we stop her?"

"You can't."

"There has to be a way."

"She's your mother's legal guardian. That gives her the same authority as a parent over a child."

"And what about my authority? I'm her daughter."

"I'm afraid that doesn't hold any weight, legally."

"This is out of control, Ben."

"Listen to me, Dawn. The last thing you need to do is to get off on the wrong foot with Nancy."

"Too late for that," snapped Dawn.

"My advice is don't make it any worse. You must abide by what she decides. Legally, you don't have a choice. If you try to stop her, she could have you arrested."

"We have to do something."

"You can try to change her mind," he offered.

"She doesn't seem the type to change her mind. Have you met her? Worked with her before?"

"I haven't, but Jerry says—"

"Don't get me started on Jerry Raven, that traitor."

Dawn questioned what had happened to the Ben she'd known. He'd been so prepared for the battle against her brothers, and they'd won. Now, he was accepting Marie's fate as if it was a good thing. With no other choice, she hung up, went inside and attempted to reason with Nancy.

"What if I get help to come in during the day?" she suggested.

Nancy raised an eyebrow. "Can you afford that kind of assistance? Besides, a single helper isn't a reliable solution. What if that person gets sick or takes vacation? You'll constantly be looking for back-ups. At the facility, your mom will have round-the-clock care by a full staff."

"Where's my mom now?"

"In her bedroom, packing a few things. I told her I'd bring the rest over later."

Dawn marched down the hall to the bedroom. Marie was sitting on the bed next to an open but empty suitcase. Dawn sat next to her and wrapped her arm around her mother's shoulder.

"Do I have to go?" asked Marie. "I don't want to, but she said it was already decided. She said it was better for everyone, especially you."

Dawn fought back tears. When nothing had changed those first few days after the ruling, she'd innocently believed that their lives could go back to normal. She expected the guardian would drop by every once in a while for an impromptu inspection, but that would be the extent of the disruption. How wrong she'd been.

"I don't want you to go, and I know you don't want to go, either."

"So why do I have to leave?"

"They say you're not safe here alone."

"Why do they think that?"

Dawn didn't have a good answer. No one, not even her mom, knew the truth. No one understood Nick's role in Marie's fall, hospitalization and misplaced medications.

After sitting in silence, Dawn offered the only answer she could. "I promise, I'll fix this."

Nancy appeared at the doorway. "Do *we* need any help packing?"

"*We* don't need anything," sneered Dawn. With no choice, she helped Marie pack, filling the suitcase with a few favorite outfits, toiletries and several large-print books.

As they rejoined Nancy in the kitchen, Marie's eyes started to water. "What about my garden? Who will tend to my plants and flowers?"

"I'll take care of them, Mom."

Nancy tried to grab Marie by the elbow, but Dawn stepped forward, blocking the advance. "I'll drive her, unless you think my driving isn't safe, either?"

Nancy acquiesced, letting Dawn have a small victory. During the drive to the facility, Marie meticulously explained the unique care required for each plant. Her instructions hummed like background noise, not sinking in, although Dawn was soothed by the calming sound of her mother's voice.

Chapter 34

The Floyd Retirement Home was nestled on the outskirts of town. Its redbrick facade was half-lost in the long shadows of aging magnolia trees. Worn, white columns, reminiscent of the Confederate South, were lined with green ferns on each side of the entryway. Next to the front door, an old woman swayed in a rocking chair as she gazed into oblivion. There was nothing specific to critique, yet something about the place was undeniably depressing.

Inside, the women were greeted by the director, Patti Floyd, a short, round woman who could've passed for Nancy's twin in her size and stature, although Patti wore more makeup and jewelry.

"Welcome, Miss Marie, we've been expecting you," said Patti. Her voice was sugary sweet, as if molasses dripped from every word. "We have your room all ready and Miss Cathy is so excited to meet you."

"Who's Miss Cathy?" asked Dawn.

"Her roommate," replied Patti, as if that should've been obvious. "Why don't we go get you settled. In the morning, we can give you a tour. Miss Nancy here has already taken care of the paperwork, so there's nothing in the world you need to do except have your supper and relax."

Patti led the group down the hallway. With each step, Dawn's Crocs squeaked against the hard linoleum floor. She'd been in such a rush to stop Nancy that she hadn't changed out of her work scrubs. The women passed door after door, all of them shut, until they reached room 112. Two plaques mounted on the wall read: MARIE SMITH and CATHY HOGAN.

Inside, the small double room was divided by a beige curtain. The space closest to the door had a single bed with rails, a nightstand, a dresser and a metal folding chair. A television hung on the wall. The room reminded Dawn of a hospital, somewhere she'd take Marie temporarily if she were sick, but it was no place to live.

Patti drew the curtain to reveal a duplicate layout on the other side, except the metal chair had been replaced by a recliner. The TV was turned on and blaring a true crime show. In the instant Dawn looked at the monitor, a lifeless, bloody body flashed across the screen. Thankfully, Marie hadn't seen it.

Mom can't be subjected to this, thought Dawn.

"Cathy," said Patti. "Look who's here. It's Marie."

No one else seemed offended by the forced excitement in Patti's voice, but Dawn was. She found it to be disingenuous and disrespectful. Marie and Cathy were adult women sharing a room, not two kindergarteners having a playdate.

Cathy Hogan was sitting in her recliner watching the show. She had porcelain skin and straight light brown hair with bangs that touched her eyebrows. She wore a long shirtdress with a matching scarf tied around her neck. Cathy reminded Dawn of an old-fashioned doll whose eyelids shut when tilted backward. When Patti made the introduction, she turned her head and blinked but didn't speak, then resumed watching TV.

"Here's the bathroom," said Patti. She opened a door at the front of the room where they could see a toilet, chrome sink and two medicine cabinets. "Marie can have the one on the right. Supper is at six, so she'll have just enough time to unpack and come to the dining hall. I'll see you a bit later. Bye-bye."

Nancy placed the suitcase on the bed. "Marie, do you need help unpacking?"

Marie stood motionless while Dawn surveyed the room. A dead fly was next to the bed. Dawn retrieved a piece of toilet paper and picked it up. She shoved the dead bug, its stiff legs protruding, in Nancy's face. "I can't leave her in this place. It's disgusting."

"I'll ask Patti to have the cleaning crew make another pass. Can we have a word?"

Dawn followed Nancy into the hallway.

There, Nancy whipped around, crossed her arms and spoke in a harsh whisper. "If you react negatively, you're just going to make it harder on her. I let you come with us as a courtesy, but if you're going to interfere with Marie's adjustment, I cannot allow that."

"You *let* me come?" Dawn put her hands on her hips and glared down at Nancy. Ben's caution to avoid antagonizing the woman was long forgotten. "Let me be clear. You being in charge of my mother was a mistake, a colossal mistake by the court that I plan to fix."

Nancy's reaction wasn't at all what Dawn expected. Instead of snapping back, she flaunted a smug grin as if thinking, *I know how the court system works, and I hold all the cards.* She pushed past Dawn and craned her head into the room. "Marie, I'll leave you to get unpacked. I'll come to check on you tomorrow."

Dawn watched as Nancy waddled down the hall and turned the corner out of sight. She spotted her mother's nameplate on the wall and had a strong urge to rip it down. Something about having Marie's name already posted made this change feel presumptuous and permanent.

Back in the room, Marie hadn't moved from her stunned position of standing by the bed. Another gruesome image flashed on Cathy's TV. Dawn pulled the curtain to block the view, although they could still hear the very loud and creepy narrator.

"Do I have to stay here?" Marie's voice cracked as she spoke.

"I'm going to do everything I can to bring you home."

"To the farmhouse?"

Dawn swallowed hard. Never before had Marie confused her current home at the duplex with their former home in the country. Marie hadn't lived at the farmhouse for almost a year. Dawn could only imagine that the stress of being ripped from her familiar surroundings was confusing her.

"Let's go have dinner," suggested Dawn, eager to get a reprieve from Cathy's TV.

The dining room was at the end of the hall opposite the nurse's station. On the far side, past the tables, a few recliners were stationed in front of a large-screen TV. Several residents sat patiently at their tables while others started to file in, mostly by wheelchair or walker.

Dawn and Marie chose an empty table and watched as two aides plated food from a serving station. Another aide approached and spoke to Dawn. "Is she new?"

"Yes, this is my mom, Marie Smith. I'm Dawn. And you are?"

"Missy. Does she want fish or barbeque?"

"You can ask her," replied Dawn, motioning toward her mom.

"I'm not hungry," said Marie.

"Which should I get her?" asked Missy, still talking to Dawn. "You can eat with her, too, but you've got to sign in. It's twelve dollars for guests."

"We'll both have the barbeque. Thanks."

Missy returned with two plastic trays, which reminded Dawn of her high school cafeteria. The mystery meat drenched in brown sauce didn't look like any barbeque she'd ever eaten. The side dishes were greasy french fries and canned green beans. Dessert was banana pudding. One sip of the iced tea made Dawn's teeth ache—it was so sweet.

Marie wasn't touching her food. She hadn't even unwrapped her silverware. Instead, she sat motionless, clutching her purse like it was her last possession on earth.

"The grocery store isn't too far away," said Dawn. "How about I pick up something else and bring it back?"

Marie nodded and reached into her bag. "Here's my list."

Daggers stabbed Dawn's heart as she took the folded sheet of paper. Did Marie not realize that she'd no longer be able to cook?

"Okay, Mom. Why don't you wait here? I'll be right back."

Dawn left the building, forcing herself not to break down. She could pick up dinner tonight, but what about all of the other nights? She couldn't bring breakfast, lunch and dinner every day. Marie had a few joys in life—cooking and gardening. Those things were being stripped away, and the last time Marie had shared a room with anyone was with her husband.

Outside, where she could speak freely, Dawn called Ben. She didn't care that it was late. Had he taken Nick's affront more seriously, they wouldn't be in this nightmare. His cell phone went to voicemail.

"Ben, this is Dawn Smith. Nancy Priest has taken my mom to the Floyd Retirement Home. The conditions are deplorable. We must get her out of there." She tried his office phone, which also went to voicemail, so she left a second message.

Dawn couldn't remember a more wretched day in her life. Little did she know it was about to get worse.

Chapter 35

Dawn arrived at the Ingles grocery store just after 6:00 p.m. She scanned the aisles, searching for food she could prepare without access to a kitchen. Settling on a Caesar salad, she stopped at the deli for fresh chicken strips to put on top. While she waited in line, images of Missy force-feeding her mom popped into her head. She knew the idea was outrageous—so why had the thought even crossed her mind?

As the woman ahead of her painstakingly made her selection of meats and cheeses, Dawn's apprehension grew. She couldn't pinpoint why she was so uneasy, but the feeling was real and not abating. A tingling sensation snaked up her neck. She rubbed her hairline. The prickling intensified. Dawn instinctively turned around.

Nick was standing uncomfortably close behind her—like it was perfectly normal.

"What are you doing here?" she shouted.

Everyone around them turned and watched.

"I had a craving for chicken fingers." He spoke quietly although his tone was mocking.

"Get the hell away from me!" she screamed.

"It's a free country, Dawn. If you don't like being near me, you can leave." His voice was calm. When he made eye contact with the onlookers, he smiled politely. Then he added the gut punch. "By the way, how's Marie?"

Dawn dropped the salad and lunged forward, wrapping her fingers around his neck. "You bastard. I'm going to kill you for this!"

Nick collapsed to the floor and fell onto his back. He flailed his arms in feigned distress. Dawn maintained her grip as she straddled his waist. She tried in vain to squeeze the life out of him.

Two store employees rushed over and pulled Dawn off him.

"Are you okay?" one of them asked Nick.

"I think so," he replied, rubbing his neck. He wobbled as he stood as if Dawn's assault had actually harmed him. "Can you just keep her away from me? She's my ex-girlfriend."

The two employees who were restraining Dawn tightened their grip.

"Let go of me!" she shouted, yanking her arms to break free. One of them let go, but the other held on. "*He's* the one harassing *me*," she protested, but it was clear whose side they'd taken. She jerked away and stormed out of the store, leaving the bag of salad on the floor. Behind her, she could hear Nick commiserating with the employees about how he'd been a victim of her abuse.

Dawn couldn't understand why Nick was still tormenting her. He'd won. He'd convinced Judge Cain and Jerry Raven that she was a threat to Marie. What more did he want from her? And why was he going to such lengths to ruin her life, given the brief time they'd dated? Whatever was in his sadistic mind had to stem from something deeper. What that was, she didn't know.

Back in her Jeep, Dawn ran her fingers through her disheveled hair. She wondered if Nick knew her Monday shopping schedule or if he'd been following her. Still needing dinner, she drove through a Chick-fil-A and ordered two chicken salads. During the entire drive back, she glanced in the rearview mirror to ensure he wasn't behind her.

At the Floyd Retirement Home, Marie was waiting patiently at the table, still clutching her purse. The other residents had dispersed, and the dinner trays had been cleared. Dawn unpacked the salads, drizzled some dressing and handed her mom a plastic fork.

She wanted comfort from the one person who'd always been her confidante. She wanted to say, "*I hate this situation. I feel helpless. What should I do?"* The problem was—her most trusted adviser was now the person who needed her to be strong.

After dinner, they returned to Marie's room. Dawn hung a few clothes in the open cubby, which served as the closet. Cathy's TV was still blaring, now playing a celebrity dancing show.

"How long have you been here?" asked Dawn, trying to strike up a conversation. Cathy nodded pleasantly and returned to watching TV. Dawn couldn't figure out if the woman even understood the question.

While Marie was in the bathroom changing into pajamas, an aide knocked on the door. She handed Dawn an invoice for the twelve-dollar uneaten meal.

They sure are quick to handle the billing, thought Dawn. It occurred to her that with all of the earlier commotion, she'd never asked how much this room was going to cost.

"What's the fee for this room?"

"Are you private pay?" asked the aide.

"I imagine." Marie's inheritance and the sale of the farmhouse had left her in very good shape financially.

"It's four thousand a month, which includes meals and laundry."

Dawn's eyes bulged. Four thousand dollars a month would drain Marie's nest egg in no time. Marie emerged from the bathroom and slipped into the bed, pulling the sheer blanket up to her neck. Dawn sat next to her on the metal folding chair.

"Do you want me to stay until you fall asleep?" she asked.

"That would be nice, dear." Marie adjusted her head on the pillow and shut her eyes. In that instant, Dawn had become the parent, and her mom had become the child.

Chapter 36

The next day, Dawn asked for the morning off from work. She imagined if Dr. Patel had to testify on her behalf now, he wouldn't be so complimentary. She'd taken more unplanned time away in the last few weeks than in her entire career.

She sat on the concrete steps outside of Ben's office waiting for him to arrive. The plush green lawn glistened with dew and the cool morning air hinted of fall. Soon, she'd trade her iced coffee for a hot brew.

Ben parked his Mercedes in the gravel lot and climbed the side stairs. When he was partially up the walk, he stopped and scowled, not hiding his annoyance that Dawn was camped on his stoop.

"Nancy Priest put my mom in an assisted living facility," blurted Dawn. "No warning. She just yanked Mom out of her home. It's the Floyd place. Have you heard of it?"

Ben glanced at his watch. "I don't have much time this morning."

Dawn stood, towering over him. "I need you to make time or tell me to find another lawyer."

Ben didn't respond but passed by Dawn and unlocked the front door. She trailed him into the building. He pointed to the conference room. "I'll meet you in there. Give me just a minute."

Dawn entered the familiar golf-themed conference room. She recalled Ben's vow the last time she and Marie had been there: *I can promise you that this VanBroklin fellow will never become Marie's guardian or conservator.* Ben had been right, but what he'd missed—what they'd all missed—was Nick's real intention. He never wanted the role. He just wanted to take it from Dawn, and he had. Somehow, Nick understood the inner workings of probate court and how to use that knowledge to his advantage.

A few minutes later, Ben rejoined her, juggling a coffee mug, binder and pen. He didn't offer a beverage and Dawn didn't care. Her focus was singular.

"How do we get Mom back home?" she asked.

"Nancy would have to agree."

"Nancy's the one who put her there. What if we remove the guardianship? Go back to court and prove Mom doesn't need one?

We only agreed to this path because we were certain it would be me."

"You've already admitted she needs a guardian, and the doctor and visitor agreed. Those opinions will be nearly impossible to reverse." Ben took a sip of coffee and placed the mug on a coaster, ensuring it was perfectly centered.

"Let's have her testify in front of the judge. He'll see."

"It might just reinforce his decision. Imagine the judge asking Marie a hypothetical question. Suppose he asks what she'd do if she needed eye surgery. How do you think she'd answer?"

"She'd ask me what I thought."

"Exactly. She'd demonstrate that she can't make decisions about her health on her own."

"It's not like that. Asking for my opinion, especially with my medical training, doesn't mean she can't decide on her own."

"It's a risk you'd be taking. And again, you can't go to court one week seeking guardianship and try to reverse it the next, just because you didn't like the outcome."

"Don't you understand?" pleaded Dawn. "She's in a tiny space with a roommate who constantly blares the TV. She can't cook or garden and the food is inedible. I can't leave her like that. I can't. What about having Nancy removed? Can we petition the court for that?"

"What evidence do you have against her? And even if we filed a motion to have Nancy removed, Judge Cain would likely ask Jerry Raven for an alternate guardian. That person may also decide that assisted living is the best option for your mother."

The sound of the front door opening made Dawn turn her head. His receptionist, Donna, passed through the lobby on the way to her desk.

"What do you know about Jerry Raven?" asked Dawn. "He visited our home, talked to my mom, gave every indication he'd recommend me for guardianship, and then he betrayed us. Some days I don't know who I hate more—him or Nick."

Ben stiffened. "I can only assume Jerry did what he thought was best. Why don't you give this some time? If you're still upset by the end of the year, we can talk more." Ben stood and walked toward the door. "Now, I really must go." What he meant was, *Now, you really must go,* and he left the room.

Dawn's phone buzzed with a text from Suzanne. *Do you know when you'll be in? We're swamped.*

She'd planned to swing by the retirement home to check on Marie, but now she couldn't. Instead, she went to the clinic to find a waiting room full of barking dogs, mewling cats and whining people. Suzanne handed her the chart for Hunter Rhodes. "He's back," she said.

Dawn took the chart and entered the exam room where Hunter and Mrs. Rhodes waited expectantly. The dog didn't appear to have any signs of distress.

"He's been bitten," said Mrs. Rhodes, frantically.

Dawn's first thought was a snake, probably a cottonmouth or rattlesnake. The clinic didn't carry the expensive antivenom, so Hunter would have to go to the emergency clinic in Greenville.

"Where was he bitten, and by what?"

"On his neck, by the neighbor's dog. We were out for our morning walk when that beast, Max, charged at Hunter. Before I knew what was happening, they were in a full-fledged brawl. I managed to pull Max off Hunter. He had my poor boy pinned by the neck in the dirt."

"Is Hunter current on his vaccines?" asked Dawn. She slid on a pair of latex gloves and examined the dog's neck, looking for teeth marks.

"Yes, he's been vaccinated. That vicious animal shouldn't be allowed to roam free. It's completely irresponsible."

"Well, I don't see any puncture wounds. I'll clean the area and Dr. Patel might prescribe a round of antibiotics." For the first time, Dawn noticed crescent-shaped red marks on Mrs. Rhodes's forearm. She pointed to the wound and asked, "Did you get bitten?"

"Oh my goodness," replied the woman, unaware of the injury.

"Maybe you'd like to wash your arm?" Dawn motioned to the sink.

"I'll do it at home, once Hunter's been treated."

Mrs. Rhodes was the kind of owner Dawn appreciated—more concerned about her pet than herself, and she didn't think twice about agreeing to any and all treatments, no matter the cost.

"May I?" asked Dawn. She escorted Mrs. Rhodes to the sink and began cleaning her forearm with so much soap that tiny bubbles floated into the air.

"Aren't you going to take care of Hunter?"

"We will, but frankly, I'm more concerned about you. That's a pretty bad puncture. A dog's teeth can act like needles, injecting bacteria into your body, deeper than you can see. When was the last time you had a tetanus shot?"

"Oh, I have no idea. I think I had one as a child."

"The tetanus vaccine is only good for ten years. If you're unsure, I'd recommend you get a booster."

"It's a dog bite," protested Mrs. Rhodes. "I didn't step on a rusty nail."

"You can get tetanus from any deep wound, including a dog bite, especially if it's been contaminated with soil."

Mrs. Rhodes examined her arm. "I appreciate your concern, but it's not necessary, really."

Dawn recalled a video she'd been shown in college as part of her training. A newborn had contracted tetanus through the umbilical cord of his mother due to the unsanitary conditions in their village. The tiny baby arched his back unnaturally and curled his feet. He couldn't open his mouth to cry, but the agony in his muffled whimpers was heart-wrenching.

"Have you ever heard of lockjaw?" asked Dawn.

Mrs. Rhodes tilted her head, confused.

"Lockjaw is the common term for tetanus. If you aren't vaccinated and the toxin gets into your bloodstream, your jaw will seize up. You won't be able to open your mouth to eat or drink. Your stomach will cramp, and your muscles will spasm. Before modern medicine, people with tetanus were believed to be possessed by the devil because their bodies would contort so uncontrollably."

Mrs. Rhodes's eyes filled with fear as Dawn described the horrors of tetanus. Both women could see that the area around the bite was beginning to swell.

"I don't mean to scare you, but that's a pretty bad bite. Why take the risk when you can get a simple booster? Keep washing your arm. I'll be back with some iodine to flush the wound, but you really should see your doctor. I can look after Hunter while you're gone."

The rest of the afternoon was a blur, treating animals in various states of distress. Dr. Patel even called Smita to come in although she was still on maternity leave. At the end of the day, Dawn stayed late to clean the kennel. This chore was typically assigned to the more junior vet techs, but she felt the need to make up for all of the missed work. She was scrubbing an empty cage when Smita entered the room carrying the last drop-off of the day, a puffy Pomeranian.

"I'm sorry you had to come in," said Dawn. "I know it was because of me."

"It's no bother." Smita's warm smile eased Dawn's guilt. "I've spent so much time with the baby that I almost put a diaper on this little guy."

They laughed, then Smita's expression became more solemn. "Seriously, how are things with you?"

"Not good. Nick did the worst thing possible. He went after my mom."

"Neil told me. He also told me about the bad review of the clinic."

"There's more. He damn near ran me over on his motorcycle, and he crept behind me at the grocery store. I thought once I lost in court, he'd stop, but he hasn't."

"Did you file the restraining order?"

"I tried, but the sheriff couldn't serve it without his exact address. No one can seem to find it. Nothing is in his name."

"Can I help?"

"Nick is crazy. Best you don't get involved. Besides, I've inconvenienced you enough."

"I've dealt with crazy before," Smita reminded her. "But seriously, you'll find a way to file the restraining order? Promise me?"

"I promise, but I suspect he'll find a way to harass me. Like with the motorcycle, he knocked me over, and I can't prove it was him. How am I supposed to protect myself?"

"Here," said Smita, reaching forward. "Hand me your phone."

Chapter 37

Around 7:00 p.m., Dawn finished cleaning the last cage. She peeled off her yellow plastic gloves and tossed them in the sink. Once the water was hot and soapy, she washed her hands and arms up to her sleeves.

The clinic was eerily quiet, with all of the humans gone and the animals asleep. Earlier, while she'd been cleaning the cages, the cacophony of guttural woofs and shrill whines was enough to make her ears ring. Eventually, the yelps turned to quiet whimpers and faded off.

Smita had offered to stay late so they could walk out together, but Dawn refused. There was no way she'd allow her problems to deprive an innocent baby of time with his mother, especially when Smita's maternity leave was coming to an end.

As Dawn approached the back door, she hesitated. Ever since Nick had shown his true colors, Alex had been accompanying her outside. Now, she wished Smita had stayed. Instead, she faced a solitary walk to her Jeep. Worse, the back of the clinic didn't have any windows, so she had no way of knowing if Nick was lurking outside.

Dawn went to the medicine cabinet, selected an eighteen-gauge syringe and gripped it like a knife. She realized the insanity of arming herself with a giant needle, but it was the only weapon she had. She slowly cracked the back door and scanned the parking lot. All was quiet. Her Jeep was the only vehicle in sight. She took a cautious step forward, as if she were placing her foot in quicksand. Since Nick's appearance at the grocery store, she feared he'd pop up like a jack-in-the-box. He'd turned a mindless activity, walking to her Jeep, into a moment of dread.

When she was about ten feet from her Jeep, she knelt and looked under the running board. The far side was clear. She slowly approached the rear and peered into the back seat. Dawn had seen too many thriller movies where the killer sprang from behind and wrapped a noose around the neck of the unwary driver. Once certain the coast was clear, she clicked the key fob to unlock the door, jumped inside and quickly locked the doors behind her.

As she drove home, the sky morphed from streaks of amber to

specks of gray. The sun set behind the trees, extinguishing the last bit of daylight. Dawn's phone beeped. She glanced at the screen. A peculiar message appeared: *AirTag Found Moving with You. The location of this AirTag can be seen by the owner.*

By the time Dawn arrived home, the night sky had turned pitch black. The half-moon cast light across the lawn, onto the shrubs and across the porch. She surveyed the path to the front door, confirming all was clear, and dashed inside.

In the security of her home, Dawn googled "AirTag" and learned that the Apple device was designed to track lost objects like keys. The location of the missing item would be displayed on the owner's iPhone. If, however, someone else's AirTag "found its way" into her stuff, her iPhone would send an alert. She read that the "errant AirTag" would eventually start playing a sound to identify its location.

Dawn went outside to inspect her Jeep. A beeping sound like Morse code was coming from the back of the vehicle. She knelt by the spare tire to take a closer look. A circular device about the size of a quarter was stuck to the undercarriage. It was so small, she would've never noticed it had it not been pinging. She pried it loose with her fingernail and inspected the tiny spy device. The melody, which was four urgent, repeating beeps, continued to play.

That's how he knew I was at the grocery store, she surmised.

Back inside, Dawn continued her research, learning it could take anywhere from a few hours to a few days for the alert to trigger. Apple provided instructions on how to electronically disable the AirTag, but Dawn preferred a simpler suggestion found on YouTube—to wrap it in aluminum foil. She took the little device to the kitchen, tore a sheet of silver foil and triple-wrapped it. The beeping stopped. She set the device on the counter with disdain, as if it were a cockroach infesting her home.

Reading further, Dawn learned there was no way for her to trace the owner. Only law enforcement had that capability by directly contacting Apple with the serial number. It didn't matter. She knew who'd placed it, but concrete proof would bolster her argument in the restraining order.

Dawn looked at the time—she'd wasted forty-five minutes with this unplanned investigation. She hurried to Marie's duplex and packed some clothes, shoes and a few pictures. Although Nancy had promised to bring more things over, her follow-through was clearly lacking. That reality is what Judge Cain had completely missed—family was always going to do more.

By the time Dawn arrived at the Floyd Retirement Home, it was nearly 8:30 p.m. The dining area was deserted. An aide who was manning the front desk didn't bother to look up as Dawn passed by and headed down the hall. Unlike her Crocs that squeaked against the linoleum floor, the rubber soles of her tennis shoes seemed to stick with each step.

When she arrived at her mom's room, both Marie and Cathy were sleeping. At home, Marie didn't go to bed until around 10:00 p.m., sometimes later. How odd that she was already down for the night. Dawn quietly hung the clothes and put the shoes at the bottom of the cubby. She placed three photos on the nightstand. One was of Dawn's college graduation. She was wearing a shiny black cap and gown with an orange sash, denoting her honors status. Another was taken of her parents just after they'd married. They were seated side by side with her dad's arm protectively around her mom's back. The last picture was her mom's favorite. Her dad was sitting on the tractor at the farmhouse, beaming with pride.

Not wanting to wake Marie, Dawn blew her a kiss and tiptoed out of the room. Back at the front desk, Dawn approached the young aide. "Hi, I'm Dawn. Marie Smith is my mother. I just wanted to ask how she was today."

"Which room is she in?" the girl asked.

"112." Dawn's concern rose. If this aide was supposed to be taking care of Marie, shouldn't she already know the room number?

The girl looked at her computer screen. "I don't see anything reported."

"I'm sorry. I didn't mean if anything was reported, but just how she's doing in general. This was her first day here."

The girl shrugged. "If there's a problem, it gets noted on her chart."

Chapter 38

At the clinic the next day, Kelly pulled Dawn aside. "You rushed out so fast yesterday. What's going on with Marie?"

"The guardian put her in a facility."

Kelly's mouth gaped. "She can do that?"

"Apparently so. She moved Mom to the Floyd Retirement Home."

"Oh no, are you aware of the rumors about that place?"

Dawn's brow creased as she shook her head.

"Let's just say I've heard they're liberal with the medications. Same way we sedate the animals to keep them calm."

Dawn recalled the previous night, with her mom and Cathy sleeping so peacefully. Maybe *peacefully drugged* was the better description. "Every time I think it can't get any worse, it does."

"Just check her meds, okay?" suggested Kelly.

"I will. Hey, I hate to ask, but can you cover for me again this afternoon? I need to leave early."

"Whatever you need. Marie comes first."

Dawn didn't share that she wasn't going to Floyd. She was heading back to Nick's place to get his exact apartment number.

That afternoon, she parked outside his complex and waited, not particularly concerned if he saw her. Maybe it would freak him out a little—the hunter being stalked by his prey. No matter what, she wasn't leaving without the information to complete the restraining order application.

A boy was playing outside in the gravel lot. He was squatting, stacking rocks into small towers. Whitish-gray dust covered his knees and palms. Upon a closer look, Dawn recognized this boy. It was Matthias Santos.

"Hi there," she said, as she approached.

He looked up, not the least bit afraid of a stranger.

"I'm looking for Nick. Do you know which apartment is his?"

Matthias pointed to the building behind them without taking his eyes off his rock castle.

"Do you know which number?" she clarified.

"Four one eight."

"Where's your mom?"

"At work."

Dawn remembered Maribel Santos testifying that she worked at the Quick Stop. She'd seen it when she and Kelly were walking to get dinner the night of the flat tire.

"Who's watching after you?" she asked.

The boy shrugged.

Dawn's nostrils flared. Not only had Maribel Santos lied under oath, but she was leaving her young son unattended. "I'm going to visit your mom right now. Would you like to come with me?"

He shrugged again.

"You can ride in my Jeep." Dawn pointed to her vehicle, and his eyes lit up.

They drove a few blocks to the Quick Stop. One entrance was blocked with an orange construction cone, marking a huge pothole. Dawn pulled into the other entrance and parked next to the building. Turning to Matthias, she said, "Why don't you wait here for a minute and then I'll come get you. I'll bring you a candy bar. What's your favorite?"

"Snickers," he cheered, clapping his hands. Particles of whitish-gray dust plumed in the air.

Dawn locked the Jeep behind her, entered the convenience store and found Maribel Santos behind the cash register. The store was empty except for the two women.

"Do you remember me?" asked Dawn. Her voice was assertive, on the verge of aggressive.

It took a second, but Maribel's look of confusion turned to recognition. "What do you want?"

"Two things." Dawn slammed her keys onto the counter. "First, why did you lie in court?"

"I didn't lie." Maribel's demeanor remained surprisingly calm, likely a survival tactic from dealing with the sketchy clientele.

"You testified that Nick babysits Matthias."

"He does."

"Then why did you tell me that you didn't know Nick? I passed you on the stairs, remember? I showed you his photo, and you said you didn't know him."

"Oh, that. Nick warned me that if his sister ever came looking for him, she was bad news. He said she was a tall blonde. I thought you were her."

"You thought I was Nick's sister?" repeated Dawn.

"You fit the description."

"So, you're telling me that Nick actually babysits Matthias?"

Maribel nodded. "On weekends."

"You pay him?"

"No. He does it for free, but I cook for him sometimes."

Dawn couldn't imagine Nick looking after a child or this clueless mother allowing it. "That leads to my second question. Who's watching your kid now?"

"He's at home."

"No, he was playing outside, ripe for any stranger to snatch. All I had to do was offer him a ride in my cool Jeep and he hopped right in." Dawn pointed to Matthias in the passenger seat. "Lucky for you, I brought him here instead of selling him to the highest bidder."

Maribel's eyes widened. "He was supposed to stay inside."

"He's a child. Too young to be left alone," said Dawn. Then she mumbled to herself, "How is it that a mother like this gets to keep her kid, but I lose guardianship of my mom?" She faced Maribel again. "I'm going to get him and bring him inside. You are going to give him a Snickers and keep him with you until you go home. And if I ever find him outside alone again, I'm reporting you to Child Protective Services. Is that clear?"

Maribel nodded dutifully.

"One more thing," said Dawn. "What else did Nick tell you about his sister?"

"Just that she lives overseas but sometimes comes home. He said she was trouble and if she tried to find him, not to tell her anything."

"Did he tell you her name?"

"I don't remember."

"Well, try."

"Maybe Sofia."

"Sophie," interjected Dawn, suddenly remembering the name Amanda Graham had mentioned. She grabbed her keys and fetched Matthias. Inside the store, Dawn knelt, facing him at eye level. "Look, buddy, can you do me a favor?"

He nodded.

"Make sure you stay with your mom. Don't go outside by yourself anymore, okay?"

"Why?" he asked.

Dawn wanted to say, *Because there are monsters like Nick VanBroklin in this world.* But apparently, Nick was decent to this kid.

Before leaving the Quick Stop parking lot, Dawn looked up "Sophie VanBroklin" on social media. The only thing that popped up was a Facebook page for a Boxer named Sophie. She tried Sophie Graham. Still nothing. Then she went to Amanda Graham's page and looked at her friends—there was a Sophie Brown. A blonde in army fatigues had a profile, although none of her information was public. Even her messenger feature was blocked. With no other choice, Dawn sent her a friend request and hoped she'd accept.

Chapter 39

Because Dawn had learned Nick's apartment number from Matthias, she didn't have to continue her stakeout. Instead, she headed to Floyd to inquire about her mom's medications. She stopped at the front nurses' station to find a different aide manning the desk.

"Hi, I'm Dawn Smith. My mom is Marie Smith, in Room 112. I'd like to get a copy of her medications, please."

"You'll have to ask the records department," said the aide.

"How do I go about doing that?"

The girl pointed to double doors behind her. "At the main office, but you'll have to hurry. They close at five."

Dawn pushed through the doors, hurried down the corridor and found her way to the main office. A sign pointed to the records department, which was nothing more than a large room lined with tan filing cabinets. A middle-aged woman sat behind a desk, sorting papers into several stacks. She looked up, somewhat startled, when Dawn knocked on the open door.

"May I help you?" she asked.

"I was told to come here to get medical records for Marie Smith. I'd like to know if her medications have changed."

"Are you a doctor?" the woman asked, eyeing Dawn's scrubs.

"No, I'm her daughter."

The woman pressed her lips together and glanced at the clock. It was 4:45 p.m.

Although Dawn didn't speak, she thought, *I dare you to tell me that you can't pull records in fifteen minutes.* Her resolve must've shown as the woman acquiesced.

"What's your mother's name?"

"Marie P. Smith."

The woman clacked on her keyboard and squinted at the computer screen. "Let's see. Yes, I found her, but she only arrived Monday?"

"That's right. I want to see if her medications have changed since she's been here."

"And your name is—"

"Dawn Smith, her daughter."

"The note in the file says the only person authorized to receive medical information about Marie Smith is Nancy Priest."

"I'm her *daughter*," repeated Dawn.

"I'm sorry, but I'm not allowed to give you any information."

"You've got to be kidding."

"I suggest you take that up with Mrs. Priest."

Dawn thought she detected a hint of glee in the woman's voice at finding a reason to be uncooperative. "I have a court order that allows me access to my mother's medical information," she countered.

"You'll need to talk to the head nurse. If she approves the release of the records, I can provide them to you, but she'll have to approve it first."

"And where will I find the head nurse?"

The woman paused, as if she was going to withhold that information. Dawn waited. The silence between them thickened.

"Katie Manning's office is up the hall, but she's probably gone by now."

Dawn marched up the corridor, reading the nameplates until she found the one for Katie Manning. The office door was shut, and no one answered when she knocked. She returned to the records office, only to find that door also closed and locked.

Back in the residential area, Marie was in the dining room, sitting with Cathy and another resident. The menu was a fried chicken leg, canned carrots, a roll and rainbow-colored Jell-O. Dawn couldn't help but think how different the meal would look if Marie had made it: the chicken would've been white meat and baked, the carrots would've come fresh from her garden and the dessert would've been a homemade work of art.

As she approached, the new tablemate looked up, "Are you her daughter?" she asked. Like Marie, this woman seemed too young and alert to be in assisted living.

"Yes, I'm Dawn Smith."

"I'm Susan Givens. I'm down the hall from your mama and Cathy. Are you from Laurel?"

Dawn nodded.

"I'm not from South Carolina," said Susan. Her voice had the rasp of someone with a decades-old, pack-a-day habit. "I was born in Tennessee. We moved here for my husband's job but ended up staying. My children are still back there. They visit when they can."

As Susan spoke, the left side of her face didn't move. Her left arm remained pinned at her side while she used her right arm to feed herself. Dawn realized Susan's affliction was likely the aftereffects of a stroke. The woman continued to share her life story about growing up in Tennessee and how she lost her husband. Dawn tried to politely listen, but she was distracted by her mother's appearance. In just a few short days, something had changed. Marie's face seemed bloated, and the rims of her eyes were bloodshot. Normally, Marie would've engaged in the conversation, but she remained uncharacteristically silent, almost introverted.

"Mom, you and Dad went to Tennessee, remember, to see Graceland?"

"We did?" asked Marie.

Seeing the family home of Elvis had been one of Marie's favorite trips. How could she not remember?

An aide approached the table. "You want a supper ticket?"

"No thanks." Dawn wasn't going to pay twelve dollars just to visit with her mom. They were already paying for Marie's meal, which she wasn't eating. Dawn nudged the plate forward. "Don't you want to try some of your dinner?"

Marie shook her head. Susan continued to reminisce about happier times in Tennessee, and Cathy ate quietly, never saying a word.

Dawn questioned how she'd tolerate long days at the clinic, followed by depressing evenings at this place. "Mom, do you mind if I head out? I have some things I need to take care of."

"Will I see you tomorrow?" Marie's weary eyes flashed with worry.

"Yes, I'll come by after work." Dawn stood and kissed her mom on the forehead. She started to leave but had second thoughts. Maybe she should stay through dinner to ensure Marie had something to eat. But no matter what time she left, she'd always feel like it was too soon. She'd always feel like she was abandoning her mom. Today, however, she couldn't bear the place a moment longer.

Back home, the dark bay window of Marie's duplex added to Dawn's depression. In the past, the kitchen light would've been on. Dawn would've popped inside for a quick chat or cup of tea. Now, the still, somber building looked as if the life had been drained from it. Dawn slammed her fists into the steering wheel and screamed. She closed her eyes and took a deep breath. Somehow, she had to find a way to end this nightmare.

Inside, Dawn searched for Katie Manning's contact information on the Floyd website and emailed a copy of the court order with a request for her mother's medications. She printed a copy of the order and tucked it in her bag, anticipating she'd be challenged again.

She was just closing her laptop when she heard footsteps outside. Someone was mounting the stairs. She sat motionless and listened intently. The footsteps stopped at her front door. Dawn waited. A normal person would knock or ring the bell, but there was nothing—only silence.

Chapter 40

Dawn's heart raced. She'd only been home for a few minutes. How did Nick know she was there? Was he watching her place? Had he followed her from Floyd? A thought occurred to her—just because she'd removed one tracking device didn't mean he hadn't placed another. She tiptoed to her utensil drawer and retrieved a large, serrated knife. Glancing at the back sliding glass door, she confirmed it was locked. Her hands shook as she opened the security camera on her phone, which would give her a view of the front porch.

On the small screen, Dawn made out the back of someone's head, but this person had long blonde hair and was dressed in tight pink yoga pants and a matching halter top. It was Cindy, her neighbor. Dawn breathed a sigh of relief. But why was Cindy just standing there with her back to the door? Something was off.

"Cindy, are you okay?" yelled Dawn, through the closed door.

"I need help!" The girl shouted back in a squeaky voice.

Dawn swallowed hard. Nick had pursued Regan at the bar. Had he switched from targeting her coworker to her neighbor? Was he in the yard, out of view of the camera? Was he threatening her in some way, pointing a gun at her?

Only then did Dawn notice that Cindy was tugging on a rope that bound her wrists. Dawn quickly exited the security camera app and opened her phone. "I'm calling 911. Tell him the police will be here any minute."

There was no reply.

"Cindy, did you hear me?" Dawn shouted. "Tell him I'm calling the police."

Nick was clearly using Cindy as bait. He'd probably charmed her, just as he'd captivated Dawn in the early days. But she couldn't open the door to save her friend. That was exactly what he wanted her to do. Dawn frantically began to punch the numbers on her phone. Before she could complete the call, Cindy cried out again.

"He's too strong for me, Dawn. I need your help."

Cindy was too petite to fend off Nick, and the police couldn't arrive fast enough. Dawn had no choice. She reached for the deadbolt and hesitated, knowing she was playing right into his hands. Dawn twisted the bolt, cracked the door and peered outside.

Cindy was now crouched on the porch, tugging a bright yellow workout band that was wrapped around her wrists. The band was stretched taut and disappeared below the height of the shrubs. Cindy's fingers grasped the rubber as she resisted the force at the other end. Dawn leapt to her side and attempted to cut the band with her knife.

"What are you doing?" questioned Cindy. "Don't set him free."

Dawn hesitated. Why would Cindy resist her help? Then she saw what was on the other end of the band. Nick wasn't tugging against them. Tied by the neck was a blonde Labrador. The culprit behind Cindy's cries for help was a dog.

Dawn's shoulders pitched forward. The adrenaline that had been pumping through her blood dissipated like a switch that had suddenly been flipped off. Prior to Nick's harassment, Dawn would've never assumed she or her friends were in danger. Now, she was on constant alert.

"You got a dog?" she asked.

Cindy shook her head. "No, I found him eating Snowball's food. He doesn't have a collar. I haven't seen any missing dog posters around, have you?"

Dawn hadn't spotted any lost pet signs in the neighborhood, something she would've noticed. She eyed the dog to gauge his behavior. Although he was being stubborn about being dragged by the neck, he wasn't showing any signs of aggression.

"What should I do with him?" asked Cindy.

"Call the humane society." Dawn's response was unusually blunt. With her profession, she was routinely expected to help strays, but today was not the day she'd agree to be the protector of all things four-legged.

"I thought about that, but what if they're overcrowded? What if they have to put him down? I don't want that on my conscience, but I can't keep him, either. Snowball is so freaked out, she won't eat."

"What do you want from me?" asked Dawn, although she already knew the answer.

"Could you keep him, just for a day or two while I try to find his owner? I'll put up signs and post on our neighborhood Facebook group. He has to belong to someone."

Dawn kneeled, and the lab gingerly walked up the steps to her—no tugging required. She rubbed his well-groomed coat and examined his teeth. When she extended her hand and said, "Shake," he obediently raised a paw.

"Somebody's got to be missing you," she concluded.

"Right?" agreed Cindy. "I promise I'll find his owner if you'll just keep him while I look."

Maybe Cindy caught her at a weak moment, or the emptiness of her mother's place had her longing for company, but whatever the reason, Dawn surprised herself and agreed. "Okay, but only for a few days."

Cindy jumped up and down with excitement. Her thin body looked like a pink pogo stick. "Oh, thank you. I'll get started looking right now. Do you need some food for him? He already ate a whole bowl of Snowball's cat food, but I can give you some more."

"No thanks. I'll get some at the clinic, and I'll check if he's chipped."

Dawn removed the makeshift leash and returned it to Cindy. Now free, the Labrador walked straight into Dawn's home and jumped on the couch as if he'd lived there all of his life.

"Be my guest, Yellow Dog," she said. Whether she realized it or not, the impersonal name allowed her to keep some distance. The last thing she needed was to fall in love with this furball only to have his owner show up and take him away.

Dawn grabbed a cold beer and sat next to the dog. He stood, stepped onto her lap and plopped down like a puppy. Then he nudged his head under her hand, forcing her to pet him. Later that evening, when she showered, he guarded the bathroom door. And when she slept, he stayed at the foot of the bed throughout the night.

The next morning, Dawn brought Yellow Dog to the clinic to check if he'd been microchipped. She waved the scanner between his shoulder blades, but it didn't alert. Thinking the rice-sized chip could have migrated, she scanned down each front leg. If he'd been tagged, the scanner would pick up the radio waves emitted by the chip and an identification number would be displayed. However, when the device finally beeped, a digital message appeared: *No Tag Found*.

In Dawn's experience, owners often forgot to update their information, especially when they moved, but with Yellow Dog, he'd never been chipped. The only hope for finding his home would be the outreach Cindy had promised to do.

Dawn poured a heaping bowl of dry food for Yellow Dog, which he gobbled down. After eating the last morsel, he stared at her with begging eyes as if she'd never fed him at all.

When Kelly arrived, she ditched her keys and phone on the break room table and knelt next to him. "He's gorgeous," she cooed. Noticing the scanner, she asked, "Is he lost?"

"Appears to be. He showed up at my neighbor's place. Doesn't have a chip."

Kelly tried several commands: *Sit. Shake. Speak.* Yellow Dog happily performed each one. Regan and Alex arrived through the back door. Alex was carrying a box of glazed donuts and a four-pack of coffee.

"One pumpkin spice latte for cleaning the kennel the other night," he said, as he offered the cup to Dawn. Yellow Dog intercepted Alex's advance, wedged his body in front of the girls and growled, showing his teeth. Alex instinctively withdrew his hand and took a step back.

"I'd say he's a good judge of character," joked Regan.

Dawn hadn't seen any signs of hostility from Yellow Dog, but given his aggression toward Alex, she was forced to lock him in the kennel until she could take him home at lunchtime. On the drive, she gave the Floyd head nurse a call.

"Yes, I received your request," Katie Manning confirmed. "I'll need to send you a form to complete and return."

"More red tape," muttered Dawn. "And once I return the form, how long before I receive the information?"

"Up to thirty days."

"You've got to be kidding. All I want is a simple list of my mom's medications. I'm also a healthcare professional, and I can assure you it would take me less than five minutes to pull her medications."

"I'm just relaying our policy, ma'am."

"What if I come to your records room? I can pull the file myself to expedite the process."

"That violates HIPPA," said the nurse. "If you work in healthcare, I would think you'd know that."

Dawn clenched her teeth at the insult. She thought about threatening this nurse with a lawsuit for violating the judge's orders but held her tongue. Marie was at the mercy of these people, so for now, she had to play nice. Once home, she begrudgingly filled out the records request form and while at her computer, completed a new restraining order request with Nick's full address.

Chapter 41

After her last appointment, Dawn headed to Floyd. Several residents were in the dining hall, including Cathy and Susan, but Marie was nowhere to be found. Dawn hurried to her mother's room. Marie was lying in bed, still in her pajamas. Her face was puffy, and the rims of her eyes were still red. Dawn questioned whether something in the facility was causing Marie to have an allergic reaction, or if the change in her appearance was due to new medications.

"Mom, why aren't you having dinner?"

"Oh honey, I'm so glad you're here. I can't seem to find my glasses."

Dawn glanced at the nightstand, the place where Marie always kept her glasses. In the morning, the first thing Marie would do was to reach for her glasses and reclaim her vision.

"Did you put them on the nightstand?" asked Dawn.

"I thought so." Marie reached to the right, groping the table as she continued to stare forward.

"Have you been in bed all day?" asked Dawn.

Marie nodded.

"And nobody helped you?" Dawn's voice rose. She rifled through the drawers of the nightstand and searched under the bed. Dawn checked the pockets of every article of clothing in the cubby and emptied the dresser—underwear, socks, pajamas and books. In the bathroom, she searched the medicine cabinet which contained Marie's toiletries, but the glasses seemed to have disappeared into thin air. Returning to Marie's bedside, she asked, "You have a spare pair, don't you?"

"At home. In my bathroom drawer."

"Okay, I'll go get them."

On her way out, Dawn stopped by the front desk. A middle-aged aide was talking on the phone. Dawn waited, not intending to eavesdrop, but she could hear the woman was on a personal call, something about dinner and leftovers. When the woman finally hung up, she approached the desk.

"Excuse me," she said. "I'm Dawn Smith, Marie Smith's daughter. I was just in her room, and it appears her glasses have been lost.

I'm not sure how. I've looked everywhere. She's legally blind without them."

The woman stared back blankly.

"Well, do you know where they could be?" asked Dawn. "She's been in bed all day because she couldn't see to get up."

"Did you look in the bathroom?"

"Of course. They aren't there."

"I don't know what to tell you." The woman shrugged.

"Has anyone tried to help her? Has she even eaten today?"

"I came on at three, so I don't know about earlier."

"Do you people communicate with each other?" Dawn's tone revealed her exasperation. "You have a woman who cannot see without her glasses. She's been left helpless in bed all day and you're just sitting here?"

The woman leaned back and crossed her arms. "The assisted living residents need to be able to get to meals on their own. If she needs to be moved to skilled nursing—"

"She doesn't need skilled nursing," Dawn interrupted, balling her fists in frustration. "She needs her damn glasses."

Dawn marched back to her mother's room to make one more pass, including looking on Cathy's side. Still, she came up empty. On the nightstand, she noticed one of Marie's framed photos was turned backward, facing the wall. Dawn picked up her graduation photo and faced it forward, figuring her mom must've moved it by accident while searching for her glasses.

On the drive home, Dawn called Nancy Priest. "I was just over at Floyd and my mom's glasses have been lost. In all the time she lived at home, that *never* happened. She hasn't been at that place a week and her glasses have already disappeared."

There was no response.

"On top of that, they left her in bed all day. No one is helping her. Do you know their staff-to-resident ratio? It's over twenty to one. When I took care of her, she had my full attention. Tell me how this current setup is better than her being at home with me?"

"Was your mother injured?" asked Nancy.

"What's that got to do with anything?"

"I'm asking if she was harmed."

"She hasn't eaten."

"Do you know that for a fact?" countered Nancy.

"I'm going home to get her spare glasses. Then I'm going to ensure she's had dinner. Then I'm going to order a few more pairs for when this inevitably happens again. As her guardian, what exactly are you going to do?"

Nancy spoke in a beleaguered tone, as if she were being unduly burdened. "I will go by and check on Marie in the morning."

"Well, luckily she has me tonight." Dawn hung up, so furious she was shaking. As she stepped onto her porch, she heard barking.

"I almost forgot about you," she said out loud. Yellow Dog greeted her at the door. She tried to fasten his leash, but he skirted back and forth several times before she could secure it. Outside, Dawn waited for Yellow Dog to relieve himself. She bagged his poop and tossed it in the garbage bin. When she tugged his leash to go back inside, he resisted, thrashing his head about.

"Come on," she pleaded. "Don't you be difficult, too." She refilled his food and water, petted his head a few times and retrieved Marie's spare glasses.

When Dawn returned, her mom was still in bed. "I found your spares," she said. "I thought about something. We didn't check your bed. Could your glasses be under your covers?"

Dawn pulled back the blanket and was hit with a familiar odor, one she'd just dealt with thanks to Yellow Dog. Her mother's light blue pants had a dark stain around the crotch that had leaked onto the sheets.

"I'm sorry," said Marie. "I was afraid to—"

"It's okay, Mom." Dawn interrupted. "Let's get you changed."

With her spare glasses, Marie was able to get out of bed and walk to the bathroom. Dawn handed her a fresh set of clothes and waited while her mother cleaned up and changed. The odor permeated the room.

"Why don't you go find the others in the dining room?" suggested Dawn. "I'll be there in just a minute."

Once Marie had left, Dawn stripped the soiled sheets. Given the number of dirty diapers Marie had changed for her, she didn't mind. And she hadn't been bothered by picking up after Yellow Dog earlier. He was good company. Still, if she had to summarize the day, one word did the trick—shit.

Chapter 42

The next morning, Dawn was stationed next to Suzanne at the front desk, refilling medications. Because of her many absences, she was no longer allowed first choice of assignments but relegated to the more expendable tasks. She didn't like it, but she understood.

Her phone rang—it was Nancy Priest.

Nice of you to finally show up, she thought. *After I already got the spare glasses, served dinner and found housekeeping for clean sheets.*

"I've just been to the Floyd home," said Nancy. "And I received some alarming news."

Dawn's heart leapt into her throat. She pictured a team of doctors and nurses surrounding her mom's bed, frantically performing CPR. "What's happened?"

"One of the staff said you cussed her out. Look, I know you don't like this situation, but I can't have you harassing the staff."

Dawn felt as if her brain had short-circuited. Here she was bracing for unspeakable news about her mom and Nancy was reproaching her.

"What are you talking about?" she asked.

"Are you denying the incident occurred?" accused Nancy.

Dawn mentally inventoried her interactions from the previous day, unable to recall any instance of *cussing someone out.* The woman in housekeeping had been nothing but gracious, providing clean sheets upon request. The aide at the front desk had been useless. Yes, Dawn had raised her voice, but she hadn't cussed at her. She tried to recall exactly what she'd said. The conversation had been so insignificant. She remembered saying that her mother needed her damn glasses. She'd said the word *damn,* a far cry from cussing someone out.

"Are you denying that you swore at one of the staff?" repeated Nancy.

"I didn't swear at anyone."

"The report I received was that you cussed and screamed at one of the aides."

Dawn couldn't believe she was having this conversation. What right did Nancy have to scold her, especially when she was mistaken? Rather than dignify the allegation with a response, she countered with her own questions. "Have you checked on my mom? Did you ensure she still has her glasses and has eaten breakfast?"

"Your mother is doing fine and displaying model behavior. *She's* not one having outbursts and upsetting the staff. Look, if I hear another report like this, I'm going to have to restrict your visits."

"Restrict my visits?" Dawn repeated with indignation. How dare Nancy make such a threat. Dawn pulled up a copy of Judge Cain's order and read it aloud. "Item number seven of the court order states: *There shall be no restrictions on contact or visitation by either petitioner or Dawn Smith with Mrs. Marie P. Smith unless limited or restricted by the treating physician or other health care provider."* She paused for effect, then added, "You do not have the authority to restrict my visits."

"I'm sure if I speak to Dr. Edwards and explain the situation, he'll agree that your disruption of the peaceful environment is not good for your mother."

"Her doctor is Ron Landis."

"No, now that she's at the Floyd home, I changed her primary care physician to Dr. Edwards. He sees all the patients there, and he has final say on who's allowed to visit your mother."

Dawn was stunned. The threat was veiled but real. Up to that point, she still believed she had a chance of freeing her mom. For the first time, she was beginning to understand that her mother had been sucked into a legal machine whose gears were grinding tighter every day.

"Then I'd like to speak to Dr. Edwards. Item six of the court order states: *Dawn Smith shall have full access to all medical records of her mother, Mrs. Marie P. Smith*. I'd like him to provide a list of her current medications."

"Why?" asked Nancy.

"I've always managed her meds and will continue to monitor them, especially with a new doctor involved. And I'd like that list before the end of the day. Is that going to be a problem?"

Dawn couldn't tell if Nancy's huff was a rebuke or an agreement. The line went dead. Nancy had the upper hand legally, but Dawn still believed her own position was stronger. It was moral, familial and just plain right.

That evening, Yellow Dog greeted her at the door, ready to go outside. As Dawn walked him around the neighborhood, she kept her eyes peeled for the green Kawasaki. She dared Nick to mess with her today. Between her foul mood and Yellow Dog's protective nature, Nick would be in for a surprise. She stopped by her neighbor's place to see if anyone had responded to the posting about the lost dog. Cindy shared that people were commenting on how handsome he was, but no one was claiming ownership. Back at home, Dawn saw a new message from Nancy.

What's that woman going to accuse me of now? she thought.

To her surprise, Nancy had sent over Marie's medications. There was no salutation or signature, just the PDF file likely provided by Dr. Edwards. With Yellow Dog stationed at her feet, Dawn sat at the kitchen table and read through the list. She recognized her mother's regular meds but there were two new ones: Zolpidem and Namenda. She knew Zolpidem. Z-drugs like Zolpidem, commonly called Ambien, and Zaleplon were prescribed to aid with sleep. Dawn googled Namenda, as it was unknown to her. She learned it was used to treat mild to severe dementia of the Alzheimer's type. The drug didn't claim to cure Alzheimer's disease but was advertised to improve memory, awareness and the ability to perform daily functions.

My mom doesn't have Alzheimer's, she thought. *Why are they giving her this?*

Next, she read the long list of side effects: nausea, vomiting, diarrhea, excessive urination, dizziness, lethargy, unusual weakness, anxiety, loss of appetite, weight loss, joint pain, bloating, skin rash and redness or swelling around the eyes.

"Oh my gosh," she exclaimed. Dawn pictured Marie's bloated face and red eyes. "It's this drug."

Yellow Dog lifted his head at the outburst and readjusted himself at her feet. Not finding a comfortable position, he hoisted himself onto all fours and headed to the couch.

Dawn read on to discover the recommended starting dose was seven milligrams, once a day. Her mom was on the maximum dose, twenty-eight milligrams. And the cost was twenty dollars a pill, which would be a six-hundred-dollar bill at the end of the month.

This is insane, she thought. *They are needlessly drugging my mom and making a ton of money doing so.*

Chapter 43

On Saturday morning, Dawn drove to a nearby park with Yellow Dog for her weekend run. She didn't want to risk another encounter with Nick, especially since he knew her routine. Here again, he was disrupting her life. She was ready to have her day in court, to secure the restraining order and force him to keep his distance.

As she ran along the nature trail, Yellow Dog trotted beside her, panting happily. Partway through the first loop, her music was interrupted by an incoming Facebook message. The text simply stated: *Do I know you?* It was from Sophie Brown.

Dawn slowed to a walk and replied. *If your brother is Nick VanBroklin, I'd appreciate talking to you.*

Sophie responded. *I can video call you on WhatsApp. What's your number?*

Not only had Dawn found Nick's sister, but it appeared the woman was willing to talk. Dawn sat on a nearby bench and texted her number. A slight autumn breeze tousled a loose strand of her hair against her cheek. She refastened her ponytail and waited.

When the video call came in, Dawn could've been looking in the mirror, except that her own face was flush from exercise. Sophie was blonde, in her late twenties and also wore her hair up. Dawn couldn't tell where Sophie was—the backdrop was a nondescript white wall and there was no background noise.

"Thanks for calling me," said Dawn.

"How do you know my brother?" asked Sophie.

"We dated for a few weeks. It was a bad breakup." Dawn recalled her meeting with Amanda Graham and instantly regretted using the same term: *bad breakup.* There was a possibility Sophie would be just as protective of Nick. Her only clue that this conversation might take a different turn had come from Maribel. Nick had warned his neighbor to steer clear of his sister, leading Dawn to believe there was acrimony between them.

"What's he done to you?" asked Sophie.

The question was so blunt that it took Dawn by surprise. Feeling she could be forthright, Dawn replied. "He's harassing me, posting bad reviews at work and sharing private photos."

"Does he know your family?" the girl asked.

"Yes, why?"

"You need to protect them. Nick won't stop with just you. He'll target the person you care about most and rip them away from you."

The sleeves of Dawn's thin pullover, damp with sweat, clung to her body, sending chills down her arms. She swallowed hard, wishing she'd talked to Sophie much sooner. "Why does he do this?"

Nick's sister shrugged. "Because he can. Because he's a sadist. Who knows? He ruined my marriage."

"How?" The question came out of Dawn's mouth before she could consider if it was too personal.

"I met my husband, Matt, when I was stationed at Fort Jackson. I was having dinner by myself. Matt and his brother, Joel, were sitting one table over. They both started flirting with me. Joel was a real charmer and probably used to getting the girl, but Matt was different. I could tell he had a real interest in me. I think they were both shocked when I chose to go out with Matt, not Joel. We dated for a few months before I was sent overseas and during my first trip home, we decided to get married.

"While I was deployed again, Nick befriended Matt. I didn't know how much time they were spending together, or I would've warned my husband. My brother said he was my best friend, as if I shared everything with him. It wasn't true, but I didn't know Nick was filling Matt's head with lies.

"One day, Matt called me out of the blue and said he wanted a divorce. I was stunned. We were still newlyweds. I thought maybe the distance was too hard, but he finally told me the reason. He said he knew that I really wanted to be with Joel and that I'd settled for him. I about fell over. It was the most absurd thing I'd ever heard. I assured him that I'd never had any interest in Joel, not ever. Joel was like a brother to me. That's when Matt brought up my own brother. He said Nick was the one who revealed my true feelings for Joel."

"What'd you do?"

"I told Matt, over and over, that Nick was lying. I'd never looked at Joel as anything other than my husband's brother. But Nick had already polluted Matt's mind, saying he felt obligated to share the truth because they'd become friends. He made it look like he was doing Matt a favor. That, along with Matt's insecurities about Joel, made it impossible for me to convince him otherwise. Plus, I was halfway around the world."

"You couldn't get him to see the truth?"

"No. Matt cut off all contact. He blocked my email and phone. The only person I could speak to was his asshole lawyer, Charles Hood, a guy Nick referred."

Dawn's eyes widened, realizing the Charles and Nick duo had struck before.

"I never realized Nick had sabotaged my marriage until it was too late."

"Has he done this to other women?" asked Dawn.

"Probably more than I know. Nick and I don't speak. I remember the girl he terrorized in college. He tore her down so completely that she agreed to do anything he wanted. He made her cut ties with her friends and family so he could isolate and control her. Once she allowed him to basically own her, to make her existence revolve around him—he dropped her, and she was totally lost. It sent her into a deep depression."

An unsettling silence filled the air.

"He doesn't know anything about my life now," added Sophie. "And I'd like to keep it that way. That's why I didn't accept your friend request, in case he checks."

"Why doesn't your family warn people? I mean, if you know he's like this?"

"Mom's in denial, and I don't know who Nick meets or dates. He stays off social media."

The fact that Nick could continue destroying others made Dawn even more determined to get a restraining order on his legal record.

"Does he have a type? His neighbor thought I was you. What did the other girl look like?"

"A tall blonde—and before you say this is some Freudian resentment toward our mother, it might be. Nick blames her for driving Dad away, but plenty of parents divorce without their kids turning psycho. And he was rotten before they split. I think Nick was born this way, and he'll probably die this way."

"Do you want me to try to find your husband?" offered Dawn. "Maybe he'd listen to me."

"He won't," said Sophie, as she rubbed her eyes. "Nick didn't just tell Matt that I wanted Joel. That wasn't enough. He manipulated evidence."

"Like what?"

"When I was away for training, Nick took my Blazer that I'd left at my mom's house and parked it in front of Joel's place. I wasn't even there, but Nick took photos and changed the date to make it look like I'd spent the night with Joel before I left. I found out about my alleged affair during the divorce. Nick put so much doubt in my husband's mind that it was impossible to undo it."

Dawn recalled all the things Nick had done early in their relationship to set her up. She realized he'd been calculating how to take Marie away from the moment they'd first met.

"But what about Joel?" she asked. "Couldn't you get him to tell Matt that none of this was true?"

"We tried. He didn't believe Joel, either. There was too much competition between them." Sophie glanced away from the screen and mouthed something to the person beckoning her. "Sorry. I have to go. Just be careful, okay?"

Chapter 44

For the rest of the day, Dawn couldn't get Sophie's story out of her head. She regretted not asking the college girlfriend's name so she could find out more.

On Sunday, she stopped by Floyd at lunchtime. The dining room was unusually crowded with family members visiting after church. The noon meal was pot roast with rosemary crust, mixed vegetables with rice, a roll and sweet tea. Dessert was pumpkin pie with whipped cream and coffee. The upgraded meal didn't fool Dawn. She'd seen the menu on days when no visitors came by, and little did the families know that dinner would be premade peanut butter sandwiches.

Marie picked at her food while Dawn observed her mom's diminished physique. The skin around Marie's collarbone was sunken, and her watch dangled loosely around her wrist, where it had once been snug.

Dawn turned to Susan and asked, "Is there a scale anywhere around here?"

"I think there's one in physical therapy, but they're closed today."

Cathy nodded and pointed to the south hallway.

After lunch, while the others played bingo, Dawn snuck Marie into the physical therapy room. A platform scale was positioned between a tattered exercise table and a set of dumbbells. Dawn asked Marie to step on the scale and tapped the cylindrical bar to reach equilibrium. Marie's weight was one hundred and sixty pounds, down five pounds.

"Mom, you're losing weight."

"I want to go home," pleaded Marie.

Dawn's heart broke into a million pieces. She wanted nothing more than to grant this request, but her hands were tied. She escorted her mother back to her room and stepped into the hallway to call Nancy.

"My mom has lost five pounds in a week," reported Dawn. "I'd like to take her home for dinner tonight. She'll eat better there."

"We've already discussed this," replied Nancy, with annoyance. "The only way for Marie to acclimate to her new surroundings is to stay put. We can discuss outside visits later."

"All I'm asking for is one dinner—a few hours. It will lift her spirits."

"Not right now."

"You're okay with her losing five pounds in a week?"

"I'll reach out to Dr. Edwards in the morning. He can prescribe Marinol to help her appetite."

"She doesn't need more drugs."

Dawn was so frustrated that Nancy would refuse something that would have an immediate positive impact. With every conversation, Nancy seemed to delay or divert. It made Dawn question how this woman was qualified to make decisions for her mother. A disturbing thought crossed Dawn's mind. She had no idea about Nancy's background or training. Other than being recommended by Jerry Raven, who Dawn considered traitorous, Nancy's credentials were unknown.

When Dawn returned to her mother's room, Marie was sitting on the bed. Cathy had her TV blaring, which amplified Dawn's irritation. On Marie's nightstand, Dawn's graduation picture was turned away—again.

"Mom, did you move my photo? Are you angry with me?"

"Of course I'm not angry with you, dear. I know you're doing your best."

"Well, how did my photo get moved again?"

Marie stared blankly at her.

The displaced photo no longer seemed random, especially since the other two had not been touched. Dawn took the frame and walked over to Cathy.

"Did you move my picture?" she asked, raising her voice to combat the TV.

Cathy shook her head and stood. She grabbed Dawn's arm and lifted her hand as high as she could. Dawn looked at her, confused. Cathy continued to grip Dawn's hand and raised up on her toes, as if trying to get taller.

Dawn's face turned white.

She scrambled for her phone and pulled up the camping picture. "Is this who moved my photo?"

Cathy nodded eagerly.

"When was he here?"

Cathy pressed her palms together, as if praying, and placed them against her cheek. She tilted her head and shut her eyes. They were playing a game of charades, but the message was clear.

"While she was sleeping?" guessed Dawn.

Cathy nodded.

"Did he hurt her?"

Cathy curled her fingers and held them up to her eyes as if she were looking through binoculars.

"Glasses. He took her glasses?"

Another nod.

Dawn felt as if she'd been punched in the gut. "Has he done anything else to her?"

Cathy shrugged, which gave Dawn little comfort.

"I have to get her out of here." Dawn hurried into the hallway and made a panicked phone call. Nancy had barely said hello when Dawn blurted, "My mom's in danger."

"What seems to be the problem?" asked Nancy, not hiding her annoyance at having her Sunday afternoon interrupted for a second time.

"A guy I used to date, who's been stalking me, has been visiting my mom at Floyd during the night."

"Did your mom ask him to leave?"

"She doesn't know he's been here, and I don't want to scare her. He's the one who took her glasses."

The line was quiet for a moment.

"How do you know he's been there?" asked Nancy.

"Cathy, my mom's roommate, told me."

"Let me speak to her."

"She can't talk." The moment the words left Dawn's lips, she grasped the irony. Her only witness couldn't explain what she'd seen.

"Can you prove he took your mom's glasses?" asked Nancy.

"Cathy can. You just have to ask her questions, and she'll respond. Look, this guy, Nicholas VanBroklin, is dangerous. I just talked to his sister. She'll tell you. Will you talk to her?"

"I don't see how your affair is any concern of mine."

Dawn bristled. She didn't have an affair with Nick. Neither of them was married. And the theft of Marie's glasses should definitely be a concern if Nancy bothered to care. Dawn's distress was falling on deaf ears. For her mom's sake, she had to try a different approach. She took a deep breath and sucked up every ounce of her pride to plead with the only person who could guarantee Marie's safety.

"Look, I know we got off on the wrong foot. I apologize for that. The reason I lost guardianship of my mother is because of this guy. He's a psychopath, and I'm certain he's been visiting my mom at night. I'm afraid he's going to hurt her because he knows that would destroy me. I'll agree to her being placed somewhere you see fit. I won't fight it. But for right now, can I *please* take her home where she'll be safe?"

"Dawn, I appreciate your concern, but your mother is already somewhere I see fit. I'm not going to change my mind about her getting adjusted. And frankly, you can't blame other people for the judge's decision. I read Judge Cain's findings. It seems to me that Nick was rightfully concerned about your mother's well-being."

Chapter 45

For the first time in Dawn's life, she understood how a person could go off the deep end in a fit of rage. She couldn't tell if Nancy was ignorant, lazy or just plain spiteful, but it didn't matter. The result was the same—every night Marie spent at Floyd, she was in danger.

With the evening drawing near, Dawn felt she had no choice but to hurry home and pack an overnight bag. Yellow Dog greeted her with a frenzied whine, upset about being left alone for so long. She was tempted to bring him back with her to serve as a watchdog, but pets weren't allowed at the facility.

When Dawn returned to Floyd, dinner was being served: a peanut butter sandwich with a bag of potato chips. Marie picked at her food for the second time that day. How Dawn wished they were savoring a Sunday baked ham or homemade lasagna. She'd taken her mom's cooking for granted, something she'd never do again if she could only bring Marie home.

Later that evening, when the plates had been cleared and the staff had thinned, an idea popped into her mind. It wasn't entirely ethical, but she didn't care. Dawn made a quick trip to her place to fetch Yellow Dog. She detoured by the vet clinic and retrieved an animal training vest, turning him into a fake service dog. He'd be the best alarm should Nick creep into her mother's room during the night.

Back at Floyd, no one seemed to mind that she had a dog in tow. A few of the residents clapped with delight and asked to pet him.

"Not while he's on duty," she fibbed, and headed down the hallway.

When they entered her mom's room, Cathy gasped and leapt onto the bed. She tucked into a tiny ball, hugging her legs. Her eyes, wide with fright, tracked every movement of the beast who'd invaded her space.

"He won't hurt you. I promise," said Dawn. She reached down and stroked Yellow Dog's back.

Cathy didn't budge from her curled position in the center of the bed.

"Would it be okay if he stayed here for just a while? I'll keep him on this side of the room," promised Dawn. "Look, I'll even tie him down." She wrapped the dog's leash around Marie's bedpost.

Eventually, Cathy turned off the TV and slipped under the covers. With both residents tucked in their beds, Dawn turned off the overhead light.

"Don't you need to go home?" asked Marie.

"I'll sit here till you fall asleep." The truth was that Dawn planned to stand guard with Yellow Dog the entire night. It wasn't a sustainable solution, but all she could do was take it one day—or night—at a time.

Marie smiled, adjusted her pillow and closed her eyes.

Dawn went to the main room and dragged a recliner down the hallway, back to her mom's room, daring anyone to stop her. It was a poor excuse for a bed but better than the floor or metal folding chair. She released the footrest and propped her feet. Yellow Dog watched with interest, then sprawled across the floor next to her. Dawn opened her laptop, the only source of light in the room, and typed *Nancy Priest Laurel South Carolina* in the Google toolbar.

A single one-star review appeared. *Nancy Priest nearly killed my son. He suffers from pulmonary fibrosis and is on constant oxygen. When Nancy became his guardian and conservator, she was responsible for ordering and paying for his oxygen tanks, but she let them run out. He called me gasping for air. I immediately called 911 and he was rushed to the hospital. He barely survived. Do not let Nancy Priest anywhere near your loved one.*

As Dawn read the review, she was unable to quell the sensation that she, like the boy, was suffocating. She inhaled several deep breaths before the panicked feeling subsided. Next, she tried to find Nancy Priest on Facebook and Instagram, but there was no match. On a lark, she searched for *Nancy Raven*, thinking there could be a connection between the two. Why else would Jerry Raven recommend someone so unqualified? Still, she came up empty.

A search on LinkedIn revealed Nancy's profile, listing her as an LPC, Licensed Professional Counselor. Dawn found the website for the South Carolina Board of Examiners for LPCs. When she entered *Nancy Priest* and clicked on the license number, she was shocked. The license had lapsed several years prior.

Thinking she might have grounds to have Nancy removed, she researched the qualifications necessary to be a guardian. After reading pages from the South Carolina code, Dawn was even more stunned. There were no required credentials to become a guardian in South Carolina. Nancy's lapsed license was not a disqualifier. All she needed was the appointment by the probate judge and her only legal obligation was to file a plan of care within thirty days of being named. South Carolina had no public guardian program and, shockingly, very little oversight.

Dawn, with her certifications as a vet tech, had to go through more credentialing to take care of an animal than Nancy did to take care of a human being. And what recourse did Dawn have if Nancy was doing a horrible job? All she could do was go back to the same judge who'd made the appointment. Dawn couldn't comprehend how the state could be so lax given the critical function of this role, and she guessed most people didn't understand the rules until it was too late.

She rubbed her eyes, irritated by the glare of the screen and the dryness of the air. Although it was early fall, the heat in the facility was blasting, making the room stifling. Dawn contemplated who she could ask for help—besides Ben. Her dad was gone. Stuart had been her closest friend the last few months, but she'd burned that bridge. Kelly was loyal to a fault, but she and her family didn't have any connections. Alex, with his intimidating size, afforded protection at work, but she couldn't ask him to guard her mom. Her only option, she concluded, was to call Ben in the morning. Maybe she could take out a restraining order against Nick on her mom's behalf?

Dawn untied Yellow Dog, reclined the chair and shut her eyes. The oppressive temperature and makeshift bed made falling asleep challenging. Just when she'd start to doze off, Dawn would jerk awake, momentarily lost to time and place. Slowly, as she made out the silhouette of her mom's bed and heard Marie's rhythmic breathing, reality would sink in. She'd glance at the clock only to discover that ten minutes had passed since the last time she'd checked.

At some point during the night, Dawn sensed a presence in the room. In her groggy state of half-sleep, she dismissed the strange feeling, but it persisted, as if something or someone was lurking just out of reach. Unable to ignore her uneasiness, she squinted one eye open. In the dark, a tall figure stood motionless just a few feet away.

Who was there? Why hadn't Yellow Dog alerted her? There was no way her dutiful guard dog would've remained quiet—unless he was forced. Dawn's heart began to pound at the realization something bad must've happened to him. With one eye barely open, she feigned sleep, keeping her body perfectly still as she watched this figure lumber about in the dark.

He began to move away from Dawn and toward her mother. She couldn't allow that. Dawn pushed against the recliner, ready to leap into action, but her limbs were immobile. Her legs remained rigid, as if she was paralyzed. She tried to scream, to warn her mom, but her muffled cry remained trapped in her mouth. Why was she unable to control her body? Had she been drugged?

The figure stopped and turned toward her.

"No!" she screamed again. This time the sound escaped. He advanced, towering over her. His hand reached toward her face. He was going to cover her mouth, suppress her cries, suffocate her.

Dawn lashed out, flailing her arms to block his advance, astonished she was now able to move. He stepped back and spoke in a high-pitched whisper. Confusion filled her brain. She didn't recognize this voice. She jerked fully awake, breathing rapidly.

"It's Wendy, the CNA. I think you were having a bad dream."

Dawn sat upright. In the dark, she made out the figure of a woman, shorter than she'd originally perceived. She looked toward her mom who was still asleep. Cathy was sitting up in bed with the covers pulled to her chin.

Dawn's heartbeat began to steady.

"You work here?" she asked in a low whisper.

"Yes."

"Where's Yellow Dog?"

"The dog? He's in the bathroom. When I was doing my rounds, I found him drinking out of the toilet, so I brought him a bowl of water."

Dawn eased her stiff body out of the chair. She ambled to the hallway, passing Yellow Dog who was sprawled on the cool tile of the bathroom floor. The glow of the overhead fluorescent lights made her eyes burn.

Wendy, who'd seemed like a giant when she was standing over Dawn, was a short woman with wiry gray hair and kind eyes.

"I'm Dawn, Marie's daughter. I must've dozed off."

Wendy nodded, acknowledging the obvious. She didn't seem fazed that a visitor was staying overnight with a dog.

"Have you ever seen anyone in my mom's room—a tall guy visiting at night?" asked Dawn.

Wendy thought for a moment and shook her head. "I haven't seen anyone, but I cover three halls on third shift so I might not."

Chapter 46

The next morning, Dr. Patel was already at the clinic when Dawn arrived. He asked to have a word with her in his office.

"You look tired," he commented.

All she could do was nod in agreement.

"Smita and I were talking. We know the stress you've been under with this lawsuit. You've had to take quite a lot of unplanned time off. We think it would be best if Smita came back early so you could take a leave of absence for a short while, until you can get these issues sorted out."

"What?" Dawn knew she'd been less than an ideal employee, but this conversation completely blindsided her.

"We wouldn't be able to pay you during this period," he added. "But you'd still have your position when you're able to return, fully committed."

A leave of absence? she thought. *I can't. I need this job and the paycheck, and I need the only normalcy I have left in my life.*

"Please, don't ask me to take time off," she begged. "I won't miss any more work. I promise."

Dr. Patel pressed his lips. He clearly didn't believe she could keep such a vow.

"And it's not fair to Smita. She shouldn't have to cut her maternity leave short because of me. Please. I'll do better."

Dawn's eyes began to water. Tears silently rolled down her cheeks. The destructive ripple effect caused by Nick's actions was affecting her personally and professionally. She had wished misfortune on people before, usually those who mistreated helpless animals, but her growing hatred of Nick eclipsed anything she'd ever known. Not only did she wish him dead, but she wanted him to suffer first.

"Alright," the vet relented. "But another unplanned absence and we'll have to revisit this conversation."

Dr. Patel left the office, giving Dawn time to collect herself. She couldn't let clients see that she'd been crying, especially not after the bad review. They might think she was upset over a dead animal—one she'd killed. She checked her appearance using her camera. Her face looked a lot like Marie's—red eyes and puffy cheeks. A realization hit her. Something that had been nagging at her since the encounter with Wendy.

Of course, thought Dawn. *Mom slept through the commotion because she's on Zolpidem.*

With renewed resolve, she called Dr. Edwards to discuss her mother's medications. The call landed on an automated message with six options. She rolled her eyes. The Village Veterinary Clinic didn't have six options. They had Suzanne, a live human who triaged calls. At the beep, she left a message asking to discuss her mom's medications, again. Her next call was to Ben's mobile.

"Hello, Dawn. What can I do for you today?" He didn't mask his impatience.

"Nick has been visiting my mom at the Floyd place."

The line was quiet for a moment. "What exactly is your complaint?" he asked.

"This psycho has access to Mom. When she was home, I could keep him away from her. But now, at Floyd, he can visit whenever he wants."

"Is she complaining about his visits?"

This conversation felt like a stale rerun of her earlier call with Nancy. "She doesn't know he's coming by, but I do. He took her glasses, and he's been tampering with my photos. Don't you see? He's making sure I know he's been there. He's up to something, and I need to find out what. I'm going to put a camera in her room."

"I would strongly advise against that," cautioned Ben. "South Carolina law doesn't allow the use of cameras in nursing homes. It's considered an infringement on the privacy rights of the other residents and the staff."

Dawn had already broken the rules with Yellow Dog and was prepared to break them again. "What if I do it anyway?"

"The footage wouldn't be admissible if it's taken illegally."

"What else can I do to keep him away from her?"

"I'm afraid there's not much you can do."

"What about filing a restraining order against him on my mom's behalf? Can I do that?"

"Legally, as far as restricting visitation, you'd have to enlist your mom's guardian, and you'd need a valid argument as to why."

"This is insane. Nancy isn't going to do anything. What about my own restraining order? Can't I extend it to Mom since she's a member of my family?"

"That would only work if she were a minor. By the way, Donna was trying to find Nick's address to have him served. She spoke to someone at the court who told her that your application had already been filed and served."

"I found his apartment number and resubmitted the paperwork last week."

"Well, the hearing is scheduled for a week from Wednesday. You should be receiving a notification in the mail."

"We need to prepare *in person* this time. I have the AirTag he put on my car. Can you have it traced as evidence that he's been stalking me?"

"Why don't you give everything to Donna, and she'll set up a time to meet. I really need to go now. We'll talk later in the week."

Dawn felt that Ben was once again downplaying the importance of her case. She didn't know if he was swamped with too many clients, if he'd become fatigued with the Smith family drama or if he considered restraining orders to be beneath his pay grade. But with the hearing only a week away, she didn't have time to find a new lawyer.

She spent the rest of the day taking on every extra task at the clinic and making sure Dr. Patel noticed. That evening, she walked Yellow Dog and then sank onto her couch, beer in hand. She was too wiped out to spend another night at Floyd, although the anxiety of leaving her mom alone made her stomach knot.

Dawn replayed the morning's conversation with Dr. Patel. Even though he'd suggested a temporary leave, she felt like she'd almost been fired. She burst into tears. Everything she'd been suppressing, combined with sheer exhaustion, drove her to uncontrollable sobs.

Yellow Dog, who was lying on the couch next to her, burrowed his face into her side. She rubbed his thick coat as she wiped away tears.

"When is karma going to get Nick?" she lamented.

Yellow Dog immediately alerted on the word, *karma*. His head snapped to attention and his ears pointed high, as if that word was familiar to him.

Dawn repeated it. "Karma."

He looked at her as if saying, "Yes?"

Chapter 47

The following Wednesday morning, Dawn arrived at the courthouse. Barely a week had passed since she'd sworn to Dr. Patel that she wouldn't need any more time off, and she was already breaking that promise. This absence couldn't be avoided. She didn't decide the magistrate court calendar, and she couldn't skip the restraining order hearing. Ben met her just after security and led her to a small conference room.

"How's your mom doing?" he asked, making small talk.

"Not good. She's lost weight and I can't stop Nick from going there. But I hope I can at least block him when I'm visiting, if we get the restraining order. Were you able to trace the AirTag?"

"I'm afraid I don't have good news on that front," he said. "The AirTag was linked to an unregistered phone."

"Well, that's just part of our case, right? I mean we can prove Nick came to my home and work, and I gave Donna printouts of his text messages."

"Yes, I have those. We still have a solid case. Would've been stronger with the AirTag." Ben glanced at his watch. "Why don't you go ahead to the courtroom? I'm going to see if I can find Charles Hood."

"Why?"

"The judge will expect that we tried to mediate prior to the hearing."

"You're not going to let Nick off the hook, are you?" Dawn's voice grew louder.

"No, this is just a formality."

Ben left in search of Nick's lawyer, leaving Dawn to enter the magistrate courtroom alone. It looked similar to the probate court, with the judge's bench, tables for the plaintiff and defendant, a jury box and rows of wooden benches. Unlike probate court, where they'd been the only people present, this courtroom was crowded and noisy. There were young, old, Black, White, loners and entire families, all crammed together in the small space. Dawn's gaze landed on Nick. He was dressed in the same dark suit and tie he'd worn to the guardianship hearing. When their eyes met, his smile broadened, which made Dawn's blood boil.

We'll see who's smiling once you're slapped with a restraining order, she thought and looked away.

Ben joined her just before the bailiff asked everyone to rise. The simultaneous swish of people standing overtook the chatter. A middle-aged white man dressed in a black robe entered and took his seat at the bench. His face was small and severe, as if his eyes, nose and mouth had all been pinched together.

"The Honorable Judge Herold," said the bailiff. "The court is now in session."

"I'm going to call the calendar," said the judge. "When I call your name, I need you to stand so I know you're here."

Dawn noticed a pattern of the men being called first, likely the defendants. Some had attorneys. Others did not. Some were present. Others were not. When the judge called Nick, he and Charles stood.

"I see you have an attorney," said Judge Herold. "Have you provided your information to my clerk?"

"Yes, Your Honor," said Charles.

Hearing Charles's voice made Dawn's skin crawl. He was complicit in Nick's treachery and deserved some of the blame for Marie being taken away.

"Is Dawn Smith present in the courtroom for this hearing?" asked the judge.

Dawn and Ben stood, and Ben confirmed that they had also signed in with the clerk. As the roll call continued, the number of absences was notable. About half the time, one of the two parties hadn't shown up. If the plaintiff was absent, the judge dismissed the case on the spot.

Dawn leaned over to Ben and whispered, "If a woman felt the need to file a restraining order, why would she be a no-show?"

Ben shrugged. "Happens a lot. She loses her nerve or maybe the couple reconciles for the time being."

In the instances where the defendant, typically the male, was absent, the judge continued with the roll call.

"Why doesn't he dismiss those, too?" asked Dawn.

"The plaintiff has the right to a hearing, where she can ask for a default judgment against the offender. She'll automatically be granted the restraining order."

At the end of the roll call, which took nearly an hour, there were only ten cases where both parties were present, including Dawn and Nick. When it was their turn, Judge Herold addressed the attorneys.

"Have you two had a chance to speak?"

"We've met, Your Honor," said Charles. "No agreement can be reached. We need a hearing. In fact, I would argue that although Ms. Smith filed the restraining order against my client, *he's* the one who needs protection from *her*."

"We'll get to that in the hearing," said the judge.

"We're prepared," Charles replied, with a tone of arrogance. "Our witness is present in the courtroom."

Dawn scanned the seats looking for Maribel Santos. Was that woman going to vouch for Nick again? The bailiff called Dawn to the front, swore her in and directed her to the witness stand. She continued surveying the room but didn't see Maribel or Matthias.

Ben stood and began his questioning, which they'd rehearsed the week prior. "Ms. Smith, can you explain the nature of your relationship with Mr. VanBroklin?"

"We went on five dates. When I realized he was a liar, I broke up with him."

"After you broke off the relationship with Mr. VanBroklin, did he continue to contact you?"

"Yes. He called and texted me nonstop, so I blocked his number."

Ben turned toward the judge. "Your Honor, I would ask to submit to the court for review, printouts of text messages of a harassing nature from Mr. VanBroklin's phone to my client's phone."

"Please hand them to my clerk," said the judge.

Ben faced Dawn. "Did he do anything else?"

"Yes. He came to my house. When I didn't answer the front door, he let himself in through the back. I was so scared, I managed to escape—"

Charles interrupted, "Your Honor, objection. Escape implies my client meant to do Ms. Smith harm. He was merely there to check on her well-being as she was unresponsive."

"You'll have your chance on cross," replied Judge Herold.

"Let's move on," said Ben. "Were there any other incidents?"

"Another time, he'd been inside my home. I could tell because—"

"Objection, Your Honor," said Charles. "Did she *see* him in the house?"

Although Dawn and Ben had practiced her testimony, at her insistence, he hadn't prepared her for the constant interruptions. Was this Charles Hood's strategy to fluster her?

"Mr. Hood, again, you'll have your turn." Judge Herold peered down at Dawn from his perch. "Ms. Smith, go on please."

Knowing she couldn't prove Nick had taken her necklace, she switched to the incident at the clinic. "Nick came to my job and threatened me. I have witnesses." Dawn relayed her account of how Nick had shown up with Snowball and pulled his jacket back to expose his gun. "If Dr. Patel hadn't interrupted us, I'm afraid of what he would've done. And he told the police officer that he was trying to return a lost cat, but at the clinic he told me that *his* cat needed treatment. Those were his exact words. He stole the cat and lied about it."

Ben yielded the floor, and Charles stood to pose his questions.

"Ms. Smith, you stated that you escaped out the window when my client came to your house. Did he threaten you in any way?"

Dawn recalled Ben's counsel to remain calm. She replied flatly, "He let himself in my home. Uninvited. To me, that was a threat."

"So, you never had any interaction with him?"

"No," she replied.

"And after you jumped out the window, did my client speak with your mother where she asked him to run an errand for her, to pick up a light bulb?"

"Well, yes, but—"

"No, that's all. Thank you," he said, cutting her off. "Do you remember an incident where you approached my client at the Ingles grocery store on October third of this year?"

"I was there, but he—"

"Didn't you physically assault my client in front of customers and staff that evening?"

Dawn remained silent, feeling an unsettling déjà vu. They'd succeeded in distorting the facts the last time, making her appear to be an unfit caregiver. Were they going to twist the truth again?

"Answer the question, please," said Charles. "Did you try to choke my client in the Ingles grocery store? Because that's what witnesses reported, one of whom is here today to testify."

Dawn looked at Ben for guidance. Nothing about the Ingles incident had come up when they'd prepared. They'd focused on Nick's actions, not hers.

"Your Honor, objection," said Ben. "Mr. Hood can address what a witness has to say once they are sworn in. I respectfully request that he keep his questions to Ms. Smith's testimony."

"I did ask a question of Ms. Smith," said Charles, as he faced the judge. He raised his arms as if helpless. "She hasn't answered."

"Can you answer the question?" said the judge, peering down at Dawn.

"Did you attempt to choke my client at the Ingles grocery store?" repeated Charles.

Dawn's jaw clenched. "I was defending myself."

"That's all, Your Honor. I'd like to call Trevor Harnage, who works at the Ingles deli, to the stand."

Dawn stepped down and for the first time, recognized the employee from the deli. He was sitting in the back of the courtroom dressed in an oversized ivory suit. He looked like an altar boy draped in a cassock as he approached the witness stand and placed his hand on the Bible.

Charles asked the standard introductory questions—his name, place of work, years at the store and if he knew either of the litigants.

"Mr. Harnage, could you tell me what you witnessed while at work the evening of October third?"

The boy cleared his throat and spoke like a cherub. "I was working at the deli. Several people were in line to place orders when, all of a sudden, this woman grabbed this man by his throat and started screaming at him. She said she was going to kill him. He fell on the floor, and she jumped on top of him. Some of us, me and a few others, tried to pull her off. She seemed like she'd totally lost it."

Dawn bowed her head. This boy's testimony was crucifying her, which is exactly what it was meant to do. He had no agenda. He'd merely witnessed a snapshot in time of Dawn's history with Nick, missing the larger picture.

"And are these two individuals in the courtroom today?" asked Charles.

Trevor Harnage identified Dawn and Nick as the two customers involved in the altercation.

"I have nothing further," said Charles.

The judge looked at Ben. "Mr. Clayton. Do you have any questions for this witness?"

"No, Your Honor."

"Mr. Harnage, you may step down. Any further witnesses?" asked Judge Herold.

"No, Your Honor," said Charles.

Dawn whispered to Ben in disbelief, "Nick's not taking the stand?"

"Like I'd told you, he doesn't have to."

When they'd prepared, Ben had predicted that Nick wouldn't testify, nor was he obligated to speak in his defense. Dawn was certain he'd take the stand. He was such a prolific liar and so arrogant that he'd surely think he could outsmart any cross-examination. But now, all the time they'd spent preparing was wasted.

"Closing remarks, Mr. Clayton?" said the judge.

"Yes, Your Honor." Ben stood. "As you'll see from the printout, Mr. VanBroklin continued to harass my client via text messages and phone calls after the relationship ended. When she didn't answer her door, he thought it was appropriate to enter her home through an unsecured but closed back door, which caused my client such fear that she left the house through the window. He showed up at her place of work with a stolen animal, pretending to be a client. He proceeded to show her that he had a gun, which would be intimidating for anyone. There is absolutely no reason for him to have contact with Ms. Smith. Therefore, we respectfully request the court to put the restraining order in place so that my client can feel safe at home, at work, and throughout her daily life. Thank you."

Charles stood for his closing remarks. "Your Honor, they were dating, they weren't dating, we know how that goes. My client did nothing but attempt to visit Ms. Smith to check on her. Instead of answering the door, like any normal person, she jumped out the window. He walked into the house because he was concerned. He'd seen her Jeep parked outside and she wasn't responding. And when he spoke to her mother, who lived next door, he ended up being entrusted to run an errand for them. Regarding the animal, my client attempted to return a lost cat by doing what we're all supposed to do when we find a stray, take it to the vet and have it scanned. He never claimed it was *his* cat. And imagine my client's surprise when he was standing in line to buy some lunch meat, and Ms. Smith turned on him and started choking him, to the point strangers had to intervene. If anything, my client needs protection from Ms. Smith. That's all, Your Honor."

"I've heard enough," said the judge. He addressed both parties. "Mr. Hood, I do see cause for a restraining order to be placed against your client to have zero contact with Ms. Smith. And Mr. Clayton, I also see cause to issue a restraining order against Ms. Smith, to have no further contact with Mr. VanBroklin. As you stated, there's no reason for the two of them to have further contact with each other."

With that brief edict, both Dawn and Nick had mutual restraining orders placed against them. They were required to remain in the courtroom until the clerk prepared the paperwork and they'd been officially served. The judge asked Dawn and Ben to leave first and kept Nick and Charles inside to ensure they wouldn't end up in the parking lot together.

Outside, Dawn felt like she'd been sucker punched—again. The system had failed her—

again.

"How the hell did I get a restraining order placed against me?" she asked.

"You never mentioned the incident at the grocery store," countered Ben.

"He creeped up behind me, and his falling to the floor was a charade. He wasn't hurt."

"You understand how it looked to other people?"

"Why the hell did I even do this?" exclaimed Dawn. "Now I have a restraining order against *me*, and Mom still isn't safe. How am I the bad guy here? This is bullshit, all bullshit."

Chapter 48

Dawn wanted to take the rest of the day off given her foul mood, but she couldn't. Smita was filling in for her, and it wasn't fair to keep encroaching on the last few days of her boss's maternity leave.

"How'd it go in court?" asked Smita when Dawn arrived at work.

Dawn shook her head. "Not good. I got the restraining order against Nick, but he got one against me, like I'm the criminal."

Smita's eyes widened. "How'd that happen?"

"It's a long story. It's a good thing I don't own a gun because I'd be tempted to—"

Dawn stopped. Even though her words were a hollow threat, she surprised herself that she'd sunk to this level of vitriol.

"But you know you *can't* get a gun," warned Smita, who'd taken Dawn's wishful thinking literally.

"I could never *really* shoot him, although I'd be doing the world a favor."

"That's not what I meant," said Smita. "If you have a restraining order against you, no gun shop will sell you a firearm. It's a question on the background check."

Nick had just delivered another blow, this time through Smita. Dawn hadn't been serious about purchasing a gun, but now she was outraged that her rights had been restricted because of him.

"Did your lawyer ask that Nick surrender his firearms?" asked Smita.

"It didn't even come up. We prepared this time, and he still missed things." Dawn wanted to pound her fist through the wall.

"I'm so sorry you're going through this. I'm already here. Why don't you go talk to your lawyer? Maybe you can have the restraining order amended to take away Nick's firearms."

"I've already missed too much work."

"Don't worry about Neil. This is more important. At least give your lawyer a call?"

Dawn nodded. Something was clearly wrong when a veterinarian was giving her better legal advice than her own attorney. She made up her mind to start looking for a new lawyer because Ben had failed her for the last time.

At the end of the day, Alex escorted Dawn to her Jeep out of habit.

"Nick isn't allowed to come here," she told him. "He'll go to jail and be fined if he violates the restraining order."

"I don't mind." Alex opened the door of the Jeep and ensured she was safely inside. How was it, she wondered, that a stand-up guy like Alex was still single and a psycho like Nick could charm any girl he wanted?

As Dawn pulled into the driveway, she noticed a sign planted in her mom's yard. A closer look revealed it was a real estate listing—*For Sale by Owner* with Nancy Priest's contact information. Dawn's jaw fell open. This woman, as conservator, could sell Marie's home and there was nothing Dawn could do to stop her. Dawn yanked the sign out of the ground and stomped on it until the metal twisted. She hurled it into the trash dumpster, went inside and plunged a corkscrew into a bottle of Cabernet. Today required more than beer. Yellow Dog, who typically followed her into the kitchen for a treat, remained planted by the back door, staring into the darkness.

"What do you see?" asked Dawn, as she flipped on the backlight. There wasn't anything out there. She returned to the kitchen and shook the bag of treats, but he had no interest. Instead, he paced from the back door to the front as if on a mission.

"What's wrong with you?" she asked. "Don't you want a treat?"

When she approached him, offering a bacon-flavored bone, he snapped at her hand. Dawn jerked her arm back, shocked that he was being so aggressive.

"Bad boy," she scolded. "No one is going to adopt you if you act that way." She grabbed Yellow Dog by the collar, clipped on his leash and tied the end to the leg of the kitchen table. It was her version of doggie time-out. "Now stay there until you can learn to be nice."

For dinner, she microwaved a frozen meal, which looked as appetizing as the food at Floyd. Even so, she had a choice, unlike Marie. Dawn sat cross-legged on the couch, still in her scrubs, wine glass in one hand and fork in the other. Yellow Dog whined. He was used to getting scraps from her plate. She was about to turn on the TV when his tone changed to a guttural growl. Dawn turned her head slightly and admonished him. "Learn not to snap and I'll untie you."

Instead of quieting, he launched into a full-blown tirade, barking ferociously and tugging at his leash with such vigor that the heavy table securing him nearly inched across the wood floor.

Dawn set her plastic plate and wine glass on the coffee table and stood to face him. "I told you—"

She froze.

Nick was standing by the front door inside her home.

Yellow Dog growled and lunged forward again, but he was tethered to the table.

Nick drew his gun and pointed it at the dog. "Shut it up or I'll shoot it in the face."

"Don't," cried Dawn, as she circled the couch and stood next to Yellow Dog. "You're not allowed to be here. You need to leave!"

Nick cast his head back and laughed. "You think a piece of paper is going to stop me?"

"What do you want?" Dawn fixated on the barrel of the gun, which was still pointed at the dog. She had a primal urge to escape, to sprint down the hall and not look back, but there was no way she could outrun a bullet.

"You know there's no point changing your locks when Marie has the new key." Nick held up a silver house key and grinned.

Only then did Dawn realize how Nick had entered her locked door. He had access to her mom's purse at Floyd. He could've easily taken or copied their house key. How had she not thought of that possibility before?

She slid her phone from her back pocket and tapped it several times before freezing. The barrel of the gun was now pointing at her.

"Put that down," he sneered. "Now."

Dawn obeyed, placing the phone on the kitchen table. Yellow Dog continued to bark and lunge forward. He must've sensed Nick outside. That's why he'd acted so hostile.

"I'm curious," said Nick. "What made you go cold?"

"What made me go cold?" she repeated. "You're a pathological liar." Dawn surprised herself at the strength in her voice. She revealed no hint of the fear she harbored inside.

"But what specifically turned you off?" he asked.

"Why does that matter? You need to leave."

Yellow Dog was no longer barking at full volume, but he was

growling with his teeth and gums exposed. His body was crouched, ready to pounce.

"It matters to me," replied Nick. Everything about his demeanor was ultra casual. He stood in her entryway, dressed in blue jeans and a long-sleeved flannel shirt, acting like he was chatting with a friend.

Dawn began to consider that Nick wasn't just evil, but truly insane. Her best tactic, she thought, was to stall. To do that, she needed to keep him talking.

"I saw you leaving the bank in the maroon SUV," she said. "The night we met, you weren't a Good Samaritan reporting an accident. *You* were the hit-and-run driver."

"Ah, that." Nick nodded slowly as if a great puzzle had been solved. "I thought you figured out how Marie fell."

Dawn stood speechless.

"I pushed her," he boasted. "Couldn't have asked for a better opportunity when you went next door for another bottle of wine. The trick was getting her to stand up, but as soon as I started to clear the dishes, she insisted on helping."

"You bastard. I know you drugged her, too. You put Lisinopril in her eggs, didn't you?"

"You told me about her medications that first dinner, remember? You really made that easy." Nick's eyes sparkled with amusement.

"You poisoned her, then took the vial while we were at the hospital and left it on my Jeep."

"What fun would it be if you thought the overdose was an accident?" The corners of his mouth turned up.

"That was a mistake. That bottle has your fingerprints."

"Nice try," he replied, smugly. "It doesn't."

Dawn couldn't figure out why Nick was so calm and self-assured. He didn't care that he was violating the restraining order, which meant he already knew how he'd get away with it. That thought sent a shiver down her spine.

"What do you want?" Her voice sounded like cut glass, harsh and emotionless. In the background, Yellow Dog maintained a constant growl.

"I'm glad you asked. But it's not what I want, it's what *you* want. I know you want Marie back home, out of that terrible place. I can make that happen."

Dawn's eyes narrowed. "Why would you do that? Your actions put her there."

"Yes, it appears they did. It's why I've been checking on her, to make sure she's okay."

"You leave her alone."

Nick's grin broadened.

Dawn understood all too clearly. He had no intention of staying away from *either* of them. With the issuance of the restraining order, Dawn naively thought she was protected. In reality, she had nothing if Nick refused to obey it.

"Do you want your mother home?" he asked.

"You know I do."

"You don't have much time, do you? Her unit is already for sale. I imagine it will go quickly at such a reduced price. But here's what I'll do for you. I'll tell Judge Cain the real story—that Marie's fall and overdose were my fault. That she's never been in any danger with you."

"It won't matter. He's already made his decision."

"I think it would matter, if he knew his ruling was based on lies."

Dawn found it impossible to believe that Nick would confess to perjury, and he wasn't the type to miraculously gain a conscience. He'd gone to incredible lengths to eliminate her rights as a daughter. Why would he offer to reverse direction now? It didn't make any sense.

"Why would you do that?" she asked.

"Because of what you're going to do for me."

Dawn eyed him warily.

"You're going to give yourself to me," he said. "There's so much more we can explore."

"Never."

"Really? Never? How else will you free Marie? You think Nancy will ever release her grip? Trust me, it will only get tighter. She's got ahold of your mom and those claws are just beginning to dig in. Your mom's a private pay ward, right? That's a cash cow for Nancy and Patti Floyd." Nick shook his head, feigning disappointment. "I'm really surprised by you, Dawn. I thought you'd be selfless to save your mom."

Nick turned, as if he was going to leave.

"How do I know you'd stick to the deal?" she asked.

He halted his retreat and faced her, visibly pleased.

"Because I like Marie, always have. I hate that she's getting so thin, and I can only imagine the cocktail of drugs they'll prescribe if her memory continues to decline. Might get to the point where she doesn't recognize you at all." He made a *tsk tsk* sound with his tongue as he shook his head. "But you have the power to stop it. You've got one minute to decide."

Dawn glanced at her phone, then at Yellow Dog, who was still crouched and ready to strike. She remembered the conversation with Sophie. Once Nick had gained total control of his college girlfriend, he lost interest. Was allowing herself to be violated for the sake of her mom his way of breaking her?

"What's it going to be?" he asked.

She lowered her head and nodded. "Okay."

Chapter 49

"Get undressed," commanded Nick, pointing the gun at Dawn.

She slowly grasped the hem of her top and pulled it over her head, revealing a white lace bra.

"Keep going," he ordered, lowering his aim to her waist.

She untied the cloth belt of her scrubs and let them fall to the floor, exposing her bare legs and white panties.

Nick glided his tongue across his upper lip as he scanned her half-naked body.

The thought of his vile mouth against her skin gave her welts. *There's so much more we can explore*, replayed in her mind. She'd been too adventurous with Nick in the woods, something she'd forever regret. Whatever he envisioned doing next would certainly breach her boundaries. Her body began to quiver. She glanced nervously at her phone, which was still resting on the kitchen table.

Nick took a step forward.

Suddenly, a burst of movement blew past her. A bright flash exploded. Yellow Dog had leapt from the floor, forcing the knot of the leash to unravel. The Labrador latched onto Nick's right arm, sinking his teeth so deep that blood began to stain the flannel sleeve. Nick frantically shook his arm, trying in vain to free himself. He dropped to the floor, reminiscent of how he'd collapsed at the grocery store, but this time was real. He curled into a ball, but the dog's aggression only intensified. Yellow Dog thrashed his head, ripping flesh while his jaw remained clamped to Nick's forearm.

Instinctively, Dawn put her hand to her stomach, which was strangely wet. She'd felt a sharp sting, like she'd been stung by a wasp. The sensation intensified from a mild burning to a bonfire, as if someone had placed scorching coals inside of her belly. She took a step toward the sink in search of water to douse the heat. The stainless-steel tub began to morph. Solid material appeared to turn into molten lava, flowing in circles before her eyes. The pendulum lamp above the sink mutated from a single bulb to a diffused halo of light. As Dawn took another step, the edges of the light began to dim, replaced with darkness. With one more step, everything turned black.

Nick's sole focus was retrieving his gun, which had been knocked from his hand during the attack. Fueled by the adrenaline of the struggle, he felt no pain, even though his arm was bleeding profusely and still lodged in the dog's mouth. If he could just get to his gun, he'd unload every bullet in his magazine into this savage beast.

As he twisted on the floor, Nick managed to grab a chair with his left hand and flipped it on its side. He wedged the seat between his right arm and the dog and pressed forward. When the dog momentarily snapped at the chair, Nick pulled his arm free and scrambled to his feet. He held the chair between them like a lion tamer to keep his distance.

Nick saw Dawn's motionless body resting on her back with blood spilling from her naked torso. He'd never intended to shoot her. His finger had been on the trigger and the muzzle had been pointed at her when the dog attacked. To him, the gun going off was a justifiable reflex. He had no idea if she was still alive and couldn't approach her to check. The dog was standing guard between them, with bloody saliva spewing from its mouth as it barked.

Nick's pistol was on the kitchen floor next to the animal. As much as he wanted to exact revenge on the filthy mutt, he risked another attack if he advanced. The wiser move was to retreat. Using the chair for protection, he inched his way backward until he reached the front door. Only then did he ease down the chair and slip outside into the darkness.

He thought he'd been clever, leaving his mobile phone at his place so there was no digital evidence of his visit. But with the unexpected turn of events, he had no time and no means to sanitize the scene. His pistol could be traced to the gun store where he'd purchased it. They'd have a record of the sale, and the bullet inside of Dawn could be linked to the gun. His blood was all over the floor and his fingerprints were on the chair and doorknob.

Nick considered his options. He could get his shotgun, return to Dawn's place, shoot the dog, retrieve his pistol and then try to sanitize any trace of his blood and fingerprints. Or he could hit the road. He had no idea if neighbors had heard the gunshot or if the police were already on their way. He knew that with the sophistication of forensics, he'd be hard-pressed to remove every trace of his DNA, even with bleach. Then again, he could explain his DNA at her place as they'd once dated. Time was not on his side, but he had to try to retrieve his gun.

He sped home and headed straight for the bathroom. There, he peeled back the flannel sleeve of his shirt to reveal the gnarly gash in his forearm. He rinsed the blood, wrapped a bandage around the wound and downed several pain pills, all the while cursing the damn dog. Next, he loaded his shotgun and grabbed plastic garbage bags and paper towels. He stole a bottle of bleach from the apartment's common laundry room and headed back to Dawn's.

When he turned the corner to her street, Nick slammed the brakes and swore out loud. From a distance, blue lights flashed from three police cars parked in front of Dawn's duplex. He didn't see an ambulance, which told him one of two things—she'd already been taken to the hospital, or she didn't survive. He'd shot her at close range with a 9mm bullet. If he had to guess, she needed a hearse, not an ambulance.

Nick raced back to his apartment to initiate Plan B. He collected his camping gear: tent, tarp, sleeping bags, portable stove, prepackaged meals, cooler, lanterns, water purifier, portable radio and chargers. He dumped everything from his pantry—cans of soup, pasta, trail mix and cereal—into a paper sack. In a large suitcase, he packed his toiletries and winter clothes: pants, shirts, sweaters, underwear, socks and several pairs of boots. Lastly, he grabbed an envelope of cash from his file cabinet. It was a few thousand dollars, which would allow him to avoid ATMs or using credit cards in the short term.

Outside, he packed Sophie's maroon Blazer. He removed a license plate from a neighbor's broken-down car and affixed it to the SUV. The stolen plate would buy him some time, although he'd have to repeat this trick to evade highway cameras.

If it had been summer, he would've headed north and camped along the outskirts of the Appalachian Trail. It would be easy to supplement his supplies by scavenging through rest stop trash cans at night, and he could camp close to a stream for water. But with winter approaching, Nick felt the better plan was to head west and then south, crossing into Mexico. If people could breach the border to enter the United States, surely he could find a way to exit the country undetected.

On the drive out of town, he spotted a CVS, parked out of range of cameras and went inside. He grabbed lighters, black hair dye, a six-pack of beer, more bandages and medicine. Although he was taking the risk of being identified by the clerk and interior cameras, Nick thought it was better to give away his position while he was still in town rather than once he was on the run.

He drove southwest on I-85 to Atlanta, where he switched to I-20, taking him through Alabama to Mississippi. Outside of Meridian, he parked out of sight at the edge of a UPS distribution center. Dinner was dry cereal washed down with beer and chased with more Advil to calm his throbbing arm. In the middle of the night, he slipped out of the Blazer and swapped license plates with one of the docked trucks. Nick wasn't sure if eighteen-wheelers had different plates than SUVs, and he had no means to research the question. Before leaving town, he'd destroyed his mobile phone and flushed the pieces down the toilet. He needed a new phone, but it was too risky to go into a store during the early days of his escape. Facial recognition technology had become more sophisticated, and he wasn't taking any chances.

The next day, he fueled up at a dingy gas station on the outskirts of town and continued west to Galveston, Texas. He hid overnight at a park, which was a few miles inland from the beach. Using the public restroom, he shaved his stubble and dyed his hair jet black. On day three, he drove just outside of Brownsville, Texas, with the intention of crossing into Matamoros, Mexico. His dilemma was how to get past the border checkpoint without showing his driver's license and passport. He also needed a new phone.

Nick disguised himself in a baseball cap and sunglasses to enter the Brownsville Walmart Supercenter. He selected a prepaid phone and picked up more bandages, a twelve-pack of bottled water, a chilled Coke and a sub sandwich. At the checkout, he stood behind a Mexican couple buying a large-screen TV, which gave him an idea. They'd come to the US to buy electronics, presumably cheaper or better quality than they could find at home. He could approach a couple like them and bribe the husband to drive his Blazer into Mexico while he hid in the back. The wife could return in the couple's vehicle. Nick retreated to his Blazer and plotted some more.

That evening, he entered a county park and drove into the woods behind the baseball diamond. With a connection to the world again, he searched the internet for news from Laurel. The shooting had been on a local Greenville TV station, and his photograph and description were being publicized along with a phone number to call with leads. Nick's darker hair made him harder to recognize, but he couldn't disguise his most prominent feature—his height. The media had also released a description of the Blazer with the original, and incorrect, license number. One thing was clear—this needed to be his last night in Texas.

He devoured the sandwich as he searched for possible camping sites in Matamoros. There was a secluded area near a water reservoir not far from an airstrip and a small church. He also searched for possible drop-off spots, assuming he could bribe a driver. As he reached for fresh bandages to tend to his injured arm, another idea occurred to him, one that was even better than his initial scheme to cross the border.

Early the next day, Nick drove to the Brownsville Community Health Clinic, which was just down the road from Walmart. He scanned the lot, noting the foreign plates. Around mid-morning, a Hispanic man, woman and young boy left the clinic and headed toward a Fiat with Mexican plates. Nick approached the couple. His arm was bandaged, and he'd wrapped a second bandage around his head.

"Excuse me," he said. "I'm sorry to bother you. I was wondering if you could help me?"

The woman looked at her husband. The boy had already hopped in the back seat of their car.

"I just had a procedure done here," explained Nick. "I was planning to drive to my sister's place for a few days to recover, but I don't think I'm up to it." He pointed to the bandage on his head. "I'm feeling kind of dizzy."

The couple stood next to their car, still listening and not openly alarmed or suspicious.

"Would one of you be able to drive me? It's not far. She lives in Matamoros, if you're headed that way? I'd pay you for your trouble."

Nick reached into his pocket and pulled out a wad of twenty-dollar bills. "Would two hundred be enough? I'd call an Uber, but I don't want to leave my Blazer here."

The husband shrugged, handed his keys to the wife and followed Nick to the Blazer. The man entered the driver's side and Nick slowly pulled himself into the passenger seat, as if every movement was a struggle. Once inside, he leaned forward, bracing his head against the glove box.

"You okay?" the guy asked.

"I'm just really dizzy." Nick handed the man his phone with the GPS already mapped to an apartment complex just over the border. "This is her address. Maybe I should just lie down for a minute."

Nick exited the Blazer and reentered through the back door, stretching his body across the seat. He'd already positioned a sleeping bag on the floor and moved most of his camping gear to the back cargo, out of sight. The man, who believed Nick's lie, shifted the car into drive and led the caravan to the border.

The Matamoros crossing station, with its rusted arch that spanned the road, looked like a poor man's version of the McDonald's yellow arches. Vehicle lanes were separated by bright yellow guardrails, while pedestrians crossed on a footpath at the outer edge. Each car pulled up to the booth and awaited a green or red light. Green meant cleared for passage and red required further inspection.

When Nick's SUV approached, he ducked under the sleeping bag. He'd already planned his strategy if he was exposed. He'd pretend to be unconscious. Hopefully, they'd rush him to the local Mexican hospital, which was less than four miles away. From there, he'd find a way to escape, although he'd have to sacrifice his truck full of supplies.

Nick felt the vehicle slow and come to a stop. He couldn't see what was happening and his mind raced with possibilities. Was the husband showing his passport? Were the Customs officers checking the license plate, which wouldn't match the vehicle? Was there a notice to stop all maroon Chevy Blazers from leaving the country?

He swallowed hard, his throat tight. He felt as if he might suffocate under the weight of the sleeping bag but didn't dare look. Instead, he remained as stiff as a corpse under the cover of his shroud. Before a full panic could set in, he felt the car move forward.

Nick peeked from underneath his cover. The bright daylight made his eyeballs ache, but all he felt was relief. He'd made it through Customs. He remained prone in the backseat as his chauffeur continued their journey. Within ten minutes, they'd arrived at the apartment complex, the fictitious residence of his sister.

"Hey, Mister. We're here." The Mexican man parked and peered in the back seat.

Nick sat up and cradled his head. "Thank you. I really don't think I could've driven myself."

"Do you want me to go with you?" the guy offered.

"No, thanks. I'll be fine." Nick pointed to the second floor. "That's her place right there. Thanks again." He counted ten crisp twenty-dollar bills and handed them to his unwitting accomplice.

The guy nodded and rejoined his wife and child, who were waiting in their Fiat. When they were out of sight, Nick plugged in the address for the deserted reservoir and headed away from civilization.

Chapter 50

A rhythmic beep pinged in her ears. A thick pillow supported her head. A soft mattress cradled her body.

This isn't my bed, she thought. *Where am I?*

Slowly opening her eyes, she confirmed she was not at home. This bed had rails on the sides. A thin plastic tube was attached to her arm, secured with medical tape and connected to a hanging IV bag. To her right, Kelly was curled up in a chair, asleep.

"Kel-ly." Dawn struggled to speak, her throat dry. She tried again. "Kel—"

Her friend's eyes popped open. "Oh my gosh, you're awake."

"Where am I?"

"The hospital, but you're okay," Kelly assured, then spoke more cautiously. "Do you remember anything?"

Dawn struggled to find context. If she could place a single memory, she could build the pieces around it. But she had nothing. "What happened?"

"I received a text message from you, that you needed help, with your home address. I hurried over and found your door wide open. You were on the floor bleeding. Yellow Dog was next to you, going crazy. I called 911. The medics and police arrived, and he tried to attack every guy who came through the door. It was all I could do to restrain him so they could stop your bleeding. Dr. Smita showed up with Dr. Patel. She told me about the app you'd installed on your phone."

Dawn's memory, which had been a blank canvas, started to fill with splotches of images. She began to recall the conversation with Smita at the clinic when she'd asked how to protect herself from Nick. Smita had taken her phone and installed a safety alert app.

"It looks like an ordinary news application," Smita had explained. "But it has the added feature of sending text messages for help. You preprogram the message and choose your trusted contacts, who will receive the alert. Let me show you."

Smita had added her information and Kelly's to the app on Dawn's phone. For the distress message, she'd written: "Need help. Activated my safety app." Then she'd selected the options to transmit the location and start the recording.

"If you're ever in trouble, triple tap on the app's icon, and the text message we just created will immediately be sent to me. It also has a GPS locator and will start recording audio of everything going on in the room."

"Are you remembering something?" Kelly's question snapped Dawn back to the present.

"I remember Smita installing a safety app on my phone."

"I'm so glad she did. You could've bled to death and none of us would've known." Kelly paused, then spoke as if talking to a child. "Do you remember who shot you?"

The confrontation with Nick flashed in Dawn's mind. "Nick."

"That's what we thought. Dr. Smita told the cops how he'd been stalking you and that you'd gotten a restraining order." Kelly paused, appearing as if she wanted to say more but couldn't.

"What's is it?" asked Dawn.

"I found you in your underwear. They asked me if that was normal. I didn't think so." Kelly waited, not prying further or forcing an explanation.

"He was trying to coerce me to—" Dawn's voice cracked. "I was stalling. I knew the app would alert you and Smita." She pointed to a plastic cup next to the bed. "Could I get some water?"

Kelly hopped up, filled the cup with water and handed it to Dawn.

"My throat is so dry."

"You've been out for a while."

"How long?"

"It's been a week."

"A week?" Dawn nearly spit out the water. "What about my mom?"

"Don't worry. I've been going over to Floyd. She's doing okay." Kelly looked sheepishly at the floor. "I told her you were in training, out of state. I just couldn't—"

"No, I'm glad you didn't tell her."

"She knows you've been gone for a bit, but I don't think she's really keeping track of time. I should get the nurse. Tell them you're up." Kelly started to leave, but Dawn had more questions.

"Did they catch Nick?"

"No. The cops went to his apartment, but he was gone. He hasn't been at the bank since that night. They have his picture on TV and are asking people to be on the lookout, but I don't think they have a clue where he is. But don't worry, you're safe here."

"How's Yellow Dog?" asked Dawn.

Kelly started kneading her hands and looked nervously around the room, avoiding eye contact.

"Cindy found his owner, didn't she?" guessed Dawn. Her heart sank. "And I was thinking about keeping him."

Kelly's eyes started to well up with tears.

"What is it? Did Nick hurt him?" Dawn tried to sit up but was met with a sharp pain on her left side. She put her hand on her belly and eased back into the bed.

Kelly's gaze fixed on the floor. Her voice was a sheepish whisper. "Like I said, he wouldn't let any male near you, not even the medics. He was so agitated. He'd seen you get shot. I had to pull him away so they could attend to you, but he kept lunging forward, trying to attack everyone. The medic yelled at me to get him out of the room, so I took him to my car."

Dawn immediately pictured the many dogs she'd treated, who'd died from heat stroke after being left in a hot car. But not Kelly—there was no way Kelly would be so reckless. Even with all of the commotion, Kelly would've known better than to leave a dog in a car.

"I cracked the windows to give him air," continued Kelly. "After you'd been transported to the hospital, I was going to take him to the clinic. You know with Kia, I couldn't take him to my place, but—"

"But what?" demanded Dawn. She needed Kelly to just spit out what had happened to Yellow Dog.

"When I went to my car, he was gone."

"What do you mean—gone?"

"I only cracked the windows a few inches, not enough for him to escape, but when I returned, the driver's window was all the way open, and he was gone. He must've pressed on the glass and forced it down. I've looked everywhere for him, Dawn. I've been going back to your place every day to see if he's come back."

Dawn could think of only one reason why Yellow Dog wouldn't return home. She pictured Nick sneaking up to Kelly's car, reaching through the slit window and rolling it down. Yellow Dog would've tried to attack him again, so Nick must've done something to stop him—something horrible. She wanted to cry, but her dry eyes wouldn't produce tears. She listened, in a fog, as Kelly apologized over and over.

Chapter 51

Nick's bullet had missed Dawn's spine, mesentery artery and liver, but it had taken out her spleen. Thanks to the app, help had arrived quickly to control the blood loss, which was the most life-threatening part of the shooting. Based on the gash on her forehead, the medical team suspected she'd knocked her head on the sink when she'd passed out from the pain. She'd suffered a minor concussion, rendering her unconscious, although her cranial CT scan showed no signs of bleeding or swelling of the skull. With instructions on how to clean and treat her wound, Dawn was discharged from the hospital at the end of the week.

A short week later, she and Ben were back in probate court in front of Judge Cain. Ben had filed an emergency order, based on new evidence, to amend Marie's guardianship. This time, Marie was present and determined to speak for herself. She, Dawn and Ben sat opposite Nancy Priest and her overpriced Greenville lawyer, Allen Dobbins. Unlike last time, when the only other people in court were witnesses, this round had several reporters in the back of the room.

Judge Cain's demeanor was markedly changed. Before, he'd displayed a haughty arrogance. Now, with Nick's disappearance headlining the news and the victim of that shooting in his courtroom, he appeared much humbler. He also seemed eager to get this case behind him, which explained why they were able to be heard so quickly.

"Mr. Clayton," said Judge Cain. "I understand you've submitted a motion to remove Nancy Priest, the current guardian and conservator of Marie Smith?"

Ben rose to speak. "Yes, Your Honor. We believe the plaintiff in that case, Mr. Nicholas VanBroklin, provided false statements regarding the suitability of my client, Ms. Dawn Smith. You're familiar with the current events surrounding the former plaintiff?"

The judge cleared his throat and repositioned himself in his chair. Ben was going to make him squirm, literally.

"I'm aware of the *alleged* case against Mr. VanBroklin," replied the judge.

"Your Honor, we have evidence that not only did Mr. VanBroklin lie under oath, but he single-handedly put Marie Smith in danger on more than one occasion."

"What evidence do you have?"

"The night of the shooting, when Mr. VanBroklin *allegedly* violated his restraining order and breached my client's home, she activated an application on her mobile phone that created a recording. I have an affidavit from the company that provided the recording. It attests to the date, time and the authenticity of the source. May I?" Ben pointed to his computer.

The judge nodded. "Go ahead."

As Ben played the recording, everyone in the room was captivated by Nick's confession. When he admitted to pushing Marie and putting Lisinopril in her food, audible gasps came from the back. Even Judge Cain leaned forward as if questioning if he was hearing the audio correctly.

The sound went quiet during the time when Dawn was undressing. The courtroom was deathly silent. Then, the unexpected explosion of the gun blast made everyone flinch. Pandemonium ensued with Nick shouting and Yellow Dog growling as he tore flesh.

Ben stopped the recording and glanced at Dawn. They'd discussed playing the gunshot in court and agreed it was necessary, even though it made her relive the nightmare. The worst part was hearing Yellow Dog, fighting for *her* life. She dabbed her eye with a tissue.

"Your Honor, my client was her mother's long-standing power of attorney and is her only next of kin. If Mr. VanBroklin's testimony had any bearing on your decision to *not* appoint the daughter who has legal priority to be Marie Smith's guardian and conservator, we ask that you reconsider."

Marie tapped Ben on the arm and whispered, "I want to testify."

He leaned toward her and replied, "I don't think you'll need to."

She crossed her arms defiantly. "I don't care. It's time I spoke my mind."

The trip to the courthouse was the first time Marie had been allowed to leave the Floyd facility in over a month. She'd almost been denied the opportunity had Ben not threatened Nancy with false imprisonment.

"Your Honor," said Ben, as he raised his hand. "Mrs. Marie Smith would like to say a few words, if possible."

Judge Cain's eyebrows rose, not hiding his surprise. He looked squarely at Marie and asked, "Mrs. Smith, can you tell me who is the current president of the United States?"

Marie, who was not sworn in nor on the witness stand, spoke. "Who's the president? That's how you want to test my competence? If you want to talk politics, why don't you ask me how your brother became a congressman? Everyone in town knows who paid for his campaign and it's not a pretty story. I'm not saying you're corrupt, Judge Cain. My late husband, rest his soul, said you were a decent man and not involved with how things went down with Congressman Cain. What else would you like to know?"

The bailiff snickered. The reporters gossiped. Dawn stared at her mother in awe. If Judge Cain had started the proceeding eating a little crow, he was now having a full plate for supper.

"I wasn't here before when a lot of decisions were made for me and my daughter," continued Marie. "And I don't agree with these decisions. I want my daughter to manage all of my affairs. I trust her. And I want to go back to my home where I can cook and garden and live in peace."

Dawn had no idea what had possessed her mom. The mild-mannered, ever-placating Marie was showing real backbone.

Judge Cain looked unnerved. People didn't speak to a judge like this, but Marie Smith was unabashed. And with a slew of reporters in the back, any judge would be mindful of how he treated an elderly woman in his courtroom. He looked at Nancy Priest's attorney and said, "Counselor?"

"Your Honor," said Mr. Dobbins. "My client has decided to resign from this appointment—for personal reasons." There was far too much publicity around the Smith family, and Dawn was becoming more famous by the day. Little did she know how much more of the story would be revealed in the coming days.

"Alright then. With no one else seeking successor guardianship or conservatorship, the court will draft a new order appointing Dawn Smith."

Dawn sat stunned. Had she just heard correctly? Was the battle really over? Could she halt the sale of Marie's duplex and bring her home in time for Thanksgiving?

Chapter 52

Marie slept in her own bed that night. As quickly as her wishes had been denied and her rights trampled, the damage had been reversed.

For Dawn, the whole ordeal felt surreal, as if she'd just woken up from a nightmare. The next day after work, she stopped by Floyd to retrieve the rest of her mom's belongings, thankful she'd never have to step foot in that place again. Cathy and Susan were in the dining room joined by an attractive middle-aged woman. Dawn felt a pang of guilt. Unlike Marie, these women were still stuck there.

"Hi ladies," she said, as she approached. "I've come to pick up my mom's stuff. She's coming home for good."

Susan looked at the woman next to her. "Why can't you do that for me?"

"It's not that easy, Mom," said the woman. She extended a hand to Dawn. "I'm Lori Griner, Susan's daughter."

Cathy reached out, clasping Dawn's arm, and formed the shape of a gun with her hand. Undoubtedly, she'd seen the news and, given her fascination with all things true crime, wanted to hear the story.

Dawn took Cathy's hand and artfully repositioned the woman's fingers. The attention she was receiving because of the shooting, especially from reporters, was making her uneasy. Dawn didn't want to highlight her newfound celebrity if the others hadn't heard about it.

"Did your mama show you what I taught her?" asked Susan.

Dawn shook her head.

Susan picked a raisin out of her soggy carrot salad, popped it in her mouth and gulped some water. Then she opened her mouth wide and stuck out her tongue to reveal the nugget of dried fruit.

"I taught Marie how to skip the Namenda." Susan chuckled with delight, then broke into a hoarse cough, covering her mouth with her good hand.

Now that Dawn thought about it, her mom's face didn't look as bloated, and her eyes were clear, not bloodshot. And she'd spoken so clearly in court.

Lori changed the subject. "How'd you get Nancy Priest to agree to let her go home?"

"I had to go back to court. We challenged some of the testimony against me. I should've been my mom's guardian and conservator all along, not Nancy."

Lori's face revealed utter shock. She stood and took Dawn by the elbow, escorting her out of earshot of the residents. "And Judge Cain agreed?"

"You know all of these players?" asked Dawn.

"Sadly, Nancy Priest is my mom's guardian and conservator. I've been through hell with these people." Lori started to share more when a Floyd employee who was sweeping the floor inched closer, clearly eavesdropping. "Let's go somewhere more private," she said, giving the worker a disdainful glare.

Outside, the temperature dropped as the sun began to set, casting orange streaks across the autumn sky. Dawn crossed her arms and rubbed them briskly to stave off the chill.

"Nancy Priest and her crew are conniving gold diggers, preying upon the elderly," said Lori. "Do you know how I found out she'd taken control of my parents? I came to visit—I live in Nashville—and my mom and dad had vanished into thin air. They weren't at their home, and I had no idea where they'd gone. Neither did my brother. After contacting the police, I learned that Nancy had filed an emergency ex parte petition."

"What's that?" asked Dawn.

"I didn't know, either, at the time. It meant that no one in my family had to be notified of the hearing. Nancy had that crooked Dr. Edwards testify that Mom, because of her stroke, needed more care than Dad could provide. They painted me and my brother as delinquents, just because we live out of state. Before any of us even knew what had happened, Nancy had taken control of everything."

"She can do that?"

"She can and she did. She moved my parents here against their will. She hired a company to clean out their house and sold all of their possessions for pennies on the dollar. Then she sold their home and paid herself a fat commission. She did all of this in a matter of weeks."

"Couldn't your parents have called you?"

"They didn't have cell phones, just a home landline. When they were moved here, they were told they would be given a new phone, so they patiently waited, all the while having no way to contact me.

After a week of not being able to reach them, I drove to Laurel. That's when I found out they'd been taken."

"Can't you fight back?" asked Dawn.

"As guardian and conservator, Nancy has the right to use Mom's money to fight *me* in court, and Mom has so little left."

"What about your dad?" asked Dawn, fearing she knew the answer.

"He died last year from a broken heart. Everything he'd worked for his entire life had been stripped from him, and he had no way of protecting Mom, which left him devastated. They have such a corrupt racket going on here. Nancy catches vulnerable people, and that vile sister of hers keeps them."

"Sister?"

"Don't you know? Nancy Priest and Patti Floyd are sisters."

Dawn's mouth dropped open. A chill ran up her arms. She'd noticed their resemblance upon first meeting Patti but had never put it together. "Is that legal?"

"This is backward, small-town South Carolina. Nobody's watching what they're doing. And most of the lawyers in town won't go up against the Floyd family. A few of them are on the payroll, like that evil Jerry Raven. During the hearing, Nancy proposed for him to be my parents' guardian ad litem. He was supposed to represent their best interests, yet he allowed them to be imprisoned here. And he charged my parents thousands of dollars for his *service*."

Dawn recalled her early research on Nancy. On a hunch, she'd checked if Nancy and Jerry were related. They weren't so she ignored her suspicion, but she'd been right all along. They were linked—just not by blood or marriage.

"Nancy Priest, Jerry Raven and Patti Floyd destroyed my parents' quality of life, and they've been lining their pockets in the process." Lori pointed inside. "Do you know how many other wards Nancy put in here with Jerry's help?"

Dawn shook her head.

"Five on my mom's hall alone, and who knows about the rest of the building. Patti Floyd charges exorbitant fees and Nancy uses the ward's money to pay the bills—first to the facility for the *care* and then to herself as conservator and guardian. It's like the court gave her a blank check."

"Isn't there anything you can do?"

"I called the state ombudsman, but she was no help. Everything's been done legally. All I can do now is drive six hours every time I want to check on Mom. I've begged Nancy to move her closer to me and my brother in Tennessee, now that Dad's gone, but she won't. She even had Dr. Edwards draft a phony medical opinion that Mom is too feeble to be moved. I ask you, does that feisty lady in there look feeble to you?"

Lori Griner was confiding in Dawn as if they were life-long friends, but Dawn understood. The feeling of helplessness was so frustrating that venting, especially to someone else who'd been a victim, provided relief.

"I only saw one review of Nancy Priest when I researched her," said Dawn. "Trust me, I plan to write another one. Couldn't you post a review about her?"

"And risk retribution? At least if I play nice, she doesn't try to block my visits."

"That's horrible. Does your mom understand what's going on?"

Lori rolled her eyes. "That's the worst part. She expects me to do something, but my hands are tied. My brother is so over it. He hardly visits anymore because she spends the whole time nagging him about going back to Tennessee."

"I'm so sorry," said Dawn. "What about Ben Clayton? Is he in on this scheme?"

"I haven't seen his name come up."

Dawn couldn't be sure, but she guessed Ben's failures were because he hadn't taken her case seriously and not because he was corrupt. He'd rallied for her and Marie in the end, although she'd find a different lawyer should she ever need one again.

Lori sighed. "I'm happy for you, really, but I'm so jealous. You managed to beat them. I don't think I ever will."

Dawn thought about the many reporters calling her for an exclusive. "If you're willing, I've got a few reporters that I think we should speak with."

The media was missing the real story. It wasn't her shooting. It was corruption in the Laurel probate system. Then she wondered—what had become of Nick?

Chapter 53

The water reservoir was bordered by a residential area to the west, a landing strip and church to the south and nothing but woods to the east. Nick set up camp on the east side where he could remain undetected indefinitely. He planned to travel farther south once he'd done some more research. If he'd learned anything from TV crime shows, staying in one place for too long was never a good idea. Passing Customs was just his first hurdle. The Mexican military was known for setting up separate checkpoints, typically outside of town. At those stops, they'd search for contraband such as cash, weapons, ammunition and drugs, and they'd have a field day with the contents in his Blazer. Until he could determine exactly where those stops were located, he needed to stay put.

With his tent pitched and camping stove lit, Nick retrieved a can of bacon potato soup. He hadn't eaten since breakfast, which was a few handfuls of dry cereal, and he craved some warm comfort food. When he looked at the lid, he became so enraged that he threw the container against a tree. It made a sharp crack and fell to the ground, dented but still intact. In his haste to depart, he'd forgotten a can opener. He scrounged through the paper bag of dry goods until he found a can of chicken noodle soup with a pull top. He grimaced as he prepared a warm, but less satisfying meal.

At dusk, Nick sprawled onto his sleeping bag inside the tent. His back ached, which he attributed to sleeping in the SUV the past few nights. In fact, his whole body ached, especially his forearm where he'd been bitten.

"That damn dog," he scowled, as he popped another Advil. Of all the things he regretted from that night, not shooting the dog the minute he'd entered Dawn's place topped the list. He searched the internet for more updates on Dawn's condition but found nothing. If she'd died, the story would've made national news. His best guess was that she was still in the hospital. He considered calling to inquire, saying he was her boyfriend, but decided she wasn't worth the risk. His focus needed to be on how to establish his life under the radar in Mexico.

The next morning, Nick made coffee using water from the reservoir and his straw filter. It was a slow process, but he didn't have anything better to do. Within a few hours, his stomach seized with pain. He inspected the filter, perplexed at how he could've ingested tainted water. The reservoir itself looked fairly clean, and he'd taken the extra precaution of filtering the water. He cussed as he threw the straw to the ground and grabbed a bottle of water from the twelve-pack he'd purchased.

His biggest irritation, besides the muscle aches, was the sheer boredom. Camping trips of the past were different. They'd been an escape from civilization but had a definitive endpoint. Now, he had nothing but time. Being on the run would be his perpetual way of life. That, plus the nagging possibility of being caught, started to play tricks on his psyche. He needed a destination, a place where he'd never have to look over his shoulder. The truth was that the instant he'd pulled the trigger, whether intentional or not, he'd erased any chance of peace.

From a distance, Nick observed the white cross of the church perched high in the air above the small building. The surrounding parking lot was empty, so he dared to approach. A simple archway led to a wooden door, which was unlocked. Inside, a crucifix adorned the back wall and pastel-colored pews lined the aisle. Nick never considered crossing himself or saying a prayer. He'd abandoned religion long ago, believing he was the master of his fate. Toward the back of the church, a door led to the kitchen. The cabinets were stocked with coffee, tea and snacks. The refrigerator had fresh orange juice and cream. This little oasis could supply him for weeks.

He grabbed a bottle of juice, unscrewed the cap and took a giant swig, but the liquid spewed from his mouth onto the floor. He coughed and rubbed his neck, feeling a tightness in his jaw. Nick resealed the cap, assuming spoiled juice had caused his gag reflex. He wiped the floor, removing any trace of his presence, stashed a few bags of chips in his pockets and exited the building.

When he was several hundred yards from his campsite, he froze. An intermittent flash of light, almost like a beacon, originated from the area. Had someone discovered his hideout? He crouched, looking for any signs of movement, and cursed himself for leaving his shotgun inside the tent. Diverting into the woods, he circled around the back of the camp. All appeared quiet. Eventually, he approached the tent and scanned the area for anything missing or displaced.

Everything seemed the same, but he couldn't relax, not knowing the source of the light.

By evening, his throat and jaw were so tight he was certain he had strep, probably contracted from that "filthy" Mexican family who had smuggled him. He skipped dinner and went to bed but tossed around restlessly throughout the night. Over the next day, his condition worsened, with aches, sweating and bouts of muscle spasms. When he reached for a bottle of water, his hand trembled. As he drew the bottle to his mouth, the jerkiness of his movement caused it to spill before he could bring it to his lips. Still determined, he sucked in a gulp and pressed his hand over his mouth, as if trying to contain the fluid. His cheeks expanded as a mixture of water and saliva dribbled down his jaw.

The next day, Nick realized he wasn't getting better and needed help. He eased himself onto his knees and gradually stood. Feeling unsteady, he took a wobbly step, then another and collapsed. He tried again, staggering a few paces before plunging to the ground. On his third attempt to reach the Blazer, he saw the burst of light again, like he'd seen from the church. The side mirrors of the SUV were catching the sun at just the right angle and reflecting the light. Nick rolled on the ground, his back arching unnaturally, as he laughed hysterically at his paranoia.

Once his fit of mania had passed, he came to a grim realization—he couldn't seek medical treatment. The risk of being recognized or caught was too high. He stumbled back to the tent to recover on his own.

Over the coming days, he endured massive headaches. The bite on his arm throbbed like a drum. He tried to take more Advil, but an abnormal pressure on his jaw was preventing him from opening his mouth, like an invisible vice was clamped around it. Then came the seizures. His body writhed uncontrollably as if an electric current had overtaken his nervous system. His arms and legs jerked and his face contorted, making his outer appearance resemble the true inner demon.

As Nick struggled to take rapid, shallow breaths, he cursed his body for betraying him. He cursed the Mexicans, believing their "dirty" water had poisoned him. Unlike Mrs. Rhodes, he'd never been educated on the potentially lethal effects of an untreated dog bite. Each breath grew progressively fainter. Deprived of the oxygen he needed to sustain life, his skin turned a sickly blue, then marble white.

Chapter 54

Dawn was just about to go next door to help her mom prepare their Thanksgiving feast—the entire staff from the clinic was coming over—when she heard a knock at the front door. For an instant, her pulse quickened. The ordeal with Nick had triggered a new panic reflex, set off by a simple tap at the door.

He's gone, she assured herself, taking a deep breath. *Besides, he wouldn't knock.*

She looked through the peephole to see the same face she'd seen on her WhatsApp several weeks ago—Sophie Brown. Dawn opened the door. Not only did they look alike, but they were the same height and dressed similarly, in a baggy sweater dress.

Sophie smiled meekly. "I'm sorry to show up without calling. I hope you don't mind."

Dawn was so stunned to see Nick's sister that it took her a few seconds to invite Sophie in.

"I'm home on a short leave for the holidays," said Sophie, as she nervously looked around the room. "I heard what Nick did to you. I'm sorry."

Dawn touched her abdomen where bandages still covered the gunshot wound. "You're not responsible for your brother's actions." She paused, then added, "And you helped me. Our conversation let me understand him better. It gave me a clue on how to stall until help could arrive."

"I wish I could've done more to stop him. He's escaped, and no one knows where he is. Aren't you afraid he'll come back?"

Sophie was reading Dawn's mind. Not a day went by that she didn't picture Nick lurking outside, intent on finishing the job. She'd try to reason with herself. If Nick was smart, and he was, he'd be hundreds of miles away by now. Still, the worry didn't subside. She thought about getting another dog for protection, but each time she decided to wait just one more day, hoping Yellow Dog might return. She also considered buying a gun—an idea that had never crossed her mind before she met Nick. But facing someone who was prepared to kill her and feeling so incredibly helpless had changed her perspective on firearms.

Dawn was momentarily lost in her thoughts when Sophie's voice brought her back to the present. "My mom told me Nick had taken something of yours." She reached into her pocket, pulled out her hand and opened her palm.

"My locket," exclaimed Dawn. Her eyes began to water. As much as she tried to pretend it was only a necklace, not as dear as a person or a pet, she'd struggled with the loss. Eventually, she accepted that she'd never see it again.

"After the police searched Nick's place, they let us go in. I found it in one of his drawers. Mom said that you'd asked about a necklace, so I figured it had to be yours. May I?"

Dawn nodded as silent tears rolled down her cheeks. She turned and lifted her hair so Sophie could drape the locket around her neck and fasten the clasp.

"There you go. Back with its rightful owner."

"I don't know how to thank you." Dawn pressed her palm against the locket as she turned around.

Sophie fought back tears as she shook her head. She didn't speak, but her expression said everything. Though not her fault, she felt the weight of her brother's sins.

"I'm having friends from work over for Thanksgiving. Will you stay?" offered Dawn. "My mom's been cooking for two days. We have plenty of food."

"Thanks for the offer, but I actually have plans." Sophie's smile broadened. "When Matt heard what Nick had done, he finally let his guard down. For the first time, he was open to the possibility that my brother had set me up. It's what Joel and I had been telling him all along, but he started to believe me. I'm going to his place for Thanksgiving. We've talked on the phone, but this will be the first time I've seen him since our divorce."

"That's huge," said Dawn. "I'm really happy for you."

"Well, I'd better get going. I wanted you to have the necklace before I went to Matt's. This needed to be my first step in setting things right. Can I ask, who are the pictures of?"

"My parents. Marie and David Smith."

Sophie stared at Dawn as if she'd seen a ghost. "Marie Smith was on the list," she whispered, as if in a trance.

"What list?"

"The police found a list at Nick's place, in his desk. It had names of people and all kinds of personal information—their address, age, marital status, banking information and assets. It was more information than he could've accessed as a teller but somehow, he had it. The police asked me if I had any idea what it was for, but I couldn't make any sense of it."

Dawn thought back to Nick's petition for conservatorship. At the time, she'd been shocked at how much he knew about Marie's finances. He'd obtained private information from the bank and several other sources.

"Was Susan Givens on that list?" asked Dawn.

"Yes," confirmed Sophie. "How'd you know?"

Dawn's thoughts crashed together as the puzzle pieces began to fall into place. She recalled Lori Griner's observation: *Nancy catches vulnerable people, and her vile sister keeps them*. Someone had to find the targets. Was that Nick's connection to Nancy and Patti? Dawn remembered the wad of cash that Nick always carried. Once she'd learned he wasn't from a wealthy banking family, but making a teller's salary, it didn't add up. But if the sisters were paying him, in cash, for confidential financial information about potential prey, that would explain the money. Nick was providing the shopping list—of wealthy, vulnerable, elderly people for Nancy to catch and Patti to keep.

This realization also explained how he'd been so clever regarding the inner workings of the probate court. He wasn't a lawyer, nor were any of his family members. Yet, Nick knew how to use the conservator and guardianship laws to his advantage. He knew how to put doubt in Judge Cain's mind to make Dawn appear to be unfit. He hadn't learned this skill on his own. Nancy Priest and Jerry Raven had coached him.

Dawn recalled the accident when she'd first met Nick. It was random, but he'd reached out not long after asking her on a date. In that time, he could've researched her mom and added her to the list. Marie was newly widowed, had inherited a good sum of money and had only one relative, a daughter, who he could target. This realization made Dawn sick to her stomach. It also explained something she'd never understood—why Nick had hurt Marie while they were still dating. When she'd ended the relationship, his acts of retaliation, although deranged, made sense. But he'd pushed and drugged Marie while they were still together. Now, Dawn saw the bigger picture. Nick had been plotting against her and her mom from the moment they'd first met.

But how could she prove it? After the shooting, Nick had been forced to leave town in a hurry. He'd missed destroying incriminating evidence—like the list. Maybe there was additional information at his apartment, like receipts for cash payments or phone logs between him, the Floyd sisters and Jerry Raven. Dawn had arranged for herself and Lori Griner to meet with investigative journalist Kimberly Hutchens just after Thanksgiving. She couldn't wait to share this lead and let the reporter run with it. Two women, who'd been wrongly taken from their families, were on Nick's list. Jerry Raven had been the guardian ad litem in both cases. Nancy Priest had been appointed the permanent guardian and conservator and Patti Floyd was housing both women at her facility. Dawn couldn't help but wonder—were there more?

Chapter 55

Dawn said goodbye to Sophie, wishing her luck with Matt, and headed next door to help Marie with the final touches for their feast. She quickly discovered that no assistance was necessary. The turkey was basting in the oven next to a green bean casserole and mashed potatoes. Two pumpkin pies cooled on the stove top wafting the sweet fragrance of cinnamon and butter. The dining room table, set for eight, was ready to host a thankful group of friends.

Suzanne was the first to arrive with her famed cranberry sauce. The Patels and baby Devin showed up next. Suzanne scooped the infant into her arms and cooed at him with delight. He smiled, revealing tiny dimples. Although he was only a few months old, the warmth and alertness in his eyes revealed an old soul, just like his mother.

Alex and Regan rode together. Her place was on his way, but they weren't fooling anyone, especially not Dawn. Their mutual crush had turned into a bona fide relationship, and they were doing a lousy job of concealing their affection.

Kelly was the last to arrive, carrying a clay pot of lavender mums. Ironically, the last person to bring Marie flowers was Nick, after the hospitalization he'd caused. Dawn reflected on that day, back when she thought he could do no wrong. It felt like a lifetime ago.

Kelly pulled Dawn into the kitchen, away from the others, and spoke in an excited whisper. "I got a raise," she beamed. "Dr. Patel said he'd noticed how much I've stepped up these past few months, taking extra shifts without complaining. He didn't realize I was doing it for *you*, so you could deal with all of Nick's crap. It's over a hundred extra dollars a week. I feel like I can finally breathe, even save a little money."

"That's great news, Kelly. You deserve it," said Dawn.

"Dinner is almost ready," chimed Marie, as she entered the kitchen from the dining room. "Oh, Kelly. Those are lovely. I'll plant them in the garden tomorrow. Dawn, would you put them on the back patio?"

Dawn carried the mums outside. When she bent down to place the pot on the concrete patio, a twinge of pain cut into her left side.

Although her stitches had been removed and her prognosis was a full recovery, her abdomen was still tender. She looked up at the gray November sky. In that moment, the sun peeked through a cloud and briefly warmed her face and shoulders. She basked in the warmth, thankful life was starting to return to normal. Had circumstances been different, Marie could've been eating her holiday meal at Floyd alone and mourning the death of her only child.

The sensation of something damp tickled the back of Dawn's calf. She ignored it at first, but it persisted. Dawn reached back to rub her leg and was met with a handful of fur. She whipped around to see a familiar gray nose nuzzling against her leg.

"Yellow!" she cried.

Dawn dropped to her knees and wrapped her arms around the Labrador. She buried her head in his fur and squeezed him tightly. In that instant, he became *her* dog, no longer a foster. The switch had been immediate and subconscious, even in the way she'd dropped "Dog" from his name.

Dawn couldn't imagine a happier day. Her mother was home. Her friends were together, and they were celebrating Thanksgiving. And now Yellow was home. Everything in her world was beautifully right, with the exception of one nagging fear.

Chapter 56

A month had passed and there had been little movement in the search to find Nick. As Detective Clyde had told Dawn at the onset, this type of case usually had one of two outcomes. Either Nick would be caught within a few days of the shooting, or it could be years before a trace of him would turn up.

Dawn was trying to make peace with the not knowing. She didn't think he'd be daring enough to resurface in Laurel. There was already a warrant for his arrest for attempted murder. Returning to finish the job didn't serve any purpose other than landing him in deeper trouble. Still, nothing of what he'd done made sense to her so could she really count on him being rational?

Dawn took comfort in Yellow's watchful eye and protective nature. He was more reliable than a house full of alarms, which is why the hair on the back of her neck tingled when he started barking at the front door.

Dawn checked the camera and breathed a sigh of relief at seeing Detective Clyde.

"I have some news," said the detective. "Do you have a minute?"

Before fully opening the door, Dawn pulled Yellow into the bedroom because he wasn't settling down. His behavior made her question if someone else was outside. Could Nick be hiding in the bushes or lurking around the corner? Even with the protection of an armed police officer, Dawn couldn't help but feel unsafe. Nick had done this to her.

Detective Clyde wasn't one for small talk. "We have reason to believe that the authorities in Mexico found Nick."

Dawn's eyes widened.

"Some kids were playing in the woods near a church south of Matamoros. They found a maroon Chevy Blazer with stolen plates at a campsite. The brand of items they found indicated the camper was American. They also found human remains inside the tent."

"Human remains?" repeated Dawn.

"They were decomposed beyond recognition. We're waiting for dental records for confirmation, but they're pretty confident they found him. The story is going to be on the evening news, so I wanted to let you know first."

For the first time, the full weight of the *not knowing* caught up with Dawn. Every time she stepped outside, she scanned her surroundings. Every evening at the clinic, she found an excuse to walk outside with someone else. Every time she went grocery shopping, she spun around at random intervals to ensure no one was behind her. The aftereffects were real and haunting, and although she downplayed her paranoia, it wasn't going away.

"You're telling me that Nick is dead, and soon you'll know for sure?"

Detective Clyde nodded.

Dawn exhaled a sigh of relief. It was finally over.

Epilogue

Just before 6:00 p.m., Dawn called Lori Griner and told her to turn on the evening news. The women watched together, phones to their ears, as the anchor introduced the headline story and passed it over to the lead reporter.

"We have a major development in the October shooting of a Laurel woman," said Kimberly Hutchens. "Authorities believe that the body found at a deserted campsite in Mexico is that of the alleged shooter, Nicholas VanBroklin. Verification is underway, and we'll be sure to bring you more details when confirmed. As our viewers may recall, Mr. VanBroklin's disappearance sparked a related investigation of the Floyd Retirement Home that we've been following exclusively. Patti Floyd, the owner and executive director, is alleged to be the mastermind behind an illegal scheme to remove vulnerable, elderly adults from their homes and place them at her facility, charging thousands of dollars in room and board. Based on evidence found at his residence, Mr. VanBroklin is believed to have participated in the scheme by finding potential victims. When we reached out for comment, neither Ms. Floyd nor a spokesperson for the facility returned our calls, but the DA shared that we are just seeing the tip of the iceberg in this case. As this story continues to unfold, we'll keep you updated. Back to you."

"Wow," said Lori. "Did you know they found Nick's body?"

"I did. The detective on the case stopped by earlier today, and Kimberly gave me a courtesy call to let me know the story was airing. I appreciate that she's honoring our deal—to not use my name."

"There's more she didn't say," added Lori. "Maybe she can't yet. Nancy Priest resigned from all of her appointments. I'm heading back to court to get guardianship of my mom. I'm going to be able to move her home to Tennessee."

"That's great news. But even if Nancy resigns, that doesn't make up for all of the damage she's done."

"It doesn't, or Jerry Raven. But look at all the evidence they have against them, thanks to us—and Nick's records. The Floyd sisters can't buy their way out of this one, now that the media has latched on to the story." Lori let out a wicked giggle. "And the DA is looking to make a name for himself with this case. We'll probably get called as witnesses."

"I'd be more than willing to testify," said Dawn. "You'll let me know how your hearing goes and when you come to pick up your mom?"

"Sure will. I never thought I'd see the day. Thank you."

As Dawn hung up, she heard a knock at the door. Yellow started barking with the same wild intensity as the night of the shooting. A cold chill raced up her spine as she imagined Nick outside. Detective Clyde said they'd found his body, but they didn't have definitive results from the dental records yet. As Dawn thought about it, the scene that the detective described seemed almost too perfect—the maroon Blazer, the campsite, the decomposed body. Nick had proven time and again that he was clever. He was cunning enough to fake his own death to get everyone off his trail. Had he fooled everyone again?

Yellow charged toward the door, barked again and looked at her expectantly. His behavior was different—it wasn't fear but excitement. Dawn's shoulders relaxed when she remembered who was outside. She opened the door, and Yellow raced out to greet the Jack Russell who was waiting for him. She'd momentarily forgotten that she'd agreed to a play date with Moose—and his dad, Austin Bailey.

Oddly, Yellow had no interest in protecting her from Austin. Either he was too interested in Moose, or he sensed this man was no danger to her.

She thought about Nick, finally believing that what Detective Clyde had told her was true—Nick was gone. Dawn wondered what had made him so evil. Had he been born that way or had his environment forged his character? Sophie, who'd been raised in the same household, was honest and decent. Dawn realized that she'd never know what had motivated Nick, and strangely, she didn't care. Time had softened some of her hatred, and she'd let some of it go on her own, believing that karma served the best justice.

ACKNOWLEDGEMENTS

Thank you to ...

Becky Smith Hendershot for allowing me into your veterinary world and for sharing so many heartwarming and heart wrenching stories. You are an angel on earth to every pet who's lucky enough to be in your care.

Dawn Hillyer, victim turned advocate, for inspiring my fictional story with your own true ordeal. You are proof that strong women not only survive but thrive.

Dawn Dolpp, Wally Wechsler, Virginia D'Antonio and **Karen Butler** for sharing your harrowing stalker stories and allowing me to borrow some of the details.

Jennifer Ross for being my trusted expert regarding all things involving police work & investigations.

Bobbi Duck and **Christy Mougin** for providing insight into camping life.

Dave Dargo, Elaine Edwards, Drew Stonecipher, Angela Humphries and **Greg Crawford** for offering medical advice.

Margarita Alvarado for sharing your stories about life in Mexico.

Carrie Ailes, Jack Auger, Rick Black, Michelle Camp, Janie Cohen-Legge, Rinda Galarneau, Terry Johnson, Charlene Masse, Paul Mirabella, Diane Nix, Andy Nunemaker, Wendy Penrod, Shannon Raab, Denise Sheehy, Linda Stamey, Dirk Swanson, Barbara Thompson and **Judi White** for being my early readers.

Evelyn Fazio, Brooke Berthelsen and **Janie Mills** for your skillful editing.

Madhavi, Mike and **Khalin Rubbo** for lending me your son's name and allowing my small tribute to your wonderful **Devin Rubbo**.

Ed McCallum for years of dedication and persistence, which led to the most precious gift of all.

ACKNOWLEDGMENTS

SUPPORT FOR LIZ

If you enjoyed this novel, we would so appreciate you taking a moment to tell others:

- Share with a friend or book club—Liz will often visit or Zoom/ Skype with book clubs if requested
- Write a review where you purchased the book—it's the best way to both thank and encourage the author
- Post about the book on your favorite social media site: Facebook, Instagram, X, Pinterest

If you would like to stay in touch with Liz, she can be reached at:

Website:	www.lizlazarus.com
Facebook:	www.facebook.com/AuthorLizLazarus
Instagram:	www.instagram.com/AuthorLizLazarus
X:	https://x.com/liz_lazarus

BOOK CLUB DISCUSSION QUESTIONS FOR *DAWN BEFORE DARKNESS*

www.dawnbeforedarkness.com

For a visit by the author, Liz Lazarus, at your book club please contact liz@lizlazarus.com.

In order to provide reading groups with the most thought-provoking questions possible, it is necessary to reveal important aspects of the plot of this novel. If you have not finished reading *Dawn Before Darkness*, we recommend that you wait before reviewing this guide.

1. OVERALL Would you recommend *Dawn Before Darkness* to a friend? Why or why not?	6. SELF-PROTECTION Dawn installs outside cameras and a safety app on her phone. What precautions have you taken to seek help if you or someone you love were in danger?
2. VET TECHS In this book, Dawn experiences the joys and sorrows of caring for animals. Did her experience change the way you look at this vocation?	7. GUN OWNERSHIP Dawn is not familiar with firearms and does not want to own one. Her opinion changes somewhat as she fears for her safety. Do you agree with her changing views?
3. STALKING Do you know anyone who is dealing with a stalker or who has sought a restraining order? How has it affected his/her life and family?	8. CHARACTERS Were the characters in this novel realistic? What more would you like to know about the characters or their history?
4. AGING & LEGAL DOCUMENTS As our parents age, it is important to have the proper legal paperwork (POA, Trusts, Wills) in place to reflect their wishes. Have you and your family had these tough conversations?	9. ENDING Were you surprised by the ending? What different ending could you imagine for this book? What other elements of the book surprised you?
5. GUARDIANSHIP & CONSERVATORSHIP Do you know anyone who is dealing with a guardianship or conservatorship case? How has it affected his/her life and family?	10. MOVIE CASTING If *Dawn Before Darkness* were made into a movie, who would you cast for Dawn, Marie, Stuart, Nick, Kelly, Dr. Patel and Smita?

Excerpt of

SHADES OF SILENCE

by Liz Lazarus

ORMOND BEACH NEWS

Coast Guard suspends search for missing Ormond Beach plane

BY GAGE HOLLOMAN

The US Coast Guard announced today that they are suspending the search for Ormond Beach pilot and restaurateur, Michael Sinise, pending further developments. Sinise's plane, a Cessna Caravan C-208, owned by charter company Island Connections, was reported missing on the afternoon of April 9th when he failed to arrive at North Eleuthera, Bahamas, for a scheduled pick-up. According to Miami Response Center, Sinise departed alone from Flagler Airport and indicated no signs of distress prior to dropping off radar approximately two hours into the flight.

Bill Cook, a Lieutenant with the US Coast Guard, directed the search, which began shortly after 5:30 pm on April 9th and followed Sinise's filed flight plan, beginning with the aircraft's last known position. The team employed Coast Guard HC-144 Ocean Sentry aircraft and Navy P-3C long range patrol aircraft equipped with radar, night vison and thermal sensors. Over the course of the next seventy-two hours, hundreds of square miles were covered with no signs of debris or oil slick.

"Thermal cameras were used at night to detect heat from an engine or even a person," said Cook. "During the day, we'd go over the same grid we'd covered the night before, but with the benefit of daylight."

When asked why the search was halted, Cook explained, "We followed the flight path and surrounding area, checked with nearby airports, and tried to locate the plane's emergency beacon but never detected a signal. Should further developments arise, we'll resume the search, but unfortunately, we don't have promising news at this time."

The Coast Guard plans to issue a preliminary report outlining the facts surrounding the search sometime next week. A final report is expected to take several more months. Further developments will be handled by the National Transportation Safety Board. Anyone with information regarding this case should contact the NTSB's Response Operations Center at 844-555-9922.

1. Julianna | Monday, July 5

I poured myself a glass of red wine from an open bottle at the bar and pictured Michael sitting across from me. We were having a nightcap now that the diners had finished their desserts and coffee and were headed home, their tummies full of pasta with homemade Italian sauce. He raised his glass to make a toast—to having me all to himself for a few weeks. I was about to do something I considered reckless: abandoning the restaurant for two weeks to go on vacation in Italy. Before Michael, I'd never been out of the country, much less on a cross-Atlantic flight, but he'd planned our adventure to the last detail. We'd never really taken a honeymoon. I was too worried about leaving the restaurant unsupervised, but he'd finally convinced me to relax. Samantha and Alex could easily handle things while I was gone.

I guess it just wasn't in my DNA to be so carefree, a work ethic I'd inherited from my father. Little by little Michael had shown me that it was okay to have fun. Taking time off for an overdue celebration of our marriage was part of enjoying life. He was a hopeless romantic.

I dabbed my eyes with a cocktail napkin. Now I was the romantic one, clinging to a distant memory. I was also feeling more hopeless—it had been ninety-five days since I'd last seen my husband.

I started to take a sip of wine when I heard a voice behind me.

"We need to talk," she said.

I whipped around to see a woman leaning against the hostess stand at the front of my restaurant. We had closed over an hour ago. My bar manager and chef had just left for the night, leaving me alone to finish some paperwork. She seemed to have appeared out of nowhere.

Her voice sounded like a girl's, but she looked more like a Real Housewife. She wore a tight navy dress with a scooped neckline that accentuated her rounded breasts. Gold bracelets adorned both wrists and her heels were so high that her feet arched unnaturally. Her bleached blonde hair was tousled about her face, and her skin was deeply tanned, the color that came from hours of soaking up the Florida sun.

"We're closed," I said, perplexed that this woman was somehow in my restaurant at nearly 1:00 a.m.

"You're Julianna, right?" she asked. Her eyes squinted slightly.

Most of my customers, even the regulars, called me Miss Sandoval. I couldn't put my finger on it, but there was something off-putting about the informal way she said my first name. Or maybe I was just irritable from a long night. Holidays were always busy, and that night's Fourth of July dinner crowd had been no exception.

"Look, I'm sorry, but we're closed," I repeated. "You'll need to come back during normal hours."

For an instant, I thought about my pistol in the safe in the back office. It wasn't that I felt in danger—she looked more like the type who'd be robbed than someone who'd do the robbing. Still, her presence was strange, especially on the one night when my stepson was out of town, leaving me to close the restaurant alone.

"He's not who you think he is," she said.

I shook my head, trying to make sense of her words. Was she drunk? High? And who was she talking about? It didn't matter. She was keeping me from going home and I was already exhausted. I reached in my jacket pocket for the key to the front door and stepped from behind the expansive bar to escort her out. As I approached, I got a better look at her face. She was heavily made-up, with contoured cheekbones, lash extensions and plumped-up lips. I reiterated that we were closed and she needed to leave.

"You stupid bitch," she sneered. "You don't have a clue!"

I stopped in my tracks. My entire body stiffened. The hatred in her voice was personal, as if she knew me, which she didn't. Before I could respond, I heard a blast outside. Glass shattered like someone had dropped a full tray of dishes onto the concrete floor.

Her eyes bulged and she gasped for air, opening and closing her mouth like a hooked fish. Her doll-like face was now oddly contorted. She stumbled forward a few steps, struggling to maintain her balance. When she tried to speak, blood spewed from her mouth.

I screamed.

She lurched forward, arms outstretched, and tried to grab me.

I instinctively stepped back and watched in horror as she clutched her chest and gasped for air.

Our eyes locked.

She stared at me, terrified. Her expression was the haunted, helpless look of someone who knew death was certain. Then she collapsed face-first to the floor.

I took another step back, turned and sprinted through the open archway toward the kitchen. I continued retreating down the hall to my office and slammed the door behind me. My heart was pounding in my ears. My fingers trembled as I struggled to twist the flimsy bar lock on the door knob.

Only then did I realize that I had no escape. My small office had no windows or other exits.

I frantically snatched the phone and dialed 9-1-1.

"Hurry, hurry, hurry," I chanted into the receiver.

"9-1-1. What is your emergency?"

"A woman," I panted. "A woman has been shot."

I glanced at the space between my desk and the back wall and squeezed myself into the small opening. My desk was made of wood. It wouldn't stop a bullet. Still, I felt safer crouched behind it.

"What is your address?" the dispatcher asked.

"Café Lily. 216 South Atlantic Avenue, Ormond Beach."

"And your name?"

"Julianna Sandoval. Please, send the police right away!"

I listened for any sounds of movement in the hallway. Whoever shot her could be coming for me next. The restaurant was eerily quiet, but that didn't mean I was alone.

"Help is on the way, Julianna. Just stay with me. Where are you?"

"In my office." My voice cracked. I tried to swallow but my mouth was dry.

"Did you see who shot her?"

I blinked, trying to recall the scene I'd just witnessed. I'd heard the gunshot and the window shattering. Why hadn't I looked in that direction? The entire time, I'd never taken my eyes off the woman. Why hadn't I tried to identify the shooter?

"Ma'am, are you still there?" the dispatcher asked.

"I'm here," I whispered.

I eyed the safe on the wall. I'd have to give up the cover of my desk to retrieve my pistol, but I had no choice. A flimsy lock wouldn't hold up against someone determined to break down the door. I stood quickly and pressed the cold metal keypad—0216, my parents' anniversary. Or was it 0212?

My mind went blank.

No, it was 0216.

With a single motion, I grabbed the gun and darted back to my hiding place. I squatted behind my desk with the phone pressed against my ear and my gun pointed toward the door. As much as I tried, I couldn't catch my breath.

"You're doing good, Julianna. The police are on their way."

But what if help didn't arrive in time?

2. Grant | Monday, July 5

By the third ring of my cell phone, I'd rolled over in bed and glanced at the clock: 1:33 a.m. As I picked up the call, I grumbled out loud, "Somebody better be dead."

I had just returned from vacation up north, visiting my aging parents in Jersey City. Let me rephrase: It wasn't a vacation but time away from work, trying to convince the two most stubborn people I knew that Florida summers, while miserably hot, were still better than freezing Jersey winters. The trip was a bust. They weren't budging, and I didn't get any rest.

I fumbled for my notepad and pen on the nightstand as my boss, Police Chief Michele Jamison, relayed the situation.

"We've got a homicide," she said, her voice somber.

My head dropped. The morning had started with a delayed flight from Newark, forcing me to take a later connection through Atlanta. Getting home should've taken a few hours; instead, it took the entire day. I'd just gone to bed and wasn't due back to work until the following morning. I wanted nothing more than a few hours of sleep.

"I need you," she added. "Hall's never worked a homicide so I'm giving this to you. Besides, he's up for vacation."

Summers were always an endless juggling act of trying to fit in everyone's time off, but it didn't matter. There was an unspoken rule that we were always on-call. Technically, this was Detective Chase Hall's case until 7:00 a.m. Monday, but he wasn't ready to be the lead on a homicide.

Chief Jamison didn't mention it, but I was certain there was another factor influencing her decision. She tended to be a few steps ahead of everyone else, a real chess player. If this case ended up going to trial, the last thing she needed was a clever defense attorney asking our newest detective how many murder cases he'd led before. It wouldn't look good.

"What do we have?" I asked.

"Café Lily. The owner said she'd locked up for the night and assumes the victim must have stowed away inside the restaurant. No signs of forced entry. According to the owner, the victim seemed to be there to talk to her, but she wasn't making sense. Then the owner heard a gunshot and the victim went down. It appears to be a single shot in the back, through the glass window. The owner didn't see anyone."

I was scribbling notes as she debriefed the scene. I'd learned over the years that information never came in the purest of forms—you can't remove the human element. It was like that kid's game of telephone. By the fourth or fifth rendition of the story, the facts changed. It wasn't on purpose. It just was. So it was important to write everything down immediately, on first hearing, when it came to evidence and crime scenes.

"Look, Grant, I need you to solve this. Quickly. It's peak season. That restaurant was packed full of tourists a few hours before the shooting. The Mayor has already called me." She sounded tense but still in control.

"I understand," I told her.

Chief Jamison was good at sheltering us from politics. It was one of the things I appreciated most about her. She was level-headed, and too smart for this small town and its petty Mayor.

"I'll see you there," she said and hung up.

I put the pad and pen on the edge of the bed and rubbed my eyes. I'd just taken a hot shower half an hour ago to decompress. Now I needed another one to wake up.

I walked to the kitchen, put a filter in the coffee maker and scooped a few heaping spoons of coffee grounds. Normally, it was already set up, my ritual before going to bed, but vacation had thrown off my routine.

Back in my bathroom, I stripped off my T-shirt and boxers and stepped into the shower. As I splashed water across my face, I could hear my phone ringing. I toweled off and picked it up—two missed calls from Detective Hall. I called him back as I grabbed my department-issued black polo shirt and tan pants.

"Hey," I said. Before I could say more, Hall peppered me with questions.

"Why didn't the chief pick me? I'm willing to put in the hours. I think I should postpone my vacation. I'll call the cruise line."

"Hold on," I exhaled. "Look, I'm trying to get out the door. We'll sort it out when I get there."

In truth, there was nothing to sort out. He and his wife had booked a cruise, their first trip since the birth of their daughter. There'd be plenty of work when he got back. Besides, no way was the chief making him lead investigator.

Outside my apartment, I walked to my usual parking spot where my black Chevy Malibu was slowly rusting in the ocean air. I would have preferred a spot in the garage, but alimony payments didn't allow for extras. I punched the address to the restaurant into my GPS, although I was pretty sure I knew the way. Café Lily was an upscale joint on the main road on the north side of town. Good for a first date, although I always felt you shouldn't set the bar too high. Take her for pizza and beer and see how she reacts. Yeah, I was jaded. Divorce tends to do that to you.

The commotion at the restaurant made it easy to spot: flashing police lights, a camera crew and a small crowd gawking at the scene. I turned into the entrance. Crime scene tape encircled the entire parking lot preventing me from going further. One of our younger officers guarded the front.

"We've had a murder," he said, with a mixture of terror and excitement.

"Yeah, that's why I'm here." I pointed to the tape which he quickly lifted, allowing me to drive in. Hall's identical black Chevy Malibu was already in the lot so I parked next to it.

The chief and the on-duty patrol supervisor, Sergeant White, were standing outside. Jamison was taller than White, even in flats. Her hair was pulled back in a tight bun. The blue lights of the patrol cars bounced off her ebony skin. When I approached, White got in his first jab.

"This shit's following you from Daytona," he said.

"This shit's why you have a job," I retorted.

"Boys." Jamison tilted her head toward the crowd and the news truck. She was right. Some banter was fine in the office, but it could be misconstrued by an outsider, especially the media.

Hall bounded up and rocked up and down on his toes. "I've canvassed the area. What else can I do? Can we go in?"

I raised my right hand above his head. "Hall, you're up there," I said. Then I lowered my hand to his waist. "And I need you to be down here."

Hall dropped his shoulders and stared at the ground. I felt like I'd just kicked a puppy. He didn't deserve my reprimand. He was young and eager, but he wasn't being reckless, not like what had happened in Daytona. I pushed all of that out of my mind and focused on the task at hand.

"Come with me," I said to Hall as I walked to the back edge of the parking lot.

"We're not going in?" he asked.

"We will, but we start here. I need to feel the scene. Our victim's dead. She won't be undead if we get in there any faster."

I surveyed the one-story building on the small private lot. The front of the restaurant was mostly glass, with a thick, concrete border at the top. Cursive lettering in purple neon lights spelled out *Café Lily*. Next to the name, a single white lily with a green stem illuminated the front entrance.

In addition to the police cars, there were two other vehicles. One, a white Mini Cooper, was parked next to the front door. The other, a blue Volkswagen Jetta, was at the edge of the lot. If I had to guess, the Jetta belonged to the restaurant owner. She wouldn't take up prime spots that were better left for paying customers.

A surveillance camera on the roof pointed toward the lot. From what I could tell, it didn't cover the front door, which was unfortunate. I'd have Hall canvass the area for other cameras from nearby shops. Maybe they'd captured a glimpse of our shooter.

Every investigation was like a bag of puzzle pieces. You never had all of the pieces, and some of the ones you did have were from an entirely different puzzle. The key was to collect enough relevant fragments to put an initial picture together.

White strolled over to Hall and me. He stood next to us and faced the building. "This just ruined our streak," he commented. "We haven't had a homicide in three years."

I chuckled. Hall wasn't the only naïve one around here. Murders were always going to happen—it was just a matter of time. Even if you lived in a bubble, bad guys still walked among us. In fact, the nicer the bubble, the better the hunting grounds.

"Jamison is talking to the Mayor," White needled, as if I didn't know.

"Yeah, well, there's a difference between solving a case and solving a crisis," I replied. "Come on, Hall, let's go."

As we approached the entrance, I observed the shattered window to the right of the door. Hall and I scanned the pavement looking for the spent brass, but found nothing. The shooter must have recovered it or he'd used a revolver, which didn't eject its casings. I assumed my killer was a "he"—most of them were, although I knew to keep an open mind.

Detective Hall and I walked to the front door, where Officer Phelps was guarding the scene. Unlike Daytona Beach, where I'd spent most of my career, Ormond Beach was a small town. Within a few months of arriving, I'd met all of the other officers. When Phelps saw us approach, he jotted down the required information into the crime scene log—our names, the date and time, and our reason for entering the building. Hall and I each took a pair of cloth booties and a pair of latex gloves from a box at the entrance. The summer humidity made the gloves hard to pull on.

"Why don't you start with photos and then do the sketch," I told Hall as I took in the scene. The smell of spices, maybe something Italian, filled the air.

Just inside the front door was a wooden hostess stand stacked with menus. Behind the stand was the dining room with white-clothed tables, the larger ones in the back to allow for maximum occupancy without sacrificing intimacy. A bar with mirrored shelves, liquor bottles and glasses covered the length of the back wall. To the left of the bar was an open archway, which presumably led to the kitchen and storage areas. Next to the hostess stand, the victim lay face-down on the floor.

"Do we have ID on her yet?" I called back to Phelps who was still guarding the door.

"Yeah, her bag was on the floor. I pulled out the wallet to get her ID. Everything's on the bar. Name's Brittany Jones. Valid license. Lives in a condo over on Myrtle Street."

Myrtle Street was a nice area of town.

"Did you run a background check?" I asked.

"No, figured you'd do that," Phelps said.

"Called the Medical Examiner?"

"Yep. They're on the way."

As Hall took photos, I approached the body. She was lying on her stomach with her head tilted to the side, her cheek resting on the shiny gray concrete. The first thing I noticed were her long legs—toned and tan. Both of her shoes had come off. They were navy heels with red bottoms. I couldn't remember the brand, but knew they were expensive, assuming they were real. Her right hand was tucked under her body and her left hand stretched above her head. Gold bracelets rested on her knuckles, thrown forward from the fall. Her nails were painted solid white, a stark contrast to her tan skin.

She had been shot in the back with what seemed like a large-caliber handgun, probably a .45. Whoever did this meant to kill her. There was barely any blood on the floor, which led me to believe the bullet hadn't exited her body.

I focused on the task at hand, gathering every piece of information. Still, I couldn't escape the strange spiritual moment I felt during most murder investigations. A human being, a young woman full of life only hours ago, was lying dead in front of me. She was somebody's daughter, sister or mother—maybe all three—and now she was gone.

I'd worked with cops who pretended not to take a case personally, but they were just lying to themselves. You have to take a certain amount of this job personally to do it well. The trick is to find the right balance. If you take too much to heart, you can't do the work at all.

She was my responsibility now and I needed to find out why someone wanted her dead. If I succeeded, she'd have justice. But if I failed, her death would become nothing more than a cold case, a file folder archived on some shelf in a warehouse. That wouldn't be right. No matter her situation, she didn't deserve to die like this. Somebody needed to answer for her murder.

"Hey, look at this!" Hall broke into my thoughts. He was kneeling by her side, pointing to her neck. I took a few steps so that I was standing next to him. At first it appeared she had a birthmark, but when I crouched to get a better look, I could see why Hall had called me over. She had a tattoo of a dagger interwoven with a vine of small flowers on the side of her neck.

"Make sure you get it when you do your close-up shots," I said as I stood.

Something was off about this woman. She had fancy shoes, nice jewelry and perfectly manicured nails. But her hair was bleached too yellow and the tattoo was kind of trashy—not the artwork, but the placement. Girls trying to be upscale choose the ankle or small of the back, not the neck.

I walked to the bar where her wallet lay open next to her other possessions. Her ID indicated that she was twenty-two years old. The photo showed a much more natural version of the young woman in front of me. Her bag, a medium-sized clutch, had a designer label: Louis Vuitton. I rummaged through the matching designer wallet to find a few credit cards: a Platinum American Express, a Bank of America debit card and a Dillard's department store card. She had $200 in cash, all crisp twenties like they were fresh from the ATM. I expected to find the latest version of the Samsung Galaxy or iPhone, but instead found a Tracfone, the kind you prepay and can't be traced. Made me wonder what kind of trouble she'd gotten herself into.

Sorting through the rest of her bag, I pulled out a makeup pouch with some powder and lipstick and tortoise-shell Coach sunglasses. Then I found the most curious item of all: a small digital recorder. As far as I knew, the only people who needed recorders were journalists and detectives, neither of which Brittany Jones seemed to be.

Hall was peering around my back. His eyes widened when he saw the recorder. I could tell he was itching to play it. I was, too, but I knew better. All evidence had to be turned over to FDLE, the Florida Department of Law Enforcement, to be sure we didn't accidentally destroy it. I'd put a rush on it, though, as I had to believe it would provide useful information.

The last item in her purse was a keychain with three keys: one for a Mini Cooper, presumably the car parked outside, and two silver door keys. A fourth key, dark green and not on the chain, stood out. The blade reminded me of an alligator snout and the hole at the head looked like an eye. We were about ninety miles from Gainesville and the University of Florida Gators. Maybe she went to college there?

I put her bag and its contents into an evidence pouch, sealed and labeled it, and then turned around to study the dining room one more time.

"What do you see?" Hall asked.

I squinted, surveying every part of the room in more detail. It was important to assess the scene and all its evidence before I talked to the witness. Once I spoke with her, it'd be too easy to focus solely on her account of the story, but there was always a bigger picture to consider.

"I'm thinking attempted robbery," he said. "Maybe the perp got spooked when he saw multiple people inside."

I shook my head. For as tech savvy as Hall was—and he was a digital whiz kid—he had yet to develop instincts for a crime scene.

"Look around," I replied. "This is an upscale restaurant. Clients pay with credit cards, not cash. There'd be nothing to rob but paper receipts. And her wallet—it still had cash and credit cards."

"Maybe there was no time," he offered.

"It would have taken seconds to snatch her bag. And why shoot one person point blank and not the other? This wasn't a robbery," I said, and then pointed to the lifeless body. "She was targeted."

"So how are we going to solve this?"

"She's the only person who might be able to tell us, and she's not talking."

Hall grew pensive, a notable change from his typical behavior, which I'd labeled "Energizer Bunny on Red Bull." If he could just learn to be still and absorb the scene, he had real potential.

Chief Jamison had hired me from Daytona to head up the criminal investigations division after the supervisor and another veteran detective retired. She had just lost over fifty years of experience and was short-staffed. My job was to rebuild the team, doing both the recruiting and the training. This case would be a good test of Hall's aptitude and an even better test of my patience.

Once I felt I had a good grasp of the scene in the dining room, I was ready to move on.

"Where's the witness?" I asked Officer Phelps, who hadn't moved from the front door. He was doing an admirable job of keeping extra folks out. People, especially other officers, wanted the chance to be involved. In reality, all they'd do was contaminate my crime scene.

"We moved her to the back office," he replied. "Jenkins is with her. Name's Julianna Sandoval." He pointed to the archway at the back of the restaurant.

"What'd she say?" I asked.

"Said the victim came out of nowhere after she'd locked up. When she told her to leave, the victim started cussing her out. Once she heard the shot, Ms. Sandoval ran to safety."

I nodded and motioned for Hall to follow me. We walked out of the dining area and down a narrow corridor. Wine crates were stacked neatly on the side and a few papers were tacked to a large bulletin board on the wall, showing daily menus and staffing charts. On the other side of the hallway were swinging double doors that led to the kitchen. Jenkins stood just beyond the kitchen, outside the entrance to a small office. I beckoned him over.

"How's the witness doing?" I asked.

"Nonstop questions," he whispered. "Who was she? Can she change her clothes? When can she go home?" He rolled his eyes. "I asked her to pull up video from the parking lot to keep her busy until you got here."

In my experience, people who witnessed violent crimes reacted in one of three ways. Some went catatonic; they completely shut down, barely able to function. Others became hysterical. The rest asked a lot of questions, probably out of a need to regain control. Not that any of the three reactions were desirable, but if I had to pick one, I'd take the third. At least you could get information out of those witnesses.

3. Julianna | Monday, July 5

A man dressed in a black polo shirt and khaki pants, with a sizeable gun holstered at his side entered my office. He had salt and pepper hair, cut in a short military style. His hazel eyes had noticeable bags, yet struck me as kind. He was tan and muscular, the type of man who might like the outdoors.

"I'm Detective Grant," he said, extending his right hand. As we shook, he cupped his left hand over mine. His palms were warm, like Michael's. I quickly withdrew my hand.

"This is Detective Hall," he added. A younger man dressed in a similar black polo shirt and khaki pants, also with a holstered gun, nodded at me but didn't speak.

"Are you okay?" Detective Grant asked.

A nervous laugh came over me.

Was I okay? I was alive, which was more than I could say for the woman in the other room.

He continued, "I know you've been through a lot this evening and I know you've been asked a lot of questions. You're probably exhausted. I just wanted to speak with you for a few minutes and we can talk more tomorrow, after you've had some rest. Would that be okay?"

I nodded and pointed to an empty chair next to my desk. He was the first person to ask if it was okay to question me. I appreciated that.

Detective Grant sat down, putting us at eye level. The younger one, I forgot his name, remained standing like a statue, guarding the door.

"Do you need something to drink? Some coffee? Water?" Detective Grant asked.

"Oh, I'm sorry. I should be offering you something. What can I get you?" I looked at his partner. "Either of you?"

"No, we're fine, thanks," the detective replied. "You're the owner of the restaurant?"

His question surprised me. I thought he'd want to know about the shooting. "Yes. My parents opened it years ago and I took over after they died."

"It must be hard to run a restaurant on your own, especially during peak season."

I tugged the edges of my jacket. His words "on your own" struck a chord.

"Well, I have help. My staff. My stepson." I paused. "And my husband…until he went missing."

The detective's head tilted slightly.

I explained, "You probably heard about it on the news. Michael Sinise. The pilot whose plane disappeared. That was my husband."

A look of recognition came over his face. "I'm sorry," he offered. "I didn't connect the name."

"Sandoval's my maiden name, but when you get married late in life, well…" I paused. "Too many people already knew my name to change it."

The younger detective stepped forward as if he was going to ask me a question, but Detective Grant held up his hand, blocking him. It was clear who was in charge.

"Can you tell me a little bit about your day? What time did you come in?"

I wondered why that mattered, but told him anyway. "I got in around ten. We have a buffet brunch on Sundays, so the menu is easy. I usually come in earlier but knew it was going to be a late night with the holiday."

"What time did you open?"

"Eleven," I replied.

"Who else was working today?"

"Let's see. Our chef and her staff. They were already here when I arrived. And the bar manager and servers came in not long after me."

"Maybe it would be easier if I could have a copy of today's schedule?"

"Of course." I grabbed the shift schedule that was still on my desk and handed it to him.

"Have you let anyone go recently or had any issues with customers?"

I shook my head. "No. No issues. Most of our employees have worked here for years, since my parents owned the place."

"And you took it over from them?"

"Three years ago. They were in a fatal car crash." My eyes drifted to the framed photo of my parents on my desk. They were arm in arm. Mom was looking at the camera, smiling, and Dad was leaning over, kissing her on the cheek. It was my favorite photo of them.

"I'm sorry," he said.

His condolences seemed sincere, not just the obligatory response that comes with tragedy. I shrugged. It sucked. I missed them every day, but the best way to honor their memory was to keep the restaurant going. For them, and for Lily.

"Did you leave at any point today?"

"No," I replied. "Wait, yes. Once. I walked over to Jamba Juice for a smoothie. I know, in a restaurant full of food, I go somewhere else for lunch." I glanced at the empty plastic juice cup still in my trash bin and wondered if he wanted proof. Instead, he chuckled slightly.

"Has anything odd or unusual happened recently?" he asked.

"No, not until *she* showed up," I said as I looked past him toward the dining room. Before Detective Grant arrived, I'd been retrieving surveillance video, but I could hardly concentrate. The whole time I kept wondering who she was and what she wanted from me.

An officer poked his head in my office. "Medical examiner's here."

Detective Grant nodded. "I'll be out in a minute."

The thought of a dead body in my dining room gave me the chills. "She's…I mean, they're going to…"

"She'll be taken care of. In case you need it, there are companies you can call for clean-up and stain removal. Your insurance should cover it."

"I have to do that?" I asked.

Detective Grant didn't reply, but reached into his pants pocket, pulled a card from his wallet and handed it to his young partner. "Give this company a call. See if they can come over tonight and wait for them outside. And see if they can secure that broken window."

"Thank you." I shuddered. I hadn't thought about having to deal with the clean-up. My mind was preoccupied. What would I say to her family? Could I have helped her if I hadn't run away? It all happened so fast. And what was she trying to tell me?

Then there were the more practical concerns. Who was going to want to eat at a restaurant where a woman had been shot? Would business suffer? I couldn't afford to lose any revenue. I didn't have enough saved to cover payroll. All I needed was a few busy summer months to replenish my cash reserve, but now that was at risk. I sighed. I shouldn't have spent so much money on our lavish vacation. It was against everything my father had taught me, but I'd allowed myself to be irresponsible.

"We can call the clean-up company," the detective said, "but you'll have to sign the paperwork. Do you mind if I ask you a few more questions, since we have to wait for them anyway?"

"Okay," I replied as I exhaled. The last thing I'd been doing before all this happened was pouring myself a glass of wine. Now I really wanted a drink to calm my nerves.

"How about we get you some water?" he offered.

I shook my head. "How about we get some wine?" I stood and walked into the hall where Alex, my bar manager, had stored a few crates of the latest delivery. I grabbed a bottle of Josh Cabernet and took it back to my office. Fortunately, I had a corkscrew in my desk because there was no way I was going back into the dining room to retrieve one. I rummaged through my drawer and found a sleeve of plastic cups, ones we used for wine tastings with vendors. I poured myself a glass and offered one to the detective.

"Can't. I'm on duty," he said.

"Oh, of course." I had no idea what had possessed me, offering alcohol to an on-duty cop. Exhaustion and the stress of the last few months were clouding my mind.

He continued with his questions. "So, can you walk me through your day? When you arrived at ten, where did you park?"

"At the edge of the lot. I drive a Jetta."

"And you said the chef and her staff were already here?"

"Yes."

"You came in through the front door?"

I nodded.

"Was the door locked?"

"Yes. We keep it locked until we open."

"When you unlocked the door, was there anything unusual about the lock or how it worked?"

"No, nothing."

"Okay," he said, jotting something quickly on his notepad. "Then what'd you do?"

"I did some paperwork in the office, the usual stuff. I double-checked the evening menu against our supplies in the kitchen. My dad always insisted on that, even though our chef, Samantha, is always on top of things. Brunch ended at three and I went out for a smoothie before getting ready for the dinner crowd."

"And then?"

"Let's see. We went over the specials—it was a fixed-price menu for the holiday—and the staff started setting up. I took a few more reservations. We reopened at five, as usual. Between the reservations and walk-ins, it was a busy night, but everyone was in a good mood. Around ten, we all poked our heads outside to watch the fireworks at the pier. Our last customers left around eleven fifteen."

He nodded, jotting down a few more notes.

"What time do you normally close?"

"Around eleven, but we don't push anyone out. I have the servers start changing the linens on the empty tables, which usually gives the hint to the stragglers that it's time to leave."

"And then?"

"We cleaned up. The staff left. Usually Samantha, Alex and I leave together."

"The chef and bar manager?" he clarified.

"Yes, they're a couple. I had some paperwork to finish, so I told them to go ahead and start their day off. I was only fifteen minutes behind them."

"What time was that?"

"Probably around twelve forty-five."

"Do you remember locking up?"

"Yes," I replied. "I locked the front door behind them."

"Are you sure?" he asked.

"Positive. I even jiggled it to make sure it was secure."

"What did you do after they left?" He shifted in the chair as he spoke.

"I came back to my office to finish closing out the receipts. It had been a long day, so I decided to get a glass of wine at the bar. I was pouring my drink when I heard the woman's voice behind me saying that we needed to talk. At first, I thought it was Samantha. I turned around and saw this woman next to the hostess stand. I couldn't figure out how she'd gotten in. I told her we were closed and then she started cussing at me. Next thing I know, I hear a blast and glass shattering."

"And then?"

"She fell to the floor. I wasn't quite sure what had happened. I mean, I think I realized she'd been shot, but it felt surreal. I ran in here, locked the door, called 9-1-1 and got my pistol. I hid in my office until the operator assured me that police were at the front door."

His brows furrowed. "Where's your pistol now?"

"In the safe. The operator told me to put it away before I opened the door for the police."

Detective Grant's partner reappeared. "Room's clear and the clean-up crew is on the way."

"Thanks, Hall," he said. "Did someone canvass the neighboring businesses for cameras?"

"Already on it," the young detective replied. "There's a nail place, a pool supply shop and a few retail stores. Looks like one of the stores has a camera. I'll call the owner in the morning."

Detective Grant shook his head. "Do it now. If it's looping, we can't risk losing the last few hours."

The young detective nodded and disappeared again. I was starting to feel the effects of the wine, which was making me more tired. All I wanted to do was to go home and I wondered when I'd be allowed to leave.

"Do you happen to have any other clothes you can change into?" he asked.

I looked down at my white shirt, dotted with blood spatter, and suddenly felt nauseous. Good thing I had skipped dinner.

"I have gym clothes in my car."

"If you could get them, please, and come right back. I'll need your clothes for evidence. But first, I'll need to swab your hands for gunshot residue."

"What?" I stammered. "You think I shot her?"

"No," he replied. "I don't think you shot a woman in the back while standing in front of her." He pointed to the blood on my shirt and his voice softened, "But I'm responsible for figuring out who did and need to collect evidence."

I exhaled with relief.

"And I'll need to temporarily secure your firearm until we get everything handled with the autopsy. Don't read anything into it. Just following procedure."

My mouth fell open. He'd just said he didn't suspect me, but he was swabbing my hands and taking my gun. How was I supposed to protect myself?

The detective repositioned himself in the chair so he could reach into his pants pocket. "Here's my cell phone number." He handed me a business card with a hand-written number. I hesitated to take it, fearing I'd somehow be tampering with my hands before they were tested. He added, "Do me a favor and give me a call tomorrow, once you get up. I'll meet you wherever you like."

"Tomorrow like today, or do you mean tomorrow like Tuesday?"

"Tomorrow like today," he said. "Okay, so let's secure that gun and get you swabbed. Once you've changed clothes and the clean-up crew finishes, you're free to go home."

I started to get up to open the safe when the younger detective reappeared. "I have a few questions. Had you ever seen that woman before? What exactly did she say to you?"

Detective Grant stood abruptly. "Hall, a word?" The two men left my office and walked into the corridor. I could hear hushed whispers. I took another chug of wine and looked at the clock. It was just before 6:00 a.m.

Detective Grant returned to my office, alone. "Sorry about that. He means well, but he's a little eager. Let's pick this back up once you've had time to rest. Is there anyone I can call for you?"

Who could I call? There were Samantha and Alex. They were more than my chef and bar manager—they were like family—but they'd find out about the shooting soon enough. Better to give them a couple more hours of sleep. As far as other friends, I had acquaintances, but no one I could think of calling to a crime scene at 6:00 a.m. I'd been so married to this restaurant that I'd had little time for anything else. Then Michael came along and revealed a whole new world I'd been missing, complete with flying, fishing, long walks and great sex.

Now he was gone.

Jasper still lived with me, but he was celebrating the Fourth in Miami with friends. How pathetic that I truly had no one to call.

When I didn't reply, Detective Grant suggested that one of his officers give me a ride home.

"I'd prefer to drive myself, if that's okay. I don't live far."

He hesitated, then asked, "You mentioned a stepson?"

I nodded. "He's in Miami for the long weekend. I assure you, I'm fine to drive home."

After turning over my gun, getting my hands swabbed and retrieving my gym clothes from the car, I changed out of my blood-spattered shirt and jacket. The detective waited just outside the bathroom. Maybe this was all protocol but I felt like I was in a precarious situation. Did he believe me or was he trying to put me at ease so I'd slip up and say something wrong?

When I emerged from the bathroom, I asked, "Do you need my key to lock up?"

"No," he replied. "Not much else we can do here. You can lock up. The window should be secure enough for now. I'll have a patrol car follow you home."

All of the police officers and cleaning crew departed with me. Detective Grant walked with me to my car at the edge of the parking lot. As I sat in the driver's seat, he leaned over and asked, "By the way, how long has your husband been missing?"

"It'll be three months this Friday."

"I imagine it's been a long three months," he said softly.

His voice was full of compassion, something I hadn't heard for quite some time. Sure, people were supportive, at first, but they changed as time passed. Now, it seemed no one wanted to talk about Michael, as if he'd never existed, which was so strange and isolating. I hadn't expected to feel comfort from a stranger, especially on such a horrific night, but for a brief moment, the massive solitude I'd felt since Michael's plane disappeared lifted.

ABOUT THE AUTHOR

Liz Lazarus is known for her gripping, fast-paced legal and psychological thrillers that keep readers on edge until the final page. Her novels are praised for their killer twist endings and emotionally charged storytelling, often centering on sympathetic heroines navigating life-changing and high-stakes situations.

With a sharp eye for detail and thorough research, Lazarus weaves complex narratives that go beyond suspense. Her stories frequently explore meaningful social causes, shedding light on real-world issues while still delivering compelling, page-turning entertainment. Through her work, she strikes a powerful balance—educating readers while immersing them in unforgettable, suspense-filled journeys.

Interestingly, Lazarus initially ignored the calling to become a novelist—instead, she tackled other ambitions on her bucket list: living in Paris and learning to speak French, getting her pilot's license and producing a music CD. But, as she explains, her first book "wouldn't leave me alone—it kept nudging me to write to the point that I could no longer ignore the calling."

Though her first novel, *Free of Malice*, is fiction, the attack on the main character is real, drawn from Lazarus' own experience. It portrays the emotional realities of healing from a vicious assault and tells the story of one woman's obsession to force the legal system to acknowledge her right to self-defense.

Reader response to Lazarus' first novel was so encouraging that she embarked on a writing career, releasing her second novel. *Plea for Justice* is a thriller that depicts the journey of a paralegal investigating the case of her estranged friend's incarceration. As she seeks the truth, loyalties are strained and relationships are tested leaving her to wonder if she is helping an innocent man or being played for a fool.

Her third novel, *Shades of Silence*, showcases the resilience of a woman faced with devastating loss, the unexpected friendships forged from tragedy and the recurring societal themes that confront every generation.

Her most recent psychological thriller, *Dawn Before Darkness*, reveals the treachery of a ruthless stalker, the alarming failure of the legal system and the unthinkable battle a daughter must face to protect her family.

Lazarus graduated from The Georgia Institute of Technology with an engineering degree and Northwestern's Kellogg Graduate School of Management with an MBA. She went on to a successful career as an executive at General Electric's Healthcare division. Later, she joined a leading consulting firm as a Managing Director and is currently head of Operations for a healthcare start-up in addition to being a best-selling author. She splits her time between Atlanta, Georgia, and Bozeman, Montana.

www.ingramcontent.com/pod-product-compliance
Lightning Source LLC
La Vergne TN
LVHW091031080826
845145LV00002B/452

* 9 7 8 0 9 9 0 9 3 7 4 7 0 *